What People Are Saying About

A Glimmer in the Hollows

I wasn't prepared for what waits in the woods. *A Glimmer in the Hollows* kept me turning the pages, ignoring my to-do list, and staying up past my bedtime. Lorna Selley delivers a highly atmospheric, eerie novel brimming with mystery and longing. It's one of my favorite reads of the year, and you don't want to miss it.
—**Debra Castaneda,** award-winning author of *The Root Witch*

This is a magical tale that will go beyond the reader's wildest imagination. Missing children, a babysitter who will never stop looking, and an out-of-town fiction writer all take their places as this mystical story unfolds. With its suspenseful, intricate plot and deep characters, *A Glimmer in the Hollows* is certainly movie worthy.
—***San Francisco Book Review***

A visceral romp through intrigue and mystery. Selley is an exciting new voice in paranormal suspense that everyone should read.
—**Rayvn Salvador,** author of the *Haunted New Orleans trilogy*

A Glimmer in the Hollows is a masterful debut by Lorna Selley, who skillfully combines elements of psychological suspense, intricate character development, and a hauntingly atmospheric setting of a town cloaked in secrets. Selley's vivid prose contributes to a gripping narrative packed with riveting plot twists that will keep you guessing and reading. This thrilling read will stay with you long after the last page. Grab your flashlight and prepare to journey into the shadows of Driftwood. I dare you to put this book down.
—**London Clarke,** bestselling author of *Until Death* and *The Neighbor*

"[A] spine-chilling story of a creepy little town. Lorna Selley took me on a roller coaster ride of intrigue, mystery, suspense, and the supernatural [...] I was guessing until the very end. It was a page-turner, and I could not put it down[...] The suspense kept me on the edge of my seat."
—***Reader's Favorite***

"A tense, vivid mystery steeped in surprises."
—***Midwest Book Review***

A Glimmer in the Hollows

A Novel

A Glimmer in the Hollows

A Novel

Lorna Selley

ROUNDFIRE
BOOKS

London, UK
Washington, DC, USA

First published by Roundfire Books, 2024
Roundfire Books is an imprint of Collective Ink Ltd.,
Unit 11, Shepperton House, 89 Shepperton Road, London, N1 3DF
office@collectiveinkbooks.com
www.collectiveinkbooks.com
www.roundfire-books.com

For distributor details and how to order please visit the 'Ordering' section on our website.

ISBN: 978 1 80341 625 0
978 1 80341 629 8 (ebook)
Library of Congress Control Number: 2023942592

A CIP catalogue record for this book is available from the British Library.

Design: Lapiz Digital Services

UK: Printed and bound by CPI Group (UK) Ltd, Croydon, CR0 4YY
Printed in North America by CPI GPS partners

For Nick

Chapter 1

Thursday, October 31, 2002

It's all my fault. I promised we wouldn't go out.

Jessica ran along the back road, skinny shins slashing the dark. Her legs were numb. The rest of her was all nerves and swinging arms, bursts of ragged breath. She didn't dare look over her shoulder. What if the shadow tried to take her, too?

A scratchy bulb lit the distance. She was nearing an intersection, where a streetlight marked the end of the gravel road. Burnished leaves and shrubbery thinned, and home was one straight stretch. The boxy contours of houses crouched ahead.

She raced past lamp-lit windows that splayed their light onto Driftwood's front lawns. Thunder rolled. The storm was chasing her home. Pine Street was quiet – the trick-or-treaters had moved on. But the jack-o-lanterns still flickered from porch steps, and toilet paper dangled from a neighbor's hickory tree.

She slowed when she saw the Garcias' car in the driveway, parked behind her parents' station wagon.

They're already home. And soon they'll know.

Her knees slackened. The surge of power that had held her together was almost gone.

Time dragged when she ran through the front door, and the hallway stretched on and on. A slice of kitchen linoleum angled into view.

Her brother slumped on the floor by a splattered spoonful of strawberry jelly. Jessica took another step, just a whisper away from the kitchen now, and found her mother. She was standing by her brother, yelling, but Jessica could only hear the thud of her own heart, loud as a punch between her ears.

Her feet touched linoleum. Paula Garcia stood behind Jessica's mother, hands fluttering like little birds. Her father appeared from the dining room doorway – his voice was the first noise to break through the beat of her heart. "Where the hell did you go? Do you know what time it is?"

Jessica searched for words. She found them shaking, just like her legs. Quivering inside her throat.

"I'm sorry," she said. "It's all my fault."

"What's your fault?" Her mother's voice was hollow and tinny, like the rattle of an empty can.

Jessica reached for more words, but they died on her lips.

"They just left! I didn't know they were gone!" her brother yelled, slicing into the silence.

Jessica's mouth fell open at the wall clock. Somehow, it had stolen hours from her.

"Where's Olivia?" her father boomed, as if the thought had suddenly invaded his head.

Jessica's knees gave in. All the fight had left her, and the darkness she'd run from folded its wings around her.

"She's gone."

Chapter 2

Tuesday, April 12, 2022

Elliot stood up from his desk and shuffled to the kitchen with his head still lost in his manuscript's prologue. Gauzy-faint figures behind shaggy evergreen branches, gemmy eyes flaying the dark. A mystery decades old, buried deep.

The kitchen light blinked on. He made coffee – he'd embraced his insomnia years ago. He could sleep when he was dead, or tomorrow on the couch, at least. In the meantime, his unwritten novel kept him awake at night.

Two weeks steeped in Driftwood conspiracy theories had left him with a dozen bookmarks in his web browser and a near-empty manuscript. He'd tumbled down the rabbit hole and lost himself in its twists and turns, its grub-hollowed crevices. Days fizzled as he paced his apartment, veering into tangents, scribbling notes into the little hours.

He returned to his desk, thinking of Driftwood's missing kids, and all the rumors he'd read.

"I saw those kids. Their eyes glow in the dark. They shimmer like opals."

"They're ghosts. They haunt the woods! They like to come out in the fog and the rain."

And the more Elliot read, the more intriguing Driftwood became.

"I was dumb enough to hike those trails alone. Sickness, dizziness, hallucinations … there's something wrong with that place."

Some blamed the nausea, the confusion and the strange encounters on the ley lines that intersected in the state park. Others insisted there was an underground laboratory, where malevolent ETs kidnapped children and dissected their bodies, miles below the forest floor. Some blamed sinister CIA experiments, and others thought Driftwood had fallen under the spell of a satanic cult. Elliot had scrambled to write down every rumor, and they'd bloomed into a cloud of possibilities. A dozen warping plot lines and characters.

He clicked his pen and thumbed through his notebook. Six months until his deadline, and he had nothing but a few scenes, a notebook full of scrawl. The pulse in his neck quickened at the thought.

Just stick to the formula.

His string of bestsellers had all followed the same recipe: the spine-chilling tales of a creepy little town, embellished and baked into a tightly woven plot.

Last year, he'd spent four months in a sleepy corner of Maine, bashing out chapters of *Black Eye* until dawn, after days interviewing locals who'd sworn they'd been abducted by aliens. Tall skinny grays with inky black eyes and sharp teeth, and nights in paralysis aboard ships shaped like spinning tops. The year before, he'd spent weeks in a haunted bed and breakfast in Vermont, writing *Gemini* and listening to the wind whistle through the rickety window frames.

Who knew if there was truth in any of it? He'd never felt the cold clammy brush of gray fingers, and he'd never seen the ghosts of the murdered twins in Vermont. But that didn't matter. His novels flew off shelves and into laps and tablets, and now his readers wanted more.

But it was too late to spend weeks holed up in some odd little town in Appalachia. He'd already lost months to procrastination and book signings. Six months was barely enough time to crank out all his caffeinated chapters.

He was scattered, restless, and he couldn't stop doubting himself. And now he felt the same prickly tickle of dread that had paralyzed him seven years ago, when he was still a reporter for the paper in Boston, typing through dawn to meet unreasonable deadlines.

What if they hate every word this time?

Elliot brushed his notes aside, irritated that success was now fraying his nerves. *Black Eye* had sent his career into overdrive. A studio optioned it, critics loved it, and it soared to the top of bestseller lists like a paper bird riding a gust of wind. But each bestseller meant the next had to be even better, and each day it was harder to spin all that hypnotic snappy prose when he spent nights worrying that he'd never pull it off again.

And then there was his weakening connection to anything that felt normal or real, he reminded himself, rolling his neck. His family, who complained that he always forgot to call, and the friends – the *real* friends from when he was still pulling twelve-hour days as a frazzled journalist – when did they fall to the wayside? He wasn't even sure.

He stood by the window and told himself to stop complaining, to be thankful for all that he had. Lights blinked off in the office building across the street. The stars hid light years beyond the streetlights, the Manhattan skyline, the smog and the clouds. But the inspiration he'd scribbled down for that prologue was still vivid, and it had left an imprint. The cloud-spearing trees, the haunting impish kids fading into the hollows.

The next book ... it's all in there. I just have to tease it out.

He returned to his desk and wrote for ten minutes, forming more half-sketched scenes. Feet dragging over pebbles and pine sprigs, limp arms swaying over a shoulder. A barbed tumble through the underbrush, a scream tearing the twiggy quiet at its seams.

But what happened to those kids, really?

He logged back on to his laptop, then clicked on a bookmarked article – a sloppy report in the *Driftwood Times* about a girl who'd disappeared twenty years ago.

Olivia Garcia was her name. The first kid who'd vanished, and the only one to make headlines. A six-year-old who disappeared in the park on Halloween. The others were a mystery, mostly. Amateur sleuths claimed at least a dozen more had disappeared. Foster kids, runaways. But evidence was thin – no police archives, no front-page reports. Elliot had almost given up, until he'd found a buried snippet about two foster kids who'd wandered into the park two years ago. Joseph

Baker, a twelve-year-old, and a boy who'd vanished two weeks later, five-year-old Anthony Walker.

Half an hour later, Elliot had a map of Driftwood State Park printed and taped to his wall in sections. He stared at it with his hands on his hips. The sheriff's department, forest rangers and volunteers had combed the woods for days, searching for Olivia Garcia. No torn clothing, no blood or remains. No sign of struggle. And locals swore that search and rescue had been just as fruitless for every other kid. As if they'd all been inhaled by the fog and the pines, sucked into sylvan lungs forever.

Joseph and Anthony didn't live in the same foster home. Olivia had vanished twenty years earlier. So what *did* they have in common? Were they just easy prey – vulnerable, fragile – or was the truth more tangled and sinister? And what sparked the rumors of their eyes glowing in the dark? It must have been coyotes or raccoons, he guessed. There was a logical explanation for every whispered tale about Driftwood, he was sure – abductions or trafficking, or a few bored locals tripping, hallucinating in the woods.

You don't have to solve the puzzle; you just have to write the damn book. Keep it unlikely, unthinkable. Keep it untamed.

He set his empty coffee mug on his desk and paced again, feet creaking over the hardwood, then threw another glance at the map. It would be so much easier to write in Driftwood, among the sloping acres of spruce and fir, the looming loblolly pines. He glanced back at his laptop, and his heart thumped at the thought that crept in, or perhaps it was just the caffeine.

No, no. He couldn't do that all over again. *Stick to the plan. Write the damn novel from here.* But he sat down at his desk, now feeling his heart thump a little more, and checked the weather in Driftwood. *Maybe I need a break from New York anyway.*

Thunderstorms all next week. So much for that excuse. His fingers hovered above the keyboard.

"Screw it," he muttered, then booked a plane ticket for a tiny airport twenty miles from Driftwood, with a two-hour layover in Charlotte. Just enough time to cancel the whole thing and book a flight home, he figured, then fell into bed.

Chapter 3

Tuesday, April 12, 2022

Jessica flinched when the power went out. Lightning blanched the dark, and the bathroom ceiling shuddered vein-blue and electric-white. The storm had flooded Jessica's driveway, drowned her yard, and now it interrupted her pen strokes as she wrote down a dream from the night before.

She dropped her pen and journal to the floor, climbed out of the tub and padded down the hallway, then searched the closet for a candle and a lighter. The candle flame cast its murky orange glow into the dark, and bathwater gurgled down the drain. She pulled on pajamas.

Something hit the ground outside, louder than the rainfall. *Just the wind toppling the trash can. I'll deal with it in the morning.*

But as she padded to the kitchen, candle flickering in her hand, a hunch made her pause in the hallway. *Was it really just the wind? Or is someone out there? One of those kids?* Jessica continued to the kitchen, shaking her head. *Too many nights alone reading rumors, and now I'm paranoid.*

Children vanished in Driftwood. The forest seemed to snatch them into its mossy fists. And according to legend, they reappeared, feral and barefoot, to roam the woods and haunt back yards, scavenging from trash cans. But the truth was buried under myths whipped up at water coolers – a tangled snare of secrets, hidden in the verdant belly of the state park.

Just let it go, Jessica told herself, knowing that she wouldn't. She'd never let it go, because 20 years ago, Olivia Garcia slipped from her side, into the trees, never to be seen again. But all those years digging through forum threads and newspaper archives hadn't erased Jessica's guilt or offered any answers. Just more questions, more haunting dreams and night sweats.

In the kitchen, Jessica set the candle on the counter and stared through the window, but the trash can was hidden around a corner. The wind hurled a sheet of rain at the window that hit as an angry, breathy slosh.

"I really need to get a grip," she muttered, thinking of the self-help books her friend Jamie had given her, now collecting dust under her bed. Tactful reminders that she could be more than a library clerk, eternally single, lost in the eerie conspiracies of Driftwood. The power of positive thinking, or something like that.

The light blinked on in the hallway, and the microwave's clock flashed. Puffing out a sigh, Jessica flipped on the kitchen light.

She busied herself with rinsing plates in the sink, then searched for something she could wrangle into dinner. The cabinets were nearly bare – just some granola bars and a pack of clumpy pasta mix. There was some almost-fresh bread in her mother's smelly plastic bread box, snug between the other junk she'd been too sentimental to throw out: chipped canisters and warped Tupperware on the ugly laminate countertop.

Now that Jessica's parents were dead, their clutter sustained her. Cancer had taken them both, but their belongings were a scaffold of memories, crammed into corners and overstuffed shelves. But those memories faded a little more every day, coiling deeper into the woodgrain, sinking into the carpet pile. There was little that was still palpable, except for a whiff of her mother's perfume from a dresser drawer, or the earthy scent of her father's hunting gear in the garage.

A car alarm shrieked, the kitchen light flickered, and Jessica could've sworn something glimmered outside. A quick, shiny blink, just beyond the corner of her eye.

I should head out there, just in case. The lawn's probably covered in trash.

She took a step toward the kitchen door.

But I'm already in pajamas, warm and dry. The trash can wait. And it's just a damn storm. A few branches, some roof shingles ready to slip and slide.

Branches scraped the windowpane like gnarled fingers. It was nights like these that she dreaded the most, when the wind howled, and thunder roared. Nights when Olivia whispered from some dark pocket of her mind: *"Why did you let me run into the woods? Why can't you remember what happened on that back road, Jessie?"*

The past had a habit of creeping in, like a draft under the door.

Don't think about all that tonight.

Instead, she leaned against the wall and distracted herself with thoughts of Elliot Reed, a dizzyingly handsome writer who never really left her mind at all. His bestsellers tucked her into the folds of wild, compelling worlds, eclipsing her own world, her humdrum life. For four years, critics had crooned about his glossy prose and gripping plot lines, but despite how many studied him, no one really seemed to *know* him, because he refused to discuss anything that veered from the pages of his novels. Instead, he gave a non-answer here and there, an evasion with a smile.

But that was all irrelevant to Jessica. *Her* Elliot – the version she'd whisked together from daydreams – was always there, somewhere between the background and foreground, and she had a different fantasy for every room in the house. The kitchen was one of her favorites: How he'd ease her onto the countertop and her legs would curl around his hips. His lips brushing her skin, a light touch sweeping her hair aside, and a feathery exhale as he slipped a hand between her thighs.

Another rattle from outside jerked her upright. A murmur, a scrape. There was *definitely* someone, or something, outside. Jessica ran to the garage and grabbed her raincoat and flashlight, pulled on sneakers, then headed for the back door.

Rain streamed from the porch awning and puddled on the ground. She stepped through the overgrown lawn. The dark enveloped her, and the storm pelted the hood of her raincoat. Water seeped into her shoes and bled through her pajama pants. She flipped on her flashlight and aimed it at the trashcan.

Two young boys stood by the toppled can, ghost-bright in the flashlight's beam. They were filthy and barefoot, shins caked in mud, ignoring the rain that drowned their ankles and cascaded from their hair and shoulders. They stared back at Jessica, fearless and feral, with opal-bright eyes that punctured the dark.

Jessica ran back inside and slammed the door closed.

Calm down. It was just the flashlight's reflection.

But intuition told her otherwise, so she walked to the living room window and peered behind the curtains. The kids were still standing by the trash can, but now they were facing the direction of the window, homing in on her, as if they expected to find her there. Again, their eyes glimmered, too bright to fade into the chaos of the storm. The youngest boy took a step toward her, and another, but the taller one tugged at his shoulder. They turned and sprinted, disappearing behind the shrubs at the end of the yard.

Jessica shivered. Rain dripped from her raincoat, onto the carpet. She kicked off her sneakers and shrugged off the coat. *Did I hallucinate?* she wondered. *Maybe I'm losing my mind. Too much time lost in tangents and what-ifs.*

She threw on fresh pajamas in her bedroom. Under the bed, next to her pile of books, hid a stack of more journals, recording two decades of haunting dreams and nightmares. She pulled the top one from its hiding place. The pages were filled with notes and sketches, scrawled in the little hours, sleepy eyes adjusting to lamplight from her nightstand.

Flipping through impatiently, she found an entry from a month ago:

> *I lay in a cave, deep underground, miles beneath the mossy underbrush and the roots of loblolly pines. I was trapped among worms and centipedes, skulls and bones. Glowing eyes stared at me in the dark, bright as gems. Murmurs echoed, and a small hand touched my shoulder. I woke up bathed in sweat.*

On a fresh sheet of paper, she sketched the two boys by the trash can. Their luminous eyes and skinny limbs, their indignant stare.

I should've called the cops, she thought, now walking to the kitchen.

And say what? I saw two glowing-eyed kids in my yard? Kids I dreamed about? Forget that. But maybe they're hungry. Maybe they'll come back.

She grabbed the granola bars from the cabinet, tossed them onto the back porch, then retreated to the kitchen and considered calling her brother.

No, he'll be over in a blink, winding me into a flutter with legends, theories, memories, she decided, pouring herself a large glass of wine.

I'm not calling anyone.

Instead, she'd escape inside Elliot's latest novel and bask in more sultry thoughts of lying entwined with him. Yes, she'd finish another bottle of cheap merlot, sink into *Black Eye,* a paranormal mystery that was dog eared from multiple reads, and lull herself to sleep.

Chapter 4

Friday, April 15, 2022

Elliot sat in the quietest corner of the business lounge. He nursed a scotch and watched the departures screen, waiting to board his connecting flight to Driftwood.

Dark clouds flanked the horizon, and gray drizzle splattered the gaping wide windows. Elliot frowned at the gloom. Soon those storm clouds would unload, and he'd be thrown around a puddle jumper. Thunder roared, only just discernible through the din of airport chatter and the clink of glasses from the bar.

Part of him wanted to forget his plan and head right back to New York, but he was spinning his wheels in Manhattan. Three more days of digging hadn't revealed much. The state park service didn't have a registry of missing people, a grumbling old man had told him over the phone. They had little interest in tracking anything but deer, it seemed. And the sheriff's department had no digitized records. Just a list of current missing persons and a typo-riddled mission statement.

He had, of course, complicated everything for himself yet again, Elliot admitted, sighing under his breath. He'd never planned on traveling to America's creepiest towns to write paranormal mysteries. When he was still cranking out articles, he'd pictured himself writing edgy police procedurals full of snippy one liners and short tempers. Tie-looseners and fist pounders and late-night coffee drinkers, chasing leads and shaking their heads at red herrings. But he'd soon grown bored of that, and found his mind wandering beyond the city limits, into the quiet hollows where wilder mysteries slept.

But this might have been the wildest mystery yet, and the rumors kept Elliot's mind sparking.

"Those kids like to dig through people's trash. My friend swears she caught them in her back yard."

"I saw them eating fungus right off a tree."

One comment robbed him of sleep more than the rest, left him blinking in the dark:

> *"I was with Olivia the night she disappeared. I still feel like it's all my fault. But I refuse to believe that she's dead."*

The poster, *Chasing_the_Void,* had since deleted the account, and he couldn't find the alias anywhere else.

Elliot pulled his laptop from his bag and logged on. Since boarding the flight from New York, his main character had taken shape, as if nearing Driftwood somehow made everything clearer. A woman haunted by the past, determined to uncover a mystery that tormented an Appalachian town.

With those hazy ideas unfurling, he threw together a back-cover blurb, typing between sips of scotch. A minute before heading to the departure lounge, he emailed it to his agent. He'd soon find it online, he guessed, tethering him to a story that he hadn't figured out.

Standing in line to board, he hatched a plan for the next three days, which included hiking the forest trails and trawling through library archives. But more than anything, he needed to siphon the town's fresh air and gossip, the dew on its pines and the coffee stains on its diner mugs. The beat of its heart, the pulse of its rumors. And he needed to figure out his new lead character. Shape her past, her motives, what she feared and what she craved.

Chapter 5

Friday, April 15, 2022

Jessica jogged the winding forest path, breath bursting from her lungs into the pine-scented air. She was chasing a child no more than fifty feet ahead. A young girl with long brown hair and nylon wings on her back.

Jessica's legs were lead-heavy, her clothes drenched in rain. Fog blurred the arrow-like trees, and the girl slipped from view, merging with the damp haze.

The fog thickened, blooming from the hollows, and twilight dimmed to a murky near-dark. Jessica reached for branches to guide her along the path. The pines were charcoal silhouettes, and dusky shadows stretched across the forest floor. But the girl, was she still ahead?

Jessica staggered up an incline, swerving from sloping branches, sending gravel tumbling down the trail behind her. The pines loomed, shaggy arms draping wide.

At last, the fog thinned enough that Jessica could see ten feet ahead, but darkness was inching in. A scuffle broke through the patter of the rain, and she followed the sound. The girl peered from behind a cluster of loblolly pines. She was skinny and barefoot, her wings tattered and her dress torn.

"Olivia? Is that you?" Jessica called, catching her breath.

The girl scurried farther up the trail, into the evergreens. Jessica tracked her, catching sight here and there of the sway of her hair.

She was gaining on the girl, so close she could see the gauzy fabric of her dress. But suddenly Jessica's legs felt heavy again, so heavy it felt like she'd run all night. A dragging, a pull from underground. It began as just a tug, and then a lurch, as if she were sinking into quicksand, dropping inch by inch. As if, at any moment, the twigs and leaves would fall away, and she'd tumble into the earth.

The girl turned to face her again, and this time smiled, amber-gold eyes shimmering in the last breaths of twilight. "Why don't you remember, Jessie? Why don't you remember what happened in the dark?"

Jessica couldn't seem to utter a sound. The girl's eyes flashed again, but now there were others, shimmering between the trees. Two boys stood to the left, twenty feet farther up the incline.

As she stepped forward, Jessica's foot collided with a heavy chunk of soil. The earth was sucking her in, walling up around her. She fell waist deep, kicking, grabbing at roots until the ground crumbled, and she tumbled through a loamy black tunnel.

Jessica burst into consciousness, jerking upright, dizzy from the sensation of falling. Her phone lay on the nightstand. 4 a.m. She flipped on the lamp and let the vertigo subside, then grabbed her journal from under the bed. The dream was already fading, but Jessica scribbled down all that she remembered. Then she turned off the light and sank into the pillow again, hoping to fall back to sleep.

But fifteen minutes of racing thoughts told her that wouldn't happen. Instead, she'd lie awake until dawn bled through the curtains and bleached the carpet. With a sigh, she threw back the covers and pulled on her robe. The frigid morning chilled her feet.

She made coffee, blinking under the glare of the kitchen light. Her stomach rumbled, but the fridge was as bare as the cabinets – just a jug of orange juice, a carton of almond milk, and a strange pie that Tabitha, her fiery-haired colleague, had thrust into her arms at the library potluck. *"You need to eat this before you waste away, Jessie,"* she'd said.

She made toast under the broiler instead. The stove leaked heat like a hole in the sun and needed an upgrade, just like the checkered linoleum that peeled at the edges, and the sofa in the living room with its ancient cushions she'd slowly been molding to the shape of her own butt.

Two more hours until she'd have to get ready for work. Enough time to read another four chapters of *Black Eye*. Heading for the living room, she heard a scrape from outside, a rustle. She set down her coffee cup and toast.

Another scrape, and now a murmur, coming from the back porch. Jessica walked to the back door.

Three children crouched on the porch, picking up the granola bars she'd left outside on Monday night. They froze, caught in her stare like startled deer. The same two boys, and now a young girl with wisps of flaxen hair tangled around her face, dressed in a muddy nightgown.

"Are you guys OK? What are you doing here?" Jessica steeled against a gust of cold wind that ruffled the hem of her robe. The kids didn't move.

Chapter 5

"We're hungry," the shorter boy squeaked, climbing to his feet. He had a mop of white-blond, semi-matted hair, caked in filth. His eyes were disarmingly sea-green and wide, and his skin was a grubby alabaster.

"Don't call the police!" the taller boy snapped, also climbing to his feet. "They want to take us away." His black hair hung in thick, haphazard dreads, and his eyes were just as clear and wide. But now fear sharpened his face. "We can't go back there. Please! We just need some food."

The girl remained on the porch floor, staring up at Jessica. She, too, had gemmy bright eyes, topaz-blue and crystalline. Goose bumps spread across Jessica's skin. Under the grime, the kids were angelic and eerily beautiful, with fine, angular features.

"I won't call the police," Jessica said, eyes darting around the dark back yard. "Why don't you come inside and get warm? You must be freezing." Nervousness crept into her voice.

All three children shook their heads. Jessica was almost relieved. *What was I thinking, inviting three feral kids into my home?*

"OK, just stay right here." Jessica left the door ajar and ran to the kitchen, where she grabbed a bag of trail mix from a cabinet and apples from the counter, then tossed them into a grocery bag. On her way back to the porch, she pulled three crocheted blankets from the closet in the hallway, her fingers moving before she could make a sensible decision.

"Here." She handed the bag to the blond boy. "And take these."

The kids draped the blankets around their skinny shoulders.

"You live around here? Your parents must be worried," Jessica said, and immediately regretted it. *They probably don't have parents. I bet they ran away from some rat-infested foster home.*

The kids remained quiet, faces twitching, as if they were holding a silent conversation among themselves.

"Do you have a hammer?" the taller boy said.

"No," she lied.

"Yes, you do." The boy's stare made the hairs on the back of Jessica's neck stand on end.

"I don't have one I can give *you*." She hid her unease. Another dozen questions were ready to spill from her lips, but the two boys grew even more skittish. The girl stood up, and they ran from the yard.

Inside, Jessica picked up her cold toast and coffee and paced the living room, still shaken. It wasn't just their eerie bright eyes, or their strange elfin beauty that unnerved her. They had an aura, a presence so strong it danced in the air and lingered like dust on her skin. Whatever it was, it felt like a tingling draft up her spine.

Jessica sighed, rapping her fingers on the bookshelf. She needed to do *something*. But what good would come of calling the sheriff's office, or child welfare? Would they even believe her? More likely, they'd chalk her up as crazy, like the locals who called about ghosts, UFOs, and wolves in their back yards. Driftwood was awash with legends.

I'll skip the details. I'll just let them know I saw three kids in my yard at 4:30 in the morning, she decided, reaching for her phone.

But she quickly set it down again, remembering how the eldest boy had begged her not to call the police. The county's child protection services ran on a shoestring, and Driftwood's foster homes were almost as notorious as its legends. Locals whispered about squalor and violence, blaming vanishing children on the town's broken homes. And as for Sheriff Clarke, he was useless twenty years ago, when Olivia disappeared, and he'd be just as useless now, she guessed.

Maybe they're safer in the forest, in whatever hideout they've made for themselves, Jessica figured. In the kitchen, she chewed through the toast.

"They want to take us away," the eldest boy had said. Take them where, and away from what? Were all three of them runaways? Jessica dropped her toast crust on the plate. Now that she thought about it, there was something vaguely familiar about the two boys. That steady, wide stare. She scraped back her chair and walked to the bedroom, then pulled aside the rickety sliding door of her closet.

A stack of folders hid in a box on the closet floor, under an old winter coat. They were crammed with articles, printed and archived, year after year. Reports on local child abductions, and articles about police procedure and repressed memories. Anything that might explain where Olivia went, and why Jessica's memory of that night had vanished like mist from the lake. What gateway to the past might still exist somewhere, and what had been severed and blocked off forever.

Jessica flipped through a stack of newspaper cuttings from the *Driftwood Times* until she found an article from two years ago. Just a column, with a few pixelated photos of two missing boys: Joseph Baker and Anthony Walker. The photos were blurry, but Jessica could make out Anthony's white-blond hair and Joseph's defiant scowl. The report offered a few sparse details about their disappearance – a thumb-sized snippet for kids who didn't matter enough to make headlines.

A driver reported seeing Joseph Baker entering the park 200 feet from Evergreen Pass, less than a mile from his foster home, the last paragraph read. Then: *Anthony Walker was last seen walking alone on the highway, also approaching Evergreen Pass.*

Jessica studied the two small photos, her pulse now a little faster. Both boys had disappeared right by Evergreen Pass, which ran along the border of the state park. A quiet dread had spread through Driftwood about the mountain pass. Cars and trucks seemed to fly over the guardrail like startled deer, and locals whispered about others vanishing there. More runaways, kids who'd slipped through the cracks. Jessica swore the surrounding woods were a pocket of eerie stillness, where the terrain seemed unreliable beneath her feet. As if the forest floor might crumble, pull her under its tangled brushwood, just like in the dream she'd woken from.

But the blonde girl was a mystery. Jessica flipped through her folders once more, then searched the local news for missing kids on her laptop. None of them looked anything like the girl who'd showed up on her porch. *Another one forgotten,* Jessica guessed. *Unless she ran away recently.*

Jessica's neck ached from tension. She tapped a pen against her desk. *What if she's not a foster kid? What if she has a family, desperately looking for her? What if those boys lured her away from her home? They look innocent, but maybe they're not.*

She glanced at her phone again, fingers ready to dial the sheriff's office, but shook her head, again remembering how the boys had begged her not to call the police.

I'll say she turned up alone. No need to mention the boys.

No, no, I can't do that. Then I'll be lying to the authorities. What if the neighbors saw all three of them? That could come back to bite. And how could they all have the same opal-like eyes? She dropped the pen on her desk and bit her lip, her finger tapping a nervous beat.

If they report her as missing, I'll call, she decided, anxiety now spreading down her spine, churning her stomach. The kids had turned up in her yard twice, and she was already worried that they'd somehow enmeshed her in their fate, their predicament.

Her alarm sounded from the nightstand. Two hours had blown by. In the bathroom, she opened the cabinet and picked up a bottle of Ativan, which she hadn't bothered to take for the last three days. All those years popping and flushing pills, and she still wasn't sure what was worse: the drowsy numbness when she washed them down, or the fidgety anxiety when she stopped. She shook a pill into her palm, then threw it back into the bottle.

No, I don't need that crutch. I'm normal. I'm fine. This time will be different. I just need to learn to stay calm.

Instead, she scribbled down a few thoughts in her journal. It eased her urge to fret and fidget.

I have that feeling again, she wrote. *That feeling that there's something I know about the park. Something that hides and breathes in the weeds. A twig in the mud, a notch in the bark that I always miss. It gnaws at me, like invisible teeth. I'm always chasing something that escapes in the mist.*

Chapter 6

Friday, April 15, 2022

It was one of those days at the library that begged for a fire drill, an emergency. Anything but another stack of mechanical engineering textbooks to catalog from the new inventory shelf. Jessica tugged her cardigan cuffs over her fingers. It was freezing in Driftwood College Library, as usual. A morgue full of books.

"Jessie, did you see a ghost? Or are you still waiting for a miracle? I can never tell when you stare into space like that." Tabitha poked her with a pencil. Jessica squirmed. Her chair – a cold scoop of plastic – let out a squeak.

"This place is full of ghosts," Jessica mumbled, lost in thoughts about the feral kids in her yard.

Tabitha nodded and sighed. "Don't wait forever, Jessie!" she whispered a minute later.

Jessica blinked back to the present, bewildered by another interruption. "Huh?"

"Don't wait too long for that miracle to come along. I waited and waited, and he never showed up, so I slept with Curtis instead, and he stuck like Velcro." Tabitha shoveled a palmful of Doritos into her mouth. Her heap of red hair had almost come undone and hung in frizzy tendrils. Her eyelashes were like spiders' legs, clumped in coats of flaking mascara.

"I barely remember what a man feels like," Jessica murmured.

"Mine feels like pudge and he stinks. Don't do what I did – don't get stuck with a Velcro guy who smells like meatballs." A cloud of orange crumbs settled in Tabitha's sweater, because she ate like she'd been raised by wolves.

"I won't. Velcro doesn't stick to me."

"You eat that pie? You're skin and bones."

"Yes, it was delicious," Jessica lied. *Maybe I'll leave it on the porch for those kids. I'm all out of granola bars and trail mix.*

Rosemary – quick-tempered, with a heavy bosom that strained her sensible shirt – peered over her cubicle and cleared her throat. Anything louder than the lazy trill of keystrokes irked the veteran cataloger. Tabitha rolled her eyes and flipped open a book.

Jessica longed for a window, a distraction from monotony. But desks with a view were reserved for management, and it was hard enough to get a box of tissues or the coveted automatic pencils from the storeroom. Tabitha settled for a roll of toilet paper on her desk, mostly in protest, and chewed on a unicorn pencil, which, like her snacks, came from the dollar store.

Cracking the spine of *Fundamentals of Fluid Mechanics,* Jessica searched for the willpower to catalog another title. The AC whirred, breathing another gust of cold air across her desk. Uncatalogued books towered by her monitor. When she hadn't been thinking about the kids in her yard, she'd lamented the heartbreaking boredom of her workday and whipped up more toe-curling moments with Elliot Reed. His lips on hers as she'd restocked aisles one through five, and his roaming hands under her shirt as she'd twisted the phone cable around her wrist, on hold with the IT department. And she'd thought about sliding down his chest, his belly, as she'd refilled her coffee cup. How she'd unzip his jeans, make him see stars.

And she'd spent at least an hour imagining him walking through the cataloging office door, into her life, then tortured herself with all the reasons why that would never happen. *Celebrity writers don't visit Driftwood. Elliot Reed has no use for a woodsy tourist trap, and he definitely wouldn't give a damn about a librarian with a messed-up head and holes in her cardigan cuffs.*

"The Walrus said I can't go home until I finish the accounting stack," Tabitha moaned. Another interruption.

"He can't strap you to your chair and..." Jessica trailed off as William poked his head out of his office and shuffled past in a mustard cardigan and tasseled loafers. He looked extra walrus-like that day, wayward whiskers sprouting from his chins. His halitosis lingered like a contrail.

Jessica checked the *Driftwood Times* website, which she'd kept open in a tab all afternoon. No headlines about a missing girl. No mention of a blonde kid on the sheriff's department's missing persons page, either.

The digits on her phone read 4:58. Close enough. She slipped out the door, jogged down the stairs, and nearly collided with Mr Fucky. No one knew how to pronounce the janitor's name. Some insisted that it was really Fachey or Fockey, that there was a subtle, important difference, but Fucky amused everyone, so it stuck.

She swung through the revolving doors to low black clouds and air that whipped her awake. Another howling storm ahead. Students emptied out of a red brick lecture hall. She wove around them, then hit the boardwalk by Lake Driftwood. The wind dimpled the lake's current, and the scowling skies turned it sulky gray.

Jessica pulled her cardigan close and walked faster. Just ten minutes to get home dry, if the clouds held on to their burden of rain. Thunder rolled – a clap from beyond the hulking cliff on the opposite shore.

But the clouds soon released a torrent that flooded the boardwalk and snaked across the road. The skies trembled and the lake sputtered. Another storm and no umbrella, so Jessica put her purse over her head. Water streamed down her neck, seeped through her shoes.

Moments from home, she glanced over her shoulder and caught a hunched-over figure in a hoodie, trailing ten feet behind her. She'd seen that hoodie on the boardwalk, she was sure. Someone had followed her home.

She turned around before hitting the driveway, rain slinking down her neck. Bright eyes blinked from across the street. Just a flash, like two tiny headlights flipped to high beams. But whoever hid under that hood quickly darted into the copse of trees lining the opposite street.

Jessica hurried inside and slammed the door, then peeled off her cardigan, toweled her hair. She kicked off her shoes, set the tea kettle on the stove, and ripped open a packet of hot chocolate. She was too on edge for coffee. Too spooked.

The powder dissolved as she stirred, and the rain drummed on the roof. She could still feel those eyes, watching her back, gleaming from across the street.

The warm mug thawed her fingertips. A few cloying sips seared her tongue. *It's because I gave them food and blankets. Or maybe they know what happened all those years ago. Maybe they know I let Olivia slip from my side, into the dark.*

She sighed through the steam of the mug, then peeled off her clothes. *No, that's impossible. They're just kids. They weren't even alive back then.*

She pushed aside thoughts of whether she was crazy or not – they left a nasty residue, a sense of hopelessness that engulfed her like a fog – and pulled on a sweater and leggings. The gunmetal sky threw its gloom across the bedroom walls.

As the dresser drawer clunked closed, something felt amiss. She looked behind her, taking in the disheveled mess – the pile of laundry, the books under the bed, the empty coffee mug.

Footprints.

A faint trail of crescents. She followed the prints into the hallway. They led to the living room door, which stood ajar. She grabbed a bat from her brother's old bedroom, then nudged the living room door with her foot. *This is when smart people call the sheriff, pop an Ativan.*

The door whined open. The words glared at her from the wall. Hurried, jagged, smudged by a fist. Black marker spanned five feet, scrawled at an angle, from shoulder height to the floor.

WAYKE THE SLEEPING
BURRY THE DED

As Jessica stared at the words, a strange white light suddenly flashed in her head. A flurry of twinkling bulbs, escaping some hidden furrow of her mind. She blinked and wobbled on her feet, startled. The writing on the wall had just unspooled a fragment, a sliver of a memory. She sank to the floor, closing her eyes to tease out more, but it left as quickly as it came. But whatever had just unfurled still breathed down her limbs. Her body *knew* those lights, that memory.

A fresh surge of adrenaline spurred her to stand up. She'd worry about the light later, when she wasn't wielding a bat, staring at creepy misspellings on her wall.

The rest of the scrawl was a soup of letters, numbers, strange symbols. Her Sharpie lay on the floor by a few browning apple cores. A heap of foliage littered her desk. She tightened her grip on the bat.

But it wasn't just a heap. It was a clumsy ring of pine sprigs and twigs, filled with shrubs and fungi, tangled in stringy roots and moss. A scattering of M&Ms, dusted in salt, hid among the flora. "Trail mix," she murmured, then dug out a few bird feathers, a bear claw.

She listened for a creak over the floor, but the rain still hammered against the roof.

Check every room, search the garage.

An avalanche of toys in her brother's old closet sent her heart thudding against her ribcage, but there were no footprints in the bedrooms. She searched on.

The concrete floor of the garage chilled her feet. Her father's toolbox was open, its tools scattered on the floor. The hammer and wrenches were gone.

Back in the kitchen, she grabbed her father's bourbon from under the sink, took a long swig and watched her fingers shake. There was a grubby handprint on the freezer. Unnoticed before, now it glared at her. She flung open the door. Someone had cleared out the top shelf.

"They've got some nerve," she muttered, returning to the bedroom, ready to snatch her phone.

The window was cracked open – she hadn't noticed that, either. The curtain hem billowed. Her phone rang from the nightstand, and she let out a yelp. Her brother's name lit up the screen.

"Mark?"

"Jess, something's going on. I saw the cops combing the woods with those bloodhounds."

She searched for words, but they were lost in white light. It still blinked, fading like an echo in her head. *The light ... what the hell was that light I saw when I stared at those words on the wall?*

"Are you listening, Jess?"

"Yeah, I'm here," she murmured. She shut the window. Her stomach had knotted itself.

"What's going on? You sound weird," he said.

"I'm OK. It's just that..."

"Just *what*?"

"It's just that I think someone followed me home, and someone climbed through my window when I was at work," she blabbered. "Someone wrote all over the wall."

Someone, or some kid.

"Wait, *what*? I'm coming over. Are you sure you're alone now? Did you call the sheriff's office? Maybe you should just get in the car," he interjected, with that staggered breath that told her he was already pulling on his shoes to run out of his apartment.

"No, Mark, I'm fine. There's no one here. Really, it's okay."

"Okay, well, just stay calm. I'm on my way. I'm guessing you haven't eaten."

"No, not yet," she said, a second after he'd hung up.

Call the sheriff.

She bit her lip, tapped her phone. *Call the sheriff's office now.*

But the scrawl on the wall had just unraveled a thread. She had no idea where it led, but it was vindicating, somehow, and she needed to know why. She needed to stew in those words, decipher that scribble. Find that memory.

Besides, Sheriff Clarke will probably decide I made up the whole thing. No sign of forced entry. Just some weird crap on my walls. A mess on my desk. They'll tell me to fix the window, get a security system. Some expensive shit I can't afford.

No, the drunk sheriff can stay out of this.

She thought of the Ativan in the bathroom again. But she grabbed the bourbon instead and slumped into a chair. Yelling at her brother between the claps of a storm hadn't eased the flutter in her chest. She took another long sip of bourbon, then reached for her journals from under the bed. A faint, near-forgotten memory had just surfaced. A memory of a moment she'd dreamed about almost twenty years ago.

Her oldest journal, a spiral-bound notebook decorated with stickers, lay at the bottom of the pile. Her adolescent cursive and collages filled every page. Elaborate, strange, intricate – her creations in paper and glue had been an outlet, a way to fill blank space inside and out. Illustrations of dreams and fading memories of Olivia, pasted together from magazine scraps, printed photos, and her own sketches in ink and colored pencil.

At the time, it had been the only way to make sense of Olivia's disappearance. An odd but calming therapy, a habit that she'd hid from everyone. *Sometimes our minds can't make sense of scary things, so we park those memories in a secret place,* the school counselor had told her, and Jessica had searched for those memories with glue and pencil strokes.

The first two pages were covered in glossy photos of pine trees. She'd added footsteps in ink, drawn as tracks along the back road to the state park, into an evergreen landscape pasted together from *National Geographic* photos.

On the third page, she'd drawn Olivia – a sketch of arms, legs and a head, around a dress made from a swatch of puffy floral wallpaper – and she was floating in the cosmos between aluminum-foil stars. On top of those she'd stuck sequins pilfered from a hideous sweater. *Where did you go? Did you forgive me?* She'd written her questions in a spiral around the sketch with a rainbow of colors flowing through the words.

But Jessica was searching for something else. A dream from later that year, when every night, she'd woken shaking, bathed in sweat.

At last, she found it. There was no sketch, no collage. Just her sloping, twelve-year-old handwriting:

> *I was in a dark tunnel, and I was running. I think I was chasing Olivia. She turned around and she said something, but I didn't understand. Then the lights came. She ran into the light. I looked around, and suddenly I was in the forest, all by myself. I ran home.*

Chapter 7

Friday, April 15, 2022

The highway was slick with rain that pooled into every dip in the road. Elliot exited the airport ring road, glowering at the bloated clouds beyond the windshield. The airplane that had shuttled him from Charlotte, a whistling tin can, washed into the blur in his rearview mirror.

The heavens had opened as he'd left the terminal, and the sprint to the rental car office had soaked his bones. His shirt clung, clammy and cold under his sweater.

The road was straight for a short stretch, before ascending to the mountain road that led to Driftwood, which sat snug in the valley of the lush state park. The air carried the faint stink of a paper mill. He watched the squeaky hypnotic wipers slash the rain and flipped on the high beams.

The blue mountain ridge loomed beyond the guardrail, smoky and somber. Elliot's mind was adrift in plot twists, forming fledgling characters. But soon the turns grew sharper, and he told himself to focus on the drive. The forested slopes shot up around him, almost obscuring the blackening sky. On the GPS, he saw nothing but faint snaking lines beyond the highway, as if he were speeding to leafy oblivion. Unmoored in looping thoughts, he hoped he'd find more than a thicket of pines and a sleepy town ahead. With a sigh, he remembered all that he'd run from in New York. His agent, Ruth, was now chewing her nails because he still hadn't sent her the first chapter he'd promised. *"I need something from you, Elliot. It's too late in the game. What am I supposed to tell the publisher? You'll give me a heart attack."*

The last rays of daylight sank into the gradient of dusky-hued trees. Only a few glowing cabin windows blinked through spruce and fir.

Fifteen miles to go, the navigation system promised, and then he'd park and dash under the wooden awning of the Driftwood Arbor, into the sparkling excess of the hotel lobby. And later that night he'd gaze out at Driftwood's streetlights. Pour a nightcap from the minibar, perhaps. Swirl it in the glass and stare into the viscous little whirlpool as he unwound from travel. And he'd shower off the airport grime, sink into crisp sheets. Lose himself more in loose ends, the plot he had to build and then unravel.

The ascent sharpened, and he pushed on the gas. Thunder roared from beyond the mountain ridge. The dark now cloaked everything but the rain pelting the windshield. A lightning fork hit the turf beyond the guardrail, and the road flashed a cold blue-white.

He eased around a hairpin turn, and as the wheel straightened, a chill whispered up his spine, pulling him from the thoughts he'd lost himself inside. It numbed his tailbone, spread to his neck, then crept down his limbs and froze his fingertips.

He blinked, flexed his fingers. *I'm just tired.*

But as he tapped the gas pedal again, an eerie stillness deadened the car's ascent. Inertia, despite the combustion of the engine, the dashed white lines spearing the dark ahead. He'd slipped inside a vacuum, separated from all that moved, breathed, bled.

Next, every noise – the hum of the engine, and the rubbery *swup-swup* of frantic wipers – ended. The rain no longer rattled the roof, and it didn't cascade down the windshield the way it should. The wipers froze, ending their dance halfway across the glass. As if fingers had clicked, or a conductor had swept down his baton, and the universe had held its breath.

A young girl, standing smack in the middle of the road, tore him from the void. Blonde hair slick with rain, eyes glinting like solitaires in the dark, she was a skinny waif drowning in just a nightgown. Elliot swerved – a sharp turn toward the mountain ridge. The crash through the guardrail split the heavy velvet quiet.

He thought he was careening upward, beyond the guardrail, the treetops, toward the stars. Piercing the hemisphere to disappear into the cosmos. It wasn't panic that seized him, and it wasn't a moment of revelation before death. It was a lead-heavy dread that told him he'd somehow left the living world without dying, just like the tires had left the road.

But all that ended when he remembered to breathe. The rain crashed against the roof as if the clouds had exhaled with him, and the wipers *swup-swupped* across the windshield. The car bounced, lurched, tore over foliage, skidded down grass. Elliot gripped the wheel, slammed on the breaks, and the airbag deployed in a cloud of powdery smoke. His head hit the bag – a spongy-fierce smack. The bumper folded around a tree, and the hood crumpled.

Branches scratched against the roof of the car. The wind whistled, and the storm roared on. Elliot slumped against the airbag, limbs limp among the shattered glass.

Chapter 8

Friday, April 15, 2022

Jessica raked aside the hangers on the closet rail and stared into the void.

A black hole of lost time, hidden behind a few unloved shirts.

It wasn't much of anything, really. Just a large black circle – craft paper taped to the wall. But when she gazed at it with her eyes half-closed, she saw two girls tumbling through the earth, into a cavernous pit.

She had no idea where the memory came from, or if it was a memory at all. But dark shapes triggered the vision. A black splash on a pale surface, an oval shadow in bright sunlight.

It began a few weeks after Olivia disappeared. The nightmares soon followed, and twenty years later, she still dreamed of Olivia decaying at the bottom of that pit, eyes hollowed by worms, organs liquefying among the insect lava and centipedes.

But she'd parked the real events of that night out of reach, hidden them in some unlit corner of her cortex. She'd gazed at the black circle for a decade, hoping to remember what happened on the unmarked road by the woods, when Olivia's hand slipped from hers in the dark. But it never yielded more than two girls falling into a hole in the ground.

Jessica checked the time on her phone. By now Mark would be driving through the downpour. In the meantime, the house was too quiet. Its silence was as loud as the breathy bursts of wind outside, the thud of rain.

She remembered the person hiding under the hoodie, following her home, and the footprints on the carpet, the scrawl on the wall. She fought the urge to look over her shoulder and search the garage again.

Instead, she grabbed a pad of sticky notes and a pen. *Wake the sleeping, bury the dead,* she wrote on one, then stuck it to the center of her black circle.

Now, when she stared at the circle until it blurred, a flurry of twinkling lights broke through the dark. She blinked, steeling against a wave of dizziness, and kneeled on the carpet.

In her journal, she wrote, *when did I see lights in the dark?*

She marched back to the living room and studied the writing on the wall, then scribbled down the letters and numbers, searching for patterns. Nothing emerged from the muddle.

Code? A dumb prank? she scrawled. *Or is it a threat? A cry for help?*

The bourbon still sat on the coffee table. She took another swig. The cold damp seemed to permeate the walls, seep through her skin. She glanced at the black sheen of the window, then pulled the drapes closed.

A moment on the phone with her brother bounced back to her. She'd been too startled to listen at the time. He'd said something about the sheriff's department combing the woods. Jessica grabbed her phone and searched for news on the blonde girl. Still nothing. Just reports of kids that looked nothing like her, plus a few articles on fentanyl deaths and the mayor's plans to gentrify more of Driftwood. She checked the time again. Her brother would be standing in line at a restaurant now, waiting to grab a bag of takeout. Spinning his keys in his hand, wishing the waitstaff would hurry up. Her stomach groaned.

She fiddled with the fraying cuff of her cardigan. The kids on her porch were more than just a worry. They nudged her toward the black circle, that pit of black shadows. It was a thorny dark burrow, the place inside her where she'd buried memories from twenty years ago, and most of the time, she wanted to run from it.

But tonight, Olivia whispered from the burrow again. *There's something you need to figure out, Jessie. There's something in the park.*

Jessica grabbed another notebook from under the bed, this one tattered and worn. It was filled with theories, mostly penned on sleepless nights, about all the things that might have happened to Olivia.

The worst possibilities had played like movie scenes, all transcribed in Jessica's fraught cursive. Thick arms dragging Olivia through the forest, throwing her in a truck, chaining her to a pipe in a basement. But intuition told Jessica that none of that was true. No, Olivia hadn't met a wandering creep, some toothy freak with a hunger for young skin. Her mystery was as cryptic as the rest.

But nothing linked Olivia to the feral kids in Jessica's yard–nothing except a hunch. She only haunted the black circle on the closet wall. She lived on in dark shadows, patches of color on white.

Jessica pulled the drapes. Mark had to be heading her way by now, chugging around the lake in his old lemon of a car.

The bourbon numbed her, blurred all the edges. But with her eyes closed, she could still see the flurry of lights, lighting up inroads to *somewhere*. Her hunch was tickled, stirred awake.

She packed away her folders. As usual, they hadn't revealed anything new. It was time to slouch into a recliner, eat something before she fainted. But then her phone rang.

Chapter 9

Friday, November 22, 2002

"Jessica ... Jessica, wake up!"

Jessica groaned, then turned on the creaky camping cot. "What?"

The full moon filtered through the curtain gap, casting gray ribbons over cardboard boxes. Her grandmother's junk room was a jungle of lampshades and storage bins, and it smelled of old people. Her father always took the spare bedroom. Some lame excuse about his restless leg syndrome, and how he needed to be close to Grandma in case she had a seizure.

"I had a bad dream. I dreamed you disappeared like Olivia, and I found you dead in the park," Mark gushed. He was sprawled over musty couch cushions on the floor.

"I'm right here. I'm not dead." Jessica turned her back to her brother.

"I'm scared we're all going to die in the woods. Something's out there." He propped himself up on his elbows, rustling in his sleeping bag.

Jessica sat up and sighed. "We're not going to die."

Mark turned a flashlight on and off, then sat up on the cushions. "It was horrible. Your body was all rotting and disgusting and your guts were coming out, and your eyeballs were gone."

"That's so gross."

"And then we were at your funeral, and I had to say goodbye to your corpse, and I threw up everywhere." He broke out of a whisper and Jessica shushed him. Dad and Grandma were just down the hallway, watching *Law and Order* in the living room.

"Now *I'm* going to throw up," she whispered back.

"Don't die."

"I won't. I promise."

They sat in silence for a moment, listening to the muffled TV voices.

"I have nightmares, too. I dream that Olivia fell into a huge hole in the ground, and now all the bugs are eating her," Jessica said. Mark turned on the flashlight again.

"That's gross. Really?"

"Yeah. I'm chasing a rabbit through the woods, and then I follow it into this giant rabbit hole. I see Olivia stuck down there, and I can't tell if she's dead or alive. I yell her name, and then I wake up."

"You think she's still alive?" Mark's voice rose again, then settled back into a whisper. Jessica's eyes adjusted to the moonlight, and she could see him sitting in his Henley pajamas.

"I don't know. I get this cold feeling in my stomach when I think about it."

"Mom and Dad are still acting so weird, like they're scared to let us leave the house."

Jessica felt heavy, like a rock on the cot. Guilt weighed a ton. More than her schoolbag full of textbooks. "I'm sorry. Everything's my fault. I ruined everything. And now Olivia's probably dead." Her whisper was soft but raspy. She tugged at the comforter.

"It's okay, Jessie."

"Something happened that night, before she ran away, but I can't remember what."

"You both ran into the living room, right after she got to our house," Mark whispered, wide eyes flashing in the dim light. "Try to remember, Jessie!"

Jessica frowned. "I can't! It's like there's a hole in my head and that chunk of time is just gone! But I know I was scared, even before we left the house."

"But you have to remember *something*."

"I remember Olivia begging me to take her trick-or-treating. You and your butthole friends were playing *Dungeons & Dragons* in your room."

"They're not all buttholes."

"Yeah, they are."

"You think something's hiding in there? In the woods, I mean?" The worry left Mark's voice. Now she just heard intrigue.

"I don't know. But sometimes I think she *wanted* to disappear. I know it sounds dumb…"

"What did she say right before she ran away? You still can't remember?"

Jessica shook her head. "I can't remember anything. Just the dark. It was *so* dark. Is that crazy? Am I crazy, Mark?"

He shook his shaggy head of curls. "No. I read about this in *Beast Hollow*." He climbed out of his sleeping bag and rummaged through his backpack with the flashlight, then flipped through a battered comic book. "There's this fucking terrible thing that crawls up from the underworld. This beast with really long arms, and I mean a whole shit-ton of arms, all waving around like snakes ... snakes with twigs stuck to them. And it tricks these kids into getting lost in the woods, and then it sucks them under, and it turns them into zombies. They start to rot and stink."

Jessica rolled her eyes. "But this is real life."

"No, no, listen. It's not as dumb as you think. I think there's something in the forest, Jess. Something that took Olivia."

"Maybe you're right," she said, surprising herself.

"Whoa, really?" He shone the flashlight in his sister's face.

"OK, you can't tell anyone about this, Mark. Not even your nerdy comic book friends. Not even Andrew Harding or Keith the Queef."

"You totally have a crush on Andrew Harding."

"Bullshit. Do you want to hear about this or not?"

"Okay, okay. Just tell me. I won't tell anyone, I swear," Mark pleaded, almost bouncing on the sofa cushions.

Jessica buzzed with nerves. "I think she was hearing voices inside her head. Sometimes I heard her talking like someone was there, but it was just her. Sometimes they scared her."

"Holy shit. Why didn't you tell me?"

"I thought she was just playing. But now I'm not sure."

"Did she hear voices that night, before she disappeared?"

"I can't remember." She closed her mouth before she told her brother about what she *did* remember. The thing that happened in the kitchen. The thing she couldn't tell anyone, not even him. And as that moment resurfaced, so did the noise of an apple falling on the kitchen floor. *Thud, thud.*

No, some things were too strange to share, and they always would be.

"It's a beast for sure. A huge beast underground," Mark gushed. "Or maybe it's a force. A dark force that's already captured Olivia's mind ... something that wants to drag us to another dimension." He stood up and raked around in the closet.

"What are you doing? Be quiet!" Jessica hissed, watching his dark silhouette pull shadows from the closet. "We're supposed to be asleep! Dad'll lose his shit!"

"I'm building a barrier. We have to do this every night," he decided, throwing coats and sports equipment in a heap by the door. "So it doesn't come for us next."

"I'll probably just break my neck if you do that."

Mark slumped onto the floor, landing on top of the coats he'd piled. "Everything sucks. I *hate* school. I hate everything!"

"Will you help me find it, Mark?" Jessica slid onto the floor and sat cross-legged.

"Find what?"

"The thing that's hiding in the woods."

"Are you kidding?"

They sat in silence again, breathing in the carpet dust.

"That's like the craziest thing you've ever said," Mark added, after the pause.

"Shhh … shut up for a second." Jessica stood up and tiptoed to the door, cringing as the floorboards groaned under the carpet.

"*You* shut up." Mark waved the flashlight at her.

Hushed voices floated in from the hallway, and Jessica swore she heard Olivia's name.

Mark stood up to follow her to the door, but the floorboards groaned again, louder than ever.

"Shh!" Jessica turned and glared at her brother. Mark slowed, wobbling as he gave his sister the finger and took delicate ballerina steps.

"They're calling off the search?" her grandmother said, her scratchy voice rising. Jessica kicked the coats aside, and a baseball glove fell to the floor. She froze, and Mark gasped behind her.

"They've been searching for two weeks and they found *nothing*," her father replied. Jessica heard the tightness in his voice, the brittle tones he'd used since Halloween. Like if he stretched too hard, he'd snap in half. "Apparently, she was admitted to the hospital before she disappeared. Matteo said she had trouble breathing and some kind of *psychological* problem. She scared the hell out of a nurse."

"What on Earth?" Her grandmother's voice rose again, ringing down the hallway.

"I didn't want to pry. They're upset enough as it is." Her father's voice grew louder, then faded into the kitchen, and Jessica heard the kitchen door close.

Mark grabbed her shoulder and whispered, "What the fuck?"

He writhed back into his sleeping bag, and Jessica slid onto the cot.

Jessica's eyes glazed over, and she suddenly felt freezing cold. She grabbed a pillow and stuffed it into her lap. "They gave up."

"Dad said she was crazy. It's the beast, Jessie! The beast was in her head!" Mark broke out of a whisper, and she raised her finger to her mouth again.

"She wasn't crazy, Mark!"

Jessica wanted to look behind her, as if someone might have been standing over her shoulder. Her hands and feet tingled, and her forehead was damp with sweat.

She reached above the cot and opened the curtains to look at the pearly moon above the trees in the yard. "But what if she's still alive?"

Chapter 10

Friday, April 15, 2022

Am I dead?

Elliot heard the voice in his head. Then, as the hammer came down, he understood it was his own.

That's what it felt like. A hammer to his skull, bruising the spongy coils of his brain. The first inkling that he wasn't dead. Then the sharp stabbing as he tried to breathe, the pressure. A numbness that was thawing, warming into red-hot pain.

Branches still scraped across the car roof. Raindrops fell from the canopy above, spitting on the dashboard through the shattered windshield. The wind howled.

How long have I been here? Minutes, or hours?

A gust of wind sprayed rain on his face. Another tug from blank sleep. Then a sensation slowly registered: a small hand, pressing against his sleeve.

He searched for his voice. It was buried in his throat somewhere, behind a croak and a cough and the maddening delay of bewilderment. Wet leaves swished, and the hand was gone. A giggle, the sound of feet hitting wet grass, then silence.

Elliot blinked through pain and whispered, "Fuck." He felt sorry for himself for ten seconds, then pushed the airbag aside to slide out the door. It was open, wedged against another tree. Just enough space to slip out.

"Fuck," he said again, worrying that moving might wreck his spine forever, or leave him with some other misery. But other than the hammer in his head and the shivers, the aches, he was okay. Nothing bleeding or broken or sickeningly contorted. He peeled off his sweater, wondering why his body didn't respond with a searing stab. The pain was fading fast – *painkiller* fast, and now only a burning rush of hot and cold sizzled inside. *Adrenaline?*

As he asked himself too many questions at once, dizziness swarmed him. The wet leaves whirled and warped. He hunched over, heaved, but nothing left his stomach. Eyes shut tight, he listened to the wet patter of rain. *A concussion? Is that what happened?* The bump on his head was now just an ache.

The walk up the embankment was simpler than it looked, because of the foliage that stopped him from skidding back down on his ass. He beamed his phone light into the thicket with one hand and grabbed on to branches with the other. Halfway toward the mangled guardrail, he remembered the girl by the side of the road. Was that who'd gripped his sleeve through the car window?

No phone signal, and twenty percent battery remaining. He climbed over the guardrail and searched both sides of the road, but there was no drenched, elfin little blonde kid anywhere.

What if she's dead? What if she's hurt? He froze, until he shook himself free. Standing paralyzed in the rain wouldn't do a damn thing. He jogged east and west, searching for her, but only desolate highway hid around the bends.

His flashlight danced over the trees beyond the guardrail. *Maybe she's in there, somewhere, but I'll never find her now. Not in the dark, with a dying phone.*

He ran toward Driftwood, hoping to find civilization before he drowned in his shoes. More thunder burst into the sky. Rain streamed down his neck. The blue mountain ridge to his left flashed white, as if illuminated by a giant flickering lightbulb. Still no phone service, and no cars or trucks to flag down.

His shoes squeaked as he ran. The wind picked up and started to bite. He jogged faster, until a light fanned across the highway at the top of an incline.

I feel fine. I shouldn't *feel fine.*

No kid, no injuries. Nothing added up. He bent over and coughed into the gravel. At the top of the incline, a rusty gas station stood by the road, next to a diner with its lights on. A rusty sign yawned back and forth in the wind.

The gas station's store stank of sweat and smoke. A huge man in a camo shirt ate a burger behind the counter, resting the wrapper on his belly.

"You have a phone I can use?"

"Next door. Diner's got a payphone," the man said, then crushed a soda can.

The diner was hospital bright and steeped in grease and coffee vapor. Elliot approached the counter, where a waitress drank him up, greedy eyes lingering on his wet shirt. He wished the night would end.

"The guy next door said you have a payphone."

"Sure, we got a payphone," she drawled, wrapping a brassy tendril around her finger. "Right over there."

He walked to the phone, then realized he had no idea *who* to call. He sighed, then walked back to the counter.

"I need a tow truck…"

"Wrecked your car?"

"Yeah."

A trucker hunching over a coffee looked up. The diner seemed still, suddenly, as if a spoon against porcelain would shatter the quiet.

The waitress swapped a fleeting look with the trucker. "Evergreen Pass?"

"I don't know the area. It was a sharp turn about a mile west."

Now two more truckers in a booth turned their heads.

"Well, you oughta call my cousin, Tyler." The waitress scrawled a number on a napkin. *"Angel"* was inked on the inside of her wrist in cursive. "I'd call him for you, but we can't get no signal here." She handed him the napkin, then watched him return to the payphone. Silverware clinked again; the rain pounded the roof.

He pulled out his wallet, a puffy fold of wet leather, stuck a credit card in the slot, and heard an angry beep. He looked up at the ceiling, ready to whisper another "fuck."

"Need some change?" the waitress yelled across the floor, so that the truckers looked up from their plates again.

He searched for cash in his wallet to exchange for the coins. Nothing.

"You can pay me back any time." She dropped the coins in his hand and swayed her hips back behind the counter. A giggle bounced out from the kitchen. A trucker scratched his mustache.

The phone swallowed the coin. The ring tone purred. Success.

"Hello?" a woman's voice said, soft, a little surprised.

"Hi. Can I speak to Tyler, please?" he asked, already sensing this wasn't the lover or mother of Tyler the tow truck driver.

"Tyler?" A quick but notable pause, as if she were holding her breath.

"Somebody gave me this number for a tow truck." He cradled the phone under his ear, stuck his wallet back in his pocket, then looked over his shoulder. The waitress stood slouching into one hip with her mouth open, then busied herself with the coffee pot.

"Elliot? Is that you?" she asked, and her question dissolved the diner.

"Who is this?" He'd softened his tone, he realized, after the fact.

Her silence brushed against his skin.

"It's … um … I think you have the wrong number." A subtle inhale, a hesitation that he somehow liked.

"How did you know my name?" He spoke to her in that same soft tone again, as if he knew her, then told himself to get it together.

"Lucky guess, I suppose." Shy, but a hint of a laugh.

"Yeah, I guess so. Well … goodnight." *Why haven't I hung up already*? But he waited for her reply.

"Goodnight, Elliot. And be careful out there."

Lightning struck the highway forty feet away, right as the tone went dead.

Chapter 11

Thursday, October 31, 2002

"John, the goddamned babysitter just canceled!"

Sarah Paige slammed the handset down. Lampshade tassels trembled on the console table. She sighed, and dinner strained her fit-and-flare blue dress. Chicken casserole, dropped on the table from oven-mitted hands, now formed a lumpy little tire. Jessica had eaten two bites with a slice of floppy white bread. The house still smelled like cream of chicken soup.

"What? She's supposed to be here already!"

John Paige was still in the kitchen, spooning a wobbly dessert into Tupperware. "Damn it!"

Jessica heard her father tear off a wad of paper towels. The echoes of howling middle schoolers filtered through the windows. The streets were crawling with trick-or-treaters, who'd already toilet-papered a neighbor's hickory tree.

"What are you supposed to be?" Jessica leaned against the living room doorframe.

Her mother adjusted a pigtail. "Dorothy from Wizard of Oz. Now let me figure this out."

"You got the number of another sitter? The Garcias are already on their way." Her father appeared from the kitchen, sweating through his scarecrow face paint.

Mark ran from his bedroom. "Mom! Dad! It's fine. We don't need a dumb sitter, anyway. She ate all the tater tots last time, and she was on the phone all night." His arms looked like matchsticks under the sleeves of his T-shirt. One sock was halfway off his foot.

"I don't even know if I want to go to this party, anyway, John. We barely know these people!"

Mark huffed out a sigh and crossed his legs on the hallway carpet.

"Sarah, we already RSVP'd. The Garcias are *literally* minutes away." John returned to the kitchen, then reappeared with the Tupperware. "And we made this damn dessert."

Sarah tapped her nails on the console table. "If we go, *promise* me you won't leave the house. None of you! No trick-or-treating. You can have some friends over, watch a movie. But nothing crazy. There's a storm coming in."

"But, Mom!" Jessica whined. "I promised Olivia..."

"It's fine, Mom," Mark yelled over his sister's protests. "Everything'll be fine. I swear."

The doorbell rang, and Sarah opened the door.

Matteo Garcia lunged through the doorway, red-faced in a giant felt hotdog. Paula Garcia shimmered in a Lycra Wonder Woman costume, frizzy hair bouncing off her shoulders. Hugs and laughter erupted.

Olivia ran to Jessica, coat hanger-and-pantyhose wings flapping, gauzy white dress floating around her calves. She carried a pink backpack.

"That's a cute costume!" Jessica led her into the living room, where they hurled themselves onto the couch.

"Look, Jessie, look!" Olivia's smile lit up burnished amber irises – eyes so bright and dazzling, Paula complained that people stopped to stare at her daughter in the grocery store.

She pulled out a paperback, a coloring book and a small pink box from the backpack. A little gold key hung from a plastic bracelet around her wrist.

"I got a magic box!" She took off the bracelet and inserted the key into the lock. A one-inch ballerina twirled as *Swan Lake* played from a tinny cylinder.

"That's so pretty!"

"I got a book from the library. It's my favorite. Can you read it to me?" Olivia thrust the book at Jessica: *Alice's Adventures in Wonderland.*

Swan Lake ended with a slow cranky whine.

"You can read just as well as I can."

"Yeah, but I like it when you do it. I like how you do the voices!"

"Okay, I guess."

"And can we go trick-or-treating?"

"I don't know," Jessica lied, then searched the room for a decoy. Olivia had talked about trick-or-treating for a month. "But we can watch movies!"

John and Sarah left with the Garcias. The doorbell rang a moment later, and Mark's friends burst into the hallway, then funneled into his bedroom.

"Read me Alice!" Olivia begged. "Read me the part about the rabbit hole!"

"You don't want to start at the beginning?" Jessica flipped through the book. It smelled of old paper.

"I already know the story!" Olivia pulled the book from Jessica's fingers. "It's near the beginning, but not *right* at the beginning." She turned a few pages, then pointed to an illustration of two girls lying on a lawn. "Start right here."

"Okay, okay. The rabbit hole went straight on like a tunnel for some way, and then dipped suddenly down, so suddenly that Alice had not a moment to think..."

"Did Alice really fall down the rabbit hole?"

"No, it's just a story."

"Did they try to trap her like a rabbit?"

Jessica lowered the book to her lap. *"Trap her*? Who?"

"I don't know. Bad people," Olivia whispered, eyes wide again, twinkling above raised eyebrows. A wisp of silky hair fell across her forehead.

"No, no one tried to trap her. She just jumped down the rabbit hole because she was bored." Jessica was a little shaky on the last word. She glanced around the room – the corners, dimly lit by lamplight, and the black sky outside the window.

"How do we know what's real and what's a story?" Olivia's voice was still just a whisper. She had a habit of asking impossible questions. *"It's because she's gifted,"* Paula had explained last week, exasperated.

"Stories are just in your head, but real things really happen," Jessica decided aloud.

"What about dreams?"

"Those are like stories."

Olivia frowned. "Sometimes I remember things and I don't know if they're real," she said.

"Like what?"

"It's a secret," Olivia whispered, shaking her head. "Read me the part about the magic door!"

A secret? Jessica tried to imagine what secret Olivia might have. *Probably just something silly,* she decided. Olivia thumbed through the book, then thrust it back into Jessica's lap.

"Alice opened the door and found that it led into a small passage, not much larger than a rat-hole: she knelt down and looked along the passage into the loveliest garden you ever saw…"

"Is there a magic door in the woods?" Olivia ran over Jessica's words again.

"No."

"Yes, Jessie. I think there is! There's a magic door and a secret place!" She gave Jessica's sleeve a tug. "I think there are monsters there! And it's so, so dark if you fall inside!"

"It's just a story, remember? Stories aren't real."

"No, Jessie, you don't understand! It's where you sleep until you're dead! You sleep with the bones and the snakes!" Olivia's eyes twinkled in the lamplight, so bright that Jessica forgot about the unlit corners, the black sky outside. But she felt cold inside, and the chill stiffened her shoulders, her neck. Those eyes were *too* bright. She looked away.

"Olivia, that's creepy…"

"You can get stuck in there, Jessie. You can get stuck and never get out."

"No, Olivia, that's not true. That's a story."

Olivia frowned again, as if she were trying to solve a puzzle inside her head. "If I remember a thing, did it definitely happen?"

Her questions were so complicated, they almost gave Jessica a headache. Jessica opened her mouth, ready to speak.

"And if I don't remember a thing, did it definitely *not* happen?" Olivia continued, confusing Jessica even more.

"I don't know. I guess that depends on what you remember. Maybe if it's super crazy, it didn't really happen."

"Can we go trick-or-treating now?"

"Why don't we color in your coloring book?" Jessica decided she'd forget the creepy things Olivia had said, the way her eyes had twinkled so bright. Erase it all, like she was erasing a pencil sketch.

"Yes, yes!" Olivia yelled, and Jessica opened the coloring book. She pulled her pencil case from the coffee table shelf.

"Draw me and you in the rabbit hole!" Olivia begged.

"But I thought we were coloring?" The chill crept back.

Olivia snatched a pencil from the case. Inside the back cover of the coloring book, she sketched two girls tumbling down a long, dark tunnel, arms above their heads and their hair disheveled like unraveling nests. Under the burrow, she drew a dark shape. Her harsh pencil strokes left indents on the paper.

"What's that?" Jessica asked. She held on to the edge of the sofa.

"It's the secret place," Olivia whispered. "Now that we're inside the story, did we make it real?"

"No," Jessica stammered. "It's still a story." *There's no way I'm getting inside that story,* Jessica decided. *Olivia can't make me jump down that rabbit hole.*

Olivia huffed out a sigh. "People say things inside my head, Jessie. But the doctor says it's not real. Is that a story, too?"

The room suddenly seemed cold now, as if the chill had spread to all the corners. "What do you mean? Who says things inside your head?"

"I don't know who they are. Sometimes they talk and talk!" Olivia stared up at the ceiling, as if she could see right through it, into the night sky.

"What do they say?"

"It's a secret."

"That's a secret, too?" Jessica's voice was shaky.

Olivia nodded and doodled spirals. "This is the way out," she whispered.

"The way out of what?"

"The way out of the bones."

"A spiral? Olivia, what are you talking about?"

Olivia ignored her question. "Can we go trick-or-treating now?"

Jessica searched for another diversion. This Halloween seemed creepier than all the rest. "But remember how the candy gives you a tummy ache?" She stood up, and Olivia followed her to the kitchen.

"I don't want the candy. I just want to go outside."

"You want to watch a scary movie instead?" Jessica opened the bread box and grabbed a loaf of bread.

"No, movies are boring. I want to go *outside*," Olivia whined. Then she pulled a jar of strawberry jelly from the fridge, holding it with both hands.

"We can't. There's a thunderstorm coming in." Jessica took the jelly from her, then spread it over slices of bread. She demolished a sandwich. Giggles and the sound of cellophane peeling from cardboard filtered in from Mark's open door. Mark was unpacking his new deluxe edition of *Dungeons & Dragons* while his friends cackled about spilled root beer and a terrible fart.

"Thunderstorm? I want to see it! I want to go outside and see the thunderstorm!" Olivia pleaded.

Jessica stifled a sigh. "No, it's not safe. You'll get cold and wet, and then you'll get sick." She handed Olivia a sandwich.

More howling echoed from the street outside. The neighbors' jack-o'-lantern glowed from their porch – evil triangle eyes above a zig-zag sneer. Mark and his friends were still cackling and snorting.

"But Jessie, *pleeeeeaaaaaase*?" Olivia tugged at her sleeve again.

"No."

Olivia scowled. She crossed her arms and glared at the counter, eyes focused on the fruit bowl. An apple from the top of the pile began to shake and teeter, then rolled onto the counter and bounced onto the floor. *Thud, thud.*

Jessica stepped away from the apple, until her back hit the kitchen counter. Her limbs had gone icy cold again. She mouthed something, but nothing left her lips.

"What did you just do?"

Olivia's lip trembled. "Nothing. It was an accident."

"But Olivia, I just saw…"

"It was nothing!" Olivia's tears began to flow.

"Okay, okay. It was nothing. Just an accident." Jessica picked up the apple. Her voice wobbled like Jell-O. *It was just my imagination. Just an apple. Maybe I can forget that, too.*

"My tummy hurts," Olivia said, staring at the sandwich in her hands. Jessica wiped Olivia's tears with a paper towel. A lump bulged in her throat. There was a rock in her belly now, too.

Olivia sniffed. "Jessie, *pleeeease* can we go?" She coughed a mouthful of sandwich into the trash and threw the crust away.

The wall clock ticked to 8:45. It wasn't fair that Mark could throw a nerdy party while she tried to entertain Olivia, who was in such a weird mood.

"Okay, Olivia. Listen. We can go for ten minutes," she whispered, putting her finger to her lips. "But we have to be real quiet, and you can't tell *anyone.* You promise me you can keep a secret?"

Olivia nodded. A glob of jelly dripped from her fingers onto the floor. "I'm good at secrets. But you need a costume, Jessie."

"Okay, come with me." Jessica cleaned her hands again, then led her down to the basement, stopping to check for noise from upstairs. Thudding and laughter. *They're probably wrestling in all the mess they made. They won't notice we're gone.*

Jessica flipped on the light and pulled an old sheet from a dresser. Her hands were still unsteady; her body reeled from that bouncing apple, even if her mind had pushed it all aside.

Back in the kitchen, she cut eye slits into the sheet while Olivia hid her giggles under her hand. "Ten minutes," Jessica repeated, then pulled the sheet over her head.

They crept out the door. The air outside was muggy, too warm for Halloween. Jessica couldn't see much to her left or right, because the sheet blocked her view like horse blinders. The clouds were dark pillows, almost hiding a thin crescent moon. Gangs of kids roamed the streets in costumes. Jessica looked behind her at Mark's bedroom window. *This is a bad idea. But we won't be long.*

But as they ran from one neighbor's home to another, time seemed to slide from the front of Jessica's mind. So quietly, so easily, that Jessica didn't notice they'd wandered from Pine Street. Not until she hit the curb and saw the shadowy right turn to the back road, the road that led along the boundary of the park. Jessica held on to Olivia's hand.

"Come on, Jessie, this way."

"No, that's too far. Mom and Dad will be so mad if they find out!"

"Just for a minute? Please? *Pleeeeaaaaaaase?*" Olivia coughed, suddenly out of breath.

"Are you okay?"

"Sometimes I feel like I can't breathe, Jessie. But let's go, okay? Come on!" She tugged on Jessica's sleeve.

It wasn't that Jessica said yes, and it wasn't that she said no. She wasn't sure what she said next, or why their feet moved forward. Again, time seemed to slip, and so did her urge to turn around. They took a right onto the gravel road, under the arching trees, leaving behind the streetlights.

Suddenly, the night was eerily quiet. So quiet, Jessica could hear herself breathe. She couldn't decide if she was excited or scared, but her feet kept moving forward. Olivia's eyes seemed too bright again – bright enough to glimmer in the dark.

The moon now hid behind the clouds, which were heavier than before, low in the sky above the branches. A roll of thunder echoed. Soon there was nothing but the dark and Olivia's hand pulling her forward. Jessica turned around, holding tight to Olivia's hand, and saw only an unlit, winding road behind her.

The sheet was pointless when no one was around to see it. She let go of Olivia's hand and pulled it from her head.

The damn thing was tangled up in a barrette in her hair. She struggled with it, wrestling the fabric over her head, then tossed it to the ground.

She threw out her hand to Olivia again. "Olivia? Olivia, come back!" she yelled, again and again, searching for her palm in the dark. But Olivia was gone.

Chapter 12

Friday, April 15, 2022

Impossible.

The floorboards replied with a creak. Jessica stopped circling the bedroom rug and sat on the bed. The call had ripped right through her boozy lull.

Some things just can't happen. Either mathematically, or because life's just a bitch that way.

No, I didn't just speak to Elliot Reed.

She tugged at her sweater cuff, blushing despite the empty room.

"This is what happens when you live on dreams and novels and toast," she murmured. "I don't even know what's real anymore." She sipped the bourbon, stinging from shame. Her obsession, her *longing,* boiled her cheeks.

The call replayed in her head. As she'd heard the voice on the end of the line, she'd been *certain* it was him. But the line between fiction and reality blurred on nights like these, when she lost herself in the rabbit hole inside her closet. Too many years living in daydreams. Too many hours alone.

It had to be another Elliot. Another Elliot who sounded exactly like him. The way he sounded in that interview she'd watched a thousand times.

And how mathematically likely is that?

She glanced at the bottle. *How much have I had? Not that much.*

Now she checked her phone. The call was logged. *Someone* had called. That she could trust.

Maybe I haven't lost it. Maybe it somehow happened.

A car door slammed outside. Her brother, at last. She ran to the bathroom, splashed water on her face, and tied up her mass of brown curls with an elastic band from her wrist. She'd have to keep this one quiet. Even Mark had his limits, and this little gem was just too far-fetched.

What if I called back? No, I can't do that. There's no plausible excuse. The awkwardness would kill me.

She opened the front door, almost elbowing the clay lion that Mark had made in elementary school. More clutter she couldn't throw away. What would she be without it? Her soul was held together with books, hideous figurines, the memories trapped in old junk.

"What the hell happened?" Mark cowered from the rain in a drenched T-shirt on her doorstep, clutching a bag of takeout. The rain flowed from the porch awning. He peered over her shoulder, expecting to find a crime scene. A siren wailed a few streets away, a steady scream in the dark.

"Relax, I'm fine," she said, wondering if it was true. She ushered him into the hallway. "What took you so long?"

He shuddered, dripping water onto the floor. "The roads are flooded. It's a disaster out there."

She tossed him a towel from the closet. He looked crumpled and tired. *Too many nights sketching and re-*

sketching, obsessing about the minutiae in his comic book art, she guessed.

"Where's the mess? Did they take anything?" He toweled his face and hair. His curls were a harried halo around his forehead.

She rattled off her list. The footprints, the tools, the freezer. The hoodie that followed her home.

"Jesus Christ," he mumbled.

She nodded toward the living room, then followed him down the hallway.

"What the hell is this?" He stared at the words on the wall, more alarmed than she'd expected.

"You tell me."

"This town is nuts. Sometimes I think we should just leave." He paced the floor.

"I thought you loved it. All the conspiracies and weird stuff." She wished he'd stop pacing.

"I do, but this is insane."

"I'm not calling the sheriff's office. They'll think I'm certifiable," she said, snappier than she'd meant. "And they won't do a damn thing."

"Only *you* would say that. Normal people would rush to the phone. Why the hell wouldn't you call them?"

Jessica searched for a reasonable answer. So much had happened, and she hadn't told her brother. The only person who really knew her, and the only one who would believe her.

He looked up when she didn't reply. "Jess, what the hell's going on?" His eyes darted to the wall again.

"Some of those kids turned up in the back yard. Twice."

"Kids? What kids?"

"*Those* kids. And their eyes really do glow in the dark. It's subtle, but it's definitely a shimmer, and it doesn't look human. Same with whoever followed me home."

Mark's lips tried to form words, but nothing came out.

"There's something weird about them. They don't look normal. The stories are true, Mark. Some of them, at least."

"Tell me *exactly* what happened." The color had run from Mark's face.

Jessica told him all that she remembered of the kids on her porch, and the newspaper report about the two boys. Her fidgeting made a fresh hole in her fraying sweater cuff.

"And you're sure these aren't just kids from the neighborhood?"

"No, Mark. As far as I know, none of the neighbors have kids with glowing eyes."

"Jesus Christ. So now what the hell are you going to do? What if these kids live with psychopaths? And what does all this *mean*? Bury the dead? How sick is that? You think they broke in here and wrote that?"

"Or someone who escaped a psych ward. Someone in need of tools and frozen peas."

"What if they come back?"

"I'll sleep with the bat under my bed."

"It looks like the woods threw up on your desk, and the wall's covered in the ramblings of a lunatic. A bat won't save you from a nutcase. You need some stuff."

Mark had been prepping for the apocalypse since college. His closet was crammed with military surplus and canned beans. By "stuff," he meant a shotgun and ammo.

"I have Dad's hunting rifle," she said, not that she had any idea how to use it. "Maybe it's some kind of barter ...exchange." She glanced at the wall. "What if they left all this stuff because they took the food and the tools? Maybe it's a cry for help?"

"There are M&Ms in here." Mark frowned, lost in the mess.

"Yeah. I gave them some trail mix. I guess they don't like chocolate."

"Jess..."

"They're probably starving."

"And apparently, they're batshit crazy. Look, I get this is thrilling and all..."

"Mark," she began, but had nothing useful to say. Rebuttals had a habit of turning up hours after she needed them.

"Jess, people who go near those kids disappear. You know how many hikers have vanished in the woods? What if you poked a hornet's nest?"

"Thanks, I'm not freaked out enough."

"Sorry," he mumbled, pushing his glasses up the bridge of his nose. "I need to eat, before I pass out." He nodded at the bag of takeout, and she unpacked it on the coffee table, stabbing forks into cartons.

"What's this? Some kind of gelatinous noodle thing?" Savory steam flew up her nose.

"It's Lo Mein." Mark took off his glasses and buffed them with his T-shirt.

Jessica eyed the disheveled mess of her living room, which was somehow only noticeable when she had company. Scattered books, a stale sweater. A candle threatening to drip wax onto the tabletop. Two pictures – an awkward sketch of a horse that her parents had bought at an antiques fair, and a map of the stars – hung askew on the wall, as if a little earthquake had rattled the room.

"What did you see in the park?" She grabbed a carton and slumped into the ugliest of the two recliners, which crouched like fat old toads in her living room. Mark tossed a fortune cookie her way.

"I went to get groceries, right before it rained. A bunch of cops were heading into the woods with bloodhounds."

Jessica stabbed the noodles. "Maybe it was that girl."

"Girl?"

"The one on the porch. I couldn't dig up anything about her."

"I guess we'll find out soon enough."

She gave up on the noodles. Her mouth was coated in syrupy sauce, each tooth wearing its own fluffy slipper. *A golden egg of opportunity awaits you,* the note inside her fortune cookie read. *Fat chance.*

A boom from the sky silenced them, and they listened to the thunder fade.

"I don't know how you can stand living here," Mark said after a moment.

Jessica shrugged. "It's free."

"It's like a museum of Mom and Dad. Why don't you throw all this crap out? I'll help if you want."

"No. It's fine. Maybe later."

Not now. This is all I have. Junk, folders full of tangents, and a bookshelf crammed with paperbacks.

Mark gave her a tight smile that meant, *"I wish you'd snap the hell out of your rut."* He'd given up asking, *"So what else is new? Been anywhere fun? Seeing anyone?"*

Because my empty replies felt like a gray cloud over his head, she figured.

"I just want you to be happy," he said, then stood up.

I just want my old sister back, he means. But it's been so long, I'm not even sure who that is.

"Stop feeding the kids, Jess. *Ignore* them, before you end up hurt." Mark waved at the wall, then walked to the kitchen. The sound of him opening the fridge door distracted her from a stab of grief.

"Eat that pie," she yelled. "It's strange, but okay, I think."

"Kind of like you, then?" she heard him say. He opened drawers.

"Spoons are in the dishwasher!" she yelled.

"I heard Dick Breath's back in town!" Mark yelled back.

Jessica turned rigid. "Screw him."

"No thanks."

She puffed out a sigh. The last thing she needed was a random encounter with Andrew Harding. The man who, eight long years ago, she'd thought she loved – the last man she'd let into her life. *"He's a piece of garbage,"* Mark had warned her back then, reeking of weed on a sunny afternoon. *"He's turned into a real asshole. You can't trust him,"* he'd insisted. She'd replied with an eye roll. *"You don't understand. He said he was sorry … he said he'll never cheat again."* But he did, again and again, and Mark had called him *Dick Breath* ever since. Casually, as if it were his real name.

"What are you thinking about?" Mark asked, his voice suddenly close, and she jumped in her seat. She turned to find him sitting on the sofa again, this time with enough pie for three people on his plate.

"Nothing," she said.

"This is the strangest pie I've ever eaten. There are whole peanuts in it."

"Tabitha made it."

Mark stared at the wall again. "It's like some kind of code."

Jessica nodded.

"Or serial numbers. Look." He pointed at the jumble of letters and numbers. "Like barcodes, or something."

"Coordinates?" Jessica said.

"Maybe. But they look too long for that. I'm guessing it's just nonsense. You need some help scrubbing it off the wall?"

"I'll do it tomorrow."

"Suit yourself."

"I guess you've heard about the new book," he said a moment later.

Jessica paused on her way to the couch. "Book?"

"Elliot Reed."

His name aloud was like a mild zap from an electric fence. She reminded herself she didn't need to share everything. "What book?"

"Seriously? I thought you'd be the first to know."

"Know what?"

"His next novel. I read about it today. It's ... um ... well, you'll see."

Jessica retrieved her laptop from under the debris on her desk, then sat back in the recliner.

On the *News* tab of Elliotreed.com, she read the synopsis of his next novel, *Chasing the Void*. She blinked, wondering if all the sense had leaked out of her head again. But no, there it was, next to a photo of him looking impossibly attractive at a book signing. She looked up and stared at Mark with her mouth open. He shrugged.

"A dark mystery haunts a lakeside town between the smoky summits of the Appalachian Mountains," she read, half muttering, half breathing through the words. *"When children begin to disappear in the fog..."* She threw another glance at her brother, then continued to mutter. *"Only one woman can unravel the truth, but she quickly learns that she'll have to face her deepest fears ... the memory of a tragedy decades ago."*

"Interesting, don't you think?" Mark stared at the floor.

"I don't even know what to say."

"A weird coincidence?"

Do I tell him about the phone call? No, not tonight.

Two hours later, after watching Mark dash from the porch to his car, she returned to her laptop and asked herself how enough synchronicity could pool together for Elliot Reed to write a novel about children disappearing into the fog and title it *Chasing the Void*. The alias she'd used on a forum.

"A weird coincidence," Mark had said. But what if it wasn't? What if he'd read her forum post from all those years ago? She grabbed her phone and plugged the number of the last caller into the browser.

The Blue Ridge Diner. Jessica laughed. *That place?* But it all made sense. He'd crashed his car, stuck with no signal on the highway, and walked there to make the call.

Crashed his car at Evergreen Pass.

The wind hushed and the rain sloshed outside. Jessica stared at the map of the stars on the living room wall, replaying everything that had happened since Monday. She traced the constellations with her finger and imagined herself falling through the gaping jaws of space, drifting into the arms of Elliot, somewhere between Earth and a distant star in the Milky Way. Then she grabbed a trash bag and cleared the foliage from her desk. Pine needles and soil escaped, settling on the carpet. It was past midnight.

Jessica flopped into bed and wrapped herself in crumpled sheets. Restless sleep followed – tossing, turning, blinking. Thoughts and dreams blended, clabbered, until she flung off the covers hours later and pulled on clothes. Lying in bed, waiting for dawn, was futile. *Those kids didn't come back tonight. Maybe they're somewhere near Evergreen Pass, where Elliot crashed his car. What if it's all related, somehow?*

She threw on her raincoat and grabbed her flashlight. The ignition coughed, and her parents' old car growled awake. The garage door clunked open.

Outside, the rain had stilled to a patter. Foliage and garbage from a toppled trash can littered the road. Only a few porch lights breached the dark. Jessica considered heading straight to Evergreen Pass, but it was a twenty-minute drive around the lake. Instead, she'd hike the trail that crested the foothills, no more than a three-minute drive away. She parked and beamed her flashlight at an opening between the trees, then stepped into the sopping thicket, toward the trail.

Other than a coo from a bird, a flap of wings here and there, the forest was quiet. The night air smelled of wet spring leaves, and the ground was mulchy, smothered in the dead layer of last year's bloom.

The rain slapped Jessica's neck, falling in fat beads from leaves above. Whatever search the sheriff had organized was over, and the forest breathed a damp calm. She aimed the light at the trail and hopped over puddles.

As the twiggy darkness thickened, she looked over her shoulder. It was a habit she couldn't break, no matter how many times she hiked the trails. The oak and hickory thinned, yielding to sky-high evergreens. As the pines closed in around her, she darted the light back and forth across the trail. Here, in the thick of it, every crunch and scurry echoed.

Her pace slackened on her way up the trail. She wasn't far from the clearing that overlooked Lake Driftwood, and soon the path would crest and descend toward a valley.

The descent was a relief after the uphill hike, and she could hear the distant hum of semis, the flash of headlights as a truck passed on the highway above the ravine ahead.

A creek bubbled by the steep slope of the ravine under Evergreen Pass. She hopped over it and landed in tall wet grass. Jessica struggled to stay upright without twisting her ankle, buckling her knees. She grabbed on to branches, reaching into the dark, clutching whatever crossed her path.

Aiming the light up, toward the pass, she found a hunk of metal shining in flattened grass. A chunk of a car's bumper. Tire tracks etched the ground.

He was right here.

But where was Elliot now? In some fancy hotel?

She looked right and left, and nausea turned her stomach. The world spun, until her hands found a tree trunk. She steadied herself and studied the ground. At first it was all just a messy knot of shrubs and weeds in the yellow beam. But she swore the grass had been trampled toward a cluster of trees. She followed the trail until the wet brush tickled her face and tangled around her feet.

Nausea churned again as her feet fought the grass. The trees parted to reveal a rubble of rocks and a six-foot hole leading right under the mountain pass. The storm had caused a mini- avalanche. She searched the area, which would have been hidden to anyone who hadn't trekked through the shrubs, she realized, looking behind her at the dark trail. Concealed on all sides by a wall of trees and the creeping underbrush, it lay in its own little lair.

She took a rain-dampened inhale, then stepped inside. It was a tunnel that drilled deep into the rock. Part of her wanted to turn around, run back to the car. But curiosity won, and her legs carried her forward, until the tunnel suddenly cratered, and she stumbled into a crevice.

The flashlight flew from her hand. She scrabbled in the dirt to secure it, kicking more soil loose beneath her. Her body skidded deeper and her arms flailed. A muted cry escaped her lips.

I'm trapped … trapped underground.

The thought strangled every other, and for a moment, it paralyzed her.

She shifted in the dirt, fighting to free her arms so she could beam the flashlight around her, find a way out. But that pulverized more soil beneath her, and she slid through a narrow hole.

Chapter 13

Friday, April 15, 2022

Tyler was hulking, with a ginger beard and a mumbling drawl that ate half his words. He smoked with both windows up and steered the tow truck through the storm toward the broken guardrail.

A bounce over a pothole pulled Elliot from thinking about the phone call. The mangled guardrail appeared in the headlights, and Tyler pulled over.

Elliot climbed out of the passenger's side. The wind howled and flowed through the damp fibers of his shirt. He clenched his jaw to stop his teeth chattering.

Tyler disappeared down the embankment with a flashlight and towing cables. "Looks like that car's 'bout a hunnerd feet down there!" he yelled, his voice almost lost to the storm.

I flew that far and I'm fine?

Elliot still didn't understand any of it, and only the cold, the drag of the cables hooked to the truck, distracted him from trying to figure it out. An hour passed as Tyler hauled the car up the embankment, stopping here and there to clear the path upward. At midnight, Elliot climbed back into the truck cab.

"I can't take you into Driftwood tonight," Tyler coughed out, pointing ahead. "The mechanic's over yonder. Wrong direction! I gotta go get another car over by Veryl's farm early in the morning. Said his engine's all *gaumed up*." He guffawed, as if an old car in a farmyard were the funniest thing he'd ever known. "But I can drop you at a motel on the way. My brother's place. It ain't The Arbor, but it's clean and dry. Ain't no taxi service workin' tonight, and you can forget about Uber."

Another cackle. *Jesus Christ, is everyone related?* Elliot wondered, checking the app on his phone. Sure enough, there were no cars available – nothing for miles. He tried to forget his earlier thoughts of crisp sheets and comfort.

Ten minutes later, he stood under the porch of a peeling-paint, gritty motel right off the highway. *The Duke*'s sign flashed neon blue above the entryway. A Pepsi machine hummed by the door.

The lobby smelled of musty upholstery and Lysol. In the dim light of a fluorescent strip above the reception desk, he caught damp stains across floral wallpaper, and a stuffed bobcat on a table in the corner.

He rang the bell. A guy in overalls and a sweat-stained T-shirt appeared behind the reception desk. An overhead bulb flashed on. Elliot blinked.

"Your brother said you might have a room for me?" His own voice sounded dry and mildly pissed. He gave a vague smile, reminded himself to not come off as a big-city asshole.

"Boy, you look like a damn drowned rat!" More cackling.

Runs in the family, Elliot figured.

"Wreck your car?"

"Yup. Flew a hundred feet down the embankment." Elliot relaxed, but felt disgusting. Like he'd bathed in a tub of rainwater and cigarette butts. But at least he was amusing the overalls man.

"Well, I'm Duke. Welcome to my castle!" he bellowed, throwing his arms out wide. "I got a room for you. Forty bucks a night. You got your own bathroom and a color TV."

Are there any black and white TVs left in the world? Elliot wondered, handing over his card.

"You crashed at Evergreen Pass," Duke said. It was a statement, not a question.

"How'd you guess?"

The wind swung the front door open, chilling the room with a blast of cold air, then flung it shut again.

"It's cursed," Duke replied, handing over a key attached to an antler. His smile was gone.

The floor creaked under Elliot's feet as he headed to his room. Inside, a no-smoking sign sat defiant in stale smoke and air freshener. A stain streaked the red carpet, and an old sock poked out from beneath a creased armchair.

He took one glance at the bed, guessing the sheets smelled of bleach and old men. *"Never sleep in those nasty motel sheets,"* his sister had warned him once. *"They're covered in cum,"* she'd explained, poised and sweet in her floral sundress.

The bathroom was just as sad, rusty and sick. He peeled off his shirt and kicked off the shoes he'd bought one frantic afternoon in Milan – lost luggage – that were now scuffed to hell and back. Under the water and whatever sludge lived in the pipes, he thought of the phone call again. *Goodnight, Elliot,* she'd said. And why hadn't he hung up before that?

No nightcap, so he sipped on a lemonade from the machine outside, chilling it with ice from the ice machine in the hallway, which he knew would keep him awake with its *chug-chug-clunk.* His stomach roared for food. The rain outside eased to a drip. The wind still howled, and now and then something ran across the roof.

He rummaged in his suitcase for his new prescription – Ambien, because he'd finally caved in. *Take it and sleep, before you ruin your health,* his doctor had ordered the day before. Her frown had dug tracks between her eyebrows. *You keep ignoring my advice, and you'll end up with high blood pressure, anxiety. Your cortisol's already high.*

Reluctantly, he unscrewed the lid and washed down a pill, then lay on top of the bedsheets.

But two hours later, as he'd predicted, the chug and clunk of the ice machine woke him. His eyes adjusted to the dark, and he traced a large crack in the ceiling, languishing between sleep and consciousness.

Evergreen Pass.

The thought stirred him wide awake. He flipped on the table lamp, grabbed his laptop, and connected to miserably slow Wi-Fi.

Duke seemed convinced the mountain pass was cursed, and the mention of it had been enough to make customers in the diner look up from their plates. Elliot searched the forums, forgetting any hope of sleep.

Sure enough, after digging through threads for ten minutes, he found a few mentions: *There's something wrong with Evergreen Pass. Too many accidents there. Too many kids disappear.*

He drummed his fingers on the dusty end table, then grabbed a jacket from his suitcase and walked to the front desk. Duke appeared, bleary eyed, after Elliot pinged the reception bell.

"Can I borrow a flashlight?"

A frown, a cough from behind the counter.

Duke raked through clutter on a shelf, then handed him a flashlight. "You better be careful out there. Ain't nobody around to come save you, this time of night."

Outside, the rain had all but stopped. Elliot jogged east, over the glistening asphalt. The wind whipped at his collar.

Twenty minutes later he climbed over the flattened guardrail, shining the flashlight into the trees. The rental car's tires had left deep tracks in the grass. He followed them down to the tree he'd hit, almost skidding down the ravine. He remembered the hand on his sleeve, and the wet swish of leaves right after. The noise had faded into the shrubbery to his left, he decided. The kid hadn't run around the car.

He studied the ground to his left. *Is the grass trampled? Or is it just the rain, flattening the tall blades?*

It was impossible to tell, but he set out in that direction anyway, pushing branches aside. It was a narrow, meandering path through the tall grass. A semi rolled by above the ravine, rattling the air.

Ten minutes into his trek, a wave of dizziness stormed him, and he leaned against a tree. His feet seemed unsteady, as if the ground were shifting under his shoes.

Maybe I really do have a concussion.

The damp grass soaked through his jeans, and he decided he'd had enough, that his midnight hike was a soggy waste of time. But as he panned his flashlight, searching for an easier route back, a pile of rocks glistened wet-black in the glow of the beam, in front of a gap leading right under the mountain pass.

He aimed the flashlight into the gap, then crouched to take a step inside. The dark swamped him, and the flashlight threw light on nothing but the rock face. He worried he'd collide with a dead end, smack his head. Instead, his feet lost their footing, and he skidded into a crevice, then, before he could throw his arms out or scream, he slid through a hole.

Chapter 14

Thursday, October 31, 2002

The forest was tomb-black and muggy, carpeted with oak leaves. The storm was still just an echo from beyond the mountain ridge, but Olivia felt its tremor in the earth beneath her feet. Her ballet shoes scuffed against the trail, pink satin snagging.

Jessica was calling her name, somewhere behind her, syllables fragmenting in the hush of rustling leaves. Olivia sucked air into her lungs, hungry for breath. *Keep running, don't stop now.*

The woods seemed to gape and yawn around her, an endless bear hug of pine trees, all bushy-black under the murky sky. Jessica called her name again.

Goodbye, Jessie.

Olivia slowed, catching her breath among the pines. Thunder rolled, wind fluted through the leaves – soon the rain would trickle, then cascade. She searched for light between the trees. *Did I get it wrong? I kept the secret, and I waited for the thunderstorm. Where are they?*

Olivia's knees grew weak. Fear spurred her to glance over her shoulder. What if someone found her, trapped her? What if they took her away, like the voices warned? But as she looked to the left, fingers gripping a knotted branch, a silver-gray light beamed between the pines, scattering its glow among tree trunks. The light spun, and Olivia ran toward it, skidding over twigs.

The light grew brighter, and now Olivia heard a low hum – a hum that danced over her skin. The pine trees feathered her hair as she swerved around branches, until the tall trunks parted, and long grass licked her ankles. A shadow descended. The hum drowned the wind – a deep, low resonance. The forest trembled.

Chapter 15

Saturday, April 16, 2022

"Hello? Help!"

Jessica yelled and howled, crouching in the dirt, aiming her flashlight into the crevice above her head. The dark seemed to breathe, sucking in the damp night air, exhaling through tree roots and soil. She'd slid into a small cavern. A dank pit. Faint rumbling filtered in – trucks crossing Evergreen Pass.

How far did I fall?

She scrabbled and clawed, but the passage above was too steep. There was nothing to hold onto, nothing for her shoes to grip.

She fought for ten minutes, clambering to gain footing, then slumped to the ground. Eyes closed, she rocked back and forth, seconds lapsing to half an hour. Each breath seemed more hopeless than the last.

The earthy tomb threatened to hold her there forever. Dread spiraled, constricting her breathing, scrambling her reflexes, but the sense of déjà vu was even worse.

I know this place. This is my dream, my nightmare. The black hole I see when I close my eyes. I'll die in here. Soon I'll be a rotting corpse.

She cried out again, hoping to silence the scenes in her head. Her ribs poking from flesh like the frame of a storm-wrecked ship, tendons and sinews twisted and strewn. Her skull hollowed by worms.

No, I can't die down here. This can't be how it ends. Someone will hear me, find me. Won't they?

She kicked out in frustration, then froze at the sound of falling rubble. Angling her flashlight down, she searched the ground, panning the light around her shoes. She'd been so desperate to climb out, she hadn't looked beyond her feet.

Ten feet from where she'd landed, there was a cleft in the ground, right by the wall of the pit. She inched toward it, then lurched back when her feet neared a precipice.

Crawling on her stomach, she neared the edge. A dull ache radiated from her hip, which had taken the brunt of her tumble.

"It goes down forever," she whispered, staring into a deep, narrow chasm. The flashlight lit large ridges in the bedrock, forming a haphazard path down.

Jessica gripped the rock at the precipice. The drop made her stomach turn. But she gripped even harder, tensing every muscle, when she heard a noise. A voice echoing, drifting up from below.

"Hello? Who's there?" she yelled.

Silence.

I can either die here, or find out what's below, she decided, and before she allowed herself the chance to change her mind, her right leg was reaching down.

Her feet found a ridge no more than three feet wide. She leaned against the bedrock, steering herself from the edge. Using her flashlight, she mapped the route down. She'd have to climb over boulders and edge down the rocky ridges.

Her shuffles echoed as she descended, and her hand held on to the rock, its surface scraping her palms. The decline sharpened, flattened, sharpened again in hairpin turns, interrupted by a smattering of rocks. She scrambled over them, sending pebbles and gravel falling.

"Hello?" she called out again. The faint voice replied, but the words were lost in the echo.

Time seemed to warp on her way down, minutes lost, others strung out. She wasn't sure if an hour or ten minutes had passed. Daydreams, nightmares, and sketches from her journals merged and blurred, sifting in and out of focus.

Am I even awake? Or is this all a dream?

A strange euphoria washed over her, despite the narrowing of the chasm, the slip of her feet here and there. Her head seemed light on her shoulders, and the pain in her hip had all but vanished. She glanced up. How far had she walked? She couldn't tell anymore, and now it didn't seem to matter.

Everything's going to be fine. This is a dream. A horrible dream.

She froze when light filtered up from below, dancing over the rock. A flashlight. Another murmur pulled her from her half-trance.

"Hello?" she called again, her voice parched and dry.

"Hello," the voice replied, now just discernible. A male voice.

Please don't be a serial killer. Please tell me you know how to get out of here.

As she descended farther, a figure came into view. A man standing at the bottom of the chasm. She was minutes from hitting flat turf.

"Are you okay?" he called.

Every nerve sparked under Jessica's skin. *I know that voice. The same voice I heard on the phone.*

She tried to form words, but they were too stubborn to leave her. "I … I think so," she managed at last. *I'm hallucinating. I quit Ativan cold turkey. Or maybe I popped a pill, and it's mixing with all that bourbon. No, I'd remember that.*

She wanted to aim her flashlight at the man below, prove to herself that it just couldn't be, but she still had another hairpin turn to clear on the ridge.

"Watch out," the voice said, right as Jessica floundered over a rock. She collided with shoulders, fell into the grip of two arms, and her feet hit gravel.

"Sorry," she mumbled, straightening. He took a step back. She was caught in an awkward fumble, thoughts and impulses arguing with themselves. *Just keep it together. This can't be real. Go with it until you wake up.*

"Elliot?" she heard herself say. She caught a blink, contours, dark hair and a collar in the light cast from their flashlights.

"Do I know you?" he said.

"No … no, you don't. I just … read your books."

He beamed his flashlight at the rock, and the light lit more of him. Despite her confusion, she couldn't help but notice that he was completely, hopelessly divine. His hair a little disheveled and a faint shadow along his jaw, as if he'd just woken from sleep.

"But I recognize your voice..."

"On the phone," she explained, reminding herself to breathe. Their words bounced from the rock.

He stood so close she caught the faint scent of his cologne on his collar, mixed with something she couldn't name – something that made her want to sink into him and forget that she was at the bottom of a giant hole in the ground. Her feet seemed unsteady, but there was nothing to cling to. Nothing but the rugged rock, and him. He must have noticed because his hand steadied her shoulder.

"So we speak on the phone after I misdial, and then I somehow find you *here*? How is that possible? Are you sure you're okay?" His hand lingered a moment – a light grip.

She nodded, but everything was still fluttering, arguing inside. "It's a small town, I guess. What are you doing down here?"

"It's a long story," he said. "I hiked down because I thought I heard a voice. A kid's voice. What are *you* doing here?"

"It's also a long story," Jessica mumbled. "How the hell do we get out of here?"

"I don't know. But if there's a way out, it's probably this way." Elliot stepped into a narrow passage between the bedrock. Jessica followed, pinching herself, again doubting that she was awake. *This can't be real. But it all feels real. The gravel under my feet, the butterflies in my stomach, the scraped skin of my palms.*

"When did you get here?" she asked, easing through the tight space. Each movement echoed, and the air was earthy and thick.

"Not that long before you did, I think. But I kind of lost track of time." Elliot paused, and they lingered in the dark. "I know this sounds strange, but I'm not sure if I'm dreaming or awake. About halfway down, I started feeling weird. In fact, now I'm almost certain this is a dream," he said, but she sensed he was talking to himself. "It started out as a nightmare, but now it's not so bad. I don't know why I'm talking to myself. Sorry." He walked on. Jessica followed close behind.

"No, I'm pretty sure I'm the one dreaming," she murmured. "I've been dreaming about falling into a black hole for about twenty years. And now I'm dreaming of *you*. Two people can't share a dream." She stopped before she rambled any further, asking herself why every moment felt so visceral, and yet so dreamlike-like and fluid.

Elliot stopped in the passageway again, and Jessica nearly collided with him. "But I could say the same thing. I'm dreaming of *you*," he said softly. "This is too damn strange."

"So we're both dreaming, somehow? I don't see how. It's just me at home on the couch, dreaming of you."

"Do you do that a lot?" He smiled, just visible in the glow from her flashlight.

"I didn't mean it like that. I just..." Her cheeks burned.

"You think you're debating with a dream version of me?"

"I'm standing at the bottom of a hole in the ground, I've known you for five minutes, and we're already debating how dreams and consciousness work. Only I would come up with something this weird," she whispered.

"What if I'm convinced of the same thing?" He was still smiling, subtly. The flashlights provided just enough light for her to follow his gaze as it skimmed her. Jessica reminded herself not to stare. But her eyes wanted to roam over his lips, his neck, the collar of his shirt beneath his jacket. He was right around six feet, she guessed.

"Then I guess we'll just have to agree to disagree."

"But why do I think I know you, when I don't even know your name?" His voice was warm, his words buttery soft, as if he were teasing a lover. She wanted to wrap herself in every word, wrap herself in him.

"I'm Jessica, and I have no idea. I still can't figure out if I'm asleep or awake, so how could I figure out that?"

He laughed softly. "Good point."

"Dreams aside, where are we going?" Jessica said. "This place creeps me out."

"This way." He moved ahead, and she followed, deeper into the passage. Gravel crunched under their feet.

"It must be the damn Ambien," Elliot mumbled. Again, Jessica sensed he was talking to himself, but she replied anyway.

"No, it's *my* meds, I think…" She shook her head. "Never mind."

They walked on. Jessica's head still felt light on her shoulders, and she wondered where all her fear had gone. But something still gnawed inside. A tussle between lust, confusion, overwhelm. Heat and shivers dancing over her skin.

The passageway narrowed, and they shuffled sideways, until the rock widened to a downward slope where the air grew humid, and water trickled down the rock walls.

Around a corner, the passageway opened to a cave. A cathedral of flowstone, with ten-foot stalactites hanging like dripping candle wax. The floor of the cave was slick, tiny rivulets flowing through its cracks, and it undulated into multiple levels, like a maze of mezzanines and stairwells.

"Oh my God," Jessica whispered, inspecting the flowstone. Its glossy spikes hung in clusters, long spears menacingly aimed at their heads. Condensation dripped from the cave walls.

They wound around stalagmites, dodging puddles, beaming their flashlights over the cave structures.

"Look." Jessica pointed toward gaps in the cave wall. "They look like tunnels."

"Maybe one of them gets us out of here," Elliot said. Something crunched beneath his feet.

Jessica crouched. "Trail mix ... I think those kids were down here."

"Kids? You mean the ones who disappeared?"

"Yes," she said, standing up. "Three of them turned up on my back porch. I gave them trail mix. Maybe this is where they hide."

Elliot glanced over his shoulder, casting his flashlight into the far corners of the cave. "Then there has to be a way out."

They searched passageways, tunnels, all dark, humid and close. Some were dead ends, others led right back to where they started. But one led them on an upward hike, where the granite was drier. Time seemed to warp again, one moment bleeding into the next.

"How long have we been down here?" Jessica unzipped her raincoat. The trek had warmed her.

"I can't even tell. Everything feels weird. But it's okay, we'll get out of here."

His words simmered in her head. *We. Like we already know each other.*

Minutes passed, or perhaps an hour, until the tunnel widened, and the incline sharpened. A steep rubble of rocks led higher. Elliot climbed to a plateau, then held out his hand. "Here."

She held on, climbing over the rocks. His palm was warm, and she didn't want to let go.

The air cooled, suddenly fresher, and the flashlights illuminated islands of moss creeping over the rock.

"We're getting close," Jessica whispered, relief and regret washing over her. Would this be where they said goodbye? After finding their way out?

A cool ray of moonlight flooded a gap in the cave, no more than two feet wide.

"You think we can squeeze through that?" Elliot crouched to inspect the gap.

"Wait." Jessica's flashlight danced over three large piles of pebbles.

"What the..." Jessica whispered, approaching the piles, which were marked with fistfuls of shrubs, feathers and twigs. They were three feet long and two feet wide, Jessica guessed.

"They look like graves," Elliot murmured.

"But they're so small?"

"Kids."

"That stuff on the top … it looks like what I found on my desk."

"What?" Elliot turned to face her.

"I think those kids broke into my house."

Elliot quizzed her about what she'd found in her living room. She replied with all that she remembered of the misspelled words; the foliage on her desk, the hooded figure who'd followed her home.

"That's insane," Elliot murmured.

"I know. And this is so strange … so creepy," she replied. "What the hell happened here?"

"I have no idea, but whoever's buried in here died a long time ago. It would stink to hell, otherwise. Maybe they just found animal bones, and thought they were people?"

"Let's get out of here."

"You go first."

Jessica dropped her raincoat and slid to her stomach. She crawled through the gap, into tall grass, then climbed to her feet and edged around a boulder. Elliot followed.

"You'd never know it led to a cave," Elliot said, pointing his flashlight at the rock they'd crawled from, which was covered in shrubs. "And it's hidden to anyone passing by."

"People around here talk about caves, but I thought it was just another myth."

The heady terpenes of pine trees filled Jessica's lungs. Branches obscured the sky, but the mariner blue of early twilight filtered through. Hours had passed.

"Where are we?" Elliot beamed his light into the pines.

"Somewhere in the park. We're nowhere near Evergreen Pass, that's for sure."

Moonlight breached the trees to their left. They followed that direction until the foliage thinned, and they arrived at a small clearing thick with wiregrass.

An abyss of stars shimmered above, freed from their cover of storm clouds, but faint beams of amber and gold speared the horizon, lighting up a rugged skyline of evergreens. Lush and monstrous, piercing the sky like feathery arrows.

Again, Jessica wondered if the whole night had been a dream. But the branches brushed her neck, and the air crept under her clothes. One thought led to another, without the random oddities of dreaming. In dreams, she never felt like much more than a quiet echo of herself. So what was this?

Water rushed from the opposite side of the clearing, and they followed the sound. Grass became crumbly terrain, and they halted by a rocky drop to a winding gorge below.

"The river runs to Lake Driftwood. That's the fastest route out of the park," Jessica said, pointing right.

They walked a trail that descended to hit soft grass just a few feet above the riverbank.

"Are you staying in Driftwood?"

"I was on my way," Elliot said. "I wrecked my car. I'm at a motel, not far from here."

"I still feel like I'm dreaming wide awake," Jessica murmured. "Like it's twilight in my head. I'm not even cold out here. Everything feels too easy. We hiked all that way underground, but it doesn't feel like it lasted more than ten minutes."

"I know. It's the weirdest feeling."

"What were you doing at Evergreen Pass? Kind of late, don't you think?"

"A little field research, I guess."

"The kids? I knew it." She smiled, kicked the dirt.

"What about you?"

Jessica blushed. "I couldn't sleep. I had a hunch you wrecked your car at Evergreen Pass. There are all kinds of theories about why cars crash there, and I got curious. Then I found the trail that led to the rock."

He smiled, soaking her up like blotting paper.

They turned at a scurry from below, and Elliot beamed his flashlight along the riverbank. A bushy tail swished, and yellow eyes flashed under tawny ears. Fangs gripped a trail of shredded meat. The beast froze in the glare, ears twitching.

"Is that a dog?" Elliot whispered.

"No. That's a wolf," Jessica stammered. "But look at the size of the head, the paws."

"It's huge. There are wolves in the state park?"

The wolf darted, dragging its prey into the dark.

"I'm pretty sure they died out about a hundred years ago."

Elliot took a step closer to the riverbank. "Maybe it's a wolf hybrid? Someone's pet?"

"No. When have you seen a wolf or a dog that size?"

Something gleamed among the pebbles by the river.

"You see that?"

"Let's take a look," Elliot replied.

They hit the pebbled ground by the riverbank. The gushing water glimmered in the gleam of their flashlights. Dodging muddy puddles, they followed the wolf's tracks.

Jessica aimed her light at blood-smeared plastic. "It's plastic wrap from a grocery store. Someone's feeding wildlife out here."

"Look." Elliot pointed his light ten feet farther up the river. "Is that a campfire?"

They neared a pile of charred branches and ashes, surrounded by a circle of stones. "The ashes are warm," Elliot said, poking the pile with a branch. "I guess we're not alone."

They searched the riverbank again, looking for movement, a flicker in the grass. The sun struggled to throw its ochre rays into the dark.

Jessica found Elliot looking at her when she turned, and it spurred another flurry of sparks under her skin.

"If this is a dream, I don't want to wake up," he said.

She nodded.

"You see the lion?" He pointed to the constellation of Leo, which was still visible in the sky. Denebola was a blinking yellow spark on his tail.

"Yes, I see him."

He pulled a sheet of paper from his back pocket.

"You study the stars, too?" she said.

"Ever since I was a kid. Always wondered what's out there."

"What's that?" She watched him unfold the paper.

"The first chapter of my new book." He frowned at the penciled notes all over the page. Then he began to re-fold the paper, again and again, until he'd coaxed all the folds into an origami lion. The skies lightened to ultramarine.

"If this is anything more than a dream, then I'll wake up without this in my pocket, and you'll find it in yours." He handed her the lion.

"Why *Chasing the Void,* Elliot?" She folded the lion into her pocket.

"I wanted to write about Driftwood, the kids that disappeared, and I found a comment on a forum from someone with that alias. It was you, wasn't it?"

She nodded. All that mattered, all that mystified her, was converging. Dawn threw out another glowing spear. A gust of wind rustled branches, and a few pale rays of sunlight crept across the pebbles. Jessica tossed a stone into the river.

"Who are you?" Elliot shook his head. "Never mind. I already figured that out."

"What do you mean?" She stiffened. She'd spent so much time reading his words, but knew so little about *him*.

"You're my muse, I'm sure of it," he sighed.

"Your muse?" She chased every word, wishing she could peer right into his mind. *His muse?*

"There's a woman. A muse I invented years ago, and she finds her way into every book I write. She's *you*. And now I'm dreaming of you, finally." He stared at her with a smile that felt sad, resigned.

Jessica searched for words again. *His* words were like scissors, snipping all the threads that linked her thoughts. She looked down, as if she might find them in the pebbles like a broken string of pearls.

"No," she said, shaking her head. "Sometimes it feels that way … like I'm only alive between the pages of your novels. But the truth is, you're *my* muse, and I invented *you*, whatever you are … a carbon copy of Elliot Reed."

"Typical, that I'd have you say that. Me playing with my own mind. How am I *your* muse?"

"I spend too much time thinking about you," she mumbled.

"I wish you were more than this." He shook his head again.

"More than what?" She threw her hands on her hips. It seemed to amuse him, but he frowned, too.

"More than a ghost. A beautiful ghost."

"A *ghost*?"

"The ghost who haunts the white space between my words. My muse, telling me what I want to hear." His eyes wandered over her, like he was staring at a piece of art he almost understood.

"Are we both high?" she muttered.

"The last time I felt like this, I'd chewed through a bag of mushrooms in college," he said. "But I hadn't invented you yet."

She wanted to shake him, fall into him, prove she was alive. "I need to sit down," she said instead, suddenly fatigued.

"Here," Elliot said, treading up the embankment, and she followed.

They perched on a rock and watched the stars fade. She turned her head to look at him stare at the sky. *This is what it would feel like to lie in bed next to you. Just an inch from you, so close I can feel you like a breeze or a sigh. Maybe I should just reach out, slip onto you, straddle your hips and unbutton your shirt ... find out how real you really are.*

"What are you thinking?" He turned and caught her stare.

"All the possibilities."

"Why don't you come to life like this when I'm awake, trying to write?" He found her hand, and his fingers folded into a grip, kindling her nerves.

"I'm alive. I swear."

He smiled. "If that's true, then meet me at Evergreen Pass tonight. Let's say eleven. I think we have more to explore down there. Maybe we'll figure out where those kids hide out."

She nodded, and they watched the last star fade into dawn.

Minutes from daylight, Jessica scanned the clearing. Rabbits bounded, zigzagging across the grass. The fattest one darted under a bush. A moment later, they heard a snap. Then another, and another still. Branches cracking under feet.

"Someone's here," Jessica whispered. They both stood up.

A grubby boy appeared from between the trees, bare feet making easy strides across the grass.

"It's one of those kids," Elliot whispered.

Jessica nodded. "Joseph Baker."

The boy stopped ten feet away, eyes glinting in the pale sun, then raced back into the trees.

Chapter 16

Saturday, April 16, 2022

Jessica lay in a bed of weeds and wild geranium, under the splayed branches of an oak tree. She woke to strobing rays of sunlight filtering through branches, thawing her night-numbed limbs.

"Motherfucker," she mumbled, sitting up, pulling grass from her hair. Daylight crumpled her. She looked at the palm of her hand, as if some trace of touch lingered there, and pictured Elliot, eyes resting on hers as dawn slunk over wiregrass. A smile that made her toes curl. And now he was gone – gone with the moon and the blazing stars.

A headache burst from the center of her head, spreading to drum across her forehead. Blinking hurt.

It really was just a damn dream. A nightmare, and then a dream.

She replayed moments from the night before, willing them to gel. But those memories were already fading, sliding off the edges of her memory, coasting into nothing.

Was any of it real? When did it all begin and end?

At least she knew where she was. The trail to her left led to the main path that took her out of the park. Somehow, she'd fallen asleep on her trek toward Evergreen Pass last night, then dreamed of Elliot and a strange cavernous underworld. Slumbered like a drunk in the grass.

All that bourbon. Or I'm crazy.

The morning chill bit through her clothes as she staggered to her feet. Her hands were frozen stiff, and her jeans were streaked with grass stains. Her back was soaking wet. She didn't look much better than the kids, she guessed. Pain radiated from her hip.

I must have slipped. What time is it?

She grabbed her flashlight from the grass, then patted her pockets. Her phone was still at home on the coffee table.

And no origami lion. The thought crumpled her even more. *Maybe it fell out of my pocket? No, stop kidding yourself.*

Rain still saturated the soil, but early sun danced over the grass. She jogged toward the trail, still turning over memories of the night before, telling herself that dreams were nothing like that. It had been too nerve-tingling, too visceral to be nothing more than her temporal lobe weaving magic as she slept. One long hallucination, perhaps? Her lonely mind up to tricks? She considered running to Evergreen Pass to search for a hole in the rock, then told herself to get home, *get a grip*.

A rustle of leaves pulled her from chastising herself. She stopped and turned, annoyed at the thought of some wholesome hiker catching sight of her looking like hell. No one was there. *Just a branch falling*.

But a minute later, another noise broke the quiet — a shuffle through the grass. She turned, but again, no one was around. *Stop being so paranoid.*

Another few steps, and she was sure there were eyes on her neck. She whirled around again, then coughed into the weeds. She ran up the trail until her feet met the downward slope that led to the wide path through the oak and hickory. The sensation didn't pass. *Someone's there.*

Out of breath, she slowed. Another noise – this time a scrape – and she spun around again, palpitations drumming against her ribs. *Ativan withdrawal. That's all this is. It's been at least four days.*

Jessica's eyes fell on a hooded figure standing between two pines. They locked eyes for three seconds, until the figure ran into low sloping branches.

Jessica's stomach churned, but she ran anyway, determined to get out from the trees, which seemed to be circling, closing in.

As she hit the path that led to the parking lot, she slowed, caught her breath. And just as calm relaxed her stride, a thought bounced in, crowding out all the rest:

Where the hell is my raincoat?

Chapter 17

Saturday, April 16, 2022

"I'm alive." That's what she said. But I was so damn distracted by everything else. The soft curves of her body under that sweater, her heart-shaped lips. Tousled hair in spirals down her back.

Elliot was tired. Tired of debating with himself and replaying every moment of his dream, or whatever it was. His long-winded head trip. But mostly, he was tired because it felt like he hadn't slept at all, and every muscle ached.

He was still reeling from waking up in the grass, soaked in mud. He'd sprinted back to The Duke, showered and thawed, then waited in the lobby for a battered cab to take him to the rental car office.

The events of the night before were a puzzle he couldn't piece together. He remembered walking to the mountain pass, nauseous as he approached the crash site, then following a trail of flattened grass to an opening in the rock on the ravine. That all happened. He was sure of it.

But he also remembered walking through that rock, then tumbling down a hole and finding a chasm, a cave. And the beautiful woman who'd answered the phone just hours earlier.

That part must have been a dream, he decided.

Yes, he must have somehow fallen asleep after arriving at Evergreen Pass and slipped into a vivid dream. Some sort of delayed reaction from the car crash, or those stupid pills, he figured. Like an idiot, he'd trekked through the soggy wilds to look for missing kids after smacking his head on an airbag, with Ambien zipping around his veins.

But the dream had been so compelling and lucid. So much so, that it was now impossible to tell where it began and ended. He remembered the strange sensation as he'd hiked down the chasm, as if the weight had been lifted from his own bones, his heavy head.

He eased into a parking space in downtown Driftwood, then cut the ignition of the new rental car.

Coffee, he decided, walking through the parking lot toward the boardwalk. He couldn't figure out a thing before caffeine. Late morning sun threw rays across the asphalt. The storm was over, and the skies were a stretch of breezy blue.

Driftwood in spring didn't disappoint. The lake was a lazy saucer of rippling current, basking in sunlight and tourist attention. Elliot leaned against the guardrail, and the wind tugged at his collar. Rambling homes and log cabins crouched by jetties farther east along the shore, where boats bobbed back and forth on their tethers. Elliot lost himself in the mellow expanse of water and wished his head would stop thudding.

He wanted to hike to the cliff overlooking the lake, explore the trails gouged into the mountainside. *Later,* he promised himself. He had coffee to drink, thoughts to unpack. So much of the night before was already fading, and now only moments, fragments remained.

Beyond the brick municipal buildings and the concrete of Driftwood's college campus, downtown was filled with pastel-painted storefronts, their windows crowded with gourmet, small-batch, hand-crafted everything. In between, there were at least three hiking stores, a vintage-looking pharmacy, and half a dozen restaurants with outdoor seating, where tourists ate syrup-drowned brunch. He skirted around the bookstore with its copies of *Black Eye* piled high in the window.

He searched for somewhere quiet, where he could disappear inside himself. A retro diner called Tiffany's had a huge gleaming espresso machine, but its bar and booths were crowded. He walked on.

Nexus Coffee overlooked the lakeshore, its bright blue shopfront sitting snug between the Driftwood Creamery and a revamped general store. The glass door hit a wind chime as he opened it.

A barista in a plaid shirt took his order. "The crème brûlée latte with tiramisu cream is amazing, especially with our chocolate-chunk artisanal biscotti," he promised in a nasal voice.

Elliot sipped on black coffee and snatched a copy of the *Driftwood Times* from an empty booth. As he read the front page, the mug all but slipped from his grip, settling with a ceramic rattle between two sloshes on the table.

"DREW COUNTY SHERIFF HUNTS FOR MISSING GIRL," the headline read, above a photo of an angelic-looking kid named Annabelle Lewis. Blonde hair in pigtails and a red jumper, groomed and tamed for a school photo. "The Drew County Sheriff's Department is looking for a six-year-old girl who went missing from her Driftwood home Friday," the subheading read. "Annabelle Lewis left home sometime between 7:30 and 9 p.m., Sheriff Clarke said."

Elliot wiped the spilled coffee with a napkin and grabbed his phone, ready to call the sheriff's office and report that he'd seen the girl at the side of the road. It had to be her. She had the same wide eyes that had pierced the dark the night before, wolf-bright on the shoulder of the highway.

But how do I know if that moment was real, either? There was no sign of her when I searched the highway. What if I'm losing my damn mind? All work and no play...

He set his phone on the table.

And Jessica – could she somehow exist somewhere beyond my own mind?

Doubtful, he decided. In a town like Driftwood, would he really find a woman like that? Would he find her *anywhere*? His muse, whisked into life?

No, it was much more likely that he'd taken the woman in his head, the woman on the phone, and whoever *Chasing_the_Void* happened to be, and blended them together in his dream.

As he stared into his coffee, his thoughts drifted to a month ago – the last time he'd spoken to his sister. *"This is why you're single,"* she'd said, shaking her head over a glass of wine, after arriving at his apartment unannounced. *"You live with your characters. There's no room for anyone else."*

Elliot pushed up his sleeves, sighing. He had more temporal things to worry about, beyond all the impossible moments, the befuddling sensation that his thoughts and dreams and prose were blurring. A looming deadline for a book that was still a mess of notes, for a start.

But first, he needed to report the incident on the side of the road, regardless of whether the girl seemed real or not, he decided. He picked up his phone and dialed the sheriff's department, then talked to a gravelly woman who spoke in a thick drawl, each word dripping out like the last splash of creamer from a jug.

"And your name, sir?"

"Elliot Reed."

"And would you mind stopping by this afternoon to provide some more details?"

Details? He'd given every detail that didn't sound absurd.

"Sorry, just passing through town," he said, then hung up.

The smell of hot brownies drifted as the barista officiously arranged a trayful in the display fridge.

Elliot grabbed a small leather-bound notebook from his pocket and pilfered a pen from the counter. He made a bullet list of neat notes, which quickly unfurled into chaotic detours, furious scribbles. After years of writing novels, his planning still morphed into tangled diagrams, tangents and what-ifs.

With a fresh cup of coffee in front of him, he scrutinized his notes. *Jessica* appeared half a dozen times. Was that the name of his main character? He hadn't named her in the back-cover blurb they'd thrown online, and he'd been toying with half a dozen names that didn't fit. But *Jessica* – maybe that was it.

"I think those kids broke into my house," he'd underlined. *A stalker. Writing on the wall. Deep rambling caves and children's graves.*

He scratched his head, lost in debate with himself again. Had he dreamed about a character in his book, or was he now writing about a dream? *What happened after that kid ran out from the trees? Was that when I woke up?*

On the next page he'd written:

Dark brown hair, wide brown eyes. Single was underlined.

He'd decided earlier that week that his protagonist was dating a detective. An easy way to weave in law enforcement, thicken the plot. But now he didn't much like the idea of that. No, Jessica was single. Very single. A hermit, almost, until she'd meet Character X.

Why didn't I kiss her? He'd written on the page after that.

Yes, he'd veered right out of the chapter and back under the night sky with Jessica. But he indulged himself anyway.

Had he been too *distracted* to kiss her? The trek through those winding tunnels, the blazing stars, the strange sensation of dreaming wide awake? No, he admitted. It wasn't that. It was because somewhere in the back of his mind, he'd wondered if she was something more. More than his muse, more than his invention. The thought was inviting, but also unsettling. *If she's real, then who the hell is she?*

His mind wandered back to his conversation with his sister. What was the other thing she'd said that night, between greedy gulps of his 2007 Ovid Bordeaux? *"You're a gentleman to a fault."*

"No, I'm not. I'm just … precise," he'd said. She'd scrutinized him and rolled on Chapstick, then smeared it all over his favorite wine glass with another sip.

"Oh yeah? So what stopped you from taking that model home … Adriana?" His sister had been three glasses in at that point, and she'd ended her question with a manly burp.

"That had nothing to do with being a gentleman," he'd explained, grabbing the bottle and pouring himself a glass while he still had a chance. *"She talked about celery juice and Instagram all night, and she had enormous feet. Every seventh word was Slovenian."*

And to that his sister had rolled her eyes. *"There's always some excuse. It's like you're waiting for someone else."*

Back to work, he told himself, draining his coffee. A middle-aged woman with a mane of blonde hair loudly ordered a decaf sugar-free vanilla latte with an extra shot, caramel and cream.

He tried to dive back into his notes, but soon felt eyes burning into his flesh. The woman by the counter stared at him with a smile that felt like a lick across his flesh. He ignored her, disappearing inside his notebook again.

The first chapter – how did it end? It opened with Jessica alone at home, peering around her curtains to find feral kids in her back yard. He scribbled it down.

But the chapter's opening was still lame. It needed intimacy, dramatic introspection. He imagined her naked, thinking about a lover – he spent much more time than necessary picturing exactly what that would look like – and penned another three pages of notes. She had a gilded imagination, as untamed as his own, he decided. A head full of baroque and eerie dreams.

His stomach begged for a brownie. The smiling woman had left, at least. Scrolling through his phone, he found the article about Joseph Baker and Anthony Walker. He wrote down the name of the journalist who'd written it, then tore out the front page of the newspaper and started to fold it, considering his next move.

He called the number listed for the *Driftwood Times*, asked to speak with Oliver Gray, and a flat male voice replied.

"What's this regarding?" the voice asked, and Elliot picked up the piece of paper, folded it again, over and over.

"I have some questions about an article he wrote. About two years ago."

"Oliver doesn't work here anymore," the voice replied, still flat, and now hesitant.

"Any idea where I can find him?"

"Try the bar," the voice said, and hung up.

He studied the folded newspaper in his hand. *Doesn't look much like a lion. More like a lame dog.* He crushed it in his hand. In his dream he'd nailed it. So much easier under the stars, next to Jessica. And sure enough, when he'd searched his jeans that morning, his pockets had been empty. No origami lion.

But that doesn't prove anything.

Chapter 18

Saturday, April 16, 2022

The Lewis' farmhouse stooped between trees and wire fencing. Foliage clogged its gutters, and a storm window clattered under the flaking porch.

Inside, Kristin Lewis sat on the sofa, stringy, frail and doe-eyed. She watched her husband pace across the living room, where dust and torment danced in the air. The floorboards creaked under his feet.

A bean bag patched with duct tape, a torn couch, and shelves crammed with garage-sale clutter – Dan and Kristin didn't have much, and now the only thing that mattered was gone.

Four years ago, when they'd adopted Annabelle, Kristin had hoped that her new baby girl would fix everything. But Annabelle hadn't repaired the gaping holes in their marriage. No, more than anything, their little girl confused them.

Each breath labored Kristin's lungs, as if there wasn't enough air in the room. It had been fourteen hours since they'd reported that Annabelle was gone, and Dan looked like hell, a hollowed-out lick of a man. A white face and hunched shoulders, his body rigid under last night's shirt.

"The damn rain's washed away any trace by now. She could be anywhere, and they wouldn't know," he hissed, clenching his fists.

But Kristin was also just a whisper, a sheet dithering in horror by a pile of crumpled tissues. And she couldn't stop reliving the night before. The last time she'd seen Annabelle.

It had been a normal evening, like any other. A dinner of leftovers and apple sauce, then sudsy, drawn-out bath time. She'd put Annabelle to bed right around 7:30 in her favorite night gown – white, with a row of tiny pink flowers around the hem – and read her half a chapter of *Harry Potter.* Annabelle's eyelids had fluttered and finally closed around 8 p.m.

Kristin stood up at the hum of an engine. She moved to the window to watch Detective Harding pull into the driveway in his beat-up navy unmarked car. He slammed the door and headed for the front porch with his notebook in his hand.

Dan stopped pacing and flung open the door.

Detective Andrew Harding entered, awkward around the dusty furniture and expectant stares. Sandy blond hair, gray-blue eyes. *Couldn't be older than thirty-five,* Kristin guessed.

"We have two possible leads on Annabelle," he said. "Mind if I sit down?"

Dan nodded at an old chair and halted his pace across the living room floor. Harding watched Kristin from the corner of his eye, but Kristin didn't notice. She was too busy thinking of her daughter's blonde hair in the sun, the sound of her giggle from the breakfast table, the way her tiny feet felt in her hands when she was two years old. A little girl she'd loved as her own, but who she'd never really understood.

She'd been too consumed by her broken marriage, her broken house, to notice that Annabelle wasn't like any other kid. The hours she spent playing in silence, all alone, and the words that flew out of her tiny mouth, years too soon.

"They've found her? Tell me they've found her." Kristin searched for light in the detective's eyes. But now she was thinking about how she'd found the front door open last night, welcoming a puddle of wayward rain, as she'd walked to the kitchen from the living room. And how she'd run up the stairs, already knowing something was wrong, to find an empty bed and a stuffed bear on the floor, her daughter gone. Her absence had filled the room.

As Harding settled into the recliner, Kristin looked up.

He killed a sigh. "Not yet. But we do have two witnesses who saw a young girl last night matching her description."

"Where?" Dan crossed his arms over his chest.

"She was spotted around midnight on that unmarked road near the southwest entrance to the park. The sheriff got a call this morning while they were canvassing."

"Who the hell saw her? Why didn't they stop her? Call 911? What was she *doing* there? Was she alone?"

"The first witness was some guy out late heading home. He said he saw her, then turned around at the crossroads, but she was already gone. He claims she disappeared so fast he couldn't get a good look at her. The guy may have been inebriated, but we can't confirm that."

"This is some damn bullshit. Y'all need to find her, God damn it. Who's out there looking for her?" Dan snapped, eyes round like pennies.

Dan's comment didn't bristle Harding. "Mr Lewis, we've got *everyone* either looking for her, or mobilizing to join the search. The sheriff and his deputies are in the park right now with the K9 unit and the park rangers, and the volunteer jeep unit's already there. We're canvassing the neighbors, and some of my colleagues from the state police are heading over as soon as they can."

"What about the other witness?" A tissue disintegrated into snowflakes in Kristin's hand.

Harding sighed, more audibly this time. "We just got a call. Someone who claims he saw her at around 8:15 last night. His description's a match, but it was over by Evergreen Pass."

"Evergreen Pass? That's clear over the other side of the park. What was she doing? God damn it!" Dan kicked a table leg, clawed his fingers.

"She was standing by the side of the road, apparently. The guy said he saw her right before he got into a car wreck. Drove his car into a ravine."

"None of this makes any sense!"

"I understand your frustration, Mr Lewis..."

"Do you, though?" Dan threw a hand into the air. Harding stole another glance at Kristin, who was quietly mumbling, "My baby girl."

"We're expanding the search. We've got staff heading over to the highway right now to start searching the area around Evergreen Pass. But in the meantime, I've got a few more questions."

"We told the deputy everything we know, and the sheriff already came by," Dan said, his frustration flaring red. "Why don't you go on and help with the search?"

"I won't keep you for long," Harding promised, scanning the report the deputy had filed.

"Did you notice any changes in Annabelle's behavior recently?"

"No ... well ... she kept telling me she's got a secret," Kristin said, looking up from her pile of confetti tissue.

"A *secret*?" Harding straightened again.

"I always figured she was just playing." A fresh batch of tears crept down Kristin's cheeks.

"What are you talking about, Kristin? This is the first I'm hearing about it." Dan whirled to face her.

"You're working outside all day, or at the damn bar. You're never *here*," she replied, defiant for the first time that morning.

The detective cleared his throat. "She say anything more about this secret?"

"No, nothing. I'd just find her playing on her own, kind of talking to herself, and when I asked her what she was thinking about, she'd tell me it was a secret. But she must've told me that twenty times. I never gave it much thought." Kristin stole a look at her husband, now asking herself if she knew him.

Harding scribbled on his notepad.

"But, you know, she had the wildest imagination," Kristin continued, nerves winding her words tight like a crank. "She's incredibly smart ... *gifted,* the teachers told me. The other kids bully her. I complained about it a bunch of times, but the teachers don't give a damn."

"Does Annabelle have trouble sleeping?" Harding asked.

"No, no. She sleeps just fine. I'm the one who can't sleep..." Kristin stammered.

"Did she say anything else unusual?"

"Well, this will sound real strange..."

Dan's knuckles whitened.

"Yes?" Harding watched them both.

"Sometimes I caught her talking to people who weren't there. Imaginary friends, I guess. And she always wanted to go play when it stormed. She'd cry and cry when I kept her inside. I guess she just loved the rain."

Harding shifted his weight in the chair. "Is Annabelle on any prescription medications? Does she sleepwalk?"

"She's asthmatic," Kristin said.

Harding frowned. "She needs an inhaler?"

"It doesn't seem to do any damn good," she mumbled. "She was having breathing problems and headaches. Like sometimes she just couldn't get enough air. The doctor said she has asthma, but I'm not so sure." She blew her nose.

"Any other health problems?"

"We had to take her to the hospital about a month ago. She had real bad stomach aches for months. EPI, it's called. I told the deputy already! She needs *medication.*" Kristin's hands fell limp at her sides.

"And she's never been admitted for any psychiatric issues?" The detective wrote in harsh strokes on the pad.

"No," Dan barked, but more questions flew: *Did anyone take a special interest in your daughter? New friends, groups, people in the neighborhood? Any new teachers? How did they describe her behavior at school? Changes to her routine? Are you sure you didn't hear anything last night? The back door was locked? The deputy searched the basement twice?*

Harding left Dan and Kristin on their porch as the wind picked up, and the weathervane on the roof whined and spun. The clouds had muscled their way beyond the mountain ridge. Kristin recoiled at the brisk air, then closed the door and retreated inside herself again.

Chapter 19

Saturday, April 16, 2022

Breakfast had been a slice of burned toast and a long stare into a coffee mug. Then a stutter of palpitations as Jessica read the front page of the *Driftwood Times*.

Call Mark? No, calm down first.

She bit her fingernails and chewed her lip. *Now I have to report that I saw her. She has a family searching for her.*

She dialed the sheriff's office and told a string of white lies: *"I think I might have seen Annabelle Lewis running through my back yard, around 4:30 in the morning on Wednesday. No, no, I don't think she was with anyone else, but like I said, it was dark outside. Maybe it was just another kid from the neighborhood, but it sure looked like her. Yes, I'll let you know if I remember anything else…"*

Catching sight of her stalker in the woods had left Jessica skittish, and spilling half-truths to law enforcement had only made it worse. She tossed crumbs into the sink, lost in the events of the last 24 hours.

Thirty minutes later, she sat on the living room floor, trimming the newspaper report with scissors as her printer spat out the last page. Annabelle Lewis stared back at her, pixelated. Jessica pasted the paper into a folder, then looked up at the writing still on the living room wall.

"Bury the dead," she murmured, remembering the graves she'd seen in her dream.

In the bedroom, she raked her clothes aside in the closet and stared at the black circle. Again, a flurry of white light broke through the dark. But she also smelled the earthy air of the pit she'd dreamed about, and she remembered the sensation of sliding, tumbling inside. *It's all blending together, confusing me even more. The past, the present. Dreams, nightmares, memories I can't trust.*

She blinked when another memory from the night before surfaced, and she opened the browser on her phone.

No, according to her search results, there definitely weren't any wolves in the park that looked anything like the huge shaggy beast she'd seen in the woods. Jessica sighed, disappointed, as if a wolf might have proven that it had all been real.

Her phone rang, and she closed the closet door.

"You see the news yet?" Mark sounded winded. A stop on his run around the lake.

"Yeah."

"I just met Keith on the trail. He knows the father, Dan Lewis." Mark panted into the phone, and she heard footfalls over gravel. Runners on their circuit, passing her brother. "And get this … she's adopted."

"*What?*"

"Jess, you have to call the sheriff's…"

"I already did," she interrupted.

"There's a search kicking off at two. Meet me at the ranger's station?" He picked up his run again.

"I'll be there, but it's a waste of time."

She hung up, closed her eyes, and wished she could return to her dream, find it somewhere beneath her eyelids. Consciousness was too convoluted when she was so damn tired. Sleep called her, and she napped until her phone buzzed again. A message from Jamie about the search.

Yes, see you soon, she replied, bleary, then texted her brother. *Jamie's joining us.* A gentle warning, so he didn't turn up in his Star Wars T-shirt with the hole in the armpit, or his ancient windbreaker that smelled of weed. His decade-long crush was as ardent and awkward as ever.

Orphaned, she wrote and circled on the *Driftwood Times* article about the missing girl. In the shower, she thought of Elliot again. He was somewhere in Driftwood, but *where*?

There were only two luxury hotels in town, but there was also a handful of glitzy vacation rentals scattered around Driftwood Heights, near the country club. Regardless, she didn't have the nerve to search him out, loiter in hotel lobbies hoping to find him. Such bravery would have led her to better things in life, she mused, cursing her introversion.

Wrapped in a towel, she opened her laptop. Elliot had one website and three social media accounts. It would be so easy to type a quick message.

She navigated to his website, clicked on *Contact*, and drafted a message. But every word seemed absurd, and the thought of hitting *Send* made her want to hide under the table. And who would receive it, anyway? Some pert publicist or assistant, who'd delete it with a smirk. She sighed and logged off.

But the chance, even crushingly slight, of bumping into him was enough to send her into a tailspin about what the hell to wear. Everything in her closet was worn out, mismatched, *hideous*. She grabbed a floaty blouse, tossed it aside.

Four outfits and two coats of mascara later, she opened the garage door, now thinking of Annabelle Lewis. Where was she now? Had Sheriff Clarke figured out anything?

He hasn't figured out shit, she decided, reversing out of her driveway. *In fact, I probably know more than he does. Either that, or I've let my mind trickle down the drain to join the weeds and algae in the lake.*

She cranked down the window because the AC didn't work and listened to Fleetwood Mac croon about thunder and rain on the radio. It was a relief to see that her neighbors' yards were still train wrecks, too. The neighborhood, a street of aging ranch homes backed by rows of glitzy subdivisions, was covered in broken branches and trash. Trees hung limp and defeated, and water pooled in front lawns like muddy duck ponds.

Most of her neighbors were a mystery. She only knew Mrs Davis, the 82-year-old widow in another decaying ranch next door. Everyone else had left, replaced by strangers.

She passed deputies canvassing the neighborhood. A woman with a golden retriever stapled *MISSING* posters to utility poles. Jessica parked and grabbed one.

MISSING AND ENDANGERED, it read in bold font above Annabelle's photo. *Drew County Sheriff's Department is asking for your help in locating six-year-old*

Annabelle Lewis. Three feet tall, 40 pounds, white female, last seen near Evergreen Pass.

Jessica slowed when she hit the back road, then parked in a muddy nook because her car was too humiliating to park in the main parking lot. Jamie waved as Jessica entered the parking lot, dodging puddles.

"Nothing wrong with a vintage Buick," Jamie said with a laugh. "You look good. All dressed up to search for a missing kid?" She swept black bangs off her face. Her fluffy sweater fell off one shoulder. Jamie was effortlessly, maddeningly stylish, while Jessica struggled with broken seams, pilled cotton, jeans that gaped at the waist.

"No, not for the kid. It's a long story," Jessica began, then saw Mark pull into the parking lot. He'd thrown on a respectable fleece and run to the barber, hopeful Jamie had dumped her latest boyfriend, Jessica guessed. A trust funder who called himself a *craft beer sommelier*.

They headed toward the ranger station, after a blushing "Hi" from Mark as he shoved his hands in his pockets, and a confident "Hi, Mark" from Jamie.

Sheriff Clarke stood by the station's rugged log siding with his deputies, yelling through the moist woody air at gathering volunteers. Bloodhounds sniffed a well-loved stuffed bear, then a deputy threw it back into a plastic bag. A dozen people hung around the sheriff, waiting as others parked their trucks and cars. Doors slammed, dogs barked, and the wind shook trapped raindrops from the leaves above.

Jessica spotted at least three people she knew and hoped she'd escape the small talk. Rosemary from the library, who waved at her in a wide-brimmed hat and sensible walking shoes. Pete from the hardware store, who'd lost half a finger to a chop saw, and John the undertaker, who made a killing from the dead.

A helicopter drowned the sheriff's voice as he spoke with deputies and K9 volunteers. He pointed east and west and growled a few words above the whirr, adjusting the brim of his hat. Jeeps rolled past, covered in mud.

"Don't look now," Jamie said, and Jessica froze.

"What?"

"Andrew Harding just pulled up over there and…" Jamie threw another look behind her. "I don't believe it."

Jessica turned. Andrew made eye contact and smiled, then joined the sheriff. A gold badge shimmered from his belt.

"Dick Breath?" Mark whispered.

"That son of a bitch is a *detective* now?" Jamie threw a withering look at Andrew. "I thought he was just a state trooper. Not bad for a failed English major who couldn't keep his pants zippered."

"Jess, you sure you want to do this?" Mark kicked the dirt.

"Yeah. It's just … it's fine."

The three of them veered northeast, trailing four other volunteers and a deputy, to the footpath that snaked its way to the cliff overlooking Lake Driftwood. The trail was still damp from the rain. Yellowroot and anemones bloomed above the brushwood, between the stocky trunks of oak and hickory.

She thought of Andrew, a few yards away, trekking the path in a navy shirt and the gold badge on his belt. And she remembered the nights years ago, waiting for him to come home, wondering who he might be with when he wasn't with her. How she'd left his apartment one bitter gray morning with her belongings in a bag and a box, deciding she'd never choose to need anyone again.

But unlike her, he'd since become something, while she'd stayed in Driftwood, cataloging books in the dusty library she'd sworn she'd leave as soon as she found something *real*. But *real* had never happened, and she'd woken up years later, still lost and alone.

Her mood soured as her feet crunched over twigs and foliage crept around her legs. In that bruised moment, what had seemed so visceral the night before now seemed absurd. *He's just a writer who doesn't know you. A man who would never give a damn about you.* The breeze blew hair into her face.

The thought made her face redden. She loathed how she'd crumpled herself into a ball and flicked off the lights.

"I heard there's all kinds of trouble at home," Rosemary bellowed, suddenly just a foot away, and Jessica swiveled her thoughts to the present. "That poor little girl. I just hope they find this one, before it's too late."

"What kind of trouble?" Jamie asked. She wrapped her hair into a bun as Mark watched the strands weave through her fingers. The skin of her neck was gold in the sunlight.

"The usual kind. Parents at each other's throats. That's what my neighbor, Jennifer, told me." Rosemary shook her head.

"I hope that hotshot detective they dragged out here has some ideas," John the undertaker said, now at Rosemary's side.

"I think it's a gang of perverts," Rosemary snapped. "Some nasty freaks taking those kids, *locking them up*!"

"Well, they haven't figured out much!" John yelled, rubbing his beard. "You're telling me they never got one useful piece of information from the parents, the park rangers, nobody?"

"Someone's hiding something, that's for sure," Rosemary said, almost muffled by the sound of her windbreaker grazing branches. "The sheriff, the news ... I'm no genius, but even I can see something doesn't add up."

They walked through dense forest for another hour, calling out Annabelle's name. Other volunteers headed north, toward Evergreen Pass. Now and then a radio buzzed, cutting through the rustle.

Jessica's legs dragged as they climbed the trail. A dog barked in the distance. John and Rosemary had wandered toward the other volunteers.

"Let's head deeper into the woods – no one's taken that path," Jessica said, pointing at a trail that joined the river.

They took the path, which descended into a skein of shrubs, winding around skunkbrush and bitterbush. Thirty minutes later, the trail veered toward the bank of a gushing river.

"I'm exhausted. Let's head back," Jamie whined, sitting on a tree stump.

"You guys wait here. I'll be right back," Jessica said, jogging farther down the trail.

"Jessica, wait!" Mark called behind her.

"Just stay with Jamie! I'll be right back!" she yelled over her shoulder, spurred by a hunch, by déjà vu.

I could've sworn I dreamed I was here last night, on this trail.

Dodging a puddle, she looked down to find something flitting at the edge of the trail. She blinked, as if she'd imagined it. But no, it was still there. An origami lion, covered in handwriting.

"Jessica! What the hell?" Mark's voice grew louder. Jessica pushed the lion up her sleeve. Her brother approached from around a shrub.

"Sorry, I thought I heard something," she said. "I guess it was nothing. Let's head back."

Jamie was still perched on the tree stump. They hiked back up the trail, calling out Annabelle's name. Jessica remembered her, standing on her lawn. Her bird's nest of hair and her grubby cheeks. *Where are you now, Annabelle? Are you hiding out with Joseph and Anthony? Or is the truth dark and wretched, as twisted as the roots that snake and coil under the brushwood?* The paper lion tickled her skin under her sleeve.

As Jessica trekked the path, the world seemed unreliable. What was real, and what could she trust? But the possibilities that hid among the lion's folds gave her buoyancy, and for the first time in as long as she could remember, she broke into a wide smile.

They reached the top of the trail. They were now just a few yards from the clearing, high above the lake. Jessica realized she'd completely forgotten about Andrew – she'd been too busy thinking about what might be written on the origami lion. Whatever those pencil strokes revealed, it seemed like the edges of her world were peeling back.

"Earth to Jessica."

She jumped at Jamie's voice, then joined her a few feet from the edge of the cliff, where Mark was gazing down at the lake, the wind ruffling his fleece.

"Want to grab a sandwich at Nexus Coffee?" Jamie asked.

"No, too expensive. Let's do Tiffany's," Jessica said.

Chapter 20

Saturday, April 16, 2022

"Why do they never find these kids? It's like they just vanish. It makes no sense." Jamie slumped into the table.

A server arrived in a *Tiffany's* T-shirt. Jessica and Mark ordered muffins and coffee. Jamie ordered a salad and a club soda after frowning at the menu.

"Who knows?" Jessica said, swapping a fleeting glance with her brother. "How's Seth?" she threw out as a diversion, then immediately regretted it.

Jamie sighed. "I feel like I never see him. He's at a retreat for lifestyle influencers all weekend, and next week he's going to some kind of martini mixologist event."

"Sounds busy," Jessica said, catching Mark's face wrinkle, as if he'd just smelled leaking sewage.

"It's fine, I guess. Gives me more time to work with my clients and stay on top of things at the store."

The diner echoed with the voices of tourists and a crowd of cackling seniors. A few deputies sat at the counter. Children whined and squealed. Audrey Hepburn watched over all of it, a black and white mural on the blue walls, gamine above the burgers and grease.

Jamie untwisted her hair and let it hang around her shoulders, while Mark pretended not to find it captivating, hiding his grief that she lay in the arms of a nitwit at night.

Jessica grabbed a flyer advertising *Driftwood Mystery Tours* from another booth – flying saucers, gangly almond-eyed aliens, and a child with electrodes stuck to her head. She cringed at the thought of a local idiot dragging tourists through the park, spreading bullshit about the kids. She folded the flyer, over and over.

They ate in silence, hungry from trekking the trails. After demolishing three muffins, Mark excused himself and walked to the restroom.

"Okay, Jessica. Who is he?" Jamie whispered. "You look *great*, better than you have in … in *forever*."

Jessica opened her mouth, ready to sling a few excuses, when Emily Murphy, Jamie's most lucrative yoga and juice-cleanse coaching client, slid into the booth with a glass of lemonade, patting down a floaty tunic. Emily dressed as if life never dragged her far from a spa. Hubby was a wealthy opioid prescriber, and home was a monstrous house in Driftwood Heights, where she struggled to blend in with her old-money neighbors. It wasn't the humble beginnings that gave her away, it was all the glitzy effort.

"Ladies!" she gushed, flicking a foot of hair extensions over her shoulder. Jessica caught fresh facelift scars in her hairline.

"Jessica! I don't know how the hell you can eat muffins like that and still look like you live on egg whites and air. How're you doing, anyway?"

"Fine, thanks. Keeping busy. And how are you doing?" Jessica asked, unconcerned with the answer. She continued to fold the flyer.

"Well, other than that poor little girl disappearing," she said, feigning horror. "They say she might be one of those *forest* kids. I just don't see how they can't put a stop to whatever's goin' on." She leaned in, revealing abundant cleavage.

Jessica nodded, too distracted to toss out a reply.

"Y'all should come to my garden party. We're raising money for Driftwood General's new pediatric wing. Mike just loves to give back to the community." Emily paused for a sip through her straw. "I have a fabulous caterer, but Daisy's still bringing her darling pimento cheese finger sandwiches, and Bonnie's making those adorable fruit skewers. Just be sure to wear a sweet little dress."

Jessica tugged at her sleeves, ready to break out in hives at the thought of trying to find a dress that would work. And then she'd stew awkwardly on Emily's lawn, twirling a wine glass.

"Anyway, why don't you two join us and inject some youth into this thing?"

"Sounds wonderful," Jessica said, and Jamie nodded in faux agreement.

"How's your store doing?" Emily asked Jamie. "I keep meaning to come in and buy myself one of those crystal necklaces hanging in the window." She swiped an eyelash from her cheek with a French-tipped nail.

"It's good. Tourists, mostly," Jamie replied, but Jessica knew otherwise, and thought of the shelves full of new-age inventory in the storage room of *The Waxing Crescent*. Dreamcatchers and incense and glossy hardbacks promising enlightenment, suffocating under their packaging.

"Anyway, I have some *delightful* gossip to share," Emily said in a loud whisper.

"Hmm?" Jamie raised an eyebrow, sipped her club soda.

"This morning I grabbed a latte at Nexus Coffee, and you wouldn't believe who I saw. I'd like to say *bumped into*, but sadly, I didn't get that close."

"The ghost of Burt Reynolds?" Jamie offered, and Jessica would've laughed if she wasn't still adrift in the folds of that origami lion. She plucked the lion from her sleeve and slipped it into her pocket.

Emily flapped her hand. "No, darlin', much better than that! Elliot Reed, that writer. He looks even better in real life."

Jessica stared at Emily with her mouth open. She dug a hand into the vinyl booth, unsure if she was excited or devastated. He'd been so damn close. Drinking coffee while she ached for him at home, cutting up newspaper headlines like a fruitcake.

Jamie eyed Jessica and Emily, her straw hovering an inch from her mouth.

"You did?" Jessica managed, after what felt like a whole minute.

"Yes, I swear it was him. Those eyes!"

Emily waved at a woman with a stroller outside, then brushed imaginary crumbs from the table. "Elliot Reed, in Driftwood! Can you believe it? He had his head stuck in a notebook, looking all academic and chiseled. So *refined*. And those eyes … did I mention his eyes?"

Jessica nodded, lips pressed together. Mark reappeared, freshly awkward, staring at the origami lion in her hand. She tucked it into her pocket to join the one plucked from the grass.

"Mark, honey, have a seat," Emily said, as if it had been her booth all along.

Jessica excused herself, then headed to the restroom. She wove between tourists in loud shirts, holding her breath as if that might increase the space between her and everyone else.

Three seconds before reaching the restroom doors, she walked smack into Andrew Harding. Right into his chest by his left shoulder, where she used to rest her head eight years ago, on the days when she wasn't trying to leave him. He smelled of the same cologne, faintly, but his chest felt harder, wider. More days in the gym, less time in the bar. He steadied her, and she stiffened as his hand touched her shoulder.

"Jessica," he said. "Have you got a minute? I really need to talk to you."

"You do?" She glanced at the gold badge on his belt. *In what capacity? As a detective, or my useless ex?*

But a paralyzing fear of confrontation made her cower from saying such things. There was a wall between her world and everyone else's that she'd been building for years – or maybe she'd let it build itself – but she was useless at defending it, she recognized in that moment, still remembering the sensation of his hand on her shoulder.

"Just for a minute." Andrew shot a look at the deputies standing at the counter, who were now throwing glances their way.

They headed outside, where sunlight bounced off store windows. Runners, dogs and strollers passed on the boardwalk across the street.

Andrew leaned against a wall, crossed his arms over his chest, and his badge glimmered. Eight years had treated him well, Jessica decided, and part of her resented it. As handsome as ever, and now with the confidence that came with a little authority, a longer leash, a car that wasn't his father's.

"You're a detective," she said, and regretted stating the obvious. "Since when?"

"Coming up on three years."

There was an awkward pause.

"What are you doing these days?" he said.

It was the lack of anything to tell that hurt the most.

"Still at the library."

She caught Mark glowering through the window from his booth. Emily was still there, tormenting him.

"You said you needed to talk to me?" She resisted the urge to fidget.

Was that cold? And did I mean it to be?

He looked beyond her shoulder, as if he were talking to someone else. "You saw Annabelle Lewis in your yard?"

Warmth spread under her skin, prickling her like hives. "Yeah. But like I explained on the phone, it was dark out, and I only saw her for a second. But it definitely looked like her." She swallowed, cutting herself off.

Andrew nodded, slowly. "I was hoping I could ask you a few questions about Olivia."

She crossed her arms. Something twisted inside. "Why's that?"

"Part of the investigation. I could really use your help. Listen, I wouldn't ask if I didn't need to. I know you don't really…" He looked at her, looked away. "I know you don't like to talk about it."

"It's in the past. I want to keep it there," she said, staring at his neck, the way his shirt clung here and there. At the gray-blue of his eyes, which used to hide so much. Now they seemed a little earnest, searching, almost.

Searching for what? She wondered, and bit her lip.

"I just want to get your thoughts on a few things, Jessica. Off the record. Think of it as a favor."

The sound of her name from his lips twisted something inside again. And had he taken a step closer, or did she imagine it? She wanted to sit down, be alone. But his eyes anchored her to the concrete, to the moment she hadn't seen coming.

This should be simple, she told herself. A simple matter of saying no. But then there was her sense of obligation. To Olivia, to Annabelle.

"I guess. If it could help, I mean."

He smiled, disarmingly warm. "Great. I'll stop by later. You still at the same place?"

Stop by? I still have all that weird shit on the wall. Goddammit, I should've called the sheriff. Now I feel like I'm hiding something.

"I live in my parents' house now," she heard herself say. A speedboat tore across the lake.

"Oh, how are they doing?"

She looked up at him and squinted as the sunlight hit her eyes. "They're dead."

"Jessica ... I'm so sorry."

There goes my name again. And now the diner's doors are opening. Mark and Jamie, and a few deputies. Her face burned.

"Don't worry about it," she said, thinking of how much she missed her parents. How much she longed to return home to the lights on, to cobbler in the oven. To Mom pulling off her reading glasses, hugging her on that ancient sofa.

Andrew's radio buzzed. Mark hovered.

"I've got to go, but I'll see you later. Thanks," he said, suddenly formal in front of Mark.

Jamie teased Mark with small talk. Jessica walked to a bench on the boardwalk and stared across the lake at the boats bobbing at their jetties. The Arbor Hotel's stone walls and wooden arches were visible through a blooming stretch of redbuds and oak.

When is later? And why the hell didn't I ask? Typical him, typical me. The same shitty dynamic, eight years later.

She looked at The Arbor again and wondered if Elliot was staying there. Typing at a desk, maybe, overlooking the lake. *No, not now,* she decided. *Not in the middle of the afternoon. He's somewhere around here. I know it.*

She pulled the two lions out of her pocket and wedged hers between the planks of wood that formed the bench's seat. Then she unfolded the other and traced the penciled words with her thumb. She read the notes, then refolded the page into an origami lion.

"Maybe I really am your muse," she whispered. "Maybe my entire life is just one of your books."

"Jessica?"

She jumped. Mark and Jamie stood at the side of the bench.

"Everything okay?" Jamie said. Jessica wasn't sure if it was scrutiny or sunlight narrowing her stare. She folded Elliot's lion back into her pocket.

"I'm fine. I think I'll head home, take a nap."

She walked to the parking lot, sensing her brother's eyes on her back. The sky was still clear, and the lake rippled under a sheen of white and gold. Jessica reversed out of the lot and headed for Pine Street, where fallen branches were now heaped at the curb.

She parked and climbed out, then froze in the driveway, turned around. Bright eyes glinted from across the street, under a black hood, and now, in the bright sunlight, she saw that it was Joseph Baker, the eldest boy who'd stood on her porch, begging her not to call the police.

What do you want from me?

She wanted to yell, demand an answer, but he was already running around the corner, vanishing again.

Chapter 21

Saturday, April 16, 2022

Elliot looked up from his laptop to watch sunlight fade over the Driftwood skyline, fingers ready to hit *Send* and email his first chapter to Ruth.

The chapter was solid, dark, compelling. His new character, Jessica, had led him down a path of fog-cloaked pine trees and forgotten memories. She was haunted by a past he still hadn't fully figured out, but he'd described her resolve to uncover a mystery that was as shadowy and winding as the forest trails.

He sent the email, then browsed his public inbox. A part of him – the part that wanted to believe that Jessica was more than just his muse – expected to see a message from her. A few cryptic sentences as spellbinding as his dream the night before.

But he just found the usual slurry of spam, fan mail and requests. Another three emails from a hoarder in Oklahoma who liked to send him photos of her cats sitting on copies of his novels – usually dressed in crocheted cardigans, but sometimes in hats – surrounded by piles of garbage. The usual mix of cute, sordid and creepy messages from strangers he hoped he'd never meet, and a string of inquiries that his publicist would bother him about later.

Before settling into a desk chair in his hotel room, he'd spent the afternoon in Driftwood. A stop at the sheriff's office proved to be a waste of time. *"All of those records are confidential. Ongoing investigations,"* the archive's custodian had insisted. Then he'd hiked the forest trails, steering clear of a search-and-rescue party. He'd returned to Nexus Coffee for an hour of bewildered daydreaming, since Tiffany's had remained too busy to venture inside, then driven back to The Arbor.

He ordered room service and considered his next move. There were a dozen bars in Driftwood. Four on the outskirts of town, most of which had reputations for pool table fights and broken glass. Another handful attached to hotels, serving garish cocktails to tourists, and one that hosted obscure college bands and, according to reviews, had vomit-splattered bathrooms. Then there was the Lakeside Tavern, which sat at the tail-end of the boardwalk, unassuming and serving locals for over thirty years. The most likely option for a journalist with a drinking problem.

He inhaled dinner then drove downtown. Darkness crept in from the shadows, and streetlights blinked on as he pulled into the parking lot.

A half-assed nautical theme cluttered the tavern's interior, and strings of yellow lights lit a beer garden. Inside, customers nursed drinks in dusty booths by glowing hurricane lamps.

Elliot sat at the bar and took his time with a scotch, scrolling through his phone to take another look at Oliver Gray's sparse LinkedIn profile.

He threw a look around the bar. No sign of anyone but a lonely looking woman staring into her cocktail at a booth. An hour passed, then another, and Elliot stood up to leave. *Dumb idea. A waste of time for a long shot,* he figured, pulling out his wallet to settle his tab.

But then a man in a crumpled shirt slumped through the doors, and Elliot recognized the straight black hair, the sunken eyes, from his profile photo.

"Oliver?"

The guy waited for the bartender, leaning into the bar.

"Yeah?" His eyes were bloodshot, slow to focus. *How many drinks in?* Elliot wondered. *Five? Seven? Nine?* It wouldn't be the first time he'd pried information from someone full of booze.

"Your colleagues said I might find you here."

"Oh yeah?" Oliver laughed. "I'm guessing you mean my ex-colleagues. Those bastards. Who are you?" He waved at the bartender.

"A journalist."

"What's your name?" Oliver's eyes focused.

"Elliot Reed," he said in a low voice.

Another laugh, louder this time. "You *used to be* a journalist."

Elliot cringed. "I need information on Joseph Baker and Anthony Walker. I read your article."

"Suddenly everyone cares. Why?"

"Just research."

"If you're buying, I'll talk. But outside. I need a cigarette."

They sat outside at a picnic table. Oliver downed a beer, ordered another, then sucked the life out of a Marlboro.

"What do you want to know?"

"Whatever you've got."

"Last time I tried sharing what I know about those kids, I got fired."

"Why did they fire you?"

Oliver took a long drag on his cigarette, holding his breath as if he didn't want to release the serpentine cloud smothering his insides. Music blared from the bar as the door swung open.

"Guess the mayor didn't much like me talking about it. Either that, or they figured I'd lost it."

Elliot nodded, waiting for whatever else would spill from him.

"I had a friend who works for the county do some digging. The rangers found Joseph Baker and Anthony Walker abandoned in the park when they were two, three years old. Neither of them spoke a word of English, and no one ever figured out where the hell they came from or how they got there. They had IQs through the roof, but they were screwed up, always in the shrink's office. And the freaky shit doesn't end there. You heard of Olivia Garcia?"

Elliot nodded again.

"I tracked down one of her teachers. She told me the kid was 'gifted but strange.' Her words, not mine. She said the girl seemed to think she belonged in a cave underground." Oliver drew quotation marks with his fingers.

Elliot feigned nonchalance. "A cave?"

"Yup."

"You said they were screwed up. In what way?"

"No idea. You'd need medical reports to find out. But this town's full of runaways and freaks. Everyone's got some story about what they've seen in the park."

The wind scattered ash across the table.

"Stories? Such as?"

"Don't tell me you don't already know," Oliver said, laughing. "Bullshit about the park being haunted, used for government experiments, whatever. And the UFOs. Everyone thinks they've seen one. Military aircraft, probably. There's a base not far from here."

"And the paper fired you?"

"Yeah. Assholes. Some of the locals put up signs in the park, warning hikers about a cult abducting and brainwashing kids. I guess that got the mayor real pissed – the old man's paranoid about losing tourists."

"And you think that's what it is? A cult?"

Oliver shrugged. "Beats me. I've heard every damn theory under the sun. I was just reporting what I uncovered. All I know is Joseph and Anthony had a reason to run away. They lived in overcrowded shitholes, and the foster parents were scum."

"What's your theory on the nausea? The dizziness people talk about after hiking through the park?"

"Could be anything. Exhaustion, heat stroke. The papermill's been spewing toxic shit into the air for fifty years, making people sick."

"The sheriff must have some kind of theory about all this."

"'The cases are still open.' That's what they told me every time I called. Look, the only reason people are gossiping about this is because it's so damn weird. Not because they give a damn about those kids." Oliver coughed for at least a minute, barking into his fist.

"I keep hearing about Evergreen Pass. About how it's cursed. What's the story there?"

The door swung open. Another drink for Oliver, another blare of music, and the sour waft of warm beer. Shadows danced across the wall as hurricane lamps flickered.

"Hillbilly legend, probably. I did hear one *real* strange rumor, though."

"What's that?"

"People who live around there … they say those kids turn up in their yards. A few even said they stole shit from someone's garage." His eyes glazed. He snorted through a laugh.

"What did they steal?"

"Tools and clothing. Venison."

Elliot threw a look over his shoulder at the lake sloshing its silvery tide under the pewter moon. "What else do you know about Olivia Garcia?"

"Only what I told you. She went missing twenty years ago. No one's seen her since. The parents left a few years after she disappeared. They divorced, moved out of state."

Elliot left Oliver with a paid tab and walked the sandy wooden slats of the boardwalk to his car, which sat alone in the parking lot. For a moment he felt hideously alone, before driving into the leafy embrace of Driftwood

Heights, where The Arbor's lights beamed between branches.

Walking through the hotel's parking lot, he sensed eyes on his neck. He turned around, stared into the trees that bordered the lot.

Nothing. He walked another few steps, now faster.

Leaves rustled. Elliot turned around again, now with a hunch that something, or someone, was just feet away.

Eyes stared back at him from the trees, bright and opaline.

He wasn't sure what unnerved him the most – those eyes, watching him in the dark, or the worry that he couldn't trust his own mind. He turned, dashed under the awning, and reached the lobby.

Must have been a trick of the light. Animals in the parking lot.

Later, surrounded by the sheen of cherry wood and a sea of buttery carpet, Elliot pored over his notes and read the news with a club sandwich on his lap. Still no sign of Annabelle Lewis. Just a promise from the county sheriff that they were doing all they could.

He answered a few text messages, distracted by his meeting with Oliver, and Jessica. Whoever she was, his muse or something more, she'd hung around his thoughts all day. He read a message from Ruth, which, judging by the typos, she'd sent over a few cocktails at the White Horse Tavern, asking for a glowing blurb for someone else's novel. Another from his mother, reminding him that she hadn't seen him since the holidays.

He lay on his back, staring at the ceiling fan, waiting for sleep that didn't come. He popped an Ambien, then slipped into a cloudy half-snooze, slung between star-spangled dreams and a roaming mind.

But he woke hours later and glanced at the clock. 10:45 p.m. A blurry memory from the night before surfaced.

"Oh shit!" he whispered, flinging off the covers. *I told her 11 p.m.*

He dressed and brushed his teeth, borrowed a flashlight from the front desk, and drove to Evergreen Pass, telling himself there'd be nothing there. No hole in a rock, no Jessica. *So why am I in such a damn rush?* he wondered, pulling into the parking lot.

Chapter 22

Saturday, April 16, 2022

Deputy Willis sat stiff in his patrol car, clutching his radio, eyes fixed on a boy by the woods that bordered the county road.

Anthony Walker. It had to be him. For the last few days, the kid had stared back at Willis from a photo on the wall behind Detective Harding's desk, eyes scowling through the black and white pixels.

The kid looked like he'd been living rough for years. Hair matted into tufts and spears; cheeks smeared in dirt. But Willis wasn't paralyzed by the sight of some kid. Lost kids turned up now and then. That wasn't what made his brow break out in sweat, the blood drain from his face.

No, it was what the kid was *doing* that sent his blood pressure soaring, so that the veins in his neck bulged.

One bad move, and that kid'll be dead.

Anthony sat on the ground by a hollowed tree trunk, tucking into fistfuls of fungus with a black bear. Barefoot, enjoying a picnic with a three-hundred-pound friend.

The kid dug his hands into the fungus, tearing off chunks, feeding it to the bear, then feeding himself. The bear grunted, slumped on its back legs, paws the size of Anthony's head, claws as long as shark teeth.

Willis opened the car door, fumbling.

"Step away, son," he said, walking toward Anthony, reaching for his weapon.

Anthony ignored him and fed the bear another fistful of fungus. "I love you, bear. You're my friend," the kid said in his pint-sized voice.

"Anthony? Is that you? Just stay real calm, and step away."

The bear turned his head and sized up the deputy.

"Don't hurt him!" Anthony yelled, holding on to the bear.

The deputy raised his pistol. "Anthony, I need you to step away. It's for your safety, son."

Anthony buried his face in the bear's ear, and the animal ran away, lumbering into the woods. The deputy fired one shot and missed.

"I hate you!" Anthony yelled, his voice shrill and tinny. He ran toward the deputy, then stood a few feet away. "Why did you do that? You could've hurt him, you asshole!"

"Mind your mouth, son," the deputy managed, stammering. "Now, what in God's name were you doing? You could've gotten killed."

"He won't kill me. He's my friend!"

The deputy considered grabbing the kid and throwing him in the backseat. "Come on, son. Get in the car."

Anthony licked his fingers and wiped them dry on his pants. "No."

"Come on, now, it's time to go. And you oughta be careful about eating that stuff," the deputy sputtered, wondering how anyone could have eyes so bright. Like shiny pebbles of sea glass.

"It's chicken of the woods. It's good for me. You eat *really* bad stuff," Anthony said, looking at the deputy's bulging midsection.

"Get in the car, Anthony."

Anthony ran into the woods. The deputy jogged after him, heavy with a gut full of cinnamon rolls. The boy darted between the trees, too agile to catch, and soon disappeared into the forest's fold. Panting, the deputy returned to his car.

He grabbed his radio, then let it fall to his lap. Sheriff Clarke would be so damn mad. *You're telling me the kid got away? I oughta write you up!* That's what he'd say. And he'd already received an earful for rolling in late. In fact, he got an earful from the sheriff just about every day.

And even if he'd grabbed that kid, thrown him in the back of his car, then what? Straight into one of those roach-filled foster homes. Some nasty place on the west side of town, where he'd spent too many nights cuffing junkies, dragging their scrawny asses to his patrol car.

No, screw that, he decided, easing back onto the road. *Some things are better left alone. Let them all think he's dead.*

Chapter 23

Saturday, April 16, 2022

Jessica re-read the headlines of another report on Annabelle's disappearance. She'd already tried to read it three times, but she was too restless, too *pissed*, to focus on anything.

Andrew hadn't bothered to show up. She'd waited for hours, persuading herself she wasn't waiting at all. After an hour of scrubbing, the writing had faded from the wall, but it left a stain, which now hid behind a bookshelf. She'd even vacuumed and tucked away the folders and notebooks on the floor, the laundry pile in the hallway that hadn't washed itself.

She told herself that she didn't give a damn, resenting the fact that he annoyed her so much. There were more compelling things to think about. Sighing, she tugged at her sleeves. She was restless one minute, sleepy the next. A pounding heart and a heavy head.

She poured a tumbler of wine and drew a bath, then perched on the edge of the tub, watching the water steam the air. She reached for the origami lion in her back pocket, asking herself if it proved that last night had been more than a dream. What if she'd somehow fabricated the whole thing? But *how*?

Maybe she couldn't even trust what was right in front of her. Was *anything* reliably real? She touched her face, stared at her palms, then rubbed the paper between her fingers. Yes, it was definitely real. She was real, *it* was real. This wasn't one of her own creations – some elaborate invention thrown together between gulps of wine and a slice of toast.

Ever since she'd heard Elliot's voice on the phone, the version of him that lived in her head – the one spun from daydreams and dust-jacket photos – had seemed clearer, closer than ever. Just a few blinks or a sigh away from finding his own breath and beating heart, ready to slip from her mind, into her bed.

And now that she'd met him, or some version of him, he seemed so close, he might as well have been in the same room. Right there in the bathroom, leaning against the doorframe.

But thank God he's not *right there,* she thought when she nearly tripped headfirst onto the floor, pulling off a sock. She yanked off the other sock, took another gulp of wine, and jumped when the doorbell rang. After a scramble to turn off the faucet and wipe the wine from her blouse, she ran down the hallway to open the door.

"Sorry I'm late." Andrew stood on her doorstep with an appeasing smile and a six-pack of beer.

Presumptuous came into her head, like a flashing beacon.

"No problem," she lied, backing up as he entered. He squeezed past her. She could still smell his cologne, a little stronger now. Did he apply more before coming over?

She took the beer. He followed her into the kitchen with his hands in his pockets, looking around as if he'd entered an antiques store.

"How long have you lived here?"

She dumped the beers on the kitchen table, handed him a bottle opener, and poured another tumbler of wine. "Two years. Mark and I inherited the place. I ended up living in it."

He threw his car keys on the kitchen table, and she already disliked the ambiguity. What might be work, what might be play. A minute in, and it already felt muddy. He seemed so much bigger than her in the old wooden dining chair. Or maybe it was just his presence that crowded her.

"So why are you on this case?"

"The sheriff asked for help. They sent me." He cracked his knuckles, drank some beer, rolled the sleeves of his shirt. She suddenly felt ashamed of everything in the room. Everything she owned, everything she was.

"Before that girl went missing?" she asked. The kitchen light was too glaring, too revealing of every feathery crease in her skin, every crack and smear on tired wood and linoleum. But the living room was too intimate and comfortable. She needed hard surfaces, the delineation of the kitchen table.

"Yeah. I was supposed to be working on the other three kids. I guess the mayor got worried about all the rumors, thinks it's bad for business." He rolled his neck. A little restless, just like her. His fingers played with the edge of the beer bottle label.

You used to hold me, press your lips against my skin, she thought, and crossed her legs under the table. Elliot had vanished to some corner of her mind, but her longing hadn't, and it opened a vacuum inside. But opposite her there was just a dead end, an old corpse. Eight long years hadn't changed that.

"Three? Olivia's case is still open?" she asked at last. He blinked.

A slip, already? Maybe he should chug that beer. And another.

"Officially, yes. Freezing cold, but still breathing."

Should've eaten something before drinking, she thought, but poured herself another glass.

"You said you wanted to ask me something?"

"A few things, actually." Half his beer was already down his throat. The hoppy scent wafted.

"Did you remember anything else about Wednesday morning? You're sure it was Annabelle Lewis?"

A knot formed in her stomach. "It looked like her. But like I said, I can't be sure. It happened so fast. She was there for just a second, and then she ran across the yard and disappeared behind the bushes. I figured it was one of the neighbors' kids. I opened the back door, and she was gone. Then I saw her picture in the paper."

What have I done? I spun myself a little bundle of lies, and now I'm stuck. Lying to you, after all those times you lied to me. She dug her feet into the floor.

"You said she was wearing a white nightgown?"

Jessica nodded.

"And there's absolutely nothing else you can remember about her?"

She shook her head. They let silence fill up the space between them, until Andrew rapped his fingers on the table.

"What do you remember about the night that Olivia disappeared? You told me once you kind of blacked out."

"I told the sheriff everything I remembered."

A corner of the label on his beer bottle peeled under his thumb. "Can you walk me through it, Jess? I know we talked about this before, but that was a long time ago."

What did you ever know about me, really? she wondered. They had a history, a threadbare connection, but it didn't run as deep as he thought. But his question hung there.

"I remember trick-or-treating and walking along the back road. The rest is gone. The only other thing I remember is running home."

"You really don't remember anything else? How long were you there? Did she say anything before she disappeared? Anything that made you think she wanted to run away?" Another brush with his thumb, and another edge folded. But his eyes were on her.

"Sometimes I got the feeling she never really belonged with her parents. But I don't know what she said that night, because I can't remember a damn thing about it. And I don't know how long we were out there. Time didn't make sense."

"Didn't belong with them? Why's that?"

"She was so smart. They didn't know what to do with her. Matteo drank, and Paula was ratty. She got irate about the dumbest stuff. I don't think they were happy, and I guess they forgot that Olivia was there half the time. She was always at our place."

Andrew tapped his finger against his beer bottle, mulling over what she'd told him. Jessica closed her eyes for two seconds and thought of Olivia's gold-flecked irises, coaxing an apple from the fruit bowl. *No, I sure as hell can't tell you about that.*

"You said time didn't make sense. What do you mean?"

"It's like I lost a chunk of it. It's hard to explain." She was halfway through her second glass of wine. *Pull back,* she told herself, taking another sip.

"Did you tell anyone where you were going? Did Olivia mention anyone new?"

"No, we didn't tell anyone anything. She didn't mention anyone."

"Did anyone follow you?"

"I didn't see anyone. It was deserted out there. I can't remember anything. Just how alone I felt when I..."

"When you?"

"It's like I blacked out, but I was standing up." She avoided Andrew's eye contact, the near-appeal of him in the subtle cling of a navy shirt. That turf between his neck and shoulder where she used to rest her head. "I heard Annabelle Lewis is adopted."

"I can't talk about that."

She wanted to slap him. The fridge's hum kicked in. "How many others disappeared? There are more, aren't there?"

"I have no idea, and if I did, I couldn't talk about that, either. So what do you think happened out on that back road, Jess?"

She slung a look around the room. At the cacti in their green planters along the windowsill, the faucet that dripped and dripped. "There was this weird lack of everything. It's like I lost time. All I remember is the dark. It was *so* dark."

"Why were you scared? Because Olivia disappeared? Or something else?" Andrew peeled half the label from the beer bottle.

"I don't know." Her face flushed again, cheeks warm as embers. Andrew watched her, and something about his look softened, but she wasn't sure why. The wine had thrown a blunting film around everything but the heat spreading down her neck.

"So where did she go? You've got your theories, I bet."

She thought of all the things she'd never found the courage to say. Her notebooks and folders, the black circle in her closet. A sense that none of this could be explained through the logic of police procedure. That busy minds at desks covered in reports and coffee cups couldn't untangle it.

"I don't know, but I don't think the parents are involved. Do you?"

"I can't discuss that."

She was ready to slap him again, but another part of her wanted to lean against him, rest for a while. "What *can* you discuss?"

"We're not ruling anything out, but..." He shook his head.

"But?"

"Forget it. I really can't, Jess. That's not why I'm here."

Why are you here, really? Are you as alone as I am? Alone and fumbling with dead ends in a town you used to know?

"What happened at the hospital, Andrew? Before she disappeared? I know she was admitted. I overheard my dad talking about it. What happened with that nurse?"

"Jess, please..." He reached for another beer, flipped off the cap, and it rattled and spun on the table.

"There's more to this than you thought, isn't there? Something you can't explain."

"The whole thing is just real fucking weird. Nothing makes sense." He took a long chug, shutting himself up. "Just forget it." He leaned back in his chair and slugged the rest of his beer, but he was still soft around the edges, she sensed. Looking for relief from what he carried around all day.

There was a pause, silent but loud in her head, until he cleared his throat. "I'm sorry. I'm just exhausted. I finished work at eleven last night."

Jessica tightened her grip on her glass. A memory jellied her legs. Elliot next to her, by the riverbank. *11 ... 11pm! What if it wasn't a dream? I have to know for sure.*

"You okay, Jess?"

"Yes, yes, I'm fine." A message flashed on his phone, and she glanced at the time. 10 p.m. *Please, please hurry up and leave.*

He sighed. "There's something else we need to discuss. I was going to ask you to come into the office, but..."

Oh Christ, what now?

"But *what*?" she said, hiding her impatience with a light cough.

"I just figured you'd want to talk about it here. But can we sit on your couch, at least? It's been a long day, and it started with a bench press at six o'clock this morning."

She stood up, hiding an eye roll. The room swayed, enough to remind her she'd already drunk too much. He followed her down the hallway, walking close behind. *Because he thinks I'm weak right now, needy because we threw a shovel into the rabbit hole.*

"This is way more comfortable than that shitty futon we had," he said, sinking into the sofa cushions, letting his arm rest along the back.

His words startled her, and she disguised a wobble as she sat at the other end of the sofa. "I guess. I barely remember." A little lie for a little distance.

"Did Olivia say anything about someplace dark? Maybe a basement?"

The question pulled her from thinking of Elliot. She searched for lost moments in the black space between her ears.

A basement? No, not a basement. But maybe a pit.

"I ... I can't remember."

Andrew leaned forward, pulling a folded piece of paper from his pocket. "Any thoughts on this?"

Jessica unfolded a photocopy of a sketch of two girls tumbling down a hole, into a cave. As she closed her eyes, the flurry of lights returned, beaming brighter, dancing in the dark. She remembered the earthy scent of wet soil, the sensation of tumbling. Her dream from last night bled into every other, converging with sketches, journal entries, fragments. She opened her eyes.

"Jess? Are you okay?"

"Where did you get this?"

"Your parents gave it to the sheriff. They found it in the living room. You don't remember seeing this? Did she draw it when she was with you?"

I'm useless. I buried everything that's useful. Everything that might lead to the truth.

"No, I don't remember anything about it."

"But what *is* this? You think it's normal for a six-year-old kid to draw this?"

"I don't know, Andrew. It reminds me of a nightmare I had, but..."

"But?"

"But that's all. It was just a nightmare."

Or maybe it wasn't, she added silently. *But it's all too tangled inside my head, and I couldn't explain it if I tried. And what else am I hiding? Why didn't I report the writing on the wall, the junk on my desk? Should I tell him now? No, God damn it, it's too late.*

"If you remember anything..." He leaned toward her, his hand brushing her shoulder, then resting by her collar.

Jessica nodded, shrinking, subtly, from his touch.

"I missed you, Jess."

He moved to kiss her, wafting the scent of his cologne and the beer on his lips. His skin was warm and flushed like hers.

She pulled back, hands ready to block his weight. "No, I can't."

"It's okay, I get it," he said, pulling back. "But can I at least sleep on the couch? I can't drive after so many beers."

"You can't get an Uber?"

"I'm way the hell out on the north side. That'll be forty bucks, and another to come get my car in the morning."

You were planning this, weren't you? You really are the fucking worst.

"You can take my brother's room," she said, then left him on the couch.

She stirred instant coffee into cold water and chugged it with a wince, willing herself to sober up, then gulped down another few glasses of water. In her bedroom, she closed the door and slumped against it. 10:40.

Her hair was flat. She fussed with it. Moving to unlock the door, she remembered her folders and notebooks. *What if he hears me leave and decides to snoop? Would he do such a thing? Maybe, and then he'll decide I'm a lunatic.*

She lingered by the door, now worrying about the words she'd scrubbed from the living room wall and hidden behind the bookshelf – the stain they'd left behind was dark, some of the words still discernible. *No, he's got no reason to move furniture around.*

Her keys were on the bedroom nightstand, but she'd left her phone in the kitchen. She couldn't bring herself to venture into the hall again, risk another awkward moment.

The only way to leave unnoticed would be through her bedroom window. Then she could tiptoe around to the garage. Grimacing, she pushed open the window and climbed out, landing with a thud on the lawn. But his car blocked the garage, and her flashlight was inside.

She unlocked the garage and pulled up the door inch by inch, clearing two feet of space. Then she rolled under the door, grabbed her flashlight, and tiptoed out. With a cringe, she pulled the door back down. *What the hell will he think if he catches me? Now I look like a criminal.*

Her keys jingled into her pocket. She jogged out of the driveway. Trees and lawns flew by, blurred by her speed and the wine cloud in her head. She had no idea what she was running to. A dream? Some strung-out fantasy? Or a man with a beating heart and breath in his lungs?

And am I nuts enough to think I'll jump into that hole under the mountain pass again?

Her feet smacked against the sidewalk, until she hit the crossroads and swung right onto the back road. She'd be at least fifteen minutes late. *Will he wait?*

The light from the streetlamps faded, and she flipped on her flashlight, crunching over the gravel. The road curved, and she searched for the gap in the trees, then hit the trail.

The forest was drier tonight, and twigs cracked beneath her feet. Spring pawed at the air, fighting off the evening chill. She jogged up the trail, stopping here and there to catch her breath. The fresh air cleared her head.

The trail flattened, and her feet slowed. Her bladder was ready to burst. She hid behind a bush and peed, feeling as feral as the forest kids. *Do I even know where I'm going?*

Jogging the descent, she wished she could run from all the doubt in her head. Tall grass reached for her calves as she neared the ravine.

A few steps up the ravine, nausea turned Jessica's stomach. She wretched and leaned against a tree trunk.

Is that a car parked at Evergreen Pass?

A metallic shimmer, like glossy car paint, flashed through the branches, but the whirling leaves obscured everything.

She walked through the copse of trees, pausing when dizziness floored her again. A man stood ahead, holding a flashlight.

Chapter 24

Saturday, April 16, 2022

Jessica turned off her flashlight and hid behind a tree. The park ranger ambled past, his own flashlight filtering through the branches. He hiked the ravine, and Jessica heard a door slam, an engine start. She puffed out a sigh, then trod through the lanky grass toward the rock under the mountain pass.

11 p.m. had come and gone, she was sure, and if Elliot had turned up, he hadn't hung around.

I was either too late, or completely deluded, she figured, heavy with disappointment. *And I bet that hole in the rock isn't even there.*

But nearing the rock, she caught sight of a dark gap in the rockface. Gingerly, she slipped inside.

The dark quickly enveloped her. Goosebumps spread down her neck. Remembering the sudden downward slope, she aimed her flashlight at the ground and found fresh tracks, as if someone had just slipped down.

Elliot? Or someone else? Or a raccoon, a badger?

Holding her breath as if the dark could drown her, she shuffled down the slope, crouching, leaning back to avoid toppling and rolling. Her feet slipped, gripped the ground, then slipped again, and she slid into the dark pit. Jessica's wine fog had all but vanished now. Her senses were wide awake.

Oh God, I'm back. This part was real, at least. This creepy, stuffy hole in the ground.

Her flashlight illuminated the drop to the chasm. She swung her legs over and landed on the ridge, then hiked her way down, fumbling through the darkness. Halfway down, time warped and blurred, just as it had the night before. A dream-like haze lacquered the dark, the thoughts shuttling into focus.

She dodged the rock she'd stumbled over before, remembering how she'd fallen into Elliot's grasp. But now she was alone, deep underground.

I'll figure this out alone if I have to. Did he forget, or was he never really here? What was real, and what did I invent?

She found the passageway that led to the cave and crunched over gravel. The chasm seemed darker, closer, without Elliot in front of her.

Five minutes into her trek, a shuffle startled her. She froze, listening. This time it came from behind her – from a narrow gap in the rock. An opening they'd walked past the night before.

"Elliot?" she almost called, but stopped herself. *What if it's not him? Who else is hiding down here?*

She eased inside, entering a tunnel, and the air soon became clammy and earthy, clinging to her lungs and skin.

Moments morphed to minutes, half an hour. The rock was pocketed with crevices that led to more tunnels.

Don't get lost in here. Just walk in one straight line.

Footfalls echoed behind her, suddenly loud in the dark, and light flooded the tunnel. Before she could decide to spin around or run, a hand gripped her shoulder. She yelped.

"It's me," a voice whispered. Elliot was right behind her. He lowered his flashlight. She exhaled, shaky.

"Sorry I scared you."

"You came back," she whispered, steeling against the urge to hold onto him, check that he was real.

He reached for her instead, and his grip released a fluttering inside, as if he'd unscrewed the lid of a jar full of moths in her chest. Their batting wings made it hard to think, hard to breathe. She forgot about what might be deeper inside the tunnel and lost herself in him. His eyes wandering over her, the outline of his chest, his neck, his jaw.

"I only remembered at the last minute. I didn't see you when I got here, and there was a ranger hanging around outside, so I hid inside the rock, then came back down to explore," he said. "Jesus, you really are real…" He trailed off.

She nodded, vindicated. *Yes, I'm alive. I'm more than the white space between your words.* "But are you real? Tell me you're real." She reddened at the longing in her voice.

"Yes, I'm real, Jessica. I swear." He smiled, squeezed her shoulder, releasing another flurry of moths from her jar.

"I still feel so confused about last night. It's all so foggy."

"I know. But let me show you something." He aimed his flashlight at an alcove in the rock behind them.

"What?"

"I can't even describe it," he whispered. His hand brushed her sleeve.

"You knew I'd come back?"

"No, I just hoped you would."

A prickly swirl turned inside her, hot and cold, stirring her senses again. His palm against her shoulder, his body so close, and whatever hid in the cracks and hollows. *Don't think about what this is, where I am. Just keep moving.*

They walked into another narrow tunnel, and soon it descended, snaking farther underground. The path was winding, rubble obscuring a deep decline. Water pattered onto stone – *drip drip slap* – trickling and splattering on their heads.

An eerie bright dust flickered in the glow of their flashlights.

"You see that?" Elliot whispered.

"Yeah." Jessica passed a hand through it, then examined her palm. The small flecks coated her skin.

"What the hell *is* that?" Elliot murmured.

"I have no idea. But now it's in our lungs."

They walked on, murmurs echoing. The tunnel sloped to a sharper decline, and another stretch of winding granite led them deeper. Glossy white clusters of flowstone bulged from the rock, puffy and slick like cotton balls dripping in candlewax.

"I wonder how deep we are," Elliot whispered.

"I have no idea. I feel like I'm lost in the middle of the Earth."

"We're somewhere under the cliff that overlooks the river, I think. Or maybe we're miles away. I can't even tell. But just keep going."

As they descended farther, a marbling of eerie blue streaked the rock. The *drip drip* grew louder, until Jessica found herself dodging puddles.

The tunnel widened, and the puddles formed a tinkling creek. Neon threads and spongy orbs slithered through the water, swelling to a sludge. Invertebrates flexed in the stream, some translucent, some veiny and gilled. More light particles danced in the dark, forming a mist.

"Oh my God," Jessica murmured, pausing to study the slimy underworld. The dust was thicker now, like vapor lining her throat.

"It's bioluminescence, I think," Elliot said.

"I've heard about caves like this, but not around *here*."

"I'm still having a hard time believing any of this is real," Elliot sighed. "There's a whole ecosystem down here."

The tunnel widened farther, and water snaked through deep cracks in the granite to form an estuary. A hum filled the void, and the trill of insect legs rose the hairs on the back of Jessica's neck. As they turned a corner, blue-green light burst from the dark.

The cave was a tangle of spaghetti-thin tentacles, scales that shimmered and slithered. Translucent fauna crawled over algae-slick rock and floated in soupy ponds. Glow-worms hung like sticky strings of pearls, enmeshed in a web of droopy blue spinnerets.

Jessica's stomach turned at the gluey throb, the bubbling lumpy sludge oozing from crevices. A frosted veiny membrane reached across the cave walls, and glowing insects scuttered around her feet, eyelash-thin legs brushing her shoes. Green larvae sputtered from a murky puddle. She put her hand to her mouth, staggering back.

A cracking noise ripped a gasp from her throat – a sharp crunch beneath her shoe. A thick chrysalis, silvery-white and wormy, had snapped under her weight.

"It's disgusting," Elliot whispered. "But the lights are so..."

"Beautiful?"

"Yeah."

"How many caves are down here?"

"I don't know. I still feel like I'm dreaming," Elliot murmured.

"Olivia ... I think she told me about this place," Jessica said, a whisper-faint memory surfacing.

"Olivia?"

"Olivia Garcia. I was her babysitter. I was with her the night she disappeared."

Elliot fell silent, piecing together a puzzle, just like her.

"She told me she had a secret. She was trying to tell me something, but I was just a dumb kid." Jessica gripped Elliot's sleeve. "Elliot, she said you could get stuck in here," she whispered, grasping at another memory rising from the deep – a memory of Halloween. "And right before she disappeared, she drew two girls falling through the earth, into a pit."

"How could she have known about this place? You think something happened to her here?"

"I don't know," Jessica sighed, as if she'd dropped a heavy load from her back, but the air suddenly seemed too close.

Elliot took her hand. "Let's get out of here. We can talk about it outside."

They hiked up the winding path of rocks and pebbles. The glowing particles bloomed in the dark, dissolved into the black.

At last, the tunnel opened to the passageway at the bottom of the chasm, and they followed the path they'd taken the night before, through the stalagmites and stalactites, into another tunnel.

As the air grew fresh and cold, a scuff echoed. Feet over stone, a murmur.

"It's coming from up ahead," Elliot whispered. They cut their flashlights, nearing the exit of the cave. Jessica found her raincoat lying on the ground, right where she'd left it.

Moonlight flooded the gap in the rock. Jessica and Elliot crawled outside, into the forest, their lungs hungry for fresh air. They stood close to the rock, listening for another noise.

Bright eyes glimmered between the pines. Metallic green and blue, watching as Elliot and Jessica scanned the woods. Branches snapped.

"It's *them,*" Jessica whispered.

"You can't catch us," a voice said.

Joseph Baker and Anthony Walker walked out of the shadows.

"We weren't chasing you," Jessica said.

"What are you doing here?" Joseph said, now just feet away. His filthy skin smelled of the forest – pinecones, sweat and soil. He scrutinized them, eyes like opaline slits. Anthony followed him, green eyes piercing the night, his face an impish saucer of milk under the pearly moon.

"It's okay. We're just taking a look around." Jessica watched as Joseph pulled something from his pocket.

"Why are you snooping on us? We didn't do anything wrong." Joseph gripped the bundle from his pocket.

Elliot shook his head. "We're not snooping on anybody."

"Who are you?" Joseph said.

"I'm Elliot."

"Jessica."

"You gonna tell the cops?" Joseph stuck out his chin. His eyes flashed a brilliant aquamarine.

Jessica shook her head, thinking of Andrew asleep in her brother's bed.

"It's okay. We won't tell anyone. We promise," Elliot said.

The two kids whispered.

"We're not going back." Joseph kicked the ground.

"We're not here to take you anywhere," Elliot said.

Anthony relaxed. Joseph stuffed his handful into his mouth.

"You get sick when you came down?" Joseph munched through his sentence.

Elliot nodded.

Joseph snorted. "You don't know anything, that's why. You need to eat this." He reached into his pocket again, then stuck out another handful. Jessica took a step closer and looked at his palm. A sticky, sweaty-sweet scent wafted from his open hand.

"What's that?" Elliot took a step closer, too.

"Mushrooms. You gotta bury them in the ground for a bit, let them get mushy, so they don't make you puke."

"Um ... not right now, thanks," Elliot said. Jessica shook her head.

"Well, I guess you can stick around, but you better stay out of the caves," Joseph said.

"Why's that?" Elliot circled the cave entrance with his flashlight.

"Because you're not like us." Anthony took a mushroom from Joseph's pocket and crammed it into his mouth.

"Not like you?" Jessica said.

"Forget it. You won't understand." Joseph kicked the ground.

"Did you guys break into my house?" Jessica asked.

The boys looked away, shrugging.

"*Why*?" she said.

"We needed stuff."

"And why did you write all over the wall? Leave that stuff on my desk?"

"We have to write everything down when the..." Anthony began, but Joseph nudged him quiet.

"It's a secret," Joseph muttered. "But we left you the stuff because it's rude to take things without giving something back."

"Is Annabelle with you?" Elliot said.

Joseph yanked down on the hem of his grubby T-shirt, dodging eye contact again.

"The girl who was with you on Wednesday night," Jessica added. "They're looking for her."

"We don't know where she is," Anthony said, eyes just as shifty as Joseph's.

Elliot glanced around the perimeter of the clearing. "Are you sure?"

"Uh-uh."

"You guys live around here?" Jessica asked.

Anthony nodded. Joseph shuffled, throwing a wary look at Anthony.

Jessica wondered what – who – might be hiding in the dark hollows between the trees. The rocks and shrubs crouching in the soil were cast in shades of black and blue, rugged angles in the dark.

"So where's home? I don't see any houses around here," Elliot said, finding Jessica's hand, weaving his fingers between hers, distracting her.

"It's a secret," Joseph said. His voice seemed too old for his skinny body, and weary, like he'd seen too much, lived too many lives.

"Another secret?"

"It's way down," Anthony squeaked. Joseph nudged him quiet again.

Do they live in those caves? Among the gnats and the sludge and whatever slithered through the water? What else is down there?

Jessica couldn't stop studying the two boys, wondering how they survived.

"It's rude to stare," Joseph said.

"Sorry," she said, surprised by his concern with manners. "So why did you run away?"

"It's safe here," Anthony said.

"The park ranger trapped us. They put us in a nasty place and made us go to school, and they told us lies and all kinds of dumb stuff. But we got away," Joseph said.

"The ranger trapped me like a rabbit!" Anthony yelled. The sensation that Jessica had felt earlier returned – a tiny fish surfacing in her murky pond of memories. Pinpricks spread over her skin.

"Trapped you? When?" Elliot said.

"When we came out."

Joseph elbowed Anthony quiet again.

"Came out of what?" Jessica glanced at the rock she'd crawled out of.

"You mean the cave?" Elliot said.

Joseph whispered in Anthony's ear, and Anthony bit his lip.

"I want to go now," Anthony whined.

Elliot took a step forward as the kids turned to leave. "Wait. What are those piles of rocks in the cave?"

"You have to bury the dead," Joseph said.

"Who died?" Jessica asked.

"Babies," Anthony murmured.

"How did they die?" Elliot's voice was softer now.

"They fell out of their beds." Anthony's shoulders slumped.

"Their beds?" Jessica said. The thought hollowed her for a moment. A sting of grief for lives she'd never known.

Anthony nodded. His hay pile of matted hair flopped, tufts sticking out like wayward straws. "When the disaster happened."

"We need to go now," Joseph interjected.

"What disaster?" Jessica said.

The boys ignored her question.

"You were at Evergreen Pass last night, weren't you?" Elliot said.

The boys shrugged again.

"Was Annabelle with you?"

Another kick of the dirt. "We have to go," Joseph insisted.

"Wait, why do I keep seeing you in my back yard? And why are you following me?" Jessica said.

"You gave us food." A stroke of moonlight lit Anthony's face.

"Do you know a woman named Olivia?" Jessica called as the boys began to walk away.

Joseph stopped, shrugged one more time.

Jessica glanced at the shadows shifting under the breeze-ruffled pines. "Are you all alone here? How do you live like this?"

"We live just fine," Joseph said.

"You need anything?" Elliot looked down at their grubby bare feet.

Joseph scrutinized Elliot. "I've got shoes. But can I have your sweater?"

Elliot pulled off his jacket and sweater, then handed the sweater to Joseph. The kid examined it like he worked in a clothing store. "Why is it so soft?"

"Merino wool and cashmere. You're welcome."

"Thank you," Joseph mumbled, pulling it over his head. The hem hung a few inches above his knees.

"Wait, what's the quickest way out of the woods?" Elliot panned the trees with his flashlight.

"They already forgot!" Joseph laughed. "I told you this morning, but you fell asleep. If you don't eat the stuff, you get sick down there, and then you get tired and you don't remember shit. It's called *disorientation* and *amnesia*. I know because I read the dictionary. And I read all kinda books about space."

Did we really just pass out in the grass? Jessica wondered. *What happened after that? Did I stumble over to that oak tree, where I woke up? Was I that spaced out? Or is Joseph just messing with us? And what the hell is down there? What did we breathe?*

"Joseph said 'shit!'" Anthony yelled. He pointed at the path that led to the riverbank. "You go that way!"

They backed away, eyes on Elliot and Jessica, then vanished into the trees. Elliot turned to face Jessica, and they stared at each other in the fading dark.

"I don't know what's real anymore," she whispered.

"Me neither."

"What is this?"

"I wish I knew." He took a step closer.

"But is it real? Any of it? Or have we *both* lost it? Did anything those kids said make any sense to you?"

He took another step closer. "Right now, I know it's real. But I don't know *what* I'll think in the morning."

"Where did you wake up? Last time?"

"Near Evergreen Pass. I was a mess. What about you?"

"Under a tree. I ran home." Her body distracted her, so close to his, craving him.

"Do you live alone? I mean, is there someone…?"

"No. I mean, *yes*. I'm alone. I'm always alone. Except now." She reached out to him, then hesitated, thoughts tangled. But he grabbed her hand and closed the gap between them, sending her jar of moths batting against their glass. She lost herself in the beat of his heart under his shirt, his collar by her cheek, the light pressure of his hands as they reached around her.

"Me too, usually in rooms full of people who think they know me. But I don't feel alone right now," he said.

"If this is another dream, I don't want to wake up alone in the grass." A wisp of dread drifted over her at the thought of the morning. The breeze picked up, except in the warmth between them.

He brushed her neck, and the moths inside were seconds from breaking free of their jar. "Then don't."

Another brush of her skin, a squeeze to bring her closer, and she wanted nothing more than his lips on hers, to succumb to her body, to his.

"Come back with me. We can talk about everything, figure it out."

She nodded, almost lightheaded, as if her feet might have drifted from the ground.

He kissed her, so that the moths burst from their jar and swarmed her heart, her tingling limbs.

"Let's go," he whispered a moment later.

They headed for the riverbank, toward the path that led to the trail out of the park. Jessica's legs were jelly. The air itself seemed alive.

Dawn lit the terrain in smoky strokes. They walked for ten minutes, but a sudden, heavy hug of fatigue soon made it hard to think, hard to move.

"Elliot, I think I need to rest for a moment," she murmured, now leaning against a tree. The forest swung by, circling, rocking back and forth.

"Me too. I feel so tired, I could sleep right here."

They settled into a patch of wiregrass, the leggy blades embracing them. Jessica blinked once, twice, at the fading stars, then sank into sleep.

Chapter 25

Sunday, April 17, 2022

Elliot woke to sunlight filtering through branches, freezing in a patch of wiregrass. He flexed at the nip of pins and needles.

"No, not again," he muttered, groggy from sleep. A low groan escaped him as he sat up. Thin mist enveloped the forest, dissolving into the sunlight. Elliot's jeans were grubby and damp, and his jacket was mud streaked.

He looked to his left and right, but there was no sign of a trail. The last thing he remembered was falling asleep with Jessica, then her hand nudging him awake hours later. Something about how she needed to leave. He'd been so swamped in tiredness that he'd simply mumbled, then fallen back to sleep.

He stood up, brushed off his jacket and reached for his phone, but he'd left it in his hotel room. He had nothing, not even his damn sweater. Just a pinecone under his foot and a background headache.

He stared into the trees and thought of Jessica. *Where are you now? Are you anywhere?* he wondered, thinking of how she'd leaned against him, testing his restraint as stars sequined the sky, and nothing had made any sense but the sound of her voice, the scent of her hair.

He needed more time with her. Time to explore the words tumbling from her lips, the soft skin under her shirt that begged to be touched. He'd hoped he'd wake up to find her next to him in The Arbor. Ringlets strewn across his pillow, her body pressed against him.

But the damp kiss of dawn had left him alone. He flexed his fingers as his numb arm woke up, and more details of the night before surfaced. A cave full of gloopy glowing fauna, and Joseph and Anthony, shrugging off his questions. The strange luminous haze clouding the tunnel. *Another dream or whacky head trip? No, we figured out it was more than that; we figured out it was real. We swore it was really happening. So why is it already hazy? Why can't I remember how one moment led to another? And why the hell do I keep falling asleep in the park, waking up alone?*

Those kids – who were they, really? And where was Annabelle Lewis? He imagined her parents pacing the floor, begging her to come home as the sheriff and his deputies botched another case.

He rolled his neck, wincing at the creak of his joints. There had to be a rational explanation for everything. *Something* had happened, but *what*?

Whatever it was, it had flung open a door to a world that he didn't want to leave. A world frosted with a mystery that seemed to breathe from its leafy shadows and the black hollows of its underworld. A place that gave him everything he wanted to gather up and spill onto the page. All those drafts and edits and late nights arguing with himself to create another world, but he wasn't convinced he could ever fully describe what he'd experienced in his first two nights in Driftwood.

He walked for an hour, winding around conifer branches until he found the trail, now remembering the rest of his life, and everyone waiting for *something*. Agents, editors, family. The loneliness of his apartment, and his neighbor's yapping teacup poodles. The weird professor who stared at him in the elevator with a look that was a little patronizing, a little evil. He had two more days in Driftwood before he'd have to return to all of it.

Somewhere along the trail the mist evaporated, and blue sky filled the fringed gaps between the treetops. A woodpecker drilled in the distance, and Elliot thought about how much easier it would be to finish the novel in Driftwood, where whatever veil that separated fact from fiction, life from dreams, seemed thinner. What he knew, what he imagined, and what he wanted had a habit of blending between the trees and the fog and the silvery laps of the lake tide. He wished he could bottle whatever hung in the air and take it home along with his muse. Jessica, who was now waking up in Driftwood somewhere, he liked to think, but where? And why had she been in such a hurry to leave?

Is she really alone, like she said, or was there someone waiting for her, at home in her bed? Or maybe she just works weekends?

The forest thinned, and pines gave way to oak and hickory. Elliot told himself to stop confusing night and day. He still wasn't completely convinced that his nighttime antics were anything more than the random output of his own neurons, those spongy folds inside his head, regardless of how real it all seemed the night before. Synapses firing in his brain as he slept. And it slipped from his memory a little more with each step.

The closer he got to the periphery of the park, the more he doubted his memories of the night before. The disorientation, the supernatural stillness of the forest, had persuaded him that every moment had been real, but now it all seemed absurd.

But he still debated with himself, back and forth about the plausibility, the impossibility of what had felt so compelling, until he knew he wasn't far from the lake, where he could find the path along the rocky incline that led to The Arbor.

An hour later, Elliot showered, scrubbing grass stains from his palm. Then he headed out the door again and drove downtown to grab a coffee, since the gourmet pod coffee at The Arbor tasted like luxury motor oil.

The boardwalk was busy with tourists soaking up the dazzling blue of Lake Driftwood, crowding the guardrail as they watched speedboats crease the current with darts of white foam.

Halfway along the boardwalk, across the street from Tiffany's diner, a flash of colored paper caught his eye, wedged between two wooden planks on a bench. He sat down, released the paper, and stared at the folds of an origami lion. His pulse quickened, and he looked over his shoulder. Along the edge of one crease, he read the words *Mystery Tour* and unfolded the paper. Then he reached for his phone and dialed the number listed on the page.

Chapter 26

Sunday, April 17, 2022

Jessica opened her eyes to a streak of white clouds, and to the sting of regret at waking up, which was swelling like a fresh welt. Memories of the night before floated like feathers through her head, past the flutter of waking eyelids and stirring senses. The damp semi-softness of a dew-filled lawn told her she wasn't in the park.

She blinked once, twice, then opened her eyes to Mrs Davis, who was leaning over her in a bathrobe, worry lines furrowed deep in her face.

"Oh, my lord! Jessica … Jessica, wake up, honey," she whispered.

The woman's Yorkshire terrier yapped, louder as it sprinted toward her. The dog barked an inch from Jessica's ear, and she winced at the pulsing ache of a hangover.

She sat up and looked around her neighbor's front yard, searching for answers in the beds of perennials, the daisies in the grass, the mud on her damp jeans. A feather in her head floated to where she could catch it – a memory of Elliot kissing her – and she scowled at the flowerbeds, at what the morning had ripped from her.

"How'd I get here?" she croaked, then put her hand to her head, which seemed like a frail egg, as thin as whatever sickening membrane separated her morning from the night before. She wondered if a cough or a sniff might crack her head open, so that her forgotten memories, all that she wanted and all that she feared, would bleed together like cans of spilled paint in the grass. Lust and dread and longing among a splattering of gray matter, a few dead moths.

"Well, I don't know, but it looks like you took the long way." Mrs Davis threw a worried look at Jessica's hair.

"I'm sorry. I don't know what happened. I must have ... I just don't know."

The wind sifted through her sweater, and another feather settled – the warmth of Elliot's body against hers, his fingertips brushing her skin above the waistband of her jeans.

"It's okay, honey. Come on, get up now, you know how these people like to talk." Urgency disrupted her motherly tone. "I don't think anybody else is up yet, but you better get on home."

Jessica stood up, and the lawn spun. Standing straight was a grating effort. Holding back a tearful, dizzy kind of rage was harder still. She brushed a twig from her shirt. She wasn't sure if it was the indignity or the hangover that was flushing her face, but it felt red-hot, and she craved a glass of water, Tylenol.

"Yes, yes I will." She picked up her raincoat, which was strewn in the grass. She walked across the yard deciding she'd have to avoid Mrs Davis for at least a year or so. Avoidance was one thing she'd mastered, even if living wasn't.

"If you need someone to help you clean up the yard, that retarded boy from up the street'll do it for fifteen dollars," Mrs Davis yelled from her porch, and Jessica cringed at the garbage and foliage still on her lawn, the words slung from her neighbor's mouth.

She was a stone's throw from her front door, grimacing at Andrew's car, when other feathers settled. Her head against Elliot's chest, the cotton of his shirt. His eyes on hers in the near dark. A cave full of glowing gloop and fungus gnats. The conversation with Joseph and Anthony that made no sense, at least not to any part of her mind that she could reach in that moment, as she fought the urge to vomit into the overgrown lawn. She cursed herself for downing all that wine before bed, for skipping dinner before she corked the bottle. She jammed her hands in her pocket, reached for her keys and opened the front door, cringing as the hinge whined. In the kitchen, she washed down expired Tylenol. Andrew's car keys lay on the table. It was almost seven, according to the digits on the microwave. She inched to her brother's room to find Andrew snoozing shirtless, his sandy head denting the pillow.

Back in the kitchen, she toyed with an idea that made her head thump a little harder. Then she reached for Andrew's car keys, gripping them tight so they didn't jingle in her hand, lifted her phone from the counter, and eased out the front door, closing it gingerly behind her.

A pile of folders sat on the passenger seat of Andrew's car. She unlocked the door, picked up the pile and leafed through reports, tossing a nervous glance beyond the driveway. *Olivia Garcia* jumped at her in boxy handwriting. A few official-looking documents were paperclipped to the sheet. Forms. She snapped photos with her phone.

Inside, after asking herself twice if she'd left the folder exactly as she'd found it, she placed Andrew's keys back on the kitchen table, then made coffee and grabbed the bottle of bourbon from under the sink. *Hair of the dog, or whatever.* A way to dull thoughts that were too loud, clanging like a dropped box of clutter in her tired head.

Footfalls sounded from the hallway. Andrew appeared in the kitchen doorway with one hand on his hip, the other raking through his hair. Right as she'd sloshed that bourbon into her coffee like a pitiful lush.

"Where'd you go last night?"

He walked into the kitchen, and his eyes didn't leave her.

"I hung out with a friend. Ended up sleeping over," she said.

"Without your car? I didn't even hear you leave."

Jessica bristled. *Are we married now?*

"I got a ride. Snuck out so I didn't wake you."

"Looks like you went for a hike while you were at it, or maybe you just did some yard work?"

He joined her at the sink, grabbed the glass she'd drunk from, and filled it with water. She handed him the Tylenol. *Did he figure out my bedroom door was locked? That I slipped out the window like a basket case?*

"I fell over." She sipped coffee and listened to the fridge, willing the pills to kick in.

"Jess, are you okay? I mean, are you *really* okay? Is there something going on?"

"No. I mean, yes, I'm fine. Really. It was just a weird night."

But when did I run home? So much of the night was already vague, moments bleeding into shadows. Alcohol had confused everything even more.

"Are you sure? Because you're drinking bourbon at seven in the morning with all kinds of shit in your hair, and your back yard's full of garbage. I saw you sleeping on that old woman's lawn ten minutes ago. What's going on?"

None of your fucking business, Detective.

"It's nothing. I just need to get some rest." She tugged a hand through her hair. A few leaves fell to the floor.

Andrew's phone rang from his back pocket. Jessica busied herself rinsing glasses. She heard him pace the hallway, hurried and officious in his police voice, another day of dead ends ahead. Police procedure that would lead nowhere, she guessed, and she thought of how his matter-of-factness – his uninspired loyalty to all that was temporal and reliable – had always bored the shit out of her.

His annoyingly handsome face appeared in the doorway again. His gray eyes were flat and tired, but they were eyes that knew an old part of her – a part she'd thought she'd thrown out years ago, when she'd really just filed it in the back of her mind. A part that knew him too well, that was somehow still *tethered* to him.

But the desire to sink into his chest and rest there for a while was gone, now that she'd felt Elliot's heartbeat, how he'd held her under a starry night sky. Andrew's presence felt like a near-betrayal to a man she'd never met in daylight, and with that thought, her self-loathing stirred again and gave her a gentle punch in the stomach. *Normal* people didn't have four-year relationships with imaginary boyfriends, who were stitched to life from dust-jacket photos and some self-love under the covers. *Normal* people didn't have folders full of conspiracy theories, or fear the black hole inside their own heads. And *normal* people didn't forget how they got home. They didn't wake up like *this*.

"I have to go. Take care, Jessica. Call me if you need anything," he said as he ran out the door, as if he'd be the first person she'd call.

Jessica trailed him to lock the front door behind him, and as she grabbed the handle to pull the door closed, she saw Jamie walking up the driveway holding coffee and a brown bag. Chic and glowing in a peach blouse and a string of citrine beads. Jessica caught her throw a wide-eyed look at Andrew and glare at him as he scowled back.

"Don't look at *me*. She woke up on her neighbor's lawn," he yelled, then climbed inside his car and slammed the door.

"What the hell is that asshole doing here? Tell me you didn't sleep with him last night!" Jamie turned to watch him reverse out of the driveway. She followed Jessica inside, listening as Jessica flubbed her way through a heavily redacted recount of the night before. Jessica stared at the breakfast Jamie had dumped on the table. More confusion, bewilderment.

"I called you twice, then messaged you to tell you I was bringing coffee. Guess you were sleeping on someone's *lawn*?"

"I didn't sleep there. I just took a nap, I guess. I have no fucking idea," she blurted out. The pills began to numb the pain. *An Ativan would* really *hit the spot right now,* she thought, watching Jamie's face contort.

"What are you talking about? You're scaring me, Jessica."

Jamie unpacked breakfast. A cinnamon roll for Jessica, and a vegan protein bar for herself.

"Something's happening. Something that doesn't make any sense." Jessica poured the spiked coffee she'd made down the sink and grabbed the one Jamie had brought her instead, out of politeness, maybe, or a bad habit of compliance.

"Evidently." Jamie pulled a pine needle from the collar of Jessica's shirt. "What the hell's going on?"

"It's a long story. I went for a walk in the park. I got kind of sick and fell asleep … it was weird."

I sound like a lunatic, Jessica thought, stuffing the cinnamon roll into her mouth. It tasted like heaven. Sunlight flickered, toyed with the shadows of the kitchen. But the trash in the garbage can stank.

"Start from the beginning." Jamie flicked her hair.

Jessica chewed and debated what she should and shouldn't say. What might sound almost plausible, and what might sound like the sad ramblings of an idiot.

"Elliot Reed called me. By accident, from a payphone at the Blue Ridge Diner," she said at last.

"What?"

"That's how it started. He was trying to get a tow truck in the middle of that storm on Friday night. And I think he found something I wrote on a forum a few years ago ... about Olivia."

A minute in, and she was already spilling too many details.

"Elliot Reed? Your *complete obsession* misdialed your number from a shithole diner?"

"Yes."

"What was he doing, starring in some reality TV show? *Survival in Appalachia's Fentanyl Belt*?"

Jessica frowned at the floor.

"Sorry, Jess. Okay. Go on." Jamie sipped her coffee, watching Jessica over the brim as steam escaped the lid.

"Last night and the night before I met him in the park, I think, but then we fell asleep. I woke up around five and remembered Andrew was here."

"What?"

"I didn't want him snooping around my house. I ran home, but my head was such a mess. I couldn't see straight, and I was so damn tired. I think I fell asleep on Mrs Davis' lawn a few hours ago..." She cut herself off as she heard the loopy words leave her mouth. "Shit, never mind. I can't explain it. Maybe I'm just losing it. Am I losing it?" She crossed her arms, felt her dignity slump a little further.

"I don't know, but I'm really worried about you. Did something else happen? Something bad? Are you sure Andrew didn't ... didn't *do* something?"

"Andrew? No, screw Andrew," Jessica said, swatting her hand at an invisible fly.

"Is it because of the missing girl, Jess?"

"Yes, that's part of it. And I'm pretty sure the others are living in the woods."

"In the woods?"

"I can't explain. Forget I said that."

"I'm so sorry. I can see why this could be … *triggering*. Maybe all this stuff with Elliot is … um … a way of dealing with it? Are you taking your medication, Jess? I don't mean to pry."

And there she was, backed into her lunatic corner. By a friend who spent her days selling ceramic angels, crystals that healed broken hearts and back pain, and books on telepathic dolphins, love spells and tantric sex. Jamie's citrine beads sparkled around her neck. Jessica wondered if she should force herself to vomit.

"Why on Earth is Elliot Reed here, really?" Jamie asked, tucking the front of her blouse into her pants so it draped flawlessly over faux suede leggings.

"I have no idea."

Time to shut down the freak show, she decided. *This morning's seen back-to-back performances.* Her face felt hot again, and her skin itched. She'd had enough of being in her own skin already, in fact, and wished she could go right back to sleep, find the version of herself she'd been last night. That girl who was freer, braver, had a real lover.

Jamie watched Jessica finish her cinnamon roll and pursed her lips into a smile. "Sweetie, I have something else I need to talk to you about. I kind of need a favor from you."

"Hmm?" Jessica asked through a mouthful, hoping it was nothing substantial.

"Emily Murphy spent a fortune in my store yesterday. I guess she's having some kind of faux-spiritual awakening. Anyway, she guilted me into going to that fundraiser at her house this afternoon."

"Oh, Jesus, Jamie. No. And I can't afford to make a donation..."

"It's fine," Jamie interrupted. "She doesn't care about that. She just wants her house full of people. Anything to make her drug-dealer husband look like less of an asshole, I guess. Jessica, *please*. I need to keep her as a client. I need the money. And I can't get through it without you. All those Driftwood Heights women..."

Jessica stared out of the window, breathed in the trash. Felt those claws digging in, dragging her toward hateful compliance.

"I'm sorry, I can't," she said at last, surprising herself. "I feel like my head's going to explode, and nothing makes any sense anymore. No."

Jamie frowned. Five minutes later she left, shaking her head.

Jessica crawled through her bedroom window and unlocked the door, then grabbed her phone, slumped into a recliner, and pulled up the photo of the photocopy she'd found in Andrew's car.

Chapter 27

Sunday, April 17, 2022

"Mystery tours are only on weekdays."

"Wait. How much would it take to get the full tour today. Just me?"

Elliot left the bench on the boardwalk and leaned on the guardrail with his phone to his ear. Deputies stood in a patrol boat, casting chains into the rippling lake, dragging its bed as tourists looked on.

He stared at the creases in the mystery tour flyer, waiting as the guy on the line fumbled for an answer.

"Dude, that's gonna be like, *super* expensive," he replied at last. He sounded mildly pissed, mildly excited.

"How much?" Elliot stifled a sigh.

"Like, *two hundred dollars*."

Elliot shot a wry smile. "Sure. Two hundred."

"Cash only."

"That's fine. Where?"

The guy had hit the bong before breakfast and was sitting in a herbal cloud, Elliot guessed. That would explain the long pauses, as vapor wafted over his mom's coffee table.

"The ranger's station, the one by the dirt road. You know it?"

"No, but I'll find it."

He hung up and walked along the boardwalk in search of coffee, past a few college girls who looked at him twice, giggling.

But the air was heavy, a taut pressure building beneath the tourist-friendly calm. *MISSING* posters were still plastered to utility poles, and patrol cars circuited the streets.

Nexus Coffee was empty except for the barista. Elliot ordered a black coffee and declined the suggestion of unicorn cheesecake, then fished out a copy of the *Driftwood Times* from under a well-thumbed *Rolling Stone.*

POLICE CONTINUE HUNT FOR MISSING GIRL, the headline read.

He looked up at the sound of the door hitting the wind chime, and a woman with black bangs and a string of yellow beads around her neck walked in with an awkward looking guy in a fleece, who pushed his glasses up the bridge of his nose as he sat down opposite her in the booth in front of his.

First date? Elliot wondered. *No, she doesn't seem to care enough.* He grabbed the mystery tour flyer from his pocket and copied the folds to recreate the lion he'd found on the bench. But he stopped, and something shimmied up his spine, when a voice from the other booth said the name "Jessica." It carried over the hiss of the steam wand frothing milk, right as he completed the last fold.

Another coincidence, he told himself, unconvinced. *One to add to the list.* He downed his coffee, then looked up to find the black-haired woman looking at him, at the paper lion, with the kind of wide-eyed stare that he dreaded. She reddened, looked away, and walked to the bathroom. He escaped out the door, tucking the lion into his pocket.

A few hours later, he climbed out of his car at the park entrance. The air had warmed, and the sun was drying shrinking puddles. He found a lanky kid in ripped jeans and a Nirvana T-shirt smoking a joint by the ranger's station. Couldn't be more than twenty-two or twenty-three, Elliot guessed.

He cleared his throat, and the guy looked up, apparently shell-shocked, then stubbed his joint furiously against the wooden siding.

"Elliot Reed," he said, raking a hand through his poker-straight, unwashed hair. He loafed toward Elliot, huge feet in beaten Chucks like wayward boats under his skinny frame.

"Yeah," Elliot said, masking a ripple of annoyance that he'd been recognized.

"I'm Chris. I've read all your books. They're *awesome*."

"Thanks." Elliot nodded, hoping he wouldn't lose the tour to talking about himself.

"Dr Sleep is like, *super* awesome." His skinny arms, like crooked sticks, hung and flailed.

"That's Stephen King," Elliot said, sighing on the inside.

"Shit. Yeah, of course. But you wrote *Black Eye*, right?" His parchment-white face flushed pink.

"Yeah, that was me." He handed the guy a wad of bills after contemplating calling off the whole thing. But he'd already dragged the kid from his sofa and his bong.

"Nah, I can't take that from you. I can just give you the tour for free."

"No, please." Elliot shook his head, smiling despite the clumsy moment. They were still lingering outside the ranger's station, under the stretch of oak branches.

Chris took the bills and folded them into his back pocket. "Thanks, man. Do you think it could really happen?" he asked, suddenly serious, dilated pupils locking on Elliot's.

"What's that?" Elliot asked, lost.

"Are we gonna end up enslaved by..." He threw a nervous look into the trees. "By an alien race? Get abducted, teleported by ETs who can manipulate time and space and shit?" He formed a limp fist, eyes still bulging. "You know, like in *Black Eye*?"

Elliot laughed, shaking his head. "I guess it's a worst-case scenario."

"But I mean ... is time even real? Is *space* even real? Or is it all just an illusion? If aliens can live outside of time, then maybe time is just in our *minds*." His eyes bulged, and he pointed his finger at his own head.

"I have no idea. I just write fiction. So ... the Driftwood kids?"

Chris stood up straight, suddenly focused. "Yeah, yeah, of course." He cleared his throat. "Twenty years ago, on the night of Halloween, Olivia Garcia disappeared without a trace..."

"Chris?" Elliot cut in.

"Huh?"

"How about we forget the tour script, and you just tell me what you know?"

"Wait ... are you writing a book about this?"

"No. Just curious," Elliot lied.

"Sure, I can do that." Another flail of Chris' arms, and a chin-led nod.

They left the ranger's station and wandered into the forest until they found a fallen tree and sat down, hunched forward like two men on a locker room bench. Birds chirped, and somewhere in the distance the blades of a helicopter whirred. The forest wrapped them in a pen of leafy green.

"What do you know about Annabelle Lewis?"

"Just that her parents live in a farmhouse about five miles from here. Kind of a dump, I heard. Some guy saw her Friday evening, alone out here."

"So she walked five miles *alone*?"

"I guess, and it was cold as hell that night, right when the storm came in."

"What about Joseph Baker and Anthony Walker?" Elliot asked, deciding Chris knew little more than he did about Annabelle.

"A bunch of weird shit. Some insane stuff went down before Joseph disappeared ... stuff at his school," Chris said, digging into the soil with his foot.

"Who's your source?" He kept his eyes on Chris, waiting for any sign that the kid had more than a handful of dog-eared rumors in his pocket.

"Someone *super* connected. She knows a ton about what's going on in that school." Chris sat up, poked his chest out a little.

"Your mom's a teacher." It was a statement more than a question.

"Yeah," he admitted, shrinking a little.

"So what happened, exactly?"

Chris shook his head. "Man, it's just unreal. You can't tell anyone about this."

"Of course."

"So, this teacher … a science guy, I think … gets to the school real early one morning. This is like two years ago, I guess. He gets in early because he wants to set up some equipment or something. So he walks in the door and sees Joseph writing all over the walls with a Sharpie. I'm not talking about a few lines on the wall. The whole classroom was just *covered*. He wrote on the walls, the floor, all over the desks and the windows. He had marker all over his face and his clothes. It was just … *nuts*."

"What was he writing?" Elliot wondered how much Chris had blended rumors with what he'd fabricated in his own head. *Or maybe that's just my problem,* he considered.

Chris shook his head again. "I don't know. This teacher told my mom it was some crazy equations or something. No one could figure it out. And a weird alphabet … hierographs or whatever."

"Hieroglyphics?

"Yeah, exactly. Some weird stuff he made up. Anyway, the teacher *loses* it, starts yelling at him, and Joseph calls the teacher an *ignoramus*."

Elliot laughed.

"But then Joseph gets mad as hell, and all this science equipment starts *breaking*. I mean, breaking on the shelves in the classroom."

"Breaking?" Elliot concealed another sigh. Chris appeared to be sliding right into fantasy now, and he cursed himself for not calling the whole thing off.

"Yeah, *breaking*." Chris pulled his phone from his pocket and scrolled.

Elliot watched as a video, shot from a shaky hand, revealed Joseph standing in a classroom, his clothes stained in black marker. Elliot's pulse quickened, just as it had at dawn, at the bench, and in the coffee shop. The same sensation of a breath up his spine as the tinny audio blared. Joseph yelled between walls black with scrawl, his bare feet on an inked floor covered in shattered glass. The lights in the classroom flickered, on-off, on-off, and voices gathered, hushed as the lens panned the room.

The leaves blurred to a choppy sea of green.

"What was the fallout from this?" Elliot's voice was still steady, but he was adrift inside.

"I guess he got suspended. Disappeared a few weeks later."

"You show this video to anyone else?"

"Hell, no. My mom would kill me. She's not even supposed to have that. Normally I just talk about tall grays and UFOs on the tour. Some Montauk-type shit."

"You think any of those rumors are true?"

"Beats me. You're the guy who wrote *Black Eye*."

He has a point, Elliot admitted.

"So what about the foster parents?"

Chris raked a hand through his hair. "My mom heard he talked about going home all the time. Not his foster home. Someplace else."

"Home?"

"Yeah. He always said that one day, he was gonna go home. He said it when he got mad."

"And the foster parents?"

"Assholes, I heard. Look, there are some good foster homes around here. They're not all bad, I guess. But where this kid lived ... it's *nasty*." He was flailing and flapping his hands again. A stick figure buzzing in his own current.

"What about Olivia Garcia? Know much about her?"

"She disappeared from right over there." Chris pointed to a grassy hollow between trees at the edge of the park. "I don't know much about her. Just that she was with another girl when she disappeared. They never put her name in the paper, I guess, but I heard it was something like Jennifer or Janet ... something beginning with J."

"Jessica?" Elliot said, as night and day collided.

"Yeah, that's it. *Jessica*."

Chapter 28

Sunday, April 17, 2020

Jessica had napped all morning, lost in dreams about the night before. Then she'd raked up leaves and trash from her yard under the cover of a hoodie, dodging eye contact with Mrs Davis, who'd peered through her curtains as Jessica hurled piles of foliage, a cereal box and a rotting lettuce into the garbage can.

But now she studied the photos snapped with her phone that morning, which she'd been too tired to make head or tail of before a nap.

Olivia Garcia: A. Barnes, incident 11/11 9:30 p.m., she made out, zooming into the first photo. Underneath, Andrew had scrawled, *EPI? Blood type? AL + OG hypoxia, missing report.*

The rest of the page was filled with semi-legible notes from a staff meeting at the sheriff's office twenty years ago. A few dull bullets about clearing shift swaps with the watch commander and other protocol drudgery.

Jessica flung back the closet door and grabbed a journal from the box. She flipped to a clean page with a pen between her teeth, then scribbled a list of questions. She marched to her laptop, slouched into a recliner, and searched for A. Barnes.

But there were dozens of A. Barnes in the county. *Incident,* she wrote and underlined, and before her pen finished the last stroke, she thought of a night at her grandmother's house twenty years ago.

She scared the hell out of a nurse, Dad said.

Jessica searched the state directory for registered nurses and found an A. Banes, an E. Barnes. But no A. Barnes. She sighed. Who the hell was A. Barnes? She slouched back into the recliner and searched obituaries instead.

Ten minutes later, she tapped her keyboard with her pen and stared at the monitor. Abigail Barnes. A pediatric nurse who worked at Driftwood General and died six years ago. *Check police archives on Monday,* she scribbled.

EPI? She underlined now. *Exocrine pancreatic insufficiency,* a quick search revealed. *A condition in which the body lacks adequate pancreatic enzymes to digest food.*

But perhaps EPI was an acronym for something else? Jessica chewed the pen cap. *No,* she decided. *This is starting to make sense. Olivia's stomach aches. Halloween candy made her sick.*

Jessica glanced at her desk. *M&Ms,* she scribbled. *Mushrooms.*

She returned to the photo. *Blood type.* Why did the sheriff care about Olivia's blood type? And what did *AL + OG hypoxia* mean? Her eyes widened, she scribbled again. *Annabelle Lewis and Olivia Garcia.* She searched for hypoxia, with a vague memory that it had something to do with oxygen. *Inadequate oxygen supply at the tissue level,* she read. *Headache, confusion, shortness of breath.*

Jessica paced again, remembering Olivia struggling to breathe, catching her breath when they played in the yard. Andrew was onto something, but what? Biological similarities, medical issues. She stared at the map of the stars on the living room wall, and a memory from the night before sent pinpricks down her neck. *"Because you're not like us," Anthony said.*

An idea hooked itself in place before the rest of her could protest. She texted Jamie:

I'll go to that fundraiser, but you need to lend me a dress.

You're the best. Be there in twenty minutes, Jamie texted back.

Jessica scrolled to the second photo, then let her phone fall from her hands.

"Olivia was adopted," she mumbled, struggling to pick up her phone and read. Her photo was blurred, but she could decipher the signatures of Paula and Matteo Garcia on the adoption papers. *Did Mom and Dad know?* she wondered.

She scribbled more questions with one eye on the time. *Who were Olivia's biological parents? Are the kids related, somehow?*

But soon Jamie would arrive. Jessica dashed to the bathroom and fretted with curls that refused to cooperate. Moments later the doorbell rang, and she dropped her comb into the sink.

"Why didn't you tell me?" Jamie stood at the front door in a jade-green sundress, with another dress draped over her arm. Ironed, sleek, flawless.

"Tell you what?" Jessica motioned her inside, still scrunching her hair with her free hand.

"Elliot Reed. I saw him in Nexus Coffee with that origami lion you made in Tiffany's. I was drinking coffee with your brother."

"What?"

"He was *right there,* Jessica. Looking ungodly hot. Did something actually *happen*?"

Jessica stumbled for an answer. The edges of reality were peeling again, like the label on Andrew's beer the night before. She stared at the empty bottles still sitting on the kitchen counter and fought to catch up with the moment.

"He must've found it. I left it wedged between the planks of a bench on the boardwalk." She imagined the paper lion in Elliot's hand. But she wouldn't tell Jamie another thing about it, she decided. The freak show's doors were still shuttered.

Jamie nodded, studying Jessica.

"I broke up with Seth. I'm so over him, I don't even give a damn." She handed Jessica the dress.

"Really?" Jessica told herself to care, but there was too much occupying her for a single thought about anyone else.

"Yeah, I found his profile on some lame dating app. Said he wanted to be spanked. What a pathetic turd. And he used my Japanese teapot as a neti pot."

"Maybe you should try a guy who isn't fresh out of diapers? Someone older than twenty-three?"

"They're all married, or gay, or incredibly weird."

In the bedroom, Jessica threw off her clothes and climbed into the dress. The tiny floral print was a little more boho than *Southern Living*, and the hem was an inch too short, but it would have to work. "You met Mark today?" she said, zipping the dress at the side.

"Yeah, but don't be mad. I didn't sleep with him."

Jessica shrugged as if she didn't care, didn't find it weird at all.

"I saw him standing in line at the ATM. Anyway, we started talking and grabbed a coffee. I guess we're both kind of worried about you."

Happy to hear you're bonding over my worrying decline.

"Well, now you've got to date him, or he'll fall into a downward spiral of gin and Star Wars."

"It was fun, but I have to admit, his prepping habits are kind of weird. He said he has a closet full of military surplus and beans." Jamie wrinkled her face.

"It's his way of dealing with anxiety. I guess it makes him feel like he has some control. But he's not a freak. He's just my awkward brother." *And you're way more dangerous than he is,* Jessica added silently.

"Look, I won't hurt him, I swear, but Jessica, I *totally* get it now." Jamie sat on the bed, smoothing her dress.

"What?"

"The thing you have about Elliot Reed. There's something about him. He's..." She blushed and went coy. "I can't even describe how it felt to look at him. But I *get* it."

Jessica shot a flat smile. But it felt like someone had kissed her lover.

"And I totally get how bad it must feel, being so alone. I've been single for like, four hours, and I feel so fucking alone already. I can see how it could make someone just go crazy. I'm sorry, I didn't mean it that way."

Sometimes I wonder if I hate you. Sometimes I wonder if all those crystals and self-affirmations are just clutter to fill the emptiness inside you.

"It's fine, Jamie. I've probably been certifiable for years." Jessica faked a laugh, then nodded through a few awkward platitudes: *"It's just that you're my best friend. We've known each other since middle school. I want you to be happy."*

"We should get going, I guess," Jessica mumbled. She slipped on shoes and grabbed her mother's shiny clutch, then walked to the kitchen, where she took a slug of bourbon. Jamie looked on, shaking her head.

"Dutch courage. You know I can't stand those women," Jessica said.

"I won't leave you alone with them, I swear."

Chapter 29

Sunday, April 17, 2022

This was a dumb idea.

Jessica walked through an ocean of cream carpet and hardwood, gripping her mouth in a smile. Women hugged and laughed their way to open French windows. She was lost in a flurry of sparkling fingers, buttery leather purses, teeth bleached pearly white. Tan calves under tailored hemlines, veiny feet in supple shoes.

What was I thinking? I'll never pull this off.

She scrunched her toes, sensing too much air on her legs, and stole glances at the décor, the furniture worth more than her home. The Murphys' house was a boxy mansion cluttered with faux Hamptons chic. White peonies, coral, and Montclair temple jars crowded coffee tables and ottomans. Washed-out coastal scenes stretched their way across canvases on vanilla walls, and the AC fluttered breezy curtains against enormous windows. The air stank of Yankee Candles and hot pie crust.

Jessica stood unmoored in the hallway, her back to the wall to avoid a collision with the hired help fanning out of the kitchen. Staff bustled past in dress shirts and bow ties, straining under the weight of canapés. Jessica dug her fingers into her clutch.

"Sweetheart, I'm so glad you came!"

Emily emerged from the glitter and hugged her, choking her in a cloud of Dior Poison. She strained the seams of a white maxi dress. Sun-speckled cleavage oozed from a smocked bodice, and her nails were magenta, long enough to pry open a clam shell. The front door opened, and she threw her arms in the air, then embraced a woman carrying a small dog in a purse. "Oh, sweetheart, you brought Archie! How adorable. Just don't let him on the couch."

Jamie had already disappeared into the crowd, forgetting her promise as women fawned over her dress, her glossy hair. Jessica's jaw tightened. Her lungs craved fresh air.

Can everyone tell I live paycheck to paycheck? That these shoes are the only dress pair I have? And my hair … is it a frizzy mess in the back?

She told herself to look at one steady object. *I really should've popped an Ativan. What's wrong with me?*

The intrusive questions spiraled, and she reminded herself of the woman she'd been the night before, who'd explored an underworld with Elliot Reed. *Which version of me is even real anymore? Because I sure as hell don't feel real right now. Let me be his muse, the woman in all those books.*

A crowd of women, all in pastel-hued shift dresses, moved as a herd toward the spread of canapés and wine bottles on the patio, and Jessica followed. She had a goal, but no real plan. *Find someone who isn't carrying a three-thousand-dollar purse. Someone with a forehead that wrinkles. Someone who's worn scrubs.*

Outside, a freshly mowed lawn undulated its way toward Lake Driftwood. A few children screamed at the bottom of the yard, running in circles, sugar-charged in their Ralph Lauren shirts and deck shoes. Raffle prizes crowded a table, glowing under the late afternoon sun – overstuffed gift baskets wrapped in ribbon and cellophane.

A sensation from the night before wandered back – Elliot's fingers slipping between hers – and Jessica held her breath to hold down something that wanted to escape. Maybe a dizzy spell of overwhelm, maybe an impulse to hurl a bottle of Zinfandel over the lawn. Or perhaps it was just a heavy sigh because she was so damn tired, so lost inside herself in a preppy sea of pastels and Lilly Pulitzer prints.

She flattened her dress, stood up straight, and poured herself a glass of the Zinfandel from a linen-covered table, agonizing over every movement, the eyes she was sure were on her back. *Jessica Paige … bless her heart.*

She recognized a few filler-plumped faces, but none that didn't make her feel a little sick inside. Anne Collins, who owned a pet-project boutique downtown stuffed with Southern Tide shirts and monogrammed sun hats. Tall, slim, immaculately preserved, and a husband who bought her jewelry every time she discovered another mistress. Jessica pictured her washing down painkillers with Pinot Grigio in her sprawling ranch, while her husband bent an intern over his desk in his office across the lake, wrapping his fist in her ponytail as she groaned into his outgoing mail.

And then there was Sarah something-or-other who lived in the giant mock Tudor across the road. Botched liposuction and bipolar disorder, according to Emily.

And what do these women know about me? Jessica wondered, tracing the stem of her wine glass. *What seeped through the cracks, found its way into their coffee mornings, their boozy soirees at the country club? Do they all know that I was the one who let Olivia disappear? I should leave now, while I can. Just slip away, find some excuse. Something about an upset stomach, a headache.*

Enough of that, she told herself. *Find someone who worked at the hospital.* She searched the patio. Women stood in circles, sipping from lipstick-rimmed glasses, laughing, throwing their heads back. None of them looked like they'd ever done anything but shopped and faked orgasms.

"Liz Claiborne's spring collection is just *miserable,*" moaned a sinewy woman with lipstick on her teeth.

"I'm so *sick* of the Caribbean. Jeff's promised me Hawaii this year," snorted another.

Jessica left the patio and ventured onto the lawn. A woman in a fuchsia dress rushed by, yelling, "Charlene, come try these darling tartlets!"

Another glass of wine later, Jessica found the courage to spring up conversation with a few women. But one was Emily's Pilates instructor, and the other was her dermatologist.

This was pointless, she decided. *Emily threw a hospital fundraiser and forgot to invite the damn staff. Or maybe they all see right through this. A weak stunt to polish her husband's reputation. I should have known.*

She found Jamie on the lawn, sipping a cucumber water as a willowy woman eyed a table full of hors d'oeuvres. The woman grabbed smoked salmon from a table covered in enough charcuterie meat to wallpaper a bedroom.

Jamie slapped on a wide smile. "Helen, have you met Jessica?"

The woman washed back a cracker with her wine. "Excuse me, I just can't resist all this finger food. Nice to meet you, Jessica."

"Nice to meet you, too." Jessica searched for something more to say. The woman's skin was leathery and tan, and her eyes were shaded in frosty shadow. "Such a beautiful party."

"Oh, I know. So kind of Emily to do this. The staff really appreciate it," Helen said, unconvincingly.

"You work at Driftwood General?" Jessica forgot her awkwardness and stood up straight.

"I used to. Pediatrics. But I quit … oh, it must be coming up on five years ago now."

"I was so sad to hear about Abigail," Jessica said, hearing nerves ripple her own voice. She tried to iron over it with a smile. Jamie watched her.

Helen cocked her head. "You knew Abby?"

Jessica coughed into her fist to hide a pause, spinning her next lie. "A friend of the family."

A child screeched about a candy bar. Helen nodded and took another gulp of wine. The freckled skin of her neck flushed pink.

"She was so kind to us when Olivia disappeared. My parents were close friends of the Garcias. It was devastating. Abby took care of Olivia when she was admitted to the hospital. I'm just so grateful she was there for her. It was right before she disappeared," Jessica said, asking herself where she'd found the nerve. *I'm a doormat, a wallflower. I can't play these games. Or can I?*

Helen stiffened. *She knows exactly what I'm talking about,* Jessica decided, thankful, for once, that everyone knew everyone in Driftwood.

"I just wish I'd had a chance to ask her a few more questions," Jessica said with a sigh. The muscles of her neck tightened.

"I'm so sorry to hear that." The flush drained from Helen's face.

Jamie cleared her throat, still watching Jessica. "Isn't the weather just perfect?"

Jessica ignored Jamie's diversion. "I remember she said Olivia was having some problems. I'm still so confused. If I'd known she had health issues, maybe we wouldn't have gone trick-or-treating…" Jessica paused. "I was hoping for closure."

Helen threw a look over her shoulder, now a shade paler. "You can't blame yourself, dear. Now excuse me, I must use the restroom." She set her wine glass on the table with a splash that bloomed yellow on the tablecloth, then trod over the lawn with a wobble.

Sweat beaded on Jessica's brow, and something fluttered inside – a fluttering as the edges of all that she knew wanted to peel a little further. Would something soon come loose?

"That was all bullshit, wasn't it? What the hell are you doing?" Jamie elbowed her so her own wine sloshed in the glass.

"Why is she so *nervous*?" Jessica whispered.

Jamie clenched her jaw. "I have no idea, Jess, but you need to *let this go*."

Jessica left Jamie squirming by the charcuterie and wove her way through a huddle of cocktail dresses, past Emily, who was holding court, complaining about her housekeeper as she twirled an ankle under her dress.

"If she hates ironing Mike's shirts so much, then she should've gone to college."

Jessica searched for a bathroom, almost colliding with another tray of canapés in the hallway. She passed an office, a kitchen twice the size of her living room, and found a seashell-wallpapered restroom with double sinks and tall, bronze faucets, fluffy towels folded on shelves. But Helen had either found another restroom or made a sharp exit.

Jessica walked down the hallway, then out the front door, but saw no sign of Helen. She headed to her car, which was parked two blocks away. A light wind whipped at her legs as she passed mile-long driveways and laser-perfect landscaping. She heard footfalls behind her and turned to see Helen crossing the street toward her car.

"Helen!" Jessica crossed the street. All her reserve had evaporated.

Helen's back tensed. She turned.

"What happened at the hospital, Helen? About a month before Olivia disappeared?" Jessica was suddenly breathless, as if she'd jogged around the block. The wind swung through her hair.

"I promised the Garcias I'd never tell." Helen grappled for her keys.

"The Garcias are gone. I tried tracking them down, but they left years ago. So please, just tell me."

Helen slumped. "It was just so…"

"So?"

"I'm sure Olivia was a very sweet girl, but…"

"But?" *Spit it out.*

"I've never seen anyone so scared. Poor Abby." Helen closed her eyes. "That girl … she wasn't…"

"She wasn't what?"

"She wasn't *normal,*" she whispered, keys clinking in her hand.

"What do you mean?" Jessica said, winded by Helen's sentence.

Helen sighed, suddenly drained, as if the memory had siphoned the lifeforce from her. "I never told anyone. No one would believe me. But I know what I saw."

"What? What did you see?"

Helen shook her head.

"Helen, please."

"I can't." She opened the car door and slung her purse on the front seat.

"What was Olivia's blood type?"

Helen dropped into the driver's seat. "Nothing we'd ever seen before. The results from the lab didn't make any sense." She slammed the car door shut, then veered into the road.

Jessica drove home too fast, pressing her thumbs into the steering wheel.

"She wasn't *normal?*" she muttered, pulling into her driveway. *What the hell did she mean by that?*

The photo she'd snapped that morning sailed to the front of her mind. The boxy handwriting on notepaper. *Missing report. A police report? Was whatever happened at the hospital enough to get the sheriff involved?*

She swung the front door open and flipped the light switch of the dimly lit hallway. The bulb flickered, hissed, and burned out. Sighing, she raked around the closet, searching for a new one. Nothing. She considered taking another swig from the bottle under the sink and giving up, but the house was already a wreck. A window with a broken latch, a roof missing half a dozen shingles, peeling linoleum. No, she couldn't let go completely and live in the dark.

The attic – she vaguely remembered seeing a stash of bulbs up there.

The stairs whined as she pulled them down. Dust danced in the glow of the attic's single lightbulb, and that flickered, too – on and off, on and off – then fizzled to a pulsing glow. *Great, now the wiring's all screwed up. Another thing I can't afford to fix.*

The attic smelled of dusty paperbacks, forgotten knickknacks. Boxes towered in stacks around her, and the rafters creaked beneath her feet.

She searched a dresser and found bulbs among fishing tackle and printer cables. Then she turned to head back down the stairs and sent a tower of boxes crashing to the floor.

Coughing through dust, she heaved each box back on top of another, rebuilding the unsteady tower. But as she lifted the last box from the floor, the base gave out, and its contents scattered. Scarves and belts unfurled around her feet. A shoe box landed with a thud, just missing her toes. She picked it up, pulled off the lid, and found an embarrassing collection of CDs that she'd treasured twenty years ago.

But inside, she also found a small pink box. Olivia's music box had been hiding in the attic ever since she'd cleared out the clutter from her adolescence. Still locked, because Olivia had disappeared with the key hanging from her wrist.

She moved toward the attic door, clutching the box, until a noise from below froze her feet to the floor.

Chapter 30

Sunday, April 17, 2022

Elliot stared out of his hotel room window, tiredness trying to weigh his eyelids shut. He made another cup of motor-oil coffee with the hotel room's coffee machine. An urge to return to the mountain pass tugged at him, but there was too much to figure out. *If I could just untangle the web, maybe I wouldn't feel like I'm losing it.*

He rubbed his forehead. He'd spent an hour writing, and now a list of everything orbiting his mind filled half the open page of his notebook: *Annabelle at the side of the road, phone call at the diner, origami lion on bench, Jessica present when Olivia disappeared?*

But that list had quickly blossomed into another dozen pages of hurried scrawl. He tore out each page, then lay them on the floor.

"Joseph's episode at school, Olivia thought she belonged in a cave … psychosis? Schizophrenia?" he read aloud in a mumble, remembering another hazy moment from the night before. He picked up the page, balanced it on the hotel's visitor guide, and wrote as he paced. *Mushrooms.*

Were the locals right? Had someone – or some freakish cult, as the rumors suggested – brainwashed those kids? Drugged them with hallucinogens?

He crumpled the page. No, that didn't seem right. Not unless parents, foster homes were involved, and he'd found no evidence of that. He read the scribble on another page. *UFO rumors.*

Late sun strobed gold across the hotel carpet. He sat at his laptop and opened a file named *Black Eye Interview Transcripts,* then scanned the text. *I was abducted by grays,* one woman had insisted, and even now Elliot remembered her glassy hazel eyes, her shaky fingers, as she'd sat opposite him in a coffee shop in Maine. *I suffered nightmares, paranoia. I saw lights in the sky through the bedroom, and then I was frozen ... paralyzed.*

Others claimed they'd suffered amnesia, and only remembered their abductions through hypnosis. *It was as if they'd wiped my memory.*

They travel dimensions, Elliot read. *They've been doing this for thousands of years.*

Elliot stood up from his desk and stared at his notes again, unsure of where his thoughts were headed.

"And what about Annabelle Lewis?" he mumbled, crushing another page, tossing it against the wall, and as the paper hit the edge of an insipid watercolor, he remembered one more foggy moment from the night before. *Did that really happen?* He blinked. *Maybe. Maybe Joseph looked away when I asked him about Annabelle.*

Bury the dead, he wrote on a fresh sheet of paper. *Babies fell out of their beds. Disaster. Earthquake?*

He crumpled that page, too. Bristling, he sat back down and researched Ambien side effects. *Sleepwalking, hallucinations, daytime drowsiness, dizziness* were just a few.

"Is all this just *side effects*?" he muttered. He threw his prescription in his suitcase. If he was going to figure out anything, he'd need to trust his own mind. No more Ambien until he was back in New York.

Maybe the truth doesn't matter anyway, he decided, exasperated. *It'll all end up in fiction. Stir it all up like spooky soup.*

A part of him longed to solve the mystery, uncover the truth with his rational mind, but another only cared about finishing his manuscript. *Just take what you need and meet the deadline. Just fucking write.*

His stomach rumbled. His mouth tasted sour from coffee. He chugged water from the minibar, then wrote a reminder for himself: *Check Driftwood College Library – police archives?*

He jammed his hands in his pockets, annoyed that his thoughts were tangled up like a messy ball of yarn. But at least he'd figured out his next two chapters – they'd gelled in his mind as he'd driven back to The Arbor, after his meeting with Chris. In the second chapter, another character would appear, an out-of-town journalist determined to solve the mystery that plagued the misty town of *Larch Hollow*. And in the third chapter, the focus would pan back to Jessica, who was just as determined to solve the puzzle, but was weary from trying to piece it together alone.

All of it was making more sense in his *novel*, at least. In fact, he'd been more inspired in the last two days than he had in months, he conceded.

He thought of what Chris had told him at the end of their meeting. And he pictured Jessica as a young girl, walking down the unmarked road with Olivia Garcia.

What happened that night? he asked himself, now circling her name on the page with his pen. *Where did Olivia go, and why didn't you go, too?*

He dropped the pen and grabbed his phone from his pocket.

"Of course there's nothing there," he grumbled, scrolling through his public email inbox. "Jessica, if you exist, then get in touch, before I go see a shrink."

Chapter 31

Sunday, April 17, 2022

"Mark, is that you?"

No, Mark would announce himself. So would Jamie.

"I said, who's there?" Jessica yelled, now thinking of her phone in the kitchen, and the bat under her bed.

Get the bat first.

She nudged the bedroom door, which whined open, then grabbed the bat and marched to the living room.

Empty. No writing on the wall, no foliage scattered. But she heard the same electric hiss, and the living room light flickered. *How? I never touched the light switch.*

The other bedrooms were empty, and the bathroom was quiet except for the faucet's lazy *drip drip drip.* The glass on the edge of the tub was half full of water. *Who would drink from the bathroom faucet? Someone who can't reach for a glass from the kitchen cabinet. A kid.*

She searched the garage. No tools missing, nothing out of place. But the freezer door hung open in the kitchen, and peering inside, she found it empty. Even the frost-bitten burgers were gone.

She heard a shuffle and whirled around. A whimper, a scratch.

Someone, or something, is inside.

But she'd checked under the beds, behind the doors. Everywhere, except her closet.

The bedroom lights flickered too. Another hiss, a crackle when she entered the room. Grimy handprints sullied the door and dresser, and a carton of almond milk sat on the nightstand.

A noise from the closet slammed her heart against her ribs.

"Who's there?" she said again, this time with a croaky tremor. She stared at the closet door handle.

Whoever's in there is more scared than I am, she decided, dropping the bat. She grabbed the handle, raked back the door.

A filthy tuft of blond hair poked out from a coat-draped lump in the corner. Jessica pulled back the coat.

Gemmy eyes blinked at her, and the lights hissed and flashed.

"Anthony?"

Anthony Walker cowered, grubby hands gripping his knees. His milky arms were covered in pen scrawl. "They're coming to get me," he said in a raspy squeak.

A whisper spread from her tailbone to her neck.

"Who's coming to get you, Anthony? What do you mean? Do you remember me from last night? Or are you here because I left you food?" Jessica crouched.

He slackened his grip on his knees. "Of course. I saw you with Elliot."

It felt like a ripple of electric current, whatever swept over her. She sat on the bed.

"Don't tell Joseph," Anthony whispered. "He says we can only come out when it's foggy or rainy or dark, so they don't follow us. The trappers nearly got me yesterday!"

The lights flickered again. The air seemed to throb and spark.

"The trappers?" she said, distracted by the light show.

"The park rangers and the cops. They want to take me to the hospital and put robot snakes on my head."

Jessica wished she hadn't chugged so much Zinfandel. "*Robot snakes*?"

"To steal the thoughts from my brain, I think."

Electrodes. An ECG. She eyed the ink on his skin.

"When did this happen?"

"When they found me. When I was little."

"You're *still* little. Who did that?"

He frowned. "A doctor, I think."

"And what happened today? You said they're coming to get you? Who?"

"A cop saw me."

"And you came here?"

He nodded.

Jessica tried to scoop her thoughts together. "What did you write on your arms, Anthony?"

"The voices came. We have to write everything down."

Schizophrenia? Is that what this is?

"What do the voices say?" She watched his eyes dart, glances hitting the walls like shuttlecocks.

He shrank back. "It's a secret."

"That's okay, you're safe here." She wondered if it was true.

"They said the voices aren't real. But they are. They tried to take them away, but they can't."

"Well, I won't call the cops, and I don't have any robot snakes, so why don't you come out of the closet?" *Did I lock the back door? Who else might be hiding around here? Who else is involved?*

"No!" he whined. "I don't want them to get me!"

"It's okay," she hushed, searching for a string of logic, some nugget of sense. "Why do you keep coming here, Anthony?"

"I need socks and milk for a baby."

"You mean *baby formula*?"

He nodded.

"I don't have any formula. Why do you need that?"

"We have to prepare," he whispered.

"Prepare for what?"

"For when the light comes. We have to get ready. We have to hide in the dark until it's time for the light."

"And you need baby formula for that?"

He nodded again.

Another dozen questions were ready to fly from her lips, but Anthony was so skittish, fingertips pressing into his legs. *Don't scare him off.*

"Anthony, I'm going to shut all the blinds and drapes. No one will be able to see inside. You'll be safe, I swear. Okay?"

He chewed his lip. "Okay."

She pulled all the blinds and curtains, checking that the front and back doors were locked, then returned to the bedroom. "Come on, it can't be comfortable squashed in that closet."

He hunched his way out from beneath her shirts. His face was a grimy moon, tiny veins threading through it.

"I guess you came in through the window again."

"Yes. Can I have some socks now?"

Jessica looked down at his battered tennis shoes, then opened a dresser drawer and handed him a pair of gym socks. He pulled off his shoes and tugged the socks onto his filthy feet. An inch of fabric hung over his toes. She caught a three-inch, deep red scratch on the inside of his arm.

"Anthony, does anyone know you're here? Did anyone see you get in through the window?"

He shook his head, and she hoped he was right. A pile of sweating frozen food bags sat on the closet floor, in the corner where he'd hidden.

"You took food from the freezer?"

He nodded.

"Because you're hungry?"

He shook his head.

"Who's it for?"

"It's a secret."

Another one, she thought, then remembered the plastic wrap, shimmering in the dark two nights ago. She frowned at the scratch on his arm.

"You're feeding wild animals?"

"We have to."

"Why?"

"They're hungry. They don't belong here."

"Then where do they come from?"

"Their souls come from the stars."

Jessica sat on the edge of the bed, flushed and shaky. "What does all this mean?" She pointed to the ink on his skin. His fingertips were smudged with it. Soil blackened the whites of his fingernails.

"I can't find the right letters for all the sounds."

"What sounds?"

"The voices ... the things they say. I see them in my head."

She nodded, despite how little she understood.

"Anthony, when you saw me in the forest with ... Elliot..."

"You don't understand," he interrupted.

She sighed. "No, I don't. What's going on in those caves?"

"I'm not allowed to say. The disaster made it," he whispered.

A gust of wind sifted through the trees outside.

"What disaster? In the forest, you said babies fell out of their beds?" Jessica's brain felt too big for her head. It pounded inside her skull.

"It's a secret."

More damn secrets. She searched his eyes, as if the truth might be hiding between the sparkling flecks.

"It messed up everything, and now we're stuck here. We have to wait for the light."

"What light?"

"It's very complicated. Like a big mess inside my brain."

Jessica frowned at Anthony's salad of sentences. Everything tangible and relatable seemed to be slipping from her palm. She searched for a thought she could grapple with, hold onto.

"Why did you leave the M&Ms on my desk?"

"We gave them back to you."

"Yes. Why?"

"We can't eat a lot of the stuff you eat."

"What do you mean?"

"It makes us sick."

"What do you eat?"

"Leaves, mushrooms, berries. Stuff that grows near the…" He was whispering again, eyes shifting from wall to wall.

"The what?"

"Nothing."

The smell of sweat and pine trees wafted up her nose. He *really* needed to take a bath. Another wave of dizziness washed over her, as if she'd just peered right over the edge of the world.

"Those caves, Anthony…"

Anthony looked away.

"What were those creatures inside?"

"We told you not to go in there!"

"But why?"

"Because you don't understand! You're not supposed to be there. And you might get lost and fall into the fog." He flopped onto her bed. She put her head in her hands, asking herself where reality and fiction began and ended, and the thought felt like an eerie déjà vu.

"The fog?"

"It's horrible there."

The room whirled. "Anthony, why do I feel so sick?"

Anthony pulled a fistful of mushrooms from his pocket and spread out his palm. "We already told you! You need to eat the stuff. It's like medicine."

"How do you know that's safe?"

"Of course it's safe. We always eat it. It makes the world stop whizzing, and you don't get sleepy. We figured it out."

"You're lucky you didn't die trying."

Jessica's vision blurred for a moment. Anthony's skinny ribs and button nose fell in and out of focus. "Anthony, what's the *fog*?"

"It's horrible. It comes from the crypt."

"The crypt?"

He nodded. "It's where the others sleep, with the bones," he whispered.

"What do you mean, the crypt? And what kind of fog?" She doubled over when her stomach churned.

"You have to eat these mushrooms right now!" he insisted, shoving the fistful toward her.

Jessica took the slimy, squishy handful. She threw it into her mouth and washed it down with a glass of stale water from her nightstand. The taste was mild. It was the smell, the texture that was so ... *gross*.

Anthony watched her. Jessica slouched against the wall on the bed, closed her eyes, and sensed Anthony's bony shoulder against hers. She opened an eye to find him leaning into her, staring into space.

Beneath her eyelids, Jessica saw the night sky, and every planet and star seemed just a stone's throw away, illuminating the haze in her head.

As her body grew heavy against the wall, she freed herself of her limbs, her bones, and began to drift up, into the eternal void. Soon she was floating through spacetime, into the spangled rays of supernovae that lit up the cosmos like Catherine wheels. She flew to Cassiopeia, whose nebulae strobed red and green and yellow and blue, then whirled around Earth and her cousins. Then she hopped through light years and solar winds to revel in the radiant pink dust of young stars bursting into the Nubecula Minor, before a weightless flight back home.

"Jessica, wake up!"

Jessica opened her eyes. Anthony was still at her side, now tugging her hand.

She stood up, relieved that the nausea had disappeared. The headache had eased, too. But something was off. Something was *different*. She peered through the drapes at the disappearing afternoon. Was it just her imagination, or was every color more vibrant? Did the leaves on the trees, the grass of her lawn, have more *dimension*, somehow? And why, suddenly, did everything seem a little more radiant and beautiful?

"Anthony … am I *tripping*?"

"What's tripping?" He eyed her as she paced back and forth across the carpet.

"When you eat those mushrooms, do they do something strange to your mind? Do they make you feel weird?"

"No, they just take the clouds away."

"The clouds?"

"People here have clouds in their heads. It's like they have dirty eyeballs. They think everything is boring and sensible. That's why they only know boring and sensible things."

Jessica leaned against the wall. Now the edges of all that she knew and believed had all but peeled and curled over. Beneath it all was a fiery, crystalline night sky.

She returned to perch on the end of the bed. The glowing flecks in Anthony's eyes flashed again, but now, with the slimy magic making its way through her digestive system, his pupils were black dots in oceans of electric color, his irises striated chronicles of some cosmic mystery.

"Why do your eyes do that?" She clutched his shoulder.

"The eyes are soul doors," he whispered, tense where she held on to him.

She released her grip. "I know. But why do yours glow like that?"

"It's just how I am. I can see in the dark, and I can see all kinds of things in the air that you can't."

Jessica tensed, too. Part of her wanted to put him in the bathtub, feed him, put clean clothes on his back. Another part wanted to run. *Who – what – is this kid? Where did he come from?*

"I'm hungry." He wandered into the kitchen, and Jessica followed. She considered calling Mark.

No, she decided. *Where the hell would I start? I don't even know where anything begins or ends anymore.*

He frowned into her fridge in the blind-dimmed semi-darkness, then picked up an apple from the table and ate it on the floor. "You need to clean the whirly thing in your fridge. Then it won't make that noise anymore," he said through a chomp, and the fridge hummed in agreement.

Jessica sat on the floor opposite him. "The fan? How do you know so much?"

"My mind is big and open like the sky."

She watched the small flowers of the kitchen wallpaper. They, too, seemed more defined, with small flecks of a deeper blue she hadn't noticed before.

"Anthony, are you and Joseph all alone? Who takes care of you?"

He wrinkled his brow. "I think Mom and Dad are in the stars with the animal souls. Now the voices are Mom and Dad."

Jessica leaned against a table leg. "My mom and dad are gone, too. But aren't you scared, Anthony?" Her voice was unsteady. Now she wanted to hug him close, even if he smelled like a wheelbarrow.

"Nobody loved me here, so I had to go back like Joseph. Everyone is so mean and angry."

Jessica swallowed a jagged lump. "I'm so sorry, Anthony..."

"You can't tell anybody about us! If you tell them, they're gonna come and get us, and trap us again!" His lower lip trembled. The lights hissed and flickered again.

"What the ... what's going on?" She stared up at the ceiling light.

"It comes from my mind and my fingers," he said, inspecting his fingertips.

The blood drained from Jessica's face. She held onto the table leg.

"Don't worry. Don't be scared," Jessica said, addressing herself as much as the little boy in front of her. "I can keep a secret."

"But what about Elliot?"

"He can keep a secret, too," she said. Her heart jittered. "But has anyone else found you? Has anyone else found those caves?"

He frowned. "Sometimes we have to take them to the fog."

A shiver raced up Jessica's spine. "Who? What are you talking about?"

"Bad people."

"Anthony, what did you do?"

"They come down and try to catch us. We run into the fog, and they follow us," he whispered. "They get lost in there. They never come out."

"And what happens to them?" she managed.

Anthony looked away. "For a while it's like they're just sleeping. But..."

"But *what*?"

"But then everything dries up and rots away. Then they're just bones."

Jessica moved her hand to her stomach. It felt like a little boat full of something sick and sour had capsized inside.

"How many times has this happened, Anthony?"

He shrugged.

"You said bad people. What kind of bad people?"

"I don't know. I just know they were bad. We can't let them inside."

"Were they wearing uniforms?"

"I think one was a park ranger. Another was a pervert, and another was a nosy person who wanted to call the cops. That's what Joseph said."

Jessica hid her horror, but her breath didn't want to leave her. Anthony and Joseph seemed so vulnerable, so pixie-little, but what had they done to survive? Who else knew? Who else was involved? What hornet's nest had she poked?

"Anthony, you need to listen to me carefully, and you need to tell Joseph, too. If you ever see anybody, anybody at all, you have to run and hide. Don't let anyone catch you, and don't tell *anyone* what you told me. Understand? And don't go raking through people's trash or stealing! It's not safe."

He nodded, lower lip trembling again. "But sometimes we need stuff."

"Tell me what you need, and I'll bring it to you," she said. *What the hell am I doing? Why am I not calling the sheriff right now? Am I concealing homicide? Murder?*

"You don't understand. You can't let them get us! Bad things happen to ones like us."

Jessica clutched the table leg again. There didn't seem to be enough air in the room, enough blood in her veins. "Did you just..."

"I saw a thought in your head. Joseph says it's rude. Sorry." Anthony sniffed, dragging his nose along his arm. "Now I'm thirsty."

"Well, you already drank the almond milk." She opened the fridge door, and the lump in her throat felt like a golf ball against her windpipe. She unscrewed the cap of the orange juice.

"Those critters let you get that close?" she said, staring at the scratch on his arm.

Anthony nodded.

"That seems kind of dangerous."

"I can talk to them."

She breathed through a succession of heart palpitations and watched the dust particles dance in the air. They seemed to shimmer. She was lost in them, alight as her world warped, stretched, ballooned into something new. She handed him the orange juice, and he chugged half of the carton, then wiped his mouth with the back of his hand. It dribbled down his shirt.

"I still don't know how you guys survive," she said, reaching to grab a napkin from the kitchen table.

He wiped his face along his arm, ignoring the offer of a napkin. The ink stained his cheek. "We don't need the things you need." He hiccupped.

"What do you mean?"

"When I lived at Stacy's, she cooked mac and cheese and ramen noodles, and I had a sore belly all the time, like knives inside. I puked."

"Stacy's?"

"She said she was my new mom. She *wasn't.*" He placed his hand on his heart, and Jessica noticed the subtle heave of his chest. "I need to go soon."

"Wait, Anthony. Are you okay?" She stood up and grabbed hold of the counter. Nothing seemed fixed or steady.

"Sometimes it's hard to breathe," he said.

"It's okay. Just take a few deep breaths. Nice and slow."

Anthony took a loud inhale, a heavy exhale.

"Can I have more socks and apples? And do you have a sweater like Elliot's?"

Jessica broke into a wry smile. "No, I can't afford merino wool and cashmere. But I might have something less fancy."

"Less fancy is good, too." He looked out the window. "I'm scared to go out, but I have to go back!"

"I'll give you a ride to the park."

"You can take me back, but don't let the trappers get me. Promise you won't!"

"Yes, yes, I promise."

Chapter 32

Sunday, April 17, 2022

Jessica grabbed Mark's old backpack from his closet and stuffed it with apples and socks, then threw in some raincoats from the garage, trying to guess what else Anthony might desperately need but would never think to ask for.

As if I'm packing his bag for summer camp. But what's he heading back to? How do I know he's safer underground?

She paused in the hallway. Anthony had found the clay lion by the front door and was making figures of eight in the air with it.

What would a normal person do? she wondered. This would never happen to a normal person, she decided, and in that moment, she sensed herself slip from everyone, everything that pinned her to the minutes, the hours that filled her day. Her job, her brother, Jamie. Work tomorrow seemed so miserably pointless that she refused to think about it. Her intrigue bloomed and clouded everything else, and fragments of truth glistened in the dark. Something more urgent and compelling than fear was rising inside, and it was tugging her toward the forest's shaggy hollows, the nooks and cracks of her own memory. She raked through a drawer for a sweater.

"This is fine," Anthony announced from behind her. He was swamped in a fair-isle hooded sweater pilfered from the closet in the hallway. The sleeves drooped from his hands like melting icicles.

"It's ridiculous, but it'll work," Jessica said. The world still seemed brighter, and even the carpet pile was fascinating.

She unlocked the internal garage door, reminding herself that she was now deep in the weeds of something she didn't understand. Something she'd have to hide from everyone, except Elliot Reed.

"You're trying to think about too many things at once," Anthony said from the backseat ten minutes later, and she nearly drove off the road.

"What do you mean by that?"

"Just think about now."

Okay, Mr Mindfulness.

But the thoughts kept looping, twisting. She caught sight of a patrol car in her rearview mirror. Anthony slid onto the car floor.

"Now I'm *really* losing it," she mumbled, wondering if her taillight was busted, or if her tags had expired. Some dumb thing she'd forgotten to do that would leave her wrangling to explain why a missing kid was in her car.

But the car passed hers, and she puffed out a sigh of relief. She thought of Andrew and the sheriff, his deputies. All chasing an elusive perp. Some assumed freak who'd been violating and brainwashing kids in a filthy basement, she guessed. But even Andrew admitted that things didn't add up, that he was in over his head. So what *did* he know?

Jessica hit the highway, toward Evergreen Pass. Anthony's head bobbed to sleep behind her. She followed the tight curves of the mountain road, passing the Blue Ridge Diner.

As she neared the pass, patrol car lights flashed in the distance.

"Anthony!"

Anthony bolted upright.

"Get down!"

He slid flat on his back. "We have to go from the other side!" he yelled. "Drive to the other side of the park!"

Jessica weighed her options. Bring the kid back home? But what if someone stopped by? No, she couldn't do that.

"No, no, I have to go back! Joseph's gonna be so mad!" Anthony cried.

"It's okay, Anthony, we'll get you back," she said, shaky hands gripping the wheel, then exited the highway and turned around. "But I swear, you keep reading my thoughts, and you'll give me a heart attack."

She drove in silence. Anthony slouched against the back window, staring up at the night sky. Fifteen minutes later, Jessica pulled into the park entrance, looking behind her to check for other cars.

Anthony opened the back door, then headed for the gap in the trees, right where Olivia vanished.

"Hold on!" Jessica grabbed her flashlight and the backpack. Anthony put the bag on his shoulders, and Jessica shortened the straps.

Wind hushed through the trees. The road was deserted, and the darkness was hermetic and heavy, but the slimy mushrooms were still in her bloodstream, and even the night seemed to shimmer.

Jessica flipped on her flashlight and followed Anthony, watching as the sweater sleeves flapped at his sides and the hem hung around his knees. A woolly triangle on tiny legs, with her backpack bouncing from his skinny shoulders.

She stopped a few feet inside the park. Anthony turned and watched her from beneath the hood.

"The sleeves," Jessica whispered, suddenly stiff, snared in fear. It had crept up on her, enveloped her like a cloak – a lost moment surfacing. *I know this fear.*

"Olivia tugged my sleeve..."

"Olivia?" Anthony whispered.

"I pulled the sheet off my head. I turned around, looked for her. I called her name ... called her name and stepped between the trees. And then I felt her tug my sleeve. She was never more than twenty feet away. But something ... something happened."

Jessica took another step forward, memories unfurling, reaching into the twiggy dark in search of an anchor. Anthony's eyes were a soft glow under her sweater hood.

She looked behind her at the gap where Olivia had vanished. "That lost chunk of time ... it's somewhere around *here*, not on that back road. I followed her."

"Who's Olivia?" he asked.

"A girl I knew a long time ago. I ... I think she was like you."

Anthony gasped. "Maybe the fog got her."

"You said you found bones."

He nodded.

A dog barked, and Jessica flipped off the flashlight, then pulled Anthony into a crevice between a rock and a hollowed tree.

Another bark, and a flashlight beamed through the trees, no more than fifty feet away. Anthony clung to her, shaking.

"Nothing over here," a voice yelled, and the flashlight dimmed, the crunch of twigs underfoot faded.

"No more flashlight!" Anthony whispered.

Jessica followed him as he hiked up the trail, his stalk-legs jabbing the soil. The stars were hidden, but the full moon soon became a beacon in the sky, escaping the cloud cover to light the path. The oaks and hickories thinned, and the evergreens towered, feathery-armed stick men back-lit by the silvery lining of charcoal clouds.

"The voices – who are they? Where do they come from?" Jessica whispered.

Anthony stopped. "They say we need to get ready. We have to wake up the sleepers in the crypt."

"Who? Who's they?"

The moon lit Anthony's face. He arched his head to look up at the sky. "They're far away." The sweater hood flopped off his head. "We can't wake them up. And now a trapper saw us. They're going to catch us soon."

"Who saw you?" She gripped his shoulder.

"A man."

"What did he look like?"

"The people here aren't ready for us. That's what they say," he murmured.

"Anthony, listen to me!" she whispered.

His eyes flashed. He pulled up the sweater hood.

"This trapper – who is he?"

"I don't know."

"How old is he?"

He shrugged. "Old people all look the same."

Jessica sighed. "Is he like a dad or a grandpa?"

"A dad. He's like a dad with yellow hair."

"Yellow? You mean blond, like yours?"

"No, not like mine. Dark yellow. I think he's a police officer. He has a badge."

"Shit," Jessica muttered. *Andrew saw him. He knows more than I thought.*

"Is Annabelle with you, Anthony? You can tell me."

Anthony shrugged again.

"Wait, how many of you are down there?"

He shook his head.

"The girl who was with you when you came to my back porch?" Jessica's throat was dry; her skin tingled.

"She tried to wake them up," Anthony whispered, staring at the ground.

"Wake up who? Anthony, where is she?"

Jessica spun around when something rustled behind her. Searching the woods with her flashlight, she found nothing but fir branches. *A squirrel or raccoon,* she decided, turning back to Anthony.

"Anthony? *Anthony?*"

She was alone. Alone among the black branches and the woody thicket surrounding her.

"Anthony, where did you go?"

She drowned in the quiet, until Olivia returned to the front of her mind – the memory that had surfaced near the entrance to the park. With the slippery spores still drifting through her insides, the silence seemed to breathe, permeating the dark corners where those memories hid. She took a deep inhale, bathing her lungs in the pine-zested air. It cleared the fog in her head, eroded the film that smothered moments from twenty years ago, until the truth emerged, fluttering free. Jessica slumped to the ground.

The memory folded itself around her again, this time blotting out everything else, rising from the moss and the brushwood. Olivia's long brown hair, flitting in the breeze. The swish of her dress and the flap of her angel wings. And Jessica, following her through the trail. Up, over the path that led to the clearing, then down to the valley, the creek, the ravine by Evergreen Pass. Jessica had begged Olivia to turn back, but Olivia's glinting eyes, suddenly opal-bright, had been all that had guided her. Just the marooning darkness under a cloud-hidden moon, and Olivia, running ahead, glancing over her shoulder, pulling off her angel wings.

Chapter 33

Thursday, October 31, 2002

"We have to go down, Jessie. We have to jump down the rabbit hole!"

Olivia's eyes were glowing amber in the jet-black crevice under the mountain pass. Jessica was tired, raked by thorns and branches. Nothing made any sense, because the fear rising from her belly stirred up every word she heard, every moment. All she knew was that she couldn't let Olivia go; she couldn't leave her alone in the woods. Home was at the end of a lost path, through the winding trail between the pine trees.

"You have to slide on your butt!" Olivia tugged at Jessica's sleeve, then skidded out of sight.

"Olivia! Olivia, no! Where did you go?"

"Come on, Jessie. Please. Hurry up!" Olivia yelled, her voice now muffled.

Jessica's knees almost buckled, but she crouched, throwing out her hands to steady herself, then followed the sound of Olivia's voice, blinded by the dark. She tumbled, crying out, then landed with a sharp blow to her hip, her knees.

"I told you it was real, Jessie. It's not just a story!" Olivia gushed.

Jessica coughed and gasped. She climbed to her feet and threw out her hands again. The earthy air was thick in her lungs. "I can't see anything! It's so dark in here! We need to go home!"

They were trapped inside a hole in the ground. A black pit.

I don't want to die underground.

Olivia took hold of Jessica's hand. "It's OK, Jessie. I can see in the dark. You don't understand, I have to wake the others. We have to run to the light soon."

Olivia guided Jessica, gripping her hand.

"You have to jump down, Jessie. This way, see? Climb over the edge."

Jessica landed on rock, this time with a yelp and a blow to her leg. Olivia's palm touched her knee, and a strange sensation washed down Jessica's leg, warming her grazed skin. The pain faded, until Jessica felt nothing at all.

"See? It's better now," Olivia said. "Hold my hand."

Jessica climbed to her feet, wobbling and unsteady. She shuffled behind Olivia, startled by every tumbling pebble. Large rocks blocked her path, but Olivia guided her over them.

"Who's sleeping? I don't understand."

Olivia ignored Jessica's question.

"I feel strange, Olivia. Is this a dream?" Jessica's feet were lighter now, and her fear was fading. Now she was just confused.

"No, it's not a dream, Jessie. It's the fog."

"Fog?"

"This way!"

They hit gravel, and Olivia tugged Jessica left, down a steep tunnel, where every scuff of their feet echoed.

"Where are we, Olivia? It's so dark."

Olivia tugged her forward, downward, until Jessica began to cough.

"Wait here, Jessie." Olivia said, eyes glimmering. "Don't move. I'll be right back."

Jessica sat down on cool stone and leaned against the tunnel wall. *Mark will be so worried by now. What if Mom and Dad are already home?*

Something damp and thick coated her lips, her throat. She closed her eyes, thoughts bleeding to daydreams, scenes playing behind her eyelids: Olivia's bright eyes, glinting in the woods, and the black branches brushing her face on the trail. Shapes shifting, hiding in the dark.

A murmur snapped her eyes open. Shuffling.

"Olivia?"

A blink in the dark replied. Then another, and more still. Shimmering eyes, watching her, hovering in the black. Jessica closed her own eyes and screamed, until a hand touched her shoulder.

"Jessie!"

Jessica opened her eyes again, hands flailing. Olivia was back at her side. The eyes had vanished, and low voices faded–a dying echo.

"I couldn't wake them up, Jessie. And now I have to go!"

"Wake up who? What are you talking about? Who's down here? I saw something..."

"I can't explain. I don't have time. Come on!"

Chapter 33

Olivia gripped Jessica's hand and led her through the darkness.

"How long have we been down here? I can't remember when we got here." Jessica shuffled close behind Olivia.

"I don't know. Just keep going!"

Jessica scrambled over more rocks, but her legs didn't grow tired. They were numb, in fact. Only her mind was exhausted, sleepy one moment, wide awake the next.

"Please let me wake up soon," she mumbled. Her eyes had adjusted to the dark, and now she could make out Olivia's head and shoulders in front of her.

At last, they reached a cave, where a gust of cool air told Jessica they were almost free. Olivia crawled onto her belly, through a narrow crack in the rock, and Jessica followed.

Outside, Jessica could make out the angles of trees and shrubs. The pines loomed; their tops still shrouded by a cloud-covered night sky. Thunder rumbled – a distant growl. Olivia took Jessica's hand once more and led her to the path out of the park, toward the back road.

"I'm so tired, Olivia. Wait, I need to rest. I just want to sleep."

"No, Jessie! Stay awake. We can't sleep!" Olivia tugged her forward.

Jessica ambled on, guided by Olivia's hand, edging in and out of sleep, snapped awake by the bony brush of branches.

Their trek came to a halt, and Olivia nudged Jessica's arm.

"Jessie, stay awake! You can go home now. Just run that way." Olivia guided Jessica right, down the unlit road. "I have to run to the light. I can't stay here anymore. They know I'm different."

"What do you mean?" Jessica's fear roared right back, now pulling her from tiredness, from anything but the sound of her own breath, raspy and serrated. Olivia ran.

Jessica followed her, crying out her name, until a louder noise made her cower – a heavy whirr. Deep and low, it vibrated through the forest, through her own bones. Light flooded the sky – a sudden burst, a whirl of spinning bulbs. Then it focused to a cold beam, spotlighting the crumbly forest floor. It illuminated Olivia's silhouette ahead, until she ran toward the beam and faded like smoke.

A scream broke from Jessica's throat. She sprinted back to the road, the last few hours already blurring, fading, escaping her memory.

Chapter 34

Sunday, April 17, 2022

"The light," Jessica whispered, still slumped on the ground among twigs and leaves. Yes, those were the hours she'd hidden from herself. The moments she couldn't accept.

"People here have clouds in their heads. It's like they have dirty eyeballs. They think everything is boring and sensible."

Anthony's words rung in her ears, and she re-heard them, over and over, watching moonlight sieve through the wandering clouds. He already understood what had taken her decades to figure out.

The truth had no obligation to make sense to her. It had no desire to fit into all the little files and categories she'd made for it. It simply *was*.

"Olivia ran to the light ... Olivia went *home,*" Jessica murmured.

Suddenly it all made sense. Their struggle to breathe, to eat. Their opal-bright eyes. Olivia's bloodwork.

Jessica's stomach was knotted, and she struggled to drag enough air into her lungs. She searched for the flashlight, hands fanning out to find it wedged in the grass behind her. A rustle startled her, and she froze. She listened for another sound, but heard nothing.

She stood up and found the trail where it forked, but she was now too disoriented to remember where she was, or which direction to follow. She wound around the branches, the tufty foliage at her feet, until, out of breath, she noticed the trail had flattened.

"Anthony?" she called again.

"You took so long!" he whined, running from behind a tree, setting her alight with fright all over again.

"Don't scare me like that!" She slumped against a tree, bathed in the tremor of her own heartbeat. The bulb of the flashlight dimmed and died, and the moon slunk behind clouds, blanketing her in darkness. She pressed the button – on-off, on-off – but only the glowing flecks of Anthony's irises lit the forest. She tried to retrace her steps, but she felt like she'd spun around a dozen times.

"I have to go now!" Anthony turned his back to Jessica and ran.

"Anthony, wait. No!" she called, running after him. "Anthony, the flashlight died!"

But his little legs moved so quickly, unburdened by heavy bones. Soon she heard nothing but the wind in the trees, her own feet crunching over the trail.

Jessica kept running, fear tearing every sensible thought from her, until she found herself teetering at a crumbling edge. She staggered back, lashing out to grab a branch, a rock that wasn't there.

The *clearing*. She'd been at the clearing overlooking the lake, too confused to recognize the turf.

Her right foot skidded forward, she fell back, and her left foot kicked out, hitting and pulverizing the soil at the edge of the cliff. Her body began to slide, gravity pulling her forward, downward.

Chapter 34

She wasn't sure what she understood first, that she was falling, or that the earth had crumbled beneath her feet. But now she was in free fall, her hair flying out in wind-fluted ringlets, until the mist-cloaked lake sucked her into its frigid fold. The impact pummeled her.

She plunged toward the lakebed, sand and pebbles grazing her skin, the cold water numbing her limbs. She somersaulted and began to surface, kicking, holding tight to the breath that wanted to burst from her lips.

But then she felt a drag at her waist. A tug at her shirt. A jagged piece of driftwood, half-buried in the sand, had caught the fabric. She was trapped, her breath still pressing to escape, her legs tangled in hydrilla. She wrestled and pulled at her shirt, moments left before water breached her lungs.

Chapter 35

Sunday, April 17, 2022

"I don't see why semicolons are such a problem, Ruth."

Elliot paced across The Arbor's carpet, then stared out at the blurry glow of streetlights along the boardwalk. After two days of heady escape, New York breathed down his neck through the phone.

"*Black Eye* was full of semicolons, and no one cared..."

"Accessible prose, Elliot. That's all I'm saying. And I'm simply echoing what your editor's going to say. I'm worried about you. Are you getting enough sleep?" Ruth rasped through her syllables with a huskiness earned from four decades of chain smoking over manuscripts.

"Yes, I'm fine. Just busy. I sent you the first chapter."

Elliot drew the curtains, unbuttoned his shirt.

"I just read it. Elliot, this is *unbelievable*."

He unbuckled his belt.

"I don't know what kind of magical muse you've got squirreled away, but you seem to be *way* inside this woman's head ... this *Jessica* character. How on Earth did you come up with all this?"

"I don't know," he lied, draping his shirt over a chair. "I guess I just got inspired." He was relieved to be in The Arbor, and not in her office, where he'd have to lie to her face. He pictured her at her desk in one of her turtlenecks, cracking a wry smile.

"Just make sure the conflict is compelling. If this character has a romantic interest, you need real tension. We've talked about this before," she wheezed.

Screw conflict. That's asinine. Cliched. I don't want any damn conflict. There'll be more than enough going on in this story without that.

"Sure," he mumbled.

"You sound nervous, Elliot. Are you drowning in research again? Do you need some Xanax? It's a lifesaver," Ruth said, and he heard a sound that told him she'd flipped off her reading glasses and dumped them on her desk.

"Ruth, I'm fine, really. I just hate that the damn synopsis is already out there. It's a straitjacket." Elliot wished he could retrieve all the words he'd spilled, because of the awkward silence that followed, and because he knew she'd be rubbing her eyes by now, trying to scrub the image of him stuck in a bind, trapped in his own words.

"Tell me you're not still spinning your wheels on this, Elliot. You've nailed a formula. Just *stick to it*," she said, and as he searched for a reply, the hotel room seemed too large for him alone, reefing him in a sea of carpet pile.

He looked through the gap in the curtains and searched for Leo in the night sky, as if he might find a convincing answer in the spangled dust snaking its way through the star cluster. And he thought of Jessica, who now held all the strings for his next novel. He unbuttoned his jeans.

"Elliot? Are you still there? Just don't forget what your readers expect from you."

"Ruth, I'll figure it out. Forget I said any of this," he said, distracted by a memory of Jessica holding on to him the night before.

"*Black Eye* was horrifying. *Seductive.* And that's exactly what they want more of."

Elliot imagined the engraving on his tombstone: *Here lies Elliot Reed, who mastered the art of horrifying and seducing people.*

"I'll make sure this is just as horrifying and … seductive," he said, still thinking of Jessica, and the muddle she'd made of his brain.

"And we really need a longer excerpt for the website. I need to see it before that airhead of a publicist uploads it." She sighed, and it seemed to sift into his ear and weigh him to the ground.

"Next week."

"And the blurb for that guy's novel?"

"Working on it."

"When are you coming back to New York?" she asked, a little weary. *She's already poured herself a nightcap from that art-nouveau sideboard,* Elliot decided, peeling off his shirt.

"Tomorrow night."

He threw off his jeans and fell into bed after narrowly avoiding a discussion as to whether the disappearance of Annabelle Lewis would help book sales. He blinked at the recessed lighting and listened to the hum of the air vents, drained from an afternoon holed up, typing furiously as inspiration tumbled around like gravel in a dryer. He'd written another chapter – Jessica sitting at her desk folding a page of notes into an origami lion, gazing at a map of the park on her wall. As she'd folded each crease, she'd unpacked the puzzle pieces: Three children who'd disappeared without a trace, in a town steeped in fear and conspiracy. Wolves roaming the forest, bright lights invading the night sky, a lake blanketed in fog. A drunk sheriff, a filthy underbelly, and a rusting rim of misery around a dying Appalachian town. Driftwood, but, as Ruth requested, a little more horrifying.

He replayed the events of the last 48 hours. Was there still some way to persuade himself that he'd let his mind run wild? That he'd deceived himself with dreams of labyrinthine caves and a muse he craved in his waking hours? Perhaps the dull and wretched truth, whatever it was, was just too much for his mushy sensibilities?

As each minute passed it seemed less likely, and his determination to find a rational explanation was waning like the argent moon. *No, I definitely hiked down that chasm. It all happened, somehow.*

He picked up his phone, scrolled to his email in search of contact from Jessica. Still nothing. He sighed, tormented by the lack of her.

But his encounters with Oliver Gray and a flailing tour guide told him that there were pieces of the puzzle that he hadn't pulled from his own head. At least that was *something* to hold on to.

But he'd much rather hold on to Jessica, he decided, and he pictured her above him, her back arched in pleasure, her body freed from clothes. He'd rather hold on to her waist, her hips as he guided her over him, he thought, closing his eyes and letting his hand wander over his stomach, under the hem of the bed sheet, until he grabbed hold of what ached for attention, teased from two nights of bliss cut short. He sunk his head into the pillow and sighed.

An hour later, after a nap that felt like a blink, he sat up in bed. *What if she heads back to the caves tonight? And there's still so much to figure out. I'm running out of time.*

He flung off the covers, pulled on clothes, and borrowed a flashlight from the front desk. The fading sun was a pink haze at the horizon, flashing between trees as he drove to the lot by the entrance to the state park. He'd hike to the cave they crawled out of last night, he decided. No more sliding into a dark pit.

The sunny afternoon had fanned the branches dry. Elliot trekked the trail toward the clearing above Lake Driftwood, then asked himself which route he'd wandered the night before. Twilight shaded the path, and the evergreens darkened to charcoal. He found a narrow trail leading deeper into the forest, where stocky shrubs and a fallen tree looked familiar. He followed the path and watched the last of daylight fade, until the north star shimmered in the sky.

By the time he reached the cave, the sky was navy blue, encrusted with twinkling constellations.

Stay awake this time, he ordered himself. There were no pills to confuse him now. He was wide awake. *Is Jessica already inside, searching with her flashlight?*

He gazed up at the stars, until something told him he wasn't alone.

Chapter 35

It was the eyes, flashing yellow, that he saw first. He flipped on the flashlight to find tawny fur, pointed ears like fluffy geodes.

He had no idea how to fend off a wolf. Yell? Throw a rock? All his survival instinct had dissolved into the traffic fumes of New York City.

But what kind of a wolf is that? The head, the paws. That thick shaggy fur. He's a monster. Does he smell my fear among the pinecones?

The wolf inched closer, eyes still locked on Elliot's. He eased around a fork of branches. Elliot backed up against a tree and felt his heart pound, his lungs scavenging air as he prepared to sprint. He kept his flashlight aimed at the wolf.

The creature moved closer still, paws light on the ground – huge downy clouds housing switchblade claws. Despite Elliot's instinct to run, his feet wouldn't move.

Any second, I'll see teeth, pink gums. Then a lunge, a bite to the neck.

But the wolf didn't snarl or pounce. Instead, he wagged his tail and let out a soft whine, then moved even closer. Elliot still couldn't force his limbs to move.

The wolf let out another whine, a grunt, then brushed Elliot's jeans with his nose. A sniff, a snort, a nudge. Elliot willed him to go away, find another lost soul to play with, but he let out another whine, still wagging his tail.

Elliot's terror muted. Thinking was easier.

The wolf leaped at him, paws almost as big as Elliot's hands pressing into his shoulders, and a thick, rough tongue licked his face, his ear, his neck. He closed his eyes to block the gloopy caress of wolf saliva.

"Hey," he stammered, now daring to pet the wolf's neck. "Where did you come from?"

A sharp whistle slashed the quiet, and the wolf sprinted into the trees. A young boy approached – a shadow in the flashlight's glare.

Joseph Baker embraced the wolf, then eyed Elliot, standing between two tree trunks. He remained a silent silhouette, until he darted from view.

Elliot leaned against a tree. Every bone in his body seemed impossibly heavy. Fatigue now suffocated his will to stay awake. He slumped into the grass, and the forest bled into a whirlpool of fever-wild dreams, curdling under the spangled sky.

Chapter 36

Sunday, April 17, 2022

"Elliot?" It came out as a croak, dissolving to a moan.

Jessica was limp in the arms of a man, scooped from the shore and carried over sand. For a moment, she enjoyed the warmth and the strength of him.

"Who the hell is Elliot?"

Shirt fabric brushed against her, and she heard his soles hitting flat terrain now, lifting her up a flight of wooden steps.

She coughed, searching for her voice again.

"Harding, what in the hell?" a voice called. Jessica opened her eyes to streetlamps along the boardwalk, smudging the dark. Andrew ... Andrew was carrying her.

"Willis, do me a favor and keep this between you and me."

He lowered her and she found more of herself. More of her senses and whatever it was that glued her thoughts together. Jessica flopped onto the backseat of a patrol car, wincing at a stabbing pain in her chest, unsure if she was mortified or just relieved to be alive. She shivered in wet clothes that stank of the lake. Sand scratched her skin under her jeans, under her sweater.

"Whatever you say, Detective. But you're cleaning the car tomorrow. Nice night for a swim. You know this chick?" the other voice said.

"Yeah, I know her."

Jessica curled up on the backseat as the deputy reversed. Her torso was laced in scratches, mottled by bruises still blossoming.

Thirty minutes later, she sat at the kitchen table in pajamas, swimming in shame. Her limbs were still thawing, despite a shower. Andrew sat opposite, nudging a cup of hot chocolate to her side of the table.

"Are you going to tell me what happened, Jess?"

"How did you find me?" She picked up the cup, playing for time to spin a story. It was becoming a habit.

"I was walking back from the Lakeside with Willis, ready to get a ride home, and I see some woman lying face down by the lake. Turns out it's you."

"Where's your car?" Another irrelevant question to buy more time.

"In the shop. Won't be ready until tomorrow morning." He shook his head with a look that told her he thought she'd lost herself entirely. "So?"

"I thought I saw a kid in the water," she said, because it was the first lie that came into her head.

Andrew stared on.

"So I ran in, swam out there. I guess I got confused. Tired out. It was so dark. I couldn't see a thing. And then … then I was struggling, sinking. I couldn't swim anymore. And I caught my shirt on a branch in the water. I somehow found the strength to get to the surface again. I just kicked and kicked until I hit the beach, and I guess I just kind of … passed out. It's all fuzzy in my mind. It was *horrible*."

Did he buy it? Most of it's true. She watched him cross his arms, lean back in the chair.

"You said you *thought* you saw a kid in the water. Do I need to call dispatch?"

"I … I don't think so. I think it might have been something just drifting out there."

"Are you sure? I need you to be completely sure."

"Yes. Now that I think of it. I'm pretty sure," she replied. A slither of paranoia crept in. She wasn't sure of *anything*.

He shook his head, elbows now on the table.

"This really doesn't make any sense. But I guess we'll find out soon enough, if some kid winds up dead, floating in the lake."

She sipped the hot chocolate and warmed her hands with the mug.

"You okay? You seem distracted."

"Of course I'm distracted," she said, jerking back to the moment with a twist in her seat. "I nearly drowned. And now I feel like an idiot."

The fridge hummed again. *"You need to clean the whirly thing," Anthony told me. Was that only hours ago?*

Andrew opened her fridge, closed it. Her parents' old wall clock ticked on, announcing that it was 6 o'clock. It wasn't.

"There's liquor under the sink."

He poured himself a glass of bourbon. She splashed a slosh into her hot chocolate.

"How's the search going?"

"It's not going anywhere. This town's full of crazy people."

"Oh yeah?" She took another sip, watched him over the mug rim.

"We got people calling about wolves in their back yards and UFOs in the woods. Then there are the freaks who say the kids are haunting the park. Some farmer said he saw Anthony Walker hanging out with a bear, for Christ's sake. Just a bunch of useless *horseshit*."

Jessica nearly spat out her hot chocolate. "That sounds pretty frustrating."

Andrew nodded, and they fell into silence.

"Who were Olivia's biological parents?"

Andrew looked up.

"I remember my parents said they thought she was adopted," she lied, brushing her fingers across the table.

"They found her in the park."

Now Jessica looked up. "What? You mean like the others? How many damn kids did they find abandoned in the woods, Andrew?"

"I don't know the real number, Jess. So many kids get funneled through the system. Forget I told you. I shouldn't have."

Jessica set her mug in the sink. Her shoulders tightened at the touch of hands. Andrew was right behind her.

"Jess, I think you might be batshit crazy, but you're beautiful. There's no one like you. And I'm so sorry for everything I did." His grip was tight, he didn't let go. She stiffened, closed her eyes as blood vessels flashed red and white, like rings of plasma under her eyelids.

"It's OK, Andrew. It was a long time ago," she said, realizing that she no longer cared. All those years wishing he'd at least apologize. Now she didn't give a damn.

"When I saw you lying on the beach, I thought you were dead. Everything I did just hit me. I felt like such a jerk." He pivoted around her, and his hand rubbed the back of her neck, his other reached for her shoulder. "I can't stop thinking about you."

Jessica looked away, absorbing all his regret, all his need, reminding herself that it wasn't hers. "Thank you for helping me, but..."

He pulled away. "Elliot. That was the name, right?"

She nodded, wondering how it could be true.

"Well, I guess I'm happy for you. I want you to be happy."

They exchanged awkward smiles.

"I guess I'll take your brother's room again, since I don't have a car," Andrew said. Jessica cringed, nodded, shuffled to the bedroom, and locked the door.

11:15 p.m. read the digits on her phone, and their white glow shocked her awake. *The caves ... will Elliot come back tonight?*

She stripped off her pajamas, wincing at a red welt on her ribs, and pulled on clothes. Her heart raced – a sensation that felt too familiar, as if her resting state was now an urgent flutter. She crept from the bedroom and grabbed her phone from the counter, then her keys from the soaking wet jeans that she'd dumped by the washer.

Back in the bedroom, she locked the door again. The breeze ruffled the drapes. The window was still cracked open. She slid out, padded over the grass to the driveway, then remembered her car was parked in the lot by the park.

"Not again," she mumbled. And her flashlight – that was now tangled in hydrilla, somewhere in the lake. She pulled open the garage door, just like the night before, slid underneath, then searched for another flashlight.

11:30. Is he there already?

Chapter 37

Monday, April 18, 2022

The moon was a tempered shield among stars. Jessica hiked into the heart of the park. The evergreens embraced her back into their fold, tufty fingers feathering her neck.

The thought of tumbling into the dark pit and climbing down the chasm alone again made her skin crawl. Instead, she searched out the small crack in the rock where they'd exited twice before.

Please be there. Don't tell me you talked yourself out of it or fell asleep. Don't tell me you already left town.

Approaching the rock, she caught sight of a dark shadow. Her flashlight revealed jeans, a sweater. A man lying in the grass. *Elliot.*

She ran to him and crouched, then nudged him softly. He stirred, and relief softened her.

"Jessica," he murmured, blinking awake. He propped himself up, grabbed a hold of her sleeve. "The wolf."

"What wolf?" She panned the flashlight behind her.

Elliot lay back down. "He's gone, I think."

"You mean like the one we saw two nights ago? That huge thing?"

"Yes. He's tame, like a dog. Jesus, I'm so tired."

Elliot pulled Jessica toward him, and she joined him in the grass. Nothing seemed unlikely or impossible anymore. She lay with her head on his chest, listening to his heart. The nerves under her skin woke up, and her heart beat a little harder, as if the moths had escaped their jar again, batting their wings against her ribs. *Will that ever fade?* she wondered. *And will I ever get to know, or is tonight the last night I'll meet him here? How many women are waiting for him in New York? I feel like I know him, but I don't know him at all.*

The stars blazed. Eternity quietly shattering, exploding above their heads. Jessica felt like she was drifting, the tiniest fleck in an infinite cosmos.

She almost fell sleep, until Elliot nudged her, and they lay on their sides in the grass. Despite the flutter inside, her body felt fluid tonight. It was easy to smile, easy to breathe.

His hand roamed to her waist. "What happened this morning? You disappeared."

"I tried to wake you. I needed to get back home," she said.

"There's so much I need to ask you. So much we need to figure out," he said, but he was already reaching for more of her. His lips grazed her neck. She curled her toes, sighed into the dark.

"Yes, so much has happened," she murmured, but she could only think of how he pulled her closer, gripped her tight. And how, as he kissed her, the ground seemed to dissolve from beneath her. In that moment there was nothing but the two of them, and her silent plead that the moment wouldn't break her later.

"Are we alone?" he said, searching for glowing eyes between the trees.

She searched too, then nodded. "Yes, I think so."

They lay under the blinking watch of constellations – Virgo, Lyra, Hercules. Other than the rustle of leaves, the forest was an expanse of timbered quiet.

He found her lips again. Their fingers flexed, interlocked. She tilted her head and closed her eyes, yielding to what felt like the beginning of another life, a better one. And as he whispered her name, sighed against her skin, she opened her legs, felt the denim of his jeans against her thighs. Each breath was a rise, a wave. And she wasn't even sure what else was rising inside. Was it tears that wanted to flow, or a sigh waiting to leave her lips? Or maybe it was just all her longing and lust, finally escaping her? And how would this moment ever be enough when she wanted to hold on to him forever?

His hand slipped between her thighs. A feathery exhale left her lips, fading into the woody air. Was this why she hadn't touched a man in eight long years? Why she'd sulked through all those days of solitude? Had it been broken trust from all of Andrew's lies, or was it that some part of her knew that this moment, somehow, could happen, and nothing else could match it?

She released one of his shirt buttons. Warm skin, a toned body, another wave of lust, and *oh God*, he was so incredibly divine. Her fingers were a little unsteady; she was hungry for all of him, and her senses fired under his traveling palm.

But what if they lost each other again? What if every question went unsaid? It was hard to focus when her skin was alight with the caress of lips and the soft, persistent brush of fingertips. But suddenly the thought of waking up alone without answers was worse than interrupting heaven.

"Elliot…"

He pulled back, propping himself up in the grass again. "Jessica … you distract me." She caught a half-lit smile.

"There's so much I need to tell you," she whispered.

"I know." He stood up, reached into his pocket. She joined him, finding her feet.

He unlocked his phone. "What's your number?"

She rattled it off, and he saved it. "Let me call you so you have mine," he said, but there was no service so deep in the park. She pulled her phone from her pocket and saved his number, too.

Now there'll be no more wondering, no more agonizing. I'll just call him in the morning if we wake up apart.

When she tucked her phone back into her pocket, a button fell from her shirt. Elliot grabbed it, pushed it into his own pocket, then tore off a button from his shirt placket, and placed it in her palm. She slipped it into her back pocket.

"A weird little keepsake," he said, pulling her close again. She folded into the scent of him, the bliss of the turf between his chest and neck. His fingers were tangled in hers. What else could he do with those hands? *Focus,* she told herself, and felt a subtle press from his hips. Had he read her mind?

A thought hurtled back, pulling her from bliss. "Elliot, I think Annabelle might be trapped inside that cave."

"What? Why?"

The day's events cascaded from Jessica's lips. The conversation with Helen, Anthony. The trek through the woods and her tumble into the lake. Her newly recovered memories, and her worry that the cops were following Anthony. She stared up at the sky, wondering if Olivia was out there, somewhere. Alive in some pocket of the cosmos.

Elliot was stunned into silence. "They're ETs," he murmured a moment later. "And you're telling me they're living among the bones of curious hikers and park rangers down there?"

Jessica nodded, and Elliot replied with his own tangled recollection of events. The video of Joseph, and the insight gleaned from *Black Eye* transcripts.

"I thought they were all nuts," he murmured.

"Who?"

"All those people I interviewed for *Black Eye*. I thought they made it all up."

"But how did the kids *get* here? Where are their parents?"

"A crashed craft – I'm guessing that's what Anthony means by *disaster*," Elliot murmured.

"A *craft*?" Jessica said, now feeling even more adrift and anchorless. Her life of burned toast and daydreams was dependable. The laundry piles, the headaches, the empty moments standing by the photocopier were reliably simple. But there was no map or compass to guide her here, no mundane explanations. "So all that stuff – that weird gunk – it was all onboard the craft?"

"I guess, but that must have been a long time ago. It's a whole ecosystem down there."

Jessica blanched at the implications of their theories. What knot were they untangling, and what hid in the weave?

"We've been inhaling all that stuff, and the fog…" She trailed off, now thinking of what might be swimming, mutating inside her. Had she exhaled all that glimmering dust, or was it now growing like moss in her lungs? Invading her cells, blooming in her bloodstream? And the fog – what was that doing to her battered brain cells, her frayed and jumpy nervous system?

"Jessica, what else did they say about the fog? Where's it coming from?"

"Anthony said it came from inside something he called the *crypt.* Whatever it is, he's scared of it. I guess it explains the nausea, the fatigue … why it feels like we're dreaming."

"And you really think Annabelle's trapped in there?"

"Maybe. But half of what Anthony says could be nonsense."

"I guess there's only one way to find out." Elliot beamed his flashlight at the entrance to the cave.

They crept inside the rock and shuffled into the tunnel.

"Can you remember anything about where you went with Olivia? Which direction?" Elliot said, his voice echoing.

"We might have turned left at the bottom of the chasm, but I was so disoriented, I can't even tell," Jessica whispered, replaying her newly recalled memories.

"It's happening again," Elliot said a moment later. "I feel like I'm dreaming."

"The mushrooms – I ate a handful today, and now I *know* I'm not dreaming."

"You *ate* that?"

"Anthony persuaded me because I felt like hell. It's some kind of antidote to the fog."

"You're braver than I am."

"Or dumber."

"Just don't let me fall asleep again."

"I won't," she murmured.

The tunnel seemed longer, narrower, without the dream-like haze distorting her sense of time. As they descended deeper underground, the same eerie particles of light shimmered, and this time, Jessica could see how they bounced and danced around her; how they scattered like dust across the rock and coated her skin.

They reached the passageway at the bottom of the chasm, where they searched for more clefts in the rock face, more tunnels.

"Here," Jessica whispered, spotlighting a small alcove. "This must be right under the mountain pass." She glanced up, shining the light at the looming chasm above.

The gap was no more than four feet tall, and just wide enough to enter. They crouched low, shuffling and stooping, then hiked down a rocky descent, into another long tunnel.

"Whatever's in the air is thicker here. I'm getting numb and weightless..."

A scuff interrupted the last of Elliot's words. They froze.

"Someone's ahead of us," Jessica whispered. The tunnel expanded. Soon a faint glow lit the distance, flickering burnished yellow. The light grew brighter, illuminating the rock, and the tunnel forked.

"Looks like it's coming from the left." Elliot aimed his light toward the flicker.

Candles burned in cans on the ground inside a small cavern, throwing smoky orange light against the rock. Cracks gaped in the cavern wall, leading to more tunnels, more caves, Jessica guessed.

"Oh my God." Jessica tightened her grip on the flashlight. She jumped when her feet hit paper, scraping the quiet.

"What the hell is this?" Elliot studied the marker-covered paper. Jagged words, numbers and symbols were scrawled over sheets on the ground and pasted to the walls. Tangled trellises of black ink, written by frantic hands.

"Did the kids really do this?" Jessica strained to read in the dim light.

"I guess so. None of it reaches that high."

A few words leaped from the chaos.

BURY THE DEDD

HIDE IN THE DARK

"Elliot, this is what they wrote on my living room wall."

"Bury the dead. Those graves, by the exit..." Elliot deciphered another stretch of typo-riddled script. "Wake the sleeping and run to the light," he read aloud. Condensation trickled, wrinkling the paper and smudging the ink. "Hide in the dark, don't let them trap you."

Jessica scuffed over more paper. "Someone's communicating with them. They're all hearing the same messages ... the same voices," she said, theorizing, unspooling more of the mystery aloud. "That's why they ran away. All of them. And they came down here to wake up whoever's asleep, if that's even real. Maybe it's all just metaphor. Unless these numbers, these symbols, really *mean* something."

"Or it's interference," Elliot murmured. "Something interrupting the transmission."

"*Transmission*?"

"Some kind of telepathy, or technology. Wherever they're from, they're light years ahead of us." Elliot sighed. "I can't believe I said any of that. It's about as absurd as my books."

"Their home planet – I wonder what it's like."

A shadow darkened the cavern behind them. They spun around. Joseph Baker stared back at them, eyes glinting under a black hood.

"Joseph," Jessica said, taking a step forward. "Did you write all this stuff on the wall?"

Joseph retreated.

"It's okay," Jessica said, louder this time. "Just tell me why you're following me."

But Joseph ran from the cavern, into a smaller alcove.

"Wait! I need to talk to you," Jessica called, running after him. They followed the sound of his feet hitting stone, into another narrow tunnel, but he quickly faded, lost to the dark.

"Damn it. Where do they run to? I keep hearing them, but we never find them." The rock seemed to vibrate to the echo of Jessica's voice.

"I guess we keep searching."

The tunnel stretched on, diverting into dead ends and circular detours.

"It's a maze," Elliot muttered.

Soon tiny rivulets snaked around their feet, merging and widening, deepening to a river that blocked their passage.

"Maybe if we climb a little, we can get around it." Elliot shone his light at an incline in the rock to their left, which formed rugged steppingstones and a narrow path. The water rippled, oil-black. Condensation splashed, dappling the surface.

Edging their way up the incline, they balanced with one hand against the tunnel wall.

But minutes in, the rock grew slick and slimy, and they both wobbled, teetered, then slipped into the water below. Jessica splashed and stumbled, gasping at the water bleeding through her jeans, between her toes. Elliot cursed, then found her hand. Flashlights dancing over the rock, they searched for a way out.

Elliot aimed his light fifty feet deeper into the tunnel, where the ridge was low and wide enough to reach. "This way." His words rang out among the patter and drip, the soft slush and whoosh.

A slither, a swoosh around Jessica's calves made her stiffen.

"Did you see that?" Her voice was almost lost to fright.

"No, but I definitely felt it."

A ripple broke the surface. Jessica squeezed Elliot's hand, but the rest of her wouldn't move.

"We need to get out of here. Come on," Elliot whispered. "Just walk twenty, thirty steps and we can climb out."

She waded one step, two steps, three steps through the water, only shallow breaths leaving her lungs.

Nine steps in – or maybe it was ten, she'd lost count – a tensile muscle swam between her legs, and an oval head surfaced, red eyes blinking as it submerged again. Jessica stifled a scream.

"What the hell was that?" she stammered.

"I don't know, but now we really need to go." Elliot tugged her hand. His palm was as tense as her own.

She tried to move, but her knees were weak. Each step felt lead-heavy, weighed down by soaked denim and dread. Her shoes threatened to slip from her feet. But she took four more steps, five, then six.

The water rippled again. Another black shadow crested. Glossy scales, the whip of a slick torso. Jessica choked another scream, fumbling to keep hold of her flashlight.

"Come on, we're almost there." Elliot tugged at her hand again, refusing to let her go when she wavered.

They reached the ridge, then heaved themselves onto it. Slumped against the granite, water streaming from their clothes, they caught their breath.

"What the hell were those … those *creatures*?"

"I don't know, but now I can barely move. I feel numb all over," Elliot said. "Jessica, I..."

A murmur echoed from deeper inside the tunnel.

"But Elliot, we're getting close," Jessica whispered. "I can hear them. I think we can make it. Look, the ridge gets wider."

"You go. I'll be right here. Whatever's in the air, it's way worse around here."

"But I can't just leave you here."

"I'm fine. Just tired. I'll wait for you."

Jessica beamed her flashlight at the water. "I don't think this is a good idea."

"I'll probably just fall asleep here. Please, go look for Annabelle."

"But what if those reptiles can crawl?"

"No, they'll never get this high out of the water. They're probably harmless. Just ugly."

"Okay," she whispered, reluctantly. "Don't move. I won't be long."

Jessica edged deeper into the tunnel, then followed the slippery ridge as it curved left around a corner, into another passageway.

The rockface was split by dozens of alcoves. She studied each one, listening for voices. A faint hush led her to the smallest alcove, no more than two feet high and a foot wide. Jessica tucked her flashlight into the waist of her jeans, then crept inside, hands searching for rocks in her path.

The sound of her own breathing filled the narrow passageway. Her wet jeans scraped across granite.

The hush morphed to a rhythmic, hollow hum, louder as Jessica crawled deeper. The air grew more humid, clogged with vapor. She suppressed a cough.

Ahead, a light flickered. She inched forward, watching the light come into focus and multiply. More candles, she realized. Flames dancing, but this time obscured, as if veiled behind a mist. The hum was louder now, a chorus of voices.

Another two feet deeper into the tunnel, silhouettes emerged from the dark, swaying, feathering into a dense black fog. Children held candles, chanting words she couldn't understand.

The tunnel opened to a cave, where she could make out ghost-like figures, cloaked in fog.

The crypt.

Jessica crouched on the ground, watching the sway, the flicker, listening to the strange, monotonous chant. Small bare feet poked out from the black cloud. Fingers, a flick of hair, and the flash of opaline eyes.

She climbed to her feet, but the children were too lost in their swaying, their chanting to notice. The candles cast a show of shadows against the granite, blurred in the vapor.

"Annabelle?" Jessica called, reaching for her flashlight.

Silence fell on the cavern, then whispering. A few eyes found Jessica, and a scream echoed, then another, another still, until the cavern sung with the cacophony of crying, feet scurrying. The children dispersed with their candles, vanishing into the fog, leaving Jessica in darkness.

She turned on her flashlight and searched the cave. The beam lit just a few feet ahead, the light fading into black fog. The ground was littered with debris, and Jessica yelped as her foot collided with something hard. She crouched to study it.

A large bone. A human femur among debris. Jessica shuddered, then walked another few steps, disoriented by the cloud, and again her foot hit something hard – rock hard and thigh-high.

The flashlight illuminated etchings. Symbols on a strange, cocoon-like pod. Jessica stepped deeper into the fog, but a sudden tiredness descended, clouding her head, weakening her stride.

Oh God, the mushrooms. The effect's wearing off. Get me out of here.

Jessica crawled back into the tunnel and shuffled through, moving as fast as her hands and knees would allow. Thoughts blurred, as if they, too, had become lost in the fog, and the dream-like, fluid haze returned. She was heavy and tired one moment, feather-light the next. Time slowed, sped, merging each moment.

By the time she reached the narrow ridge by the water, she wasn't sure if she'd been gone an hour or ten minutes, but worse still, there was no sign of Elliot. She called his name, and it bounced from the rock, the echo answered with silence.

I have to find him. But I have to get out of here, before I fall asleep and never wake up.

Jessica ran through tunnels, calling out Elliot's name, losing herself in the network of passageways, the endless turns and forks in her path.

I'll get stuck down here. I'll die down here, like Olivia warned. This is what she was afraid of. The snakes, the bones, the fog.

Her need to escape throttled every other, thwarting the fatigue that wanted to floor her. Landmarks guided her out. A rubble of stones, a sharp turn, the creeping moss on the tunnel walls, the fresh air that told her she'd almost escaped.

Moonlight lit the exit. She crawled through, staggered to her feet, took ten steps, and collapsed in grass.

Chapter 38

Monday, April 18, 2022

Elliot lay on his back on a patchy yellow lawn. He blinked, and a garden gnome came into focus. Clouds hung above him, but they'd already released their burden of rain. Most of it was in his shoes, his jeans, he figured. He stood up, sopping wet clothes clinging to his skin, and threw a bewildered glance at a swampy swimming pool, where leaves and a dead bird glistened in dew and rain.

The back yard belonged to a house that seemed empty, some derelict vacation home, but he ran toward a main road before he found out for sure. From the road, he could see The Arbor dug into the hillside above, and the lake below, still and moody gray. He'd wandered into a subdivision on the edge of the state park, but when?

The last thing he remembered was a sudden, desperate impulse to escape whatever had dulled his mind and burdened his body. An ominous, terrifying premonition that if he didn't get out there and then, he never would. He'd staggered out of the cave, roamed the forest in a heavy torpor, delirious and horrified, until he'd collapsed under a tree. Then, hours later, still under the spell of whatever black magic had possessed him, he'd rolled into someone's back yard, it seemed.

"The fog," he murmured.

Jessica. Where is she? Did she escape the fog? The mushrooms. They kept her awake. She's fine. Asleep somewhere, I bet. But if she isn't, I'll never forgive myself.

He jogged out of the subdivision, into the park, then took the trail that led to the small hole in the rock. He crawled through the gap, back into the cave, and fished the flashlight from his pocket. The winding passageways led him to the small crevice directly under the mountain pass, and he steeled against the desire to crumple and fall asleep again.

But his search was futile. He called Jessica's name, retracing their route, until he knew he couldn't go farther – not without the mushy fungal antidote that Anthony had given Jessica.

Time was running out. He still had to shower, pack, and throw his suitcase in his rental car. He'd have just enough time to scrape his head together and send Ruth the damn book review she'd begged for, then catch his flight back home.

She got out, he told himself. *If she was still down here, I would have found her by now. But she probably thinks I'm dead. Eaten by a reptile or trapped in supernatural fog.*

As he jogged out of the park, toward The Arbor, regret descended on him. The thought of leaving Driftwood without finding Jessica, without solving the mystery that had led him here, seemed to snuff out half the light streaming from beyond the clouds.

A memory from the night before sent his hand reaching into his back pocket. Yes, he'd definitely saved her number in his phone. He grabbed the phone and grumbled a string of expletives. The screen was cracked and waterlogged. A little lagoon under splintered glass.

His hope dissolved, and he jammed the phone back into his pocket. But as he released his grip, something slid against his finger. A little white button, as pearly as the moon. Staring at it, another memory flitted to the front of his mind.

I could've sworn she told me she worked in a library.

Chapter 39

Monday, April 18, 2022

Jessica stirred at the sound of her alarm, wincing as she turned. Her tumble off the cliff had left an ugly bruise along her torso. The earthy scent of the rainwater that had soaked her on the run home now filled the room. How long had she slept, after creeping inside and checking the time? An hour, max.

She tried to silence the alarm, but it wouldn't respond. The screen was obscured by a watermark and vertical lines. She groaned, powered off the phone, and covered her face with her hands. She was wired and exhausted, as if her eyes had never closed. She couldn't decide if she was too hot or too cold.

Elliot. He got out. Tell me he got out.

He's fine, he just left before he fell asleep, she told herself. *And now he's wondering where I am. Who I am. Or maybe he's worried I'm stuck down there – maybe he thinks I'm dead.*

There was something else to worry about, though. She stood up, tiptoed to Mark's bedroom, and found Andrew still asleep, his clothes in a pile on the floor by a beer bottle. Sandy hair ruffled, an arm draped over the edge, and a beefy erection straining his underwear.

As she thought of all the reasons why he needed to get the hell out of her house, moments from the night before returned to her. The bliss and the horror, replayed crisp and clear. This time, there was no dream-like haze clouding her memory, because the mushrooms had worked their miracle.

The red-eyed reptiles and the kids swaying in the fog; Joseph's gleaming eyes under his hood – she remembered all of it, just like she remembered the beat of Elliot's heart, the warmth of his palms on her skin. The lack of him was already a draining, punchy kind of ache.

Andrew snored, delicately. She nudged him awake.

"What the hell happened to you?" He sat up, ran a hand through his hair, and croaked out his words from the fog of sleep.

She was in no mood to lie. "I needed to go see a friend again."

"You're acting so damn weird," he muttered. "I guess this guy must be really something."

"Yes, he is." She pushed damp hair from her face. She would've been humiliated, if she wasn't so tired, so sick of him.

"You're *welcome*, by the way."

"Huh?"

"For getting you home last night."

She considered a rebuttal but didn't care enough. Her tumble into the lake seemed like days ago, and morning dramatics with Andrew felt like a tired rerun on daytime TV.

"Yeah, thanks," she mumbled.

Half the buttons on her shirt had escaped their buttonholes. She marched to the dryer, where she pulled out wrinkled clothes.

"Can you give me a ride?" he yelled. His belt buckle clinked as he dressed.

Shit. Her car was still in the lot by the park.

"I left my car downtown," she yelled back.

She heard a sigh, a scrape as he grabbed his gun. His phone rang, and he answered by grunting his own name.

"How can both kids have errors in their bloodwork? I'm not a scientist, but…" His voice rose, then faded when he pulled the bedroom door shut. Jessica's heart flung itself against her ribs.

He hung up, then rattled Jessica with a sudden turn of the door handle. After a huff down the hallway, he left with a gentle slam of the front door. Jessica's shoulders relaxed.

Thirty minutes until she had to leave, and she was still in her pajamas. She busied herself with what to wear. What to throw in her purse, and where the hell she'd left her leather flats, the ones that didn't have holes in the soles. She dragged butter across her toast and remembered Elliot's lips on her neck, the rise of her hips as he'd pulled her closer.

All that, before she remembered that they'd swapped numbers. Her heart took another leap against her ribs.

But her phone. Her damn fogged-up phone. She opened the pantry and grabbed a bag of rice, poured it into a Ziplock bag, and stuffed her phone into it.

In the shower, she lingered to let the hot water melt the tension in her back, then toweled off and threw on pants, yanked a shirt from a hanger, and tried to hide the bags under her eyes. She scrambled to button her blouse.

A weird little keepsake.

She grabbed last night's jeans from the floor. A small white button fell from the pocket, into her palm, and she sank into a spell of longing-laced bliss. She threaded the button onto a thin chain from her jewelry box and fastened it around her neck.

But work, and all the hell of it, was waiting. She ran to the front door clutching her copy of *Black Eye,* because having it with her was like having a little of Elliot, and stepped into the morning sun. The button bounced on her collarbone as she jogged to work.

The library lobby smelled of fresh photocopies and musty jackets. Jessica hiked the stairs and slid into the office.

Rosemary lowered her bifocals. "The Walrus is looking for you," she muttered, then rolled the sleeves of her sensible flannel shirt.

"He can kiss my ass," Jessica hissed back, flushed and warm despite the AC. Rosemary recoiled behind her cubicle screen.

Jessica searched for her uncomfortable chair and found it tucked under Tabitha's desk. She brushed off Cheeto dust from the seat, then doused it in lens cleaner. "Fucking gross," she whispered on her final swipe.

She sat down and checked that the button was still on the chain around her neck. Yes, it was still real, even inside the concrete monolith she worked in, with its buzzing fluorescent lights and narrow windows, too small for sunlight or suicide. But Elliot's number was still hidden behind the drowned screen of her phone, which she'd left in the bag on her kitchen counter.

I'll email him instead. But did he really make it out of that tunnel? I should run back there, she decided, eyeing the door. But she had no more mushrooms, and the thought of going anywhere near those reptiles filled her with dread. *And what if someone sees me crawling inside that rock? I can't go in daylight. Andrew knows something's up.*

Chatter distracted her from arguing with herself. The office was busier than usual, tired faces huddling around the water cooler and printer. The lack of privacy was infuriating – she was shipwrecked in a sea of seventies flooring with Tabitha, exposed to wandering eyes, at a desk against the wall by the door. She'd have to wait until at least three people resigned, or died, to move a rung up the seating ladder.

Just a moment. That's all she needed. A minute alone to navigate to Elliot's website, send an email away from prying eyes. She opened her browser, began to type, then abandoned her plan. A herd of women from accounting had gathered behind her, chatting about grocery store coupons and munching their way through someone's coffee cake. "I stocked up on Febreze. It's just perfect for refreshing my Pomeranian's blankets," said Margery, the accounts payable clerk. Jessica flexed her fingers, suppressed a sigh.

Coffee would be essential to get through the morning, she decided. That or a lobotomy. The air was stale, the colors drained and flat. Everyone seemed gray and pudding-limp.

In the kitchen, burned coffee stank on a hotplate. She grabbed a mug that had *Badass Grandma* emblazoned on both sides in electric purple font, as it was the only one unsoiled by other people's coffee stains.

"Jessica," the Walrus barked from across the office. "Try to get to work on time. Lots of new titles to be cataloged. Aisles 1 to 10, A through J."

"Got it," she mumbled.

He sauntered into the kitchen. Corduroys and a plaid shirt, and some spiffy suspenders, she noticed. Rolled shoulders, a bowtie and Birkenstocks.

"Might be a little chaotic today," he added. His chins undulated and shook the random hairs poking out like dead flies from his flesh.

"No problem, William." She looked at mugs on the drying rack instead of him.

"Good, good!" he said to her breasts, then turned on his corked heels and squeaked out.

She remembered her car, still sitting in the lot by the park, and borrowed Tabitha's phone to text Mark, asking for a ride over lunch. *I'll bring burritos,* he replied.

Tabitha hiccupped, and William chortled about his fishing trip. Angeliki, the IT manager from Greece who in no way appreciated the nickname *Leaky Angela,* yelled about server upgrades and ISP outages. Apparently, there would be internet interruptions all day.

Jessica sighed, loud enough to stir a response from Tabitha, who was chewing on her unicorn pencil. "You look like baked shit, Jessie. Like you didn't sleep a wink."

"Thanks. I didn't."

Rosemary gushed and tutted about Annabelle and how useless the sheriff had been at leading the search. Jessica survived the morning because of headphones and the promise of a burrito with Mark. There was some loud maneuver of files going on behind her, and any hope of emailing Elliot vanished into the commotion of boxes and internet interruptions. "New project in the archives section," Tabitha explained through a mouthful of cereal. "A bunch of old police reports."

Jessica's thoughts wandered to Olivia. Was she still alive? Living in another world, another universe? And what about Annabelle? Was she really trapped in the fog? Jessica considered running to the park again, but seconds later, the Walrus dumped a tower of books on her desk.

"These all have errors. I know I can trust you to fix them," he breathed into her ear.

Half an hour before lunch, Jessica began to cough. Not a regular cough from the dust billowing from the antique HVAC system, or from Mr Fucky's caustic cleaning fumes. It was a grating, hacking cough, so loud that bifocals peered above cubicle walls, and the Walrus poked his head out from his mildew-scented office.

She ran to the bathroom and leaned over a sink. The cough became a choke, a gag into the porcelain, until she hacked up a slimy film of iridescent light. It landed in the sink and released its spores – shimmering dandelion seeds that danced into the bleach-stung air and vanished. Whatever it was that glimmered underground was still inside her lungs, her sinuses. And now it was escaping her.

Her heart flung itself into another round of palpitations. *What have I done? How much does Andrew know? Errors in their bloodwork…*

A door slammed in the hallway, and Jessica jumped. The button hit her chin as she leaned over the sink. She stared at her own eyes until they blurred to a blotting of black and brown. The gunk slid down the drain. Reluctantly, she returned to her desk.

"Jessie, you sure you're okay? You look like you're about to puke," Tabitha whispered. "You want some Pepto Bismol? I got some Alka-Seltzer, too."

"No, I'm fine. Must have been something I ate."

At 11:55, Jessica ran down the stairs, through the revolving doors to a cool breeze and a light gray sky. She waited for Mark on a bench by the boardwalk, anxious because she still hadn't emailed Elliot. *As soon as I get home after work.*

The sun crept out, splashing gold all over the lake. Someone tapped her on the shoulder, and she turned to find Mark at her side with two burritos.

"Lunch in the woods?" She climbed into his front seat. The car was a wreck of candy wrappers and papers. His windbreaker and a box of jumper cables sat on the back seat, next to a *Hellboy* omnibus hardcover. Mark handed her the burrito, and she pried it from the wrapper.

"How come your car's there?" he said, reversing out of the parking lot.

"I ran the trails then grabbed a drink with Tabitha." She regretted lying.

Mark nodded slowly, as if he was trying to decide if he believed her.

"Speaking of drinks, I heard you had a few with Jamie."

Mark beamed. "Yeah, I did. I was thinking about getting her flowers. What flowers does she like?"

Jessica sighed, quietly, as an old longing to protect her brother surfaced. A longing to protect him from himself, and his own romance illiteracy.

"Mark, if you're interested in Jamie, the best thing you can do is play it cool. Act like you barely even care. Tell her there's a book in her store you really want to read, and turn up with coffee. But please don't buy her flowers."

He turned onto the back road. "Too early, you think?"

"The flowers can wait until you're at the hospital, when she's birthed your first child."

"Women are so damn complicated. I thought you all liked flowers."

They parked in the lot and walked into the forest, still demolishing their burritos. They found a fallen tree in a shady hollow and sat down.

"Are you still being stalked?"

Jessica shook her head. *A can of worms too writhing and strange to open over lunch.*

"Tell me you fixed the window."

"I couldn't get a hold of anyone over the weekend. This week," she said.

"That's a weird necklace." Mark looked at her neck, chewing through tortilla and cheese.

Jessica felt the weight of everything she couldn't say. "Thanks."

Mark led himself into a tangent about an upcoming comic conference, and Jessica zoned out, into the blurring leaves.

"I guess Jamie told you about Elliot Reed."

Jessica hid her nerves in the wrapper of her burrito. "Yeah, she said he was at Nexus Coffee."

"Yup. I guess he really is writing about Driftwood. I'm surprised you're not more … I don't know, *giddy* about that?"

"I'm giddy. I just hide it well."

"When did you get contacts?"

"Huh?" she said through a munch.

"Did you get those colored contacts or something? Your eyes look kind of different."

"It's um … eye drops." She buried her face in the wrapper again and pushed her knees together to stop them from shaking.

Chapter 40

Monday, April 18, 2022

Looks like a literary gulag, where Stalin would've locked up the books he didn't like, Elliot decided, stepping into the lobby of Driftwood College Library. *This place is freezing, and the windows are as narrow as tray slots.*

He climbed the stairs and glanced over the railing at students filing out of the library, remembering the months he'd spent aching over his thesis in grad school, while his roommate made waffles in a T-shirt and slippers and nothing else. And he remembered how lucky he'd felt to land the job at the paper, cranking out skimmable prose for a paycheck that was swallowed by rent.

Nearing the top of the stairs, he clung to a fading hope that he might find Jessica. He'd already searched the two other libraries in Driftwood, which had only yielded a dismissive headshake and a curious stare.

But if there was no Jessica here either, he'd comb through the archives, he'd decided. Do something useful, other than search hopelessly for a woman he'd never met in daylight.

At the top of the stairs, he found an open office door by a scratched chrome sign that read *Cataloging and Acquisitions.* A well-thumbed copy of *Black Eye* sat on a desk between a coffee mug and a stack of textbooks. He searched for any sign of life without putting a foot too far inside the door.

A woman appeared from behind a cubicle wall and stared at him over reading glasses.

"Can I help you?"

I'm looking for Jessica. Curly hair, about 5'6." She likes to read my books…

"I'm looking for the archives department," he said instead. *I'll wait until the owner of that book gets back to her desk. Maybe then I won't have to ask.*

She hesitated. A dash of a smile, and then she moved toward the door. "I'm headed that way. Marianne'll help you."

He followed the woman down a dark hallway that smelled of bleach and the yellowed pages of unloved books. A few lonely typists hit keys behind cubicle walls. A sigh and a cough here and there. The sound of life passing by.

They reached a room – a chaos of boxes and files – and a woman greeted them with another scant smile. She sighed into the dust that glimmered in a ray of sunlight from a tray-slot window. Elliot guessed she'd been there as long as the scratched sign by the cataloging office. Piles of manila folders towered, one after another on a long table. Staff pulled more files out of Xerox paper boxes.

"1990 through 2005 over there," a guy with a six-inch beard said to another, then took a bite out of a nasty looking donut

"Excuse all this," the woman said, toying with a paperclip. "Can I help you?"

"I was hoping I could take a look at your police records," Elliot said.

"Oh lord, I'd love to help you, but as you can see..." she trailed off, throwing a hand through the air.

He let silence hang between them as he smiled at her, a trick he'd learned years ago, when he'd had deadlines to meet and no one would say a word. She shifted her feet and blushed, until she talked to fill the void.

"This project for the sheriff's office ... all these files haven't been scanned and uploaded. They didn't digitize anything until about fifteen years ago." She moved a hole punch and other vintage office supplies aside to make room for more files. "What are you looking for, specifically? We mostly have historical records in that back room ... births, deaths, property deeds from the last hundred years or so. But there are some police records, too, I believe."

The men with beards disappeared, mumbling about coffee.

"Those files right there," Elliot said, pointing to the pile that the beards had been stacking. "Did I hear they were archives from 1990 through 2005?"

"Yes, but I don't think I'm supposed to let you look through those. They moved all these files over in such a hurry, and they need another audit. The sheriff's archive custodian told me he wanted to oversee that, and he won't be here for another hour. I'm so sorry. If you come back in a few days..."

A voice interrupted from the hallway. Something about a meeting in the staff room, and then feet shuffling, echoes from inside an office.

"William's birthday," Marianne said, as if Elliot knew the man. "I have to go to the staff room and help set up. Like I said, if you come back in a few days…"

"Of course. No problem. Thank you," he replied, and headed for the stairs.

But three steps into the hallway, he almost collided with a woman covered in crumbs, who was clutching the book he'd seen on the desk. She grinned beneath a hive of wiry red hair. Her eyes seemed too big for her head.

"Elliot Reed," she whispered, then sunk her hand into his arm.

"Yes?" He ignored her grip.

"Could you please sign this? It's for Jessica." She handed him the book.

"Jessica?" He took the book and opened the front cover, swallowing, as if he could swallow his own racing heart.

"She's read everything you've written about fifty times. And she acts like she doesn't adore you." She giggled.

Whispering spread down the hallway. A man in suspenders walked by.

"Is that right?" he said, holding back a smile, and the feeling he'd had when he'd stared at the sign by the door returned. A sensation that wanted to be more than an inkling, that wanted to flood him.

Jessica? Could it be the same Jessica? How many could there be in Driftwood? How many who read my books?

She handed him a pen from behind her ear and he opened the cover. He could have sworn she'd told him her last name, but he'd lost it somewhere along the hallways of sleep. What if he asked? The thought of raising questions, stirring gossip among this odd gaggle of librarians – no, he couldn't do it.

He was frozen, mad at himself for stumbling through thoughts with a fuzzy head. The red-haired woman was staring right at him, still biting her lip, and he couldn't think. *It has to be her,* he decided, momentarily. But the coffee mug on her desk had *Badass Grandma* written on it, for God's sake. Jessica was many things, but she definitely wasn't someone's sassy grandmother.

He signed the book, reached into his pocket, and grabbed the origami lion he'd found stuck in the planks of a bench two days ago. He tucked the lion under the front cover of the book, then handed it back to the woman covered in crumbs, who was looking at him like she might want to take a bite out of him.

"Is Jessica around?"

"She ran out for lunch." She hushed, like she'd shared a secret.

"That's too bad." He straightened but sank inside. There was a bench in the hallway. *I could wait there,* he considered. No, he couldn't do that. Jesus Christ. If it wasn't *his* Jessica, every option would be horrifyingly awkward. And he couldn't hang around the dusty shelves all afternoon. Not if he was going to catch his flight.

"Tabitha, you're supposed to be organizing the beverages!" the woman in the reading glasses called from the cataloging room. A few others carried Tupperware and soda bottles.

"Coming!" she barked back like a drill sergeant, then grabbed the book and walked down the hallway. "Thanks, Elliot," she said over her shoulder, now cute as a button, then ran into the office.

He moved toward the stairs, lost in regret and furious with himself, then snapped out of it. The archives room was empty. Everyone was distracted with a birthday party, and the custodian still hadn't arrived to scrub the files of anything useful.

He slipped inside, ducking out once to check the coast was clear. The pile of records from the sheriff's office still lay on the table. He flicked through, stopping now and then to listen for footfalls.

Whoever's been archiving and storing all these files is an idiot, he decided. It was mostly a jumble of traffic violations and domestic violence reports. A hold-up at a gas station ten miles out of town, and a failed attempt to rob the Driftwood Credit Union. He attacked another stack. More parking tickets and DUIs. Voices drifted from the cataloging room, a door opened down the hallway, and he picked up the pace, scanning each page.

He found something, right before giving up. A handful of police reports with Olivia Garcia's name on them. He grabbed the papers and folded them into his notebook.

He walked out, past a janitor who looked like he had nothing but hate for the world, then stole another glance at the cataloging office. The desk was still empty. He walked down the stairs, out the revolving doors, into the gathering clouds.

Chapter 41

Monday, April 18, 2022

Jessica flew through the library doors, a little nauseous from a stomach full of burrito. She slid into the office and faked a professional calm, organizing the clutter on her desk. But the office seemed empty, except for voices flowing out of the staff room.

At last, I can email Elliot. She logged on to her computer. Elliot's website loaded, and her fingers hovered over the keyboard.

Just write something. Anything. Do it.

But she was too wired and tired to put one word in front of another. She walked to the kitchen to refill her coffee cup, deciding she'd email him as soon as she got back to her desk.

"You're late!" Tabitha hissed, creeping out of the staff room.

"I had to go get my car!" Jessica hissed back, holding her refilled cup in her hands.

"I guess you didn't look inside your book yet, Jessie. He was here!" Tabitha crept to her desk.

The coffee quivered. Jessica gripped the mug handle. "*What?*"

"That writer you like. The one with the baby blues. He was *right here*. I bet you wanna take a look inside that book." She giggled and dug a Twizzler out of its wrapper.

"Don't mess with me, Tabitha." Jessica wanted to look up, tell her to be quiet while she walked back to her desk. But now the coffee lapped at the rim of her mug. Its ebb and flow gained momentum. A tiny splash.

"Ten minutes ago, Jessie. He was looking for something in the archives room. In Driftwood! Who could believe it? I *touched* him."

The cup felt heavy – heavy and burning hot. The heat scorched her fingers, but the rest of her was just a heart and mind suspended in jelly. The coffee kept building its wave.

And then Marianne chimed in, as she poked her gray head from around the staff room door. About how she couldn't believe it. About how she'd never forget meeting him. About how he'd asked to see something in the archives, and she'd probably come off cold because she'd tried so hard to keep her cool. A nod, then she disappeared back inside the staff room, into chatter about cake and a waft of candle smoke.

The coffee wave swelled, sloshing back and forth. Jessica let go of the mug so it hit the floor with a crash, and the liquid scalded her feet and ankles. Chips and shards flew across the floor and coffee splashed up a filing cabinet. Tabitha scrambled to help Jessica, her blouse billowing like a mainsail as she raced across the floor.

"Fuck!" Jessica whispered, again and again. Tabitha skidded through coffee on her way to the paper towels.

"You're welcome, by the way," Tabitha whispered, wiping off the filing cabinet. Jessica cowered at hearing the phrase for the second time that day. She scrubbed at the floor with a wad of paper towels.

"I told them you went to IT, so you gotta pretend your computer's all messed up. They threw a birthday party for the Walrus. We were all supposed to be there," Tabitha said, tossing mug chips in the trash.

"Screw his shitty birthday." Jessica sat at her desk and sponged coffee off her pants, furious with herself for missing Elliot, for throwing coffee all over the floor. Her paperback sat on her desk, the front cover arching into the air, teasing Jessica to flip it open. She opened it and found the origami lion that she'd made on Saturday morning. On the first page, she read:

Jessica,
Sorry I missed you.
Elliot
X

Overwhelm wanted to floor her with another embarrassing episode, but she scraped herself together, clutching the book. She was running on fumes and a ragged heartbeat, and she longed for solitude, her crumpled bed covers.

"Jessie, you look like you're gonna faint," Tabitha whispered. Her heap of hair had come undone and stuck out in all directions, like a rebel topiary.

"I'm okay," Jessica mumbled.

"Why did he give you that origami lion? That's kind of neat … but kind of weird, too."

"It's a long story," Jessica said, then changed the subject before Tabitha could probe any further. "You said he was looking for something in the archives?"

"Yes, he was right outside the door when I found him. I asked him to sign your book."

"Do you know what he was looking at?"

"I heard him ask Marianne about the folders from the sheriff's office. But she said he wasn't allowed to look through them."

"So he left empty-handed?"

"I don't know, Jessie. I didn't see anything. Except..."

"Except *what*?"

"Except, Rosemary asked me to grab paper towels from the storeroom. I ran out to get them, and I stuck my head in the door. He was gone, but I swear there was an empty manila folder open on the desk. I think he took a file."

The staff room door opened, and voices burst out. Jessica stood up and brushed the dust off her pants, steeling against another wave of dizziness. She was lightheaded one minute, lead-heavy the next – a head full of feathers and stones.

The room seemed darker. Clouds had appeared on the horizon all over again – heavy gray-black pillows, just visible through the sliver of a window. Feet shuffled in the hallway. Marianne was talking to someone, her voice a pitch higher than usual. Jessica peered around the doorframe to find Deputy Willis pacing back and forth with his hat in his hand. He looked pale and tired like a wrung-out dish rag. Jessica ducked her head back inside.

"Willis!" another voice yelled, too loud for a library. Sheriff Clarke.

"Yes, sir?"

"What the hell's going on here?" the sheriff barked. "I didn't tell you to sign off on this! They already unpacked all this shit? I told you I needed to look through them one more time. Get those files back in those boxes, God damn it. Well don't just stand there! Jesus!"

"I'm sorry, sir. I thought you wanted me to..."

"Stop thinking and start doing what the hell I tell you to do! Some of those records go with cases we're still working on, damn it. I swear. Is Harding here? Where's Harding?"

Jessica heard more shuffling, and now grunting – Deputy Willis and two interns, both with long beards and patterned sweaters, were carrying the Xerox boxes back to the sheriff's office.

Jessica held on to her chair – the walls seemed to be closing in, expanding again. She needed fresh air.

"I have to go to the clinic. I'm getting sick," she lied, tucking her book into her purse.

"Be sure to log any time off in the system, Jessica," the Walrus said. His version of "feel better."

Hail pounded the roof as she walked down the stairs, and thunder rattled the skies. Andrew stood by the revolving doors, taking notes as Mr Fucky whispered. He raised an eyebrow when Jessica passed, then returned to the murmuring janitor.

Jessica jogged along the boardwalk, hoping her phone had dried out so she could call Elliot. The hail sprayed the wooden planks and bounced from the asphalt. Lake water churned and crashed against the wet sand, but the hail's rattle drowned out the frothy gush of the tide. Nearing the end of the boardwalk, she looked ahead at the parking lot, just in time to see Andrew rushing to his car, clutching a manila folder.

Chapter 42

Monday, April 18, 2022

Elliot drank espresso in a dimly lit coffee shop by a decaying strip mall on the outskirts of town. A bored barista looked out at the parking lot, and nineties radio serenaded empty booths.

Ignoring his coffee, Elliot stared down at the police report from the library. He wasn't sure what unsettled him more, the words on the paper, or the impulse that had spurred him to steal it. He pushed the burned espresso across the table and re-read the report:

On 10-9-1999 at approximately 2309 hrs, I, Ptl. Holmes #15 received a radio call to respond to reports of a disturbance at Driftwood General Hospital. Upon arrival at the hospital's emergency room, I observed a white female nurse who appeared to be in severe distress. Two hospital orderlies were restraining her when I arrived at the scene. One of the orderlies, Sean A. Galvin, reported they had restrained her because she was running down the hallway and causing a disturbance. The nurse, Abigail Barnes, agreed to remain calm and speak with me privately in a vacant physician's office. When I asked Barnes why she was upset, she claimed that a patient admitted at 2200 hrs, Olivia Garcia, aged six, caused objects in her room to move and fall

> *to the floor without touching them. Barnes was under the impression that Garcia has supernatural abilities, and claimed the incident distressed her. Upon further questioning, it was clear that Barnes had no proof or evidence of the event she described. Approximately ten minutes into our conversation she altered her account of the incident to deny it happened, and claimed that work-related stress and insomnia had caused her to hallucinate.*

Elliot turned over the report and found a short list of notes penciled on a piece of paper tucked between the pages. Bullets scribbled after some detective had read a transcript from an interview with the Garcias, he guessed.

Admitted for severe stomach pains and possible psychological disturbance, he made out, between a string of words he couldn't decipher.

He folded the report back into his notebook. *If the sheriff's department knows this much, what else do they know? Or has the incident since been forgotten, lost in their mess of a filing system? Has anyone put the pieces together? What if they're days … moments from figuring it all out?* He drummed his fingers on the table, anxiety unfolding. Soon he began to cough.

Just a tickle, at first, until it burst into a hacking cough, grating against his throat. He ran to the bathroom.

It was a glimmering glob, whatever landed on the porcelain. Nausea churned his stomach. Or perhaps it was panic – he couldn't tell because his lungs were leaping into his throat. After he hacked and gagged for another minute, a cluster of luminous spores escaped their goo and dispersed into the air.

Elliot gripped the sink and stared at the gunk. A sudden desire to run, to self-preserve, took hold. For the first time since he'd arrived in Driftwood, his fear demanded more attention than his curiosity. The last three days crashed like breaking waves, swirled like a whirlpool.

What have I done? What's this stuff going to do to me?

He took a deep breath and tried to shake it off, but his anxiety only spiraled. *What if someone saw me walking through the park, toward that rock? Jessica said a detective was already following Anthony. She said those kids lured people into the fog to die. And what happened all those nights, after I passed out in the grass? If this gets out, they'll quarantine me, lock me up. They'll decide I'm a threat to national security. I'll never see daylight again.*

He splashed water on his face. His phone was well and truly dead, and the clock on the wall outside told him his flight was just two hours away. The last time he'd checked his email on his laptop, Jessica still hadn't contacted him, and he had no way of knowing if she'd tried to call.

But I need to leave, before it's too late.

He cursed, coughed again. It wasn't that simple. If Annabelle Lewis really was stuck inside that cave, then he and Jessica were probably the only people who could help her. Her only chance of getting out of there. *And Jessica – I don't even know if she's OK. If she got out. What if that wasn't the same Jessica at the library? What if I wrote in some other woman's book?*

There was too much to consider, too much to figure out, and he'd run out of time.

If we didn't find Annabelle last night, we probably never will. Not without getting stuck in there and dissolving into dust and bones. What if it's a trap? What if those kids want to lure us in there, too? And I have no proof that Annabelle's even there. No, I have to go.

He slumped back down at his table, half relieved that he'd made a sensible decision, half disappointed in his own lack of courage.

Stalling, he grabbed his laptop from his bag and checked his email one more time. Still nothing from Jessica. *It's been three days, and she still hasn't contacted me. The strangest freaks send me emails, but she hasn't.*

Drumming his finger on the table, he remembered how she'd left him lying in the grass two nights ago. How she'd been in such a hurry to run home. And he could've sworn she'd seemed flustered when he'd asked if she was single. What if there was someone else? Someone asleep in her bed?

The thought was a slap in the face.

Conflict. I didn't want any damn conflict. This is too messy, too fucked up and fraught.

He checked the local news for any mention of Annabelle Lewis.

Police continue search for missing girl, the *Driftwood Times* headline read. *Locals on high alert.*

A headache began to tap his skull. *You can't just leave now, asshole,* he told himself, but his hands were already teasing out a bill from his wallet to leave by his coffee, and soon he was headed for the door.

The skies roared as the car hit the highway. Clouds hung like a puffy counterpane, glowering above the mountain ridge. The first beads of hail hit the windshield, bouncing from the hood and scattering across the asphalt.

Soon Driftwood's suburbs gave way to trees, and Elliot glanced in the rearview mirror with a sense of regret that seemed to hollow out and flatten him at the same time. Charcoal brushstrokes darkened the sky, and there were rumors of canceled flights across Appalachia tomorrow. He hit the gas pedal.

I'll come back, and I'll find Jessica. When she calls me or emails me, because a button is too small to hold on to, and I feel like I'm losing my mind.

A low rumble echoed, and leaves scattered across the highway. Elliot's mind conjured a haunting image – Annabelle Lewis, alone in black fog, life slowly leaving her.

Soon the hail swelled to gravel-sized beads, metal drum-loud, like tin cans flung at the roof. The bends in the road were almost hidden by the fury, and he worried he'd fly over the guardrail all over again. Only hazy headlights told him he wasn't alone on the road. He crawled for five miles, miles that seemed to go on and on, following the dashed white lines as the wipers swished and wailed. At a sharp bend in the road, he narrowly missed a semi creeping into his lane. With a tight swerve, he aimed for the shoulder and parked by the guardrail.

Listening to the hail, he watched each minute pass. If he was going to make his flight, it would need to be a seamless, lightning-quick drop off at the rental car office, and a sprint through the parking lot to the terminal. So why wasn't he easing back onto the road?

The hail eased, but he stayed at the side of the road, tapping the steering wheel. His headache sharpened. There was Tylenol in his luggage, he was sure. He leaned back and unzipped his suitcase on the back seat, then ferreted his belongings to find the pills. They washed down with a slug from the bottled water in the cup holder. But a loud crack of lightning startled him, and water ran down his sweater.

He leaned back again, this time searching for napkins, which he swore he'd stuffed into his suitcase.

Napkins. Napkins!

He flung open the door, hail pelting him, and opened the door behind the driver's seat. Unraveling the laundry in his suitcase, he tugged free a pair of jeans, then dug his hands into the pockets and found a crumpled napkin. *Tyler's phone number.* His resolve to leave Driftwood evaporated.

He'd misdialed on the first try, misreading a digit, but which? Friday night seemed like weeks ago. He settled back into the driver's seat and eased toward the road. Soon the gas station's sign came into view, swinging on its rusty chain.

He took the turn and parked outside the diner. Lightning seared the sky as he ran to the door.

The brassy blonde waitress looked up from her pad. "You got some change this time?" she said through a mouthful of gum, then giggled.

Elliot nodded, then picked up the receiver of the payphone.

Chapter 43

Monday, April 18, 2022

Thunder roared as Jessica flung open the front door. The fresh air had cleared her head.

She paced up and down the hallway, again toying with the idea of running back to the caves to search for Annabelle, then reminded herself of all the reasons why that was a terrible idea.

If Annabelle's stuck down there, how much time does she have left?

Jessica grabbed the bourbon from under the sink and took one long swig.

I need more mushrooms, and I need Elliot.

She grabbed *Black Eye* from her bag and read Elliot's message, tracing his handwriting with her index finger. The origami lion sat between the front cover and the first page. She turned it over and discovered it was also covered in handwriting, mostly hidden under the creases, penciled on the back of the mystery tour flyer. She unfolded the paper and found a quote:

> *"Nature shows us only the tail of the lion. But I have no doubt that the lion belongs with it even if he cannot reveal himself all at once."*
>
> *–Albert Einstein*

The flutter in her chest returned, the wings of those moths still batting against their jar.

She looked down at her palms, thinking of all that hid beneath her skin, and the mushrooms from Anthony's pocket that made everything shimmer. The strange gloop coughed up from her lungs, and her brother's words as he'd stared at her in the park. *"Your eyes look kind of different."*

At the bathroom sink, she studied her own irises. Had her trips underground changed her body, her DNA? She pictured her atoms with their electrons like satellites in orbit, formed light years ago in galaxies beyond the Milky Way, transported to Earth by the winds of exploding stars. The blood cells blooming in marrow, shuttling oxygen to her cells, and the twisted cellular prisms of her organs, her skin – was all that convoluted synchronicity changing somehow? She took one more swig from the bottle, then placed it back under the sink.

But there was no time to get lost in the cosmos, or the gunk inside her own lungs. She ran to the kitchen and plugged in her phone.

At last, the charging icon appeared on the screen. The rice trick had worked, but there were no voicemails, no messages.

Nothing. She searched for Elliot's number, then dialed in a storm of heartbeats. His phone was switched off, and he hadn't set up voicemail.

Maybe his phone got messed up, too.

Instead, she sent a message from his contact page.

Hi, this is Jessica. My phone broke. I'm sorry I didn't contact you earlier. I didn't know what to write. Everything I could think of sounded insane, and I wasn't even sure you were real.

It seemed so lame after three wild nights underground, but she was too frayed to whip up anything profound. She showered, lingering under the hot water as it thawed her hands and feet.

The storm would rage on and off for another few days, the weather app on her phone warned. She pulled on pajamas and corked a bottle of wine. Branches and leaves had scattered across her freshly raked lawn.

But inside didn't look much better. She threw her hands on her hips, abandoning her glass of wine. For the first time since her parents had died, she felt a burning urge to throw all their clutter into the trash. Everything suddenly seemed pitifully stale, washed out, chipped. And none of it felt like *her*.

"Why did I think I needed all this junk?" she muttered, grabbing a roll of trash bags and tearing one off with a brisk rip. Throwing out all the garbage in her house would distract her from fretting, pacing, pining. Hail pounded the roof.

She moved room to room, hurling whatever looked ugly or useless into the bag. The tomato sauce-stained Tupperware with the cracked lids, the hideous figurines on the bookshelf. Her parents' clothes, marinated in that old-clothes stink. She unhooked the awkward horse portrait from the wall and threw that in, too, along with her mother's romance novels. *I'll never read* The Cowboy and Gentleman, she decided, laughing at the brawny hunk in a billowy shirt on the front cover. The Writer and the Detective, *perhaps.*

She flung the trash bags into the garage and grabbed her glass of wine, then slouched into the sofa with the unfolded origami lion, remembering how she'd made it in Tiffany's and left it on the bench.

The wine slipped down her throat with a gentle burn. In the bedroom, she threw on a sweater. The wet cold had seeped through the window with the broken latch. Sliding the dresser drawer shut, her eyes fell on Olivia's music box.

A wiggle with a coat hanger unlocked it. *Swan Lake* played, tinny and tired, as the ballerina twirled. Inside, there was a small satin pouch. A flap she almost missed. Jessica pulled out a one-inch piece of folded paper.

A string of letters and numbers filled the page – Olivia's child-like handwriting in red pencil.

Before she could take in what she'd found, her phone rang from the table on the entryway, where she'd set it down to throw a few coats into a trash bag. She raced down the hallway.

As she hit the green answer button and lifted her phone to her ear, she knocked the clay lion from the table. It crashed to the floor, and the lion's tail broke from its body and bounced over the carpet.

"Hello?"

A pause. "Jessica?"

A fresh jar of moths exploded inside.

"Elliot?"

"So you really do exist." His light laugh unraveled her.

"Yes, I think so. I mean yes, I do."

"Yes, I think so?" You idiot, she thought, but she laughed, too. *I exist, and I really am alive.*

"What happened last night? You disappeared," she said.

"I'm sorry. I had to get out of there. I went back inside this morning. I was worried you didn't get out. My phone died."

"My phone died, too. I just pulled it out of rice. Thanks for the message … in my book."

"So it was the right Jessica." He laughed again, softly, and she liked it so much, she curled her toes into the carpet.

"Yes. I ran out for lunch," she said. Every second was aglow.

"What happened last night, after I left?"

"I found the crypt. Where are you?" she asked.

"I'm in the diner again."

"Is the coffee that good?"

"No, it's terrible. I pulled over to call you. I was driving to the airport, when I remembered the number I wrote down for a tow truck. I guess I managed to misdial again."

Her bliss sank like a pebble. "You're leaving?"

Another pause. "I turned around. I couldn't leave town without finding you. Can you meet me downtown?"

The weight inside dissolved, and she was buoyant again. She looked down at the lion's tail on the carpet. "Yes, of course. When?"

"How about seven at Nexus Coffee?"

"I'll be there," she said.

A moment later, she threw off her pajamas and dressed, choosing her least worn-out cardigan and clean jeans from the dryer. Her stomach roared, but she was too nervous to eat. Instead, she fussed with her hair. She rummaged for makeup – her newest eyeshadow, her unopened mascara. She eyed the Ativan from the cabinet.

I waded through water infested with reptiles and survived a tumble into the lake. I escaped the fog. I don't need you anymore, she decided, tossing each pill into the toilet bowl.

She took one last look in the mirror, tucked Olivia's cryptic note into her purse, then grabbed her umbrella and ran to the car.

Chapter 44

Monday, April 18, 2022

The splinters and shards had scattered into every corner, settled in the grooves in the floorboards. Now they shimmered like rhinestones in the filth.

Dan Lewis had flung all the glasses from the cabinet onto the floor, so Kristin sipped stale wine from a coffee mug.

But Dan was also in pieces. He'd been slowly cracking and crumbling for years, filling the holes with beer and farm-chore distractions, or fixing some rusty junk car.

Annabelle's disappearance had shattered whatever remained of him. The remnants of Kristin's husband – a concave, puckered soul – had finally disintegrated like plaster under a hammer, and he'd taken half the tableware with him. Flung plates to the ground, sent a chair sailing into the living room wall. Kristin had cowered in the corner, hating him, aching for him, wishing he'd left instead of Annabelle.

She didn't care about the damn plates or glasses. They could litter the floor for eternity. She didn't even care about the hole in the wall that the chair leg had left. It was Annabelle's drawing, swiped from the fridge by Dan's hip as he'd trashed the kitchen, that hurt. *Mommy and Daddy and me,* Annabelle had written in green crayon, above a sketch of the three of them. There was a tear right down the middle of it, which Kristin had sealed with tape.

But now the house was empty – empty and storm-rattled – its peeling exteriors whining and creaking.

Dan had left hours earlier, slamming the front door so hard that Kristin wondered if the wood might break from its hinges. He'd moved into his father's shitty trailer at the end of the corn field, simmering in rage with a thermos full of liquor. His father was dead, but the space heater and the stove still worked. There was even a greasy, mildew-stained comforter he could stew under.

It had been five days since Annabelle disappeared. *The first 72 hours are critical,* she'd read again and again. The *Driftwood Times* had even stressed the fact in the front-page article about her daughter.

But those 72 hours had come and gone, and the police had nothing but a few sightings that didn't add up. Hope faded hour by hour. Kristin paced and drank, when she wasn't searching the woods, calling her daughter's name, or face down in crumpled sheets.

She wasn't sure what she mourned the most – Annabelle's presence, which she'd taken for granted every day, or the mother she should have been. The time wasted fighting with Dan, while Annabelle played alone. A little girl so self-sufficient, it was easy to forget she was there.

Yes, their little girl, the bright-eyed treasure that the park ranger had found all alone in the forest four years ago, was her own private universe.

But Annabelle wasn't always quiet. There were days when her questions had exhausted Kristin, frustrated Dan. *"Why do deer have antlers? Why can't I walk through the mirror and play with the Annabelle on the other side? What's thunder made of? Why can't I live in the woods?"*

"I don't know. It just is. Because I said so." So many dumb answers thrown back.

And Annabelle hadn't just asked questions. She'd questioned the answers, relentlessly. *"Why don't you know? Why don't you care? Why are you angry? Why is everyone so mean to me?"*

But where was she now? Was there any possible way her baby girl was still alive and unharmed? Annabelle had always been so trusting, so bewildered by loud voices, thumping fists. So tiny and fragile, like a hummingbird.

A reel of hideous possibilities had played in Kristin's head for the last three days. Annabelle lured, trapped, whimpering in wire grass, beaten and bruised, or dragged and flung like roadkill. Violated by some sick beast.

And if she's still alive, who's she calling for? Mommy? Daddy? Or is she answering the voices she hears in her head?

"It's nothing to worry about," the doctor had said. *"Just a vivid imagination. It's common in gifted kids."*

But what if those voices had lured her out the front door, into the dark?

Or maybe there was something else, Kristin figured, unable to shake the feeling that she'd let some horror go on right under her nose. *Some clue I missed – something that should've warned me.*

Kristin glanced at the laptop on the kitchen table, tempted to log on again. But she'd already tortured herself enough, reading about hallucinations, schizophrenia.

The conspiracy theories about Driftwood, where the children went.

She left the shattered glass to pace in the living room. Each thunder crack and lightning strike rattled her bones. Her back had frozen stiff, but she paced on. Every muscle ached. Worry had wormed into her core; her stomach churned like sloppy concrete. The quiet seemed to suck the air from her lungs.

She considered calling the sheriff's office again. But she'd already called four times today. *"It's her again,"* she'd heard the receptionist whisper in a deadpan drawl.

That new detective – was he any better than the rest? He hadn't come up with a damn thing yet.

Annabelle's raincoat hung on a hook by the door. The sight of it sent another deluge of tears down Kristin's cheeks. She ran up the stairs, craving the air of Annabelle's bedroom. Her presence still lingered there, fading but palpable.

She eyed each corner of the room. Her search for something out of place, some kind of clue as to where her daughter went, had yielded nothing.

Perched on the edge of Annabelle's bed, she flipped on the rainbow night light and breathed in a teddy bear from the comforter. She sunk into Annabelle's throw pillows and stared at the ceiling, watching the night light turn the walls red, orange, green, blue. *One glass too many,* she realized, floating into a wine-steeped lull.

The rain's rhythmic drum hushed her to sleep, and she dreamed of Annabelle, smiling with a wreath of leaves in her hair. A blissful moment, where Annabelle walked through the door, her blue eyes glinting in the glow of the night light, her bare feet muddy from playing in the yard. She held her mother's hand. *"Don't be sad, Mommy. I'm going to a special place. I'm safe now."*

Peace washed over Kristin, like morning sunshine on her skin, but her dream didn't last long. Soon, it faded, and Kristin's waking mind surfaced, bleeding into the bliss.

Someone stood just a foot from her, a black silhouette in the dark. Dan, clutching his liquor. She climbed to her feet.

"Harding just called me," he said, his voice cracked and dry. "He wants to see Annabelle's medical records."

"Fine," Kristin said, turning her back to her husband and walking to the window. Dan disappeared down the stairs.

She pulled the curtain aside, shaky hands fumbling with the fabric, and found a message written in the fog of the window, small fingered letters streaking the glass. A remnant of her daughter that the deputy, the detective had missed.

Goodbye, Mommy. I love you.

Kristin fell to her knees, grasping for the peace of her dream. The moment lingered in her memory, but the sensation was gone.

"Goodbye, sweetie," she whispered, choking through a lump in her throat, and in that instant, she understood that Annabelle wouldn't come home.

Chapter 45

Monday, April 18, 2022

Jessica steered gingerly through the downpour, praying her umbrella would survive the sprint from the parking lot to Nexus Coffee. The car tires plowed through puddles with a *whoosh*.

The clouds all but eclipsed the remaining rays of daylight, cloaking Driftwood in a moody shroud of shadows. Jessica parked, then headed for the boardwalk.

The lake was still a saucer of choppy gray, sloshing under the pillowy cloud cover. Rain puckered the sand and slopped from the burdened trees along the boardwalk, colliding with Jessica's umbrella and splattering at her feet.

She stepped off the curb, stealing a glance from under her umbrella, and caught sight of Nexus Coffee's blue door. Was Elliot already inside, drinking coffee? Or maybe he was still on his way, a few steps behind her? A sheet of rain snaked across the road, and water bled through her shoes. She gripped her umbrella and frowned at her wet feet.

Just a few more steps, and she'd hit the sidewalk, open that blue door. Another five seconds, and she could stop asking herself if he was already there.

She froze at the screech of tires. Time slowed. A second warped to an idle pause. She dropped her umbrella a foot from the curb, stunned by the grainy glare of headlights.

Maybe she'd looked before stepping off the curb, and maybe she hadn't. Maybe she'd been too distracted by her soggy shoes, her wandering mind, to see the car approach. She'd never know for sure, but she would remember the hands of a hooded, rain-blurred figure who stood on the sidewalk, palms facing Jessica as if to warn her, as a voice yelled "Stop!" a second too late.

The first blow hit her left thigh. The impact tore her from her feet, knocking her left leg out to swing skyward, her right lazily following the arc. The tires screeched on, the car slid forward, and now her thighs, her pelvis hit the edge of the hood. And as her torso fell and her legs rose higher, she left her body, just as she had the day before, when she'd sat on her bed with Anthony. But this time, she didn't drift into the fiery vacuum of space to bask in the glow of exploding stars. Instead, she lingered weightlessly above herself, watching her body turn like a clunky windmill. Her left arm crushed under the weight of her shoulders when she hit the windshield, her head smacking against the glass. She was a supernova, a cataclysm, and she watched every explosive break and tear. Calm, freed from gravity and consequence.

The car skidded forward still, and Jessica was airborne, head down, all four limbs adrift. She wavered, still detached and free, until she merged with her body again, just in time to slam spine-down onto the hood.

The pain began as an ache, spreading from her legs, her pelvis, her head, radiating into her chest, her belly, her arms and legs. Dull at first, until it breathed into every cell, stabbing and suffocating. She considered floating north again, like a feather from a swan's back. Above the rain and the curdling pain, into the embrace of whatever waited beyond, where she'd free herself of her breaking body. Perhaps Mom and Dad would meet her there, arms outstretched as if she'd just jumped off the school bus.

The rain crashed against her skin and bounced from the hood, almost drowning the wail of sirens, the gasps and door slams and cries to call 911. A second before closing her eyes, she blinked through puddled lashes to find Elliot staring down at her, and she felt the soft grip of his hand holding hers.

Chapter 46

Monday, April 18, 2022

Jessica came to, sailing through a corridor on a backboard. A paramedic in front and hurried feet behind, moving her past pale green walls. Bright lights above, and 409-drenched air.

"Jessica, can you hear me?" a voice called. Shoes squeaked over a rubber floor, and double doors swung open. Jessica mumbled from under an oxygen mask, a cervical collar, a mess of straps and blood and tape. Pain stung back at her, tearing down her neck, into her chest. *I was in an ambulance,* she remembered. *And I was hit by a car, I think. Something terrible happened in the middle of the road. Yes, it had to be a car.*

But she was sure of one thing. Elliot had been there, right by her side, staring down at her. So where was he now? Why, yet again, had she woken up alone? Alone among the scrubs and squeaky crocs, with her body ripped and torn?

"Autoped!" another voice yelled. "32-year-old female. Laceration to head, injuries to upper and lower legs and shoulder, possible pelvic fracture. Loss of consciousness at scene 20 minutes."

"All the moths are dead," she mumbled, or perhaps she only thought it.

"Jessica, are you in any pain?"

What a stupid question, she thought.

"Yes," she said, her voice just a breathy squeak. She blinked through tears. Where was her purse?

The gurney stopped under surgical lights, more scrubs peering down at her.

How much of me is left? What will I be when this is over? A tragedy? A miracle held together by pins and a steel cage?

Rage. That's what she felt. Or perhaps it was just the sharp edge of regret. *Something* was simmering inside her, like a hateful stew. But she was too stunned, too bashed and flattened to let it boil.

A pair of gloved hands touched the sides of Jessica's head, and an upside-down face looked down at her. Chubby hands removed her oxygen mask.

"Open your mouth, please."

Each breath was a knife in her chest. She was hot and cold, stiff but jelly-weak. A barbed-wire ball of ice and fire.

Now the doctor was searching her mouth, loosening the cervical collar to examine her throat. "16 breaths per minute!" the doctor yelled, then turned to the nurse. "More oxygen! 15 liters!"

Cold metal touched her skin and skimmed along the middle of her chest. Scissors slicing through her shirt, exposing her to the faces peering down at her.

"Normal percussion!" the doctor said, tapping Jessica's chest. "Pulse is 72 and regular! Jessica, can you still hear me? Blood glucose normal."

Jessica whimpered "Yes," and needles slid into both arms. The doctor yelled more orders. "FBC, CFTs, amylase, clotting!"

More staff crowded, their hands reaching for her limbs, prodding and pressing her chest, her lower back. "Does that hurt? Does *that* hurt?"

"Yes!"

"Chest and pelvic X-ray! Can you move your fingers and toes?"

Jessica tried, felt nothing.

"Get her a CT scan. And we need an ECG," the doctor yelled, shining a penlight into her eye. Her breath was sour-sweet. "Is there someone we need to contact?"

"My brother."

A nurse flung Jessica's purse into a plastic bag, scribbled down the number that Jessica croaked out, then disappeared into an office.

Whatever swam through her veins was now dulling the lights, the pain, the thoughts that came and went between stretches of white fog. Sleep. Maybe she could just sleep through all of it. She drifted into a pharma-numb nothingness, where pain only lurked like a wolf behind trees.

But an hour later, she lay on the bed of a CT scanner, freezing in her flimsy hospital gown as the X-ray tubes orbited her.

Parked outside radiology, she overheard voices.

"...pelvic fracture. The socket joint's a mess. She's homodynamically stable, but we've got to fix that leg. We'll get her into theater tonight. Eight hours, I'm guessing. It's a complex surgery. She's lucky she's alive..."

Eight hours? They're going to operate on me for eight fucking hours?

Panic *hurt*, she realized. *What do I look like? Is my face a train wreck?*

A porter left her in a small room with a curtained door. He dimmed the lights, and long shadows stretched across the ceiling. She sobbed silently.

The roof thrummed. The rain had returned, or was it more hail?

"Jessica!"

Mark skidded in, shedding rain from his raincoat. He looked flappy and sunken, limbs in a nervous dither. She'd never been so relieved to see him.

"What in the hell happened? Oh, Jesus ... look at you." He dropped a bag on the floor. The blood left his face.

"I got hit by a car."

"Who hit you?"

She hadn't thought about the driver. *Someone* had hit her. "I don't know. An asshole."

"But ... you're going to be OK?"

She cried. "I don't know. I have to have surgery. Everything hurts." Snot ran from her nose. Mark snatched a tissue from the nightstand and gingerly dabbed her face. It stung, like everything else.

He paced back and forth, spooked and trembling. "Oh, God, don't die."

"I'm not going to die."

"You promise?"

"Yes. But I'll probably be cranky for a while." She winced as a splash of pain trickled through the painkiller numbness. "Pass me my phone."

He fussed with the plastic hospital bag and handed her the phone. She tried to hold it, but it fell flat.

"Check for calls."

"What's the pattern lock?"

"The letter 'E,'" she mumbled.

"Of course," Mark muttered. "No calls or messages. The service is terrible in here. How the hell did this happen? What if you're all messed up forever? This is a total shit tornado."

"You're stressing me out." More tears overflowed.

"I'm sorry. I don't deal with stress very well. I think I'll take one of those pills in your bathroom."

"I threw them in the toilet."

"Fuck. Well, there's a bunch of your stuff in here," he said, placing the bag by the bed. "I didn't know what to bring because women baffle me. But I figured you'd want your toothbrush and some clothes and my Rubik's Cube, so you don't get bored. Or do you want my Game Boy?" He pulled out the cube and placed it on the nightstand.

Jessica smiled. Even that hurt. "Thanks. No."

Other than a colander or a box full of fishing tackle, she couldn't think of anything in her house she needed less than a Rubik's Cube. The Game Boy was a close second.

"I called the library and spoke to Tabitha. She's the only one I can stand. Anyway, I told her to tell your boss that you're not coming for like, *weeks*. Shit, I'm supposed to be helping Jamie. There's a leak in her roof and I said I'd find a contractor and get a sump pump. She's got two inches of water in her kitchen."

Shoes scuffed down the hallway, and Tabitha sailed in, swinging a grocery bag.

So many damn people. I haven't been this social in years, Jessica mused.

"Jessie! Oh my God, Jessie!" Tabitha dropped the bag and threw her hands to her mouth. "Oh, I can't believe that idiot hit you. What a *bastard!*"

Jessica blinked, combing through Tabitha's drama-crinkled words. Mark's mouth hung open.

"Who?" Jessica said.

Tabitha looked at Jessica, at Mark. Her hair was a floppy cloud of fuzz. "Oh God, you don't know..."

Chapter 47

Monday, April 18, 2022

It was just minutes before 7 when Elliot heard the screech of tires.

People who don't know how to drive in bad weather, he thought, until he heard the thump. Louder than the storm and the white noise of the coffee shop.

A tiny earthquake tremored under his skin, through his veins, along the plumage of nerves coursing his spine. He stood up, sending his coffee cup into a lazy whirl. Frothy beads of cappuccino splattered a napkin.

His legs moved first, then his mind. One step and another, toward the blue door. Outside, voices broke through the percussion of the rain. A dissonant yell, a grating screech. *"Call 911!"*

He pulled open the door, and the wind chime jingled. A crowd gathered around a navy car. Sirens wailed and headlights gleamed – foggy cinders in the vapory gloom. The clouds had thickened, now bruise-black and huddled low.

He stepped off the curb, over the flooding gutter and a nest of twigs and litter that bobbed like a clumsy raft. He edged his way through the crowd – a polite "Excuse me" and a firm nudge – until he reached the hood of the car.

No, that's not right. That's just an ugly idea that invaded my mind, he thought. Jessica couldn't be splayed on the hood of a car, her leg sickeningly twisted. He blinked, but it didn't erase the truth of her lying there, so he held on to her hand, as if a light grip might propel her back to her feet. But her eyes were fluttering closed.

His shirt button hung around her neck, and her hair was a mane of wet ringlets. *No, this isn't the ending,* he told himself, watching her fade. A mermaid on a rock, broken, marooned.

Elliot's rage only surfaced when he heard the car door slam. The driver staggered out. As the guy moved closer, raking a hand through his dark blond hair, Elliot noticed a gold badge on his belt.

A cop. A *detective.*

The cop put his hands on the hood, hung his head in the pouring rain, and Elliot's mind split in two. One part held on to Jessica, refusing to let her go. The other watched the cop, who was now clutching his radio. Elliot wanted to grab his collar, slam him into the sidewalk, leave him as smashed and ruined as his beautiful muse. Instead he glared at him, feet pinned to the ground. The rain flooded his shirt and seeped into his shoes.

The sirens grew louder. An ambulance whined to a stop. A patrol car followed, then parked to block traffic.

Elliot stepped back when paramedics approached. "Ma'am? Can you hear me?" one called. Steady, ironed-out – that calm-in-the-storm medical tone. Jessica didn't respond. She was already somewhere else, but where? In a deep abyss?

"What's her name? What happened, exactly?" a paramedic asked, gloved hands checking her airway, placing a stethoscope on her chest.

"Jessica Paige. He hit her as she was crossing the road," Elliot said, nodding toward the cop. The detective nodded back, still too stunned to speak.

What kind of a cop are you?

The sheriff arrived. "Harding? Jesus Christ, what in the hell happened here?" Elliot heard, but the rest of his words drowned in the rain.

Now the paramedics were stabilizing Jessica's head, placing a cervical collar around her neck. "One, two, three," one said, before they log-rolled her onto a backboard.

One, two, three. The numbers rang in Elliot's head. He wondered again if he could erase the moment with a blink, a shake of his head. *Three, two, one.*

"Are you a friend or relative?" a paramedic asked Elliot, his bald head slick with rain. Another placed a non-rebreather over Jessica's face and pumped oxygen into her lungs, then dressed her head.

"A friend."

Is that all I am? Elliot wondered, watching as they pushed her toward the ambulance. *Three, two, one. No, I can't undo it.*

"You're riding along?"

Elliot nodded and walked toward the ambulance.

"Elliot Reed!"

Elliot turned around. The detective stood behind him. *How the hell does he know my name? Doesn't look like the reading type.*

"I'm going to need you to come down to the station, answer a few questions," he barked out, hands on his hips.

"Am I under *arrest*?"

"Would you like to be?"

Elliot used all his restraint to stand still. "Are you serious? You just ran over a pedestrian, and you want to question *me*?" *I should really punch you in the face.*

The detective yelled over the rain, hands still on his hips, gray eyes flaring. "I have reason to believe you stole confidential police records from the Driftwood College Library. If you're interfering in my investigation, then you can bet I have some questions for you."

"You're keeping confidential records in a public library? I guess I shouldn't be surprised." Elliot glanced at the detective's car, the dent in the hood.

The detective stuck out his chin. "We can either do this quietly, or I can make a real public scene. You see those gawkers across the street? That kid with his phone out?"

Elliot hesitated, scanning the street and deciding he was trapped. His feet were swimming in rain.

"Fine. But I'm not getting in a patrol car. I'll meet you at the sheriff's office." He shook his head at the paramedics. The ambulance's siren flashed, and the vehicle disappeared into traffic, taillights glowing misty red in the downpour.

"I'll have Deputy Willis follow you there while I finish up here. Wouldn't want you getting lost in this weather."

"Finish up? You plan on running over anyone else? I know how to drive. Never mowed down a woman once."

Elliot walked to his rental car, slammed the door closed, and punched the address into the GPS, thumping the wheel before reversing out. He grabbed his sweater from the front seat and toweled his face.

He drove with the deputy's headlights beaming into his rearview mirror. The rain cascaded over the windshield, and Elliot told himself to focus on the road. Not the gash on Jessica's head, her twisted leg, or how much he wanted to punch the detective, wring his neck.

Chapter 48

Monday, April 18, 2022

The sheriff's office was dark, musty and wood-paneled, like an old man's hunting cabin. An American flag and a buck's head hung on the wall. Deputy Willis led Elliot to a small gray room and shut the door.

Ten minutes passed. Elliot tapped his fingers on the table. He'd studied cops for long enough, and this guy wasn't the pull-over-and-save-a-puppy kind. No, this asshole might fudge a report, screw him over somehow.

Just play his stupid game for a while, then get to the hospital, and hopefully she won't wake up alone.

The clock on the wall ticked on. Another thirty minutes passed, and Elliot was ready to throw his chair across the room. Either Harding was playing with him, or he was late because the sheriff still had him pinned to the wall.

Voices echoed. Yes, the sheriff was definitely still tearing him a new one for running over Jessica. Elliot slumped into the flimsy chair and stared at the pot-holed wall. Another ten minutes later, the detective walked in and threw a manila folder on the table.

"Start talking."

Big shot. "About what, exactly?"

"You want to tell me why you walked out of the library with the files from this folder?"

"If it was confidential, why was it in a public library?"

You've got nothing, Elliot figured. *Nothing but a chip on your shoulder. But about what?*

The detective cracked his knuckles. "Do you usually steal from libraries? Is that how you do your research?"

"What makes you think I took it?"

"We got a witness."

"That morose janitor?"

The detective crossed his arms, almost breaking into a sneer. The fluorescent light strip flickered.

"Those files are part of an ongoing investigation."

"An even better reason not to leave them in a public library. Which case? One of those missing kids? Or are those cases all stone cold?" Elliot leaned back in his chair.

The detective stood up and leaned in. "What the hell are you doing in Driftwood?"

Elliot sighed. "Detective, are you going to charge me with something? Because if you're not, then I need to go see the woman you ran over."

"Just answer the question, Reed. What are you doing here? Because when you called dispatch on Saturday morning, you told us you were just passing through town. What do you know about Annabelle Lewis?"

"The missing girl? About as much as you do. So nothing."

"I can see why you're a writer. You sure can tell a story."

"The story of a small-town cop in over his head?"

"You want to say that again?"

"You heard me the first time." Elliot stood up.

"Sit down."

"I'll stand." He leaned against the wall. Harding looked Elliot up and down, as if he were already in a line-up for some fantasy crime.

"Here's what I don't understand. You tell us you saw Annabelle Lewis on the side of the road, but we've got a witness saying they saw her clear on the other side of the park that same night. You make up some bullshit about passing through town, then you steal a police file. Your story doesn't add up."

Elliot shrugged. "I *was* just passing through town. Until I met Jessica Paige. I reported exactly what I saw. And you're trying to pin a missing file on me, based on what one person in a library said?"

"Other employees at the library confirmed you were there."

"Yeah, I was there. Did they all say I stole a file?"

Harding bristled. "What's your involvement with Miss Paige?"

"I don't see how that's any of your business."

The detective burned red. *Ouch. He didn't like that. There's something there,* Elliot figured. *Don't tell me this is her ex.*

"Here's what I think. I think you conspired with Miss Paige to steal those files."

"Now who's telling stories? You seem pretty interested in Jessica. Did she break your heart, Detective? Or did she just tell you to fuck off?"

The detective cracked his knuckles again. "How about I let you cool off in a cell for a while?"

"If you're going to charge me, then charge me. Otherwise, quit wasting my time."

Harding stared at Elliot, stretching out seconds so they felt like minutes. "Get the hell out of here, Reed. We're done for now. But if you keep interfering with my investigation, I swear…" Harding opened the door.

"Good luck with the sheriff. He seems about ready to take your badge," Elliot said, loud enough for the receptionist to hear.

"I'm *state police.* He can't do *shit,*" the detective snapped.

Elliot jogged down the steps outside, and the rain showered his clothes all over again. Driftwood's streets were backed up and flooding. A tree had fallen at a crossroads and knocked down a utility pole a block from downtown, and traffic had piled up in every direction, taillights like cats' eyes in the dark. Dusk was just a hush from black.

He sat in traffic for an hour, soaking his seat, his blood boiling all over again. He thought of his phone, then remembered it was useless. Was Jessica still unconscious, or waking up under surgical lights? Was she numb and sleepy from morphine, or drowning in pain? Was someone beside her, or was she all alone? Elliot pressed against the wheel, his foot hovering over the gas pedal. At last, traffic moved again, and men in fluorescent coveralls directed cars around the debris.

Elliot took the road to Driftwood General, sloshing through ford-sized puddles, until he entered a ring road and parked frustratingly far from the entrance to the ER. He jogged toward the revolving doors.

Chapter 49

Monday, April 18, 2022

Tabitha sat down in a chair by Jessica's hospital bed.

"I called my cousin. She works at the front desk in the sheriff's office. It was Andrew Harding. He was the driver."

"Dick Breath?" Mark yelled, loud enough to wake the dead, or the dying, at least.

"Shhh!" Tabitha put her finger to her lips, and Mark flushed. "Dick Breath?" she whispered.

"It's his other name," Jessica murmured. She pictured Andrew standing in her kitchen, reaching for her. Brushing her neck, sleeping in her brother's bed. All the times she'd wished he'd leave, and all the nights years ago, when she'd wished he'd come home. And now he'd just plowed right into her, sent her skyward. Too tired and distracted by a case he couldn't solve.

"But get this," Tabitha said. Jessica pulled herself back to the present – the anxious faces watching her, the scratchy sheets beneath her.

"What?"

"She said he even had the balls to haul some guy to the sheriff's office for nothing, right after the accident. Some shit about a stolen file! She said the guy was *stupidly* sexy ... like, it was just *dumb* how good-looking he was. Jessica, it *has* to be Elliot Reed. You and I both know there are no good-looking men in this town. He took that file from the library, and someone snitched!"

Mark frowned, looking perplexed and insulted.

"Fucking Mr Fucky," Jessica mumbled, wincing.

"Oh God, Jessica, what's going on? I feel dizzy. Are you dating him? I mean, I knew something was up when he put that origami lion in your book—"

"Can someone please tell me what the hell's going on?" Mark interrupted, his face now red and blotchy, as if the confusion were enough to bring him to tears.

"Elliot and I ... we have something, I think. I mean, I think we're seeing each other. I can't explain it. I was crossing the road to meet him at Nexus Coffee."

"Just so I understand, you're secretly dating Elliot Reed? And Dick Breath hit you with his car, then dragged Elliot to the sheriff's office over a stolen file?" Mark paced, hands jammed on his hips.

"I guess. But what the hell's going on at the sheriff's office?" Jessica's stomach churned at the thought of Andrew interrogating Elliot.

"Oh, don't worry about that," Tabitha said. "He's just waving his dick around. He doesn't know shit."

Mark sat in another squeaky chair and shook his head.

"Now are you going to tell us how you met Elliot Reed?" Tabitha grabbed the grocery bag and pulled out a bag of cookies. "These are even better than the peanut butter pie you took home. In case you get hungry."

"Thanks. It's a long story. A whole novel, I think."

"He's writing a book about you, isn't he?" Mark paced again. Jessica wished he'd stop.

"I don't know."

"What do you mean?" he asked.

"There's a lot I don't understand," Jessica said, her head suddenly heavier.

"I'm going to kill Dick Breath. Aren't you mad? It's like you don't even care."

"I'm more worried about walking again. And at least now I know why Elliot isn't here ... why I woke up alone. I'm so tired. I have to sleep."

Tabitha nodded furiously. "Yes, we're being selfish. Sorry, Jessie."

"No, you're not being selfish. Just tell the Walrus to go to hell. Same goes for Andrew, if you see him. Tell him he's a terrible driver, and that he was a boring, selfish lover."

Tabitha patted Jessica's hand. "I sure will."

They disappeared around the curtain, and the worried look on Mark's face lingered minutes after they'd left. She felt hideously alone, and her loneliness crowded the empty room. She released a throttled howl.

Olivia's music box.

The thought flung itself into her head like a shuttlecock, sailing through the soupy-thick pharma haze. She stopped crying and searched for strings of logic in her battered brain. Those letters and numbers had to mean *something*. A message that was important enough for Olivia to write down and tuck inside her music box.

A nurse shuffled in and gave Jessica more morphine. She fell into a leaden sleep, where she dreamed she was tumbling into the lake again, sinking through the frigid current and hydrilla. Her folders and journals sank with her, words leeching into the murky water like ink from a squid. A cardigan, a shoe, an origami lion, all on a downward drift.

When she collided with the lakebed, she sensed that she wasn't alone. Someone was right by her side. But that someone was on the other side of sleep, waiting for her to open her eyes. She blinked awake.

Joseph Baker stood in the corner of the room, under the cover of a wet black hoodie. Rain streamed from him, puddling on the floor. He moved to the side of the bed.

"Why are you following me?" Jessica croaked.

"You have to help us." He spoke in a hurried whisper.

"But why me?"

"We're connected, somehow. That's what they say."

Jessica tried to raise her head, then sunk back into the pillow. "Connected? Who told you that?"

"I don't know. People from home. I hear them in my head. They say you knew one of us."

"Olivia," Jessica murmured. "She's ... she's alive? She's..."

"I don't know," he interrupted.

Jessica blinked at the ceiling, struggling to unpack what she'd heard.

"Why didn't you just tell me? Why creep around?"

"I didn't know if we could trust you."

"How did you get here? I don't understand how you all – "

"I woke up. My bed opened."

"Your bed?"

Joseph shook his head. "I can't explain."

"Who are your parents, Joseph? Your *real* parents?"

"They're *dead*."

"I'm sorry. What do you want from me?"

"We have to wake up the sleepers, so we're ready." He looked up at the overhead lights.

"Ready?"

"They're coming soon, to take us home. I think I figured it out."

Footfalls echoed, then passed in the corridor. A sharp pain took Jessica's breath away.

"You hurt *everywhere*," Joseph whispered, squeezing Jessica's hand. Jessica nodded, and tears pooled and trickled to her ears again.

"Be quiet. Don't yell." Joseph closed his eyes, and heat began to radiate from his palm. It snaked up Jessica's arm, down her torso, into her head and limbs. She opened her mouth and stifled a cry as the fire spread. A bloody inferno burst into her veins, searing her nerves. Sweat poured, her muscles spasmed; her head was a skull full of embers. Blood swelled under every wound.

She whimpered when something moved beneath her skin. An army of ants was crawling up her legs, her pelvis. Or was something swimming under her flesh? She throttled a scream, dug her hands into the sheet. Now she was more than a supernova. She was an entire tortured universe, exploding, merging in one breath.

A burst of stars lit up behind her eyelids. Fractals spiraling, replicating. A blazing itch crept over her skin. Some force was knitting her together, pulling, purling, stapling. She begged to leave her body again. To drift beyond the ceiling tiles, back into the rain. But she was too stunned to cry or move, too locked in fire and pain to rise like a feather again.

I'm going to die, she thought. *Whatever he's doing, it's killing me.*

Joseph lifted his hand, and the heat dissipated.

"I'm not killing you. I'm *helping* you." He left a squishy handful of mushrooms in Jessica's palm, then walked toward the door, looked both ways, and disappeared into the corridor.

Jessica shivered in a pool of sweat, teeth chattering. The pain ebbed, moment by moment, until she only felt surges of heat, splashes of cold, pooling, swirling, settling. Tiredness crept up on her. She closed her eyes and began to drift, thoughts slipping to scattered patterns, errant sensations, like a string of beads breaking, dissolving into the liquid flow of dreams.

But a moment before surrendering, she opened her eyes and realized she could flex her fingers and toes. The pain now felt like a heavy bruising, a tenderness that ached, but wasn't shattering. She gingerly turned her head to the left and right, flexed her fingers again. Then, hoping she didn't destroy herself all over again, she lifted her arm, moved her leg.

Moments later, she raised her neck, her shoulders, propping herself up with her good arm. She gasped again, this time in disbelief, then leaned over the bed and vomited onto the floor.

Chapter 50

Monday, April 18, 2022

Voices rushed by behind the curtain. The trauma center pulsed with a frenetic beat, just afloat on a cresting wave of emergencies. Jessica's heart quietly thumped, lost in the tumult of alarms and thunderclaps.

"We're close to full capacity," a doctor complained outside. "One car wreck after another. This storm…"

Jessica sat up in bed, shoved a mushroom into her mouth, then stared at the palms of her hands, timidly flexing, shifting her arms and legs. She pulled up the hospital gown and inspected herself. Large red welts, still puffy and warm, lingered on her skin. She touched one on her shoulder, spongy-hot and tender.

It took all her resolve to resist scratching under the dressing on her leg and forehead. Her body itched as if she'd rolled in poison ivy. She prodded her head with her fingertips and crept under the bandage. Her fingers found a strip of swollen skin above her eye, freshly healed and slick beneath her fingers. The fabric peeled off with a tug, and she threw it in the trash.

The smell of vomit made her wretch all over again. Something revolting was somersaulting in her belly. Writhing hot snakes, it felt like. She chugged water from the nightstand.

The churning and itching eased, little by little. The horror of the evening waned, and a glassy-bright sheen slid over the world – the mushrooms were swimming through her. Shoes approached and she stiffened, but they passed by the curtain, too busy with another emergency. The IV bags above the bed were less than a quarter full. Any minute now, a nurse would rake the curtain aside. And wasn't she scheduled for surgery soon?

I need to get out, she decided. *There's no way I can explain this.*

She wrapped the remaining mushrooms in a tissue, pulled the needles out of her arms with a wince. Then she peeled the electrodes from her chest, and the monitor began to beep. *Beep, beep, beep!*

Jessica leaped out of bed and fell to the floor. Her legs wobbled, pulpy-weak. She crawled to the outlet and pulled out the monitor plug, then forced herself to her feet.

Vomit still burned her throat. She fished her toothbrush out of the plastic bag and brushed her teeth with the last of the water by the bed, thankful that her brother had found the sense to throw in a tube of toothpaste. Mark had packed a pair of jeans, an odd assortment of T-shirts and underwear, and an old gray sweater and tennis shoes. She dressed and hurled her belongings into the bag, then stared at herself in her phone's camera. A faint pink gash lined her forehead, above her right eye. Her hair was a bird's nest. She tied up her curls with an elastic from her purse and wiped the mascara from under her eyes.

She opened the curtain and slipped down the hallway, into the screaming bright clinical light, and turned a corner. A baby wailed from a crowded waiting room. She swung through revolving doors. Tiredness tugged at her, surfacing again, this time thick and heavy.

The rain still fell in sheets outside, and streetlights beamed angular rays into the dark. The silence reminded her that she was still alone, so tired she could warp and bend, fold in half and sleep on the ground. She sheltered under the hospital's glass canopy and reached for her phone. The pain had all but faded, and now only a strange heat in her belly remained.

"Jessica?"

She heard him before she saw him. She looked up.

"Elliot."

He jogged out of the darkness, rain-drenched in a wrinkled shirt, as heart-stoppingly handsome as every other time she'd stared at him, stolen glances in the half-dark. But now he was right *there,* interrupting her bleak and bewildering evening, breaking the scene like an interlude and eclipsing everything else.

"What the ...? I saw you..."

"Joseph," she said. "He held my hand ... he *did* something. It healed me, somehow."

"What? But, Jessica, you had a broken leg. I was worried you might be..." He shook his head.

"I don't understand it, either. And I can't explain it right now. I'm so tired, I could sleep right here."

"I'm not sure I understand anything anymore. Just that I needed to come here, find you. You're okay, really?"

Jessica nodded. Relief felt so much better than morphine.

"I'm sorry. I should've been here two hours ago. I..."

"It's okay. I know what happened."

"You do?"

She nodded. "This town is way too small."

He took a step closer, found her hand, her waist.

"Tell me this is real. Tell me you're really here," she whispered. He folded around her, wet shirt, warm skin. She dissolved into him.

"I'm here. This isn't a dream. None of it was."

She looked up at him – the rain running down his neck, the bright blue of his eyes – and he frowned at the fading gash on her forehead.

"Are you in pain?"

She shook her head. "No, not anymore."

He kissed her, pulled her close. Hands firm on her hips, lips soft and lingering.

"Why don't I take you home?" he said.

She followed him to his rental car. He opened the passenger door, and she settled into a leather seat. And as the car grew warm and Elliot laced his fingers between hers, she closed her eyes and let sleep drag her under, into its umbral hollow.

Chapter 51

Tuesday, April 19, 2022

Elliot steered the car through the rain, which hadn't eased since the clouds had broken their silvery seal. The traffic had all but cleared, and only piles of branches and a few bleary headlights remained.

"Where do you live?" he said at a crossroads.

He glanced at Jessica when he heard no reply. She was already asleep, curled on her side with her purse on her lap. He squeezed her hand. Nothing but a soft murmur.

Nudge her awake? No, she looked too peaceful, slumbering in the passenger seat. It was only then that he remembered he had no hotel room reserved. The last time he'd thought about booking a room, he'd been in Nexus Coffee, reading Jessica's email, moments before he'd heard the screech of tires. He eased onto the shoulder, then dialed The Arbor.

"I'm sorry, sir, all of our rooms are fully booked," a tired voice said.

Elliot sighed. "You really have *nothing*?"

A pause. "Hold on one moment, please."

He waited, watching the rain blur the shadows outside. The first moment of calm that day.

"We don't have any rooms, but we do have one bungalow available. It's the honeymoon cabin."

Elliot shot another look at Jessica, cringing. Four days in, a honeymoon cabin seemed presumptuous. But he wasn't about to book her into The Duke. "I'll take it."

The woman on the phone pulled up his account. Heavy drops splattered the windshield, tempered and sloppy. The storm was muting to lazy rain. He reserved three nights, unsure how long he'd stay or what lay ahead, then eased back onto the road.

The dashed white lines guided him through the dark, like the tracks of some invisible runner who never grew tired. He glanced at Jessica again – a mystery sleeping peacefully in the passenger seat. A stranger he'd met by chance, luck, a tumble into a rabbit hole, who already seemed familiar.

He parked in The Arbor lot and closed the car door slowly. In the chandelier-lit lobby, he waited by an enormous vase of lilies that threw their clovey scent into the air. A porter busied himself with drying the shiny wooden floor, which was streaked with muddy footprints.

A woman with helmet-like hair checked him in, told him everything he already knew about the hotel, then pushed a resort map and two key cards across the desk. He ignored every word, and instead thought of Jessica asleep in the passenger seat.

"It's the last bungalow at the top of the hill," he *did* catch, then ran back outside to the car. Jessica was still asleep.

A winding road behind the hotel cut into the hillside. Elliot drove past cabins lit by lamplight and solar garden torches.

Chapter 51

The honeymoon cabin sat in a leafy hollow near the top of the hill. Elliot parked and took another look at Jessica. She slept on, her chest rising and falling silently.

He dashed to the front door and flung his suitcase inside, taking in the interior. The same cherry wood and buttery carpet as the hotel, bathed in the burnished glow of a few chandeliers. He walked past an overstuffed sofa and a stone chimney to find a small kitchen – minibar overflowing with fifteen-dollar pistachios and small bottles of pinot noir – and a bedroom with a canopied four-poster bed.

Either I'm in bed with her or I'm on the couch, he figured, then ran back outside and opened the passenger door.

"Jessica." He nudged her shoulder.

"Hmm..." she murmured, still asleep.

He scooped her up, lifted her out of the car, and thanked himself for all those boring hours in the gym.

The rain splattered her forehead as he carried her inside, but it didn't wake her. He lay her on the bed and sat at the edge, swiping the flimsy canopy aside.

"Elliot," she murmured, then turned on her side, eyes still closed. Elliot smiled, asking himself why he liked hearing her say his name so much. Then he pulled off her shoes and left her to sleep.

He closed the front door and leaned against the wall, wired but exhausted, each perfect, horrifying and impossible event of the day replaying. His nerves were shredded; he still wanted to punch that cop. But now his muse slept in the next room, swamped by the folds of an opulent bed.

He looked at the couch. It was a loveseat more than a sofa. *No,* he decided, then showered. As much as he wanted to crawl under the sheets in his underwear, he threw his jeans and a shirt on, flipped off the lamp, then lay down next to Jessica and listened to her sleep, remembering his sister's words: *You're a gentleman to a fault.*

Chapter 52

Tuesday, April 19, 2022

Jessica stirred, blinking through questions in the dark.

5:00, small glowing digits read.

She didn't own a digital clock. Like the rest of the world, she relied on her phone. No, only hotel rooms still had those. And wherever she was, it was somewhere quiet, free of the hum of cars, the gleam of streetlights.

The sound of breathing pulled her from a rubble of dreams. Lungs that weren't her own, a faint and mellow respire in the suede-thick dark. She turned above a downy comforter.

She found vague shadows as her eyes peeled back the darkness. Elliot slept on top of the comforter next to her. Still in his clothes, the collar of his shirt a muted angle against his skin. She resisted the urge to reach for him.

Instead, she sat up and waited for her eyes to strip away more of the dark. A door stood ajar, and she hoped a lump on the floor was her purse. Her throat was dry; her bladder was ready to burst.

Yes, the lump on the floor was her purse, she discovered, creeping from the bed and lifting it from the carpet. The open door led to a bathroom. She walked in, closed the door, and screwed her eyes shut at the glare of the overhead light.

She found a hot tub, a pile of fluffy towels, a gloriously spacious shower. A sign politely asked her to reuse her towel, for the sake of the environment. *Or your laundry costs,* she figured, reading The Arbor's logo at the bottom of the card. She chugged a glass of water.

How about a new wardrobe, so the front desk staff don't assume I'm the new janitor?

She peed, praying that Elliot didn't wake to the sound of her tinkle.

I probably stink, she realized with horror, eyeing the fluffy towels. She showered, squirting a dollop of the complementary shower cream into her palm. It smelled like rich people on a boat. Cologne, sunscreen and a freshly laundered polo shirt.

She toweled off, studying herself in the mirror. Her injuries had all but disappeared. Just the faintest line on her forehead, a red mark along her calf. She brushed her teeth and reached for the phone in her purse.

Just as she'd guessed. A dozen missed calls from Mark, five from Jamie, three from Andrew. *Screw Andrew,* she decided. Instead, she read an anxious text from her brother:

> *The hospital called me. They said you left??Did someone kidnap you?*

Stop worrying. I can't explain how, but I'm fine. I'm at The Arbor with Elliot, she replied. It was absurd, but there was no reasonable, rational explanation to fold into a lie and send him. She texted Jamie with a message just as rushed and unlikely, then tossed her phone back into her purse.

Some more drama for them to bond over, she figured. But was her brother asleep with Jamie in the crook of his arm, or had he spent the evening drowning in floodwater and unrequited love? *Are you still entertaining her, or did she chew you up and spit you out?*

Jessica was still exhausted. Heavy-limbed and singed, as if she hadn't slept in a week. The thought of lying in her clothes any longer made her nose wrinkle. Would Elliot care if she climbed under the covers in her underwear? *No,* she decided, remembering his roaming hands the night before. He probably wouldn't mind at all.

She tiptoed back to bed, pulled back the comforter, and sunk into the mattress. Elliot sighed in his sleep.

Jessica's mind swayed between sleep and rambling thoughts. A sense of urgency kept her eyelids fluttering, and she fought to put the events of the last three days into sequence.

Joseph said he needs my help.

Her eyes flashed open. An idea – a half-formed inkling – stirred her wide awake. Easing out from the covers, she slid her feet to the floor and grabbed her purse, then rummaged for a shirt and tiptoed out of the bedroom.

A single floor lamp lit corporate-angled furniture and bland canvases – a living room buffed to a shine, free of the scuffs and scrapes of drudgery. Apples and a spa menu occupied a coffee table. The carpet felt like a springy sponge beneath her feet.

Jessica pulled on the shirt and slumped into a loveseat by a fireplace, then searched her purse for her phone and the folded paper from Olivia's music box.

"I think I figured it out," Joseph had said. As if he cracked the code.

Jessica's inkling had already slipped from her grasp. Despite the gnawing urgency, her head was still steeped in a morphine hangover. But there was something out there, that *inkling,* just beyond her reach. Something about Joseph's haunting wide eyes when he'd said, "They're coming soon, to take us home."

She studied the faded handwriting on the paper. Among the creases, a number was just discernible. *0231102240.* Her eyes lingered over *02.*

2002. The year that Olivia disappeared.

It clicked, at last. Halloween, 2002, written backward, along with a time. 10/31/2002, 22:40.

The moment when she ran into the light.

Jessica searched for more strings of numbers, teasing out another three among letters and symbols. *071462250, 1217122145, 17257255.*

Her mind sharpened, spurred by successful decoding. Three more dates and times, all around five years apart. *UFO sighting in Driftwood,* she typed into her phone's browser.

Twenty minutes later, she'd identified three UFO sightings that lined up with the decoded dates. She flipped over the sheet of paper and found one more number, so faint it was easily missed. *2219400.* The hair stood up on the back of her neck. *Tomorrow. Midnight.*

Another line of numbers, just as faint, followed: *35.432882.2503.* Jessica frowned. That didn't make any sense at all.

The door handle turned, and Elliot shuffled in, bleary, his shirt half open. His entrance scattered all her focus. Suddenly the room seemed warmer.

"Can't sleep?" He scratched his head, eyes adjusting to the light.

Jessica shook her head, pulling her thoughts back together. "I think I figured something out."

She wished she'd thrown on more than a shirt. Its hem only skimmed her thighs. She walked to the bedroom and grabbed her jeans, then returned to the loveseat.

Elliot smiled. "Please don't get dressed for my sake."

"Likewise," she said, glancing at his open shirt.

He joined her on the loveseat. There was just enough room for the two of them, and his hip was snug against hers.

She handed him the slip of paper. "I found this in Olivia's music box. She left it at my house before she disappeared. Look, the numbers *do* mean something."

"Wait, Jessica, are you sure you're okay?" Elliot scanned her, as if he expected to find a broken limb. "What happened in the hospital? What did Joseph do?"

Jessica relayed the moment when Joseph appeared at her side, and the blazing force that healed her.

"I was worried you—"

"That I'd die?"

"Or that you were alone, suffering. I tried to get there, but that detective decided to screw around."

"I know, I know. A friend from work told me. Her cousin works at the sheriff's office. I'm fine, I *think*. But yesterday morning I coughed up this weird glowing gunk."

"Me too. That light in the caves, whatever it is."

Jessica nodded. "What happened with you and Harding?" She stopped herself from saying *Andrew*, then listened to Elliot's story unfold, cringing.

"He seems to know you," he said.

Jessica wanted to cringe again, but this time she hid it. "He thinks he does. And maybe he almost knew me, a long time ago. But the truth is, he never really knew me at all."

Elliot smiled, but it didn't last long. "Well, I guess he doesn't like the fact that I'm getting to know you now. He wants to pin something on me. And I'm worried he'll drag you into it."

"He's all talk. I'm more worried about the kids, what he knows about them."

Elliot made coffee with the hotel suite's mini coffee maker. "This coffee is awful. The worst that the best has to offer."

"I usually drink the best that the worst has to offer," she replied. "The hot garbage they brew in the office."

"You said you found the crypt last night."

Jessica described the kids swaying, chanting in the fog.

"What the hell?" he murmured. They let silence fold over them for a moment, while Elliot stirred the coffee.

He returned to the loveseat, handing Jessica a mug, then studied the piece of paper from Olivia's music box. She explained what she'd deciphered.

"So they've been picking up kids every five years, taking them home?"

"And they're coming back tomorrow night. But I still can't figure out what this is. These numbers here." She pointed to the string of digits punctuated by periods.

Elliot studied the numbers, then disappeared into the bedroom. He returned with his phone.

"Coordinates," he said, after entering, then studying, the numbers. "There's supposed to be a space between the two eights. Look, it's the clearing, above Lake Driftwood."

"That's where Olivia disappeared. We were at the top of the trail, and she ran through the grass. Right before a storm."

Elliot looked at the dates again, then returned to his phone. "The other sightings also coincide with a storm. And it's going to rain again tomorrow night."

"So they've been using weather as a cover? How do they see so far…" Jessica paused, answering her own question. "They're outside of time, like in *Black Eye*."

"If they can travel this far, then yeah, they're probably not stuck inside linear time." Elliot knit his brow, as if he were struggling to believe himself.

Jessica fell silent. A fresh dose of overwhelm saturated her. The boundaries of her world had dissolved. There were no edges, no margins to anything. "Is this all nonsense we're making up?"

"At this point, I wish it was."

"But why not just send a team to rescue them? Why leave it up to the kids to decode all those cryptic messages?"

"We're not ready for them – isn't that what Anthony told you? My guess is they know this is the only way to do it. Something quick and swift. I doubt the government likes visits from extraterrestrials."

Jessica sipped coffee. "The cocoon-like things I saw last night – now I'm wondering if they're ... no, that's insane. Never mind."

"You think they're ... stasis pods? Something like that?"

"I know it sounds insane. But Joseph said he *woke up*. He said his *bed* opened. They keep talking about beds, but that can't be right. There are no *beds* down there. Maybe that's why they were chanting. They were trying to wake up whoever's still asleep in the other pods."

"You said, 'decode,'" Elliot murmured. "The symbols and writing all over the walls – maybe it's more than just instructions for their ride home. Maybe it's code that the kids are trying to crack and repeat."

"To open the pods, or whatever they are?"

"Yeah. But you said they looked like cocoons?"

"It was hard to see in there. They looked *old*. Those kids could have been asleep for eons, frozen in those things."

"Shame you weren't around when I was writing *Black Eye*." Elliot smiled again, and this time it lingered. She smiled, too, a fire inside warming her cheeks.

"I wonder how many they've already taken home. Kids written off as dead, lost forever. Like Olivia," Jessica said.

Elliot stood up to stare out the window. Dawn was electric – a deep red glow on the horizon, smoldering in the dark.

"They need our help. They can't stay here," Jessica said, unsure if she'd meant to say it aloud. *I owe this to Olivia.*

Elliot rapped his fingers on the windowsill. "I know," he said, a hint of anxiety breathing through his words. "But I don't see how the hell we'll get those kids out of there without getting stuck."

"I have some mushrooms. Joseph gave them to me. But I don't think it's enough. The kids must have built up a tolerance to the fog. Or they're popping shrooms all day."

"I'm more worried about what we're inhaling. It's not just about staying awake. We already coughed up some weird gloop."

Jessica hesitated. "I have an idea. It's probably a stupid one."

Elliot turned from the window. "What's that?"

"Respirators. Or gas masks."

"Gas masks?" Now Elliot paused. "I guess that could work. But Jessica, what if there are dozens of kids down there? You really think we can get them out? And how do we get them to the clearing, if the park's crawling with cops?"

"We need to talk to Joseph. Figure out how many are down there."

"Where do we find gas masks? Harding will be watching every move we make."

Jessica chewed her lip. "What if someone helps us?"

"Who?"

"My brother. He's been prepping for the end of the world since college. I'm sure he has gas masks, or he knows where to find them. He has the weirdest stuff."

"But can he handle this, and then keep quiet about it?"

"He's spent his whole life reading comic books and playing computer games, and he's the most awkward person I know. It'll break his mind at first, but I think he'll get over it, and he sure as hell won't tell anyone. He's way too paranoid for that."

Elliot settled into the loveseat again and took a hold of her hand. "You realize what'll happen if we get caught?"

Jessica pictured herself cornered by hazmat suits, hurled in the back of a van. "Yes, I know."

Elliot puffed out a sigh. "Okay. But let's sleep some more first. I still can't believe you're out of the hospital." He brushed her neck, dissolving a little more of her hospital hangover, then leaned in and kissed her.

Chapter 53

Tuesday, April 19, 2022

Hours and dreams later – dreams of Elliot, freed of his clothes, and dreams of ghost-faint children swaying in the dark – Jessica heard Mark's car pull up outside the bungalow.

Jessica untangled herself from Elliot, who'd fallen asleep next to her, enveloping her in warmth and a heady lust they'd been too tired to ignite any further. But it sparked in the background, even in sleep.

On the phone, her brother had been a coil of stutters, questions, expletives. Words wound tight, tiny explosions in his syllables as he'd tried to understand why his sister had left the hospital, and why she wanted him to bring gas masks to The Arbor's honeymoon suite.

But now he stood in the doorway in his windbreaker, and bewilderment had washed all that aside. Now he was lost, eyes too wide, so baffled and disturbed, it hurt to watch.

"Come in," Jessica said, ushering him inside. "Did you bring the masks?"

Mark nodded, unzipping his windbreaker. He was wearing his Star Wars T-shirt. "And everything else. Now are you going to tell me what the—"

Mark fell silent when Elliot entered from the bedroom, and Jessica wished she could wave away her brother's shock, his klutzy shyness, like a plume of smoke.

"Elliot, this is my brother, Mark."

Twenty minutes later, after introductions and a debrief that sent Mark's fumbling into overdrive, Elliot's fluid confidence began to rub off. Tension slid from Mark's face, but he was still befuddled. It took another hour and a stiff drink from the minibar for him to relax enough to do more than ask timid questions. But slowly, they hashed together a plan.

They sat at a table in the small kitchen, where lamplight shed gold into the gloomy afternoon. Outside, lead-gray clouds sulked low in the sky, promising another deluge.

Elliot stood up to retrieve his sweater from the bedroom.

"Mark, you swear you won't mention this to Jamie?" Jessica leaned into the table.

"Jamie? She'd think I was batshit crazy. Besides, I'm starting to think I'm just entertainment for her. And a handyman. She has a temper. She yelled at me for picking up her Japanese teapot. I only wanted to take a look at it. I spent all those years wishing she'd notice me, and now I don't think I even like her."

Thank God, Jessica wanted to say, but didn't.

"And you're not going to freak out when we're down there? You're okay with the plan?" she asked instead.

A streak of confidence lit up his face. "Maybe I'm just as nuts as you are, but I think I might have been waiting for something like this my whole life."

"We were right, even when we were kids. There really *is* something in the woods." Jessica tugged at her sleeves.

"We should get moving soon. It might take hours." Elliot returned to the table and hovered by Jessica.

Outside, they stared into the trunk of Mark's car. Leaves danced and swirled around their feet.

"Holy shit," Jessica murmured into the stuffed trunk.

They hauled backpacks, shopping bags and a suitcase inside.

"And you're sure these are legit?" Jessica knelt on the carpet, pulling four gas masks out of the suitcase.

"Of course. They're made for the Czech army. Brand new filters. One for each of us, plus a back-up," Mark said. "How much oxygen is down there?"

"It's not like we measured." Jessica rolled her eyes.

"I mean, can you breathe normally otherwise?" Mark rolled his eyes, too.

"Yes, of course," she said.

"And is there any detritus?"

"Any what?"

"Are the particles grainy or dusty? Are they going to clog the filters?"

"No," Elliot said, approaching with the last bag from the trunk. He flung the door shut.

"Then we're fine. They're designed for nuclear fallout, so I'm assuming they'll block black-magic pharmaceuticals and fairy dust, or whatever it is we're about to subject ourselves to."

Jessica pulled her father's revolver out of the suitcase. "Mark, what the hell?"

"You didn't tell me all the details over the phone. I packed for all scenarios."

"Maybe a gun isn't a bad idea, in case we run into any more reptiles," Elliot said.

"Reptiles? No one mentioned reptiles. What kind? I fucking hate snakes." The color drained from Mark's face.

"I don't know what they are. They have red eyes and they're ugly." Jessica shut the suitcase.

"They look like Komodo dragons, but skinnier, and they swim," Elliot added.

Mark turned even paler.

"You can't back out now, Mark. We need you." Jessica glared at her brother.

"I'll deal with it," he muttered. "But if I get eaten by a beast from an alien underworld, I want it noted in my eulogy. I want it announced at Comic-Con."

"What's all this?" Jessica unpacked granola bars, baby formula and electrolytes.

"You said we have to rescue kids. I assumed they'd be hungry and dehydrated. I even bought diapers. I spent four hundred dollars on this stuff. Here are the hoodies," he said, flinging sweaters from bags.

"I'll pay for it," Elliot insisted.

"Thanks," Mark mumbled, reddening, but a noise from outside interrupted him. A shadow danced at the window, then vanished.

"Who the hell is that?" Mark hissed, scrambling to pack the revolver and gas masks into the suitcase. "We look like terrorists throwing a baby shower."

"It's probably housekeeping. We had the *Do Not Disturb* sign on the door handle all day." Elliot looked through the peephole, then opened the door.

But it wasn't a maid or the concierge. Joseph Baker stepped inside, and Elliot shut the door behind him.

"Have you been following us *everywhere,* Joseph?" Jessica stood up.

"No, you're just easy to find." He looked down at the supplies on the carpet. "You're going to help us." His aquamarine eyes beamed from under his hood, which he lowered.

"Yes, but you need to explain exactly what's going on. Those beds – they're stasis pods, right?" Jessica said.

Joseph nodded.

"And we need a code to open them?"

He nodded again, staring at Mark.

"This is my brother— "

"I know," Joseph interrupted. "I need the codes," he added. "I think I figured it out, but I'm missing something. I think Anthony wrote it on your wall. We're running out of time."

Mark was a deer in headlights, eyes fixed on Joseph.

"So it *was* code..." Elliot murmured. "Joseph, is Annabelle down there? The girl who was with you last week?"

Joseph frowned at the carpet. "The fog took her."

"What do you mean, it took her?" Jessica said. Dread bled its way through her. "Is she *alive*?"

"Yes, but she's in a kind of..." Joseph glanced at the carpet again. "Coma. She went in too far. We couldn't get her out. The mushrooms don't last long in the fog."

"We brought gas masks," Mark said, nervously. He pointed to the suitcase.

"Those will scare everyone."

"Well, what else are we going to do?" Jessica said.

"I guess. But I need the codes." He gesticulated impatiently.

"Come on, let's go. I scrubbed the writing off the wall, but it left a stain. I think we can still make it out." Jessica grabbed her brother's car keys from the coffee table, her fear for Annabelle now quickening her reflexes.

"Wait, we need to get all this stuff ready," Mark said, his face tight with alarm.

"I can go with Jessica, and you guys can stay here," Joseph said, too confident and authoritative for a fourteen-year-old. "It's better that way, anyway."

"Why's that?" Elliot looked up from a worried pace across the carpet.

"Because you and Jessica keep distracting each other."

Chapter 54

Tuesday, April 19, 2022

"He's falling in love with you," Joseph declared, watching trees fly by from the passenger seat. "He thinks about you all the time, and he doesn't want to go back to New York. Now you don't have to keep asking yourself the same questions."

Jessica gripped the wheel. "Thanks," she managed. "Keep your hood up. Don't let anyone see you."

They listened to the hum of the engine. Jessica eased around the bends of The Arbor's leafy drive. She wanted to lose herself in Joseph's revelations about Elliot, absorb them like sunlight, but the gravity of what they were about to do weighed on her.

"The fog – where's it coming from?"

"The craft is slowly dying. It's leaking sleep fog. They used it to keep people frozen in time. To let their souls dream."

"The craft?" Jessica's eyes left the road.

"The parts of it that are left. Most of it's gone now." Joseph slumped into the seat, his voice a little mournful. Jessica gripped the wheel tighter.

"What kind of craft?"

"An ark."

"An *ark*?" Jessica pictured a boat full of animals sailing the cosmos, sails flapping among the stars. But Joseph interrupted her chain of thought.

"No, not like that. It wasn't a *boat*." He shot a look at Jessica.

The mental intrusion was a jolt, a slap. Jessica told herself to be careful about where her thoughts wandered, in case they ended up in Joseph's lap again. "I'm sorry. If you haven't noticed, this is a little much to get my head around. What do you mean by an ark?"

"It had everything on it to start a new world. There were animals, frozen in sleep, DNA, embryos. All kinds of plants and bacteria. But we crashed here. Something went wrong."

"We?" Jessica glanced at Joseph again. He was hurling puzzle pieces at her, but the pieces were puzzles of their own, all cryptic and mystifying.

"All the children were sleeping. That's why we survived. Our parents died, trying to save the craft. Sometimes we hear messages they recorded for us."

"Wait, how?"

"The people from home – they play them, and we hear them."

"What do they say?"

"They tell us to hide and keep our secrets safe, and to always remember the instructions from home. They tell us to never let them catch us, or we'll be trapped…"

"Like rabbits," Jessica murmured, a swathe of goosebumps puckering her skin.

Joseph nodded. "And they tell us to remember who we are. That we were loved. To not be afraid."

Something twisted in Jessica's chest. It wanted to rise to her throat, spill from her tear ducts. "When did they record these messages?"

"When they knew they were going to die. They sent the messages home, so we could hear them when we woke up."

"But that must have been such a long time ago."

"Yes, but time isn't really one long line. Not for them."

"Outside of time," Jessica mumbled, remembering her conversation with Elliot the night before.

"Yes. The future is just the most probable outcome. They see them all and try to make the best choices."

The car fell silent. Low afternoon sun glinted from car windows. Jessica held tight to the steering wheel, grappling with the physics of time and space.

"The crash – when did it happen?"

Joseph shrugged. "About two thousand years ago, I guess."

"*What?*" Jessica's eyes left the road again. "How is that possible? You're telling me you were sleeping that whole time? Just ... *in stasis*?"

"Yes."

"Anthony said there are other people trapped in there. People who found their way inside the caves. He said they're ... dead."

"You don't understand. We had to take them there," Joseph snapped. "They were going to tell the police."

"I'm not judging you," Jessica said, grazed by Joseph's defensiveness. *He's just a kid,* she reminded herself. "The people who got stuck in there – how come they died, but you all— "

"You can't survive in the crypt without a bed," Joseph interrupted. "The bed is a whole life-support system, and the fog is just there to shut down your body and keep you asleep."

Silence fell between them again. Jessica mouthed the start of a sentence, but gave up, too dumbfounded. The truth she'd been searching for wasn't evil or sinister, it was a miracle, a tragedy, too convoluted to fully unravel.

"So how did you wake up?" she said, breaking the silence.

"The beds are supposed to last forever. They only open with a code, but sometimes they break apart, because the parts of the craft that are left are dying. Things are malfunctioning."

Jessica pictured Olivia in her pod, tumbling through space, colliding with bedrock, encased in a hermetic shell. Waking up alone in a new world, roaming the tunnels, searching for daylight. A soul thousands of years old, flung to a distant corner of the universe, another blink in eternity. She shivered, even though the dappled sun warmed the car.

"All those symbols and numbers – what do they mean?"

"You wouldn't understand. They're teaching us about the universe. They wanted to make sure we didn't grow up stupid."

Stupid like us, Jessica assumed, trying not to bristle. She navigated the downtown traffic, praying she didn't end up anywhere near a patrol car. "And no one figured this out?"

"It's easy to hide the truth here. People only believe the things that feel normal."

Jessica hit the brakes at a stop sign, feeling dull and basic. A primitive terrestrial life form. Could she ever accept that Joseph's story was as real as the mundane purr of the car engine, the traffic and boxy buildings outside? How could reality ever be so familiar and so alien at the same time?

"How do you know all this, Joseph?"

"They tell me. In my head. We don't need to phone home."

"You just ... hear them?"

"Yes."

"Why didn't they come and rescue you? I'm guessing they have the capability..."

"It's too dangerous," he interjected. "They showed us what would happen if they tried. It was horrible. This planet is hostile. And now that cop is figuring stuff out. Soon the forest will be full of trappers, coming for us. We need to leave."

The thought released a wave of adrenaline that buzzed in Jessica's fingertips. She turned onto Pine Street. The neighborhood seemed more neglected and dilapidated than ever. The street was empty, except for trash cans, overstuffed with storm debris.

"We'll get you out," Jessica said, hoping it was true. She coughed. "The other stuff – the dust that glows down there— "

"You'll see."

"What do you mean by that?"

"I can't explain now."

Jessica cut the ignition inside the garage. They sat still for a moment, staring through the windshield into the dimly lit garage. "What's it like? The place where you come from?" Jessica opened the car door. She led Joseph inside.

"It's like here, but not nasty. There haven't been any wars there for a very long time."

"Is it in our galaxy?"

Joseph shook his head. "It's so far away, you can't even measure the distance. It's in another space and time."

Inside, the clay lion with its broken tail lay on the floor. Joseph picked it up. "You were happy when this broke."

Jessica smiled. "Yes."

"But now you're scared."

Chapter 55

Tuesday, April 19, 2022

Roiling clouds, oppressive and foreboding, had eclipsed most of the remaining daylight by the time Jessica pulled up outside the honeymoon suite. Joseph had spent the ride back to The Arbor staring out of the window, pensive and silent.

Elliot answered the door, and for a moment, Jessica wished she was alone with him. Ten minutes to lean against his shoulder, let the world dissolve. But inside, Mark sat on the floor, stuffing backpacks with granola bars, electrolytes and hoodies. A quiet anxiety radiated from him, fussy and twitchy. Tabitha's cookies, pilfered from Jessica's purse, lay by his feet on the carpet.

"Did you get the codes?" Elliot seemed on edge too, but he hid it better.

"I think so." Joseph set a roll of tape and sheets of paper on the table, then taped the sheets together. He pulled a pen from his pocket and sketched until a maze of tunnels and caves emerged from rapid strokes. "Here's a map."

"Wait, what's all this?" Jessica pointed to what looked like a spiral under a billow of fog.

"The lower floors of the crypt."

"I still don't understand what this crypt *is*," Mark said with a hint of frustration, rummaging for a cookie.

"Do I really have to explain all this now?" Joseph sighed.

"Yes, you do, if you want us to help you," Jessica said.

"It was supposed to be a place where you could sleep forever. A place that no one could break into. But it was all blown to pieces. Now it's just beds and whatever's making all the fog down there."

"You said there are *floors*?" Elliot stood by Jessica, his hand resting on her shoulder.

"Well, they *were* floors. Now they're just caves full of empty beds. Sleeping pods that survived the crash. We were down there, away from the leaking fog. That's how we survived."

Mark joined them at the table. His hair was frizzier than ever, and dark circles hung under his eyes, like bruised crescent moons.

Joseph pointed at the spiral again. "It goes down and down and down." He twirled his finger downward. "The lowest floor connects to a tunnel. Our beds malfunctioned and opened, and that's how we got out. It's the ones on the top level that are trapped in the fog." He traced a long winding thread at the bottom of his sketch. Thunder rolled, distant and dissonant.

"So these beds, or pods, or whatever you call them – they're full of the same fog that's leaking all over the top level?" Mark leaned in to examine the map.

"Yes, but when they open, the fog disappears. It gets sucked into some tube or something, and whoever's sleeping wakes up," Joseph said. Mark nodded slowly, frowning at Joseph's vague answer.

"So that's how you got out and ended up in the park? You walked down that spiral, into the tunnel?" Jessica said. A memory of Olivia drawing spirals woke up the hairs on the back of her neck.

"Yes, it connects to the tunnel that takes you to the cave with the door in it."

"Door?" Mark looked up again.

"The way out, into the park. The *exit*," Joseph over-enunciated.

"The magic door," Jessica whispered.

"Huh?" Joseph wrinkled his face.

"Never mind," Jessica said, shrugging off another memory of Olivia.

"We walked until we saw light coming in through the gap in the cave. We got lost in the park. The cops took us away. But we escaped. We came back." He smirked.

"This goes on forever. It's huge. We didn't even see a tenth of it, I bet," Jessica replied.

"But where's the fog leaking from?" Elliot asked.

"Some broken part of the craft. Whatever technology they used to supply fog to the beds and keep us asleep. It never seems to run out."

"Jesus..." Mark muttered.

"So we grab the kids and get them out through the lower tunnel?" Elliot said.

"No. That tunnel collapsed."

"What do you mean, it collapsed?" Jessica looked up from Joseph's map.

"It caved in. We have to go in and out from the top level."

"*What*?" Mark said under his breath.

"You're telling me you want us to take a bunch of traumatized kids through a reptile-infested tunnel, and the crypt is right above ground that's caving in?" Elliot said.

Mark's jaw hung slack for a few seconds.

"We don't have any choice, and the more we talk about it, the less time we have to get them out," Joseph snapped.

"We'll be lucky if we don't all end up…" Elliot glanced at Mark. "Never mind."

Joseph pointed to another spot on the map. "Here's the egg. We need to go there first. We can get mushrooms there."

"*Egg*?" Mark said.

"The main capsule. We call it the egg. I can't explain *everything*."

"And then we get Annabelle from the crypt?" Jessica said.

"Yes, and then we unlock the other beds."

They lingered in silence, heartbeats skipping from adrenaline, then stood up from the table.

"I have some of the mushrooms you gave me at the hospital." Jessica rummaged through her purse.

Joseph shook his head. "It won't be enough. It's going to take a long time to get everyone out. We need to get more."

"How many kids are we talking about?" Elliot said, his voice snappier than usual.

Joseph shrugged, with no regard to the building tension in the room.

"The reptiles— " Mark began.

"Stay away from them." Joseph glanced at the door. "We need to go now."

"But it's still light outside," Jessica said. "What if the cops are already out there?"

"We can't wait that long. You don't understand. This is going to take a long time."

"Okay, let's go." Elliot snatched his car keys from the coffee table. "We'll need to go in through the hole. We don't have time to hike into the park."

"What hole?" Mark pushed his glasses up the bridge of his nose.

"You'll see." Jessica picked up a backpack. Elliot grabbed another, then a cookie from the bag. He scrunched his face. "Is there ... *licorice* in these?"

"Tabitha was probably baking with Twizzlers again," Mark mumbled.

Mark handed out headlamps and gas masks. Joseph watched the three of them pull on hooded sweatshirts.

"Wow, you really were prepared," Jessica said to her brother, easing the backpack onto her shoulder.

"I was expecting the apocalypse. Turns out you need the same equipment to rescue alien kids."

"Don't say alien," Joseph barked. "It's rude. We're not aliens. We're people from another place."

"Sorry," Mark muttered.

Mark and Joseph climbed into the back of Elliot's rental car. Jessica rode in the passenger seat and gave a recount of what Joseph had told her in the car earlier. Joseph interrupted with frequent corrections.

Mark stayed silent, fiddling with the strap of his mask, while the others talked. Words came in short bursts, buffered by moments of nervous quiet.

"What happened with Annabelle? The night she disappeared?" Elliot asked Joseph.

"She knew it was time."

"Yes, but what actually *happened*?" Jessica said.

"We met her in the parking lot, and we walked through the park with her. We were helping her get back to the caves. But she knew Elliot was going to crash. She saw it, in her head. She wanted to help him."

"Wait, *what*?" Mark said under his breath.

"She just knew? Like a premonition?" Elliot said.

"Yes."

"But how did you meet up with her in the parking lot? How did you know she'd be there?" Jessica asked.

"I told you. We don't need phones."

Approaching Evergreen Pass, Jessica caught the flash of black metal between leaves. A row of SUVs, all with government plates.

"Holy shit, it's the FBI – the FBI and who knows who else," Mark whispered. "Or maybe it's the CIA, or the DOD. What are we *doing*?"

Jessica dug her fingers into her seatbelt.

"We'll have to hike in from farther out." Elliot sped over the pass, drove a mile, then turned onto a narrow road next to a gas station and parked at the back of the building, behind a tall dumpster enclosure.

The wind teased Jessica's hair, and a few raindrops skidded into her scalp. The air crackled with static. She hung back by the dumpster and divided the remaining mushrooms among the four of them. She pulled up her hood.

Mark swallowed, his face contorted.

"Wow, that's gross." Elliot grimaced, too.

They walked to the highway, heads under their hoods. The road was quiet, except for the clatter of distant thunder. *How can life ever be the same after this?* Jessica wondered, stepping over the guardrail, glancing over her shoulder for oncoming cars. *How can I go back to work? To coffee breaks with Tabitha and those long afternoons staring at the clock? And what does tomorrow even look like?* She watched her brother clamber over the guardrail, asking herself what she'd dragged him into. What she'd dragged *herself* into. And Elliot, now squeezing her hand, pausing a moment to kiss her under the cover of the trees.

"It'll be okay," he whispered, and again, she longed to freeze time, to capture ten minutes alone with him. *Where will you be tomorrow? Here, with me? Or will you run from all this, fly back to New York?* She clutched the sleeve of his hoodie. The thought tightened her throat, constricted her breath, until she shook free of it and walked on.

Chapter 56

Tuesday, April 19, 2022

The trek through the knee-high grass was long and winding, and the backpack was unwieldy on Jessica's back. Joseph marched ahead, his skinny frame a willowy hooded stalk.

"You realize there's no going back from this?" Mark scanned for movement from the highway. "There are laws about this shit. Soon the whole park will be crawling with hazmat suits. If we get caught, we're all completely—"

"We're not going to get caught. Not if we keep our heads down and stop talking," Jessica whispered. They hiked on, and Jessica tried to forget her brother's words. A sensation washed over her that was both chilling and reassuring. A sense that her fate was already decided – that she was treading through the weeds and brushwood toward some unavoidable destiny. The wind snapped at her hood and toyed with errant strands of her hair. She held on tight to the strap of her backpack.

The ravine was a cloister of shadows. The anemic sun, fully shrouded by oyster-gray clouds, was ready to sink into the scruffy horizon. Thunder clattered again, this time louder, and the clouds seemed to pool and thicken above their heads.

"Everything's glowing," Mark mumbled, his voice faint under the rattling sky. "I think I'm tripping."

Jessica swiped the spindly fingers of a shrub aside, then gazed up at the clouds again. The mushrooms were quickly releasing their magic, and now a flickering iridescence hung around the clouds like nebulae. Elliot stared into the distance, as if his mind was already captured by whatever danced in the air in front of him.

They followed Joseph through the hidden path between the trees, feet crushing knee-high grass.

Other than the rumble of a truck and the cars parked by Evergreen Pass, there was no sign of life. Whoever had arrived in the government vehicles had moved deeper into the park, but Jessica glanced over her shoulder regardless, checking for movement beyond the branches.

They huddled by the gap in the rock.

"There's a drop inside," Jessica said to Mark, following Joseph and Elliot inside. "You have to slide down it. Don't overthink it. Just do it."

"Wait, what?"

She ignored his question and slid down, throwing her backpack in front of her. Mark followed, cursing when he landed with a thud.

They switched on their headlamps. Mark's face was pained in the glow. Joseph took the lead down the chasm, light-footed and swift, with no need for a headlamp.

At the bottom of the chasm, he led the way toward the bioluminescent cave. Their backpacks scraped the rock in the narrow passageway.

"What the hell is this?" Mark murmured, approaching the neon fauna. "Is it real, or is it the mushrooms?" He jumped at a burp from a soupy pond.

"Of course it's real." Joseph disappeared into a cleft in the rock on the opposite side of the cave, and the others followed. The route snaked deeper underground, and their path was riddled with twists and turns, littered by rocks, like a rugged underground staircase. The air was close and earthy, the space tight and claustrophobic.

"It must have been horrible, waking up down here," Jessica thought aloud. "How did you all get out?"

"We didn't. Some of us died down here." Joseph led them deeper still.

"And you buried them?" Jessica said, her voice quaking at the thought of it.

"They were just bones. I guess others woke up a long time ago, and got lost, or stuck."

The earthy scent grew stronger, until Jessica was sure she smelled damp soil. A clicking, trilling noise floated in – the drone, the whirr of insect wings.

"Bugs," Joseph said.

"*Bugs*?" Mark and Elliot said in unison. Jessica's skin crawled.

Joseph didn't reply.

They turned a tight bend, and a smattering of light spangled the narrow downward path. Misty-bright, glimmering spores formed an eerie pale haze, illuminating an explosion of foliage that crept up the widening tunnel walls. The passageway opened to another cave, three times the size of any other – a belly of towering ferns and creeping vines, vaulted in walls of gneiss and moss and fungi. The flora loomed twelve feet tall, half-lit in the spectral glow. The cave's gloomy pockets were a tapestry of murky gray and bottle green, its fronds and plumage puckered, spongy, *alien*. Vines snaked along the cave floor, rope-thick and knuckled, forming a knotty underbrush. The smoky light reached a few far corners, limelighting the velvety caps and shaggy gills of fungi. Now the air was zesty and musty, as if they'd stumbled into a botanical hothouse.

A six-inch millipede snaked around Jessica's foot, but she was too stunned to recoil. Mark and Elliot looked just as spooked and awestruck, heads arching to take it all in.

"How the hell is this possible?" Mark murmured.

"The light. It keeps everything alive, makes things grow, like sunlight," Joseph said, swiping his hand through a cluster of spores. "It was on the craft, and it self-replates."

"Self-*replicates*?" Elliot said.

"Yes, that's what I said."

"So what's it going to do to *us*?" Mark stared at the glowing dust on his fingers.

Joseph shrugged, unmoved by his concern, and guided them along a narrow path, swiping tall leaves to steer through the sultry subterrane. Bugs scuttled, buzzed, slithered, and a small, bat-like creature nose-dived into a dark leafy pocket. Something swished among the vines.

"What was that?" Jessica said.

"I don't know what they're called. They eat the big bugs." Joseph waved his hand, dismissing the question, then parted two eight-foot ferns, revealing something akin to a filthy marble wall.

As they walked closer, Jessica realized the wall was curved, arcing so high that its top was obscured by the haze. Edging closer still, she saw it wasn't a wall at all, but the shell of an enormous egg-shaped vessel, veined and dappled in pale shades of gray and blue. It seemed to hum and vibrate, like the din of the insects around her – a strange resonance she could feel under her skin. Vines and moss colonized it in clusters, and its base was buried in roots and creepers.

"If feels ... *alive*." Jessica touched it, surprised that the texture was like a sea mammal's skin – a shark or a dolphin.

"That's because she is," Joseph said. "But she's dying, slowly."

"But what *is* it?" Elliot touched it, too.

"This was the biggest lab on the craft," Joseph said, his voice now soft with reverence. "Our parents worked in here. They were scientists."

"But it's alive?" Jessica traced the strange marbling with her finger.

"The craft has a soul. She feels. She wants to sync with you."

"What do you mean, 'sync'?" Elliot said. Mark hovered five feet back.

Joseph sighed, exasperated with their questions. "It's like a hive. Everything in here connects to the craft. Kind of like sharing a heartbeat, or a pulse, or a brain."

Joseph approached a small crack in the shell, and they slipped inside, into the mottled ruins of the interior, which was just as colonized by moss and ferns. The stumps of walls and structures were now trellises for more creeping foliage, carving and dividing the space into vine-snared geometry.

"This whole place is buzzing," Mark said under his breath.

The glowing haze lit the craft in patches, but its corners hid in moody gloom. Nestled among the moss and vines was a rubble of pilfered supplies – tools, clothing, browning apple cores, a can of baby formula, an open bag of diapers, peanut shells. Thumb-sized bugs feasted on the decay.

Deeper inside, gem-like eyes blinked from the unlit sockets of the craft. Two young boys – identical twins with matted white-blond hair – peered behind the fan-like leaves of a tall plant. They crept forward, their feet feline-light among the vines. They were just as feral as Joseph and Anthony, with crystal-clear irises, black soles and fingernails, and rings of snot around dirt-caked nostrils. One had a bitemark halfway up his arm, and the other clutched what looked like a bone.

"They don't speak," Joseph said. "They only go out at night."

"What are their names?" Jessica whispered.

"That's Slug and that's Sparrow," Joseph said, pointing.

"What's he holding?" Elliot asked.

"His brother."

"His *brother*?" Mark repeated.

"His *dead* brother. It's one of his ribs. He takes it with him everywhere."

Jessica swallowed a gasp. The two boys stared back. One sniffled, then spat into the vines at his feet.

"I told them you might be coming," Joseph said. "So they don't freak out."

A snort and a rustle came from a thicket behind them – two girls with raven-black, greasy matted hair, curled up among the foliage, clutching balls of dark fur.

The furballs were wolf pups, Jessica realized, when a fluffy head turned her way. The girls stood up and took a few timid steps forward. They had pen-stained limbs, inked with more strange symbols, letters and digits. One girl had a gap in her front teeth. She held out a bloody tooth to Joseph, triumphantly.

"This is Bean, and this is Cricket." Joseph pointed at the girls.

"Hi," Jessica said meekly.

Bean grinned, and Cricket picked her nose.

"The wolves…" Elliot said.

"They came here with us," Joseph said. "Those two lost their mother."

Joseph led them deeper into the craft. The kids followed, huddling, all eyes focused on Joseph.

"They're communicating. It's a whole conversation," Elliot whispered.

The buzz in the air intensified, until a frenetic pulse beat under Jessica's skin

"I told them it's time to leave, and that you're here to help," Joseph said. "They're excited, but they're scared, and they're sad to leave the craft. She's their mother."

Joseph's words left an imprint that seemed to travel through the buzz of the craft. Jessica held back a sudden welling of tears. She was awash in sensation – a heavy sorrow and thrumming, electric excitement.

"You feel that?" Elliot whispered. He squeezed her hand, and the sensation intensified. They stared at each other, lost in the current, then refocused.

The kids flew into a flurry of movement, rifling through the loot among the vines. A young voice gurgled behind them, and they turned to find a rake-thin boy holding a baby with disarmingly green eyes. The infant was dressed in a long, grubby white robe.

Joseph took the baby, jiggling the child on his hips. "Her bed opened two days ago. Take her. She's heavy." He thrust the baby into Elliot's arms.

"What's her name?" Elliot held the baby at arm's length, perplexed, then let her rest against his chest.

"We don't know," Joseph said. "She hasn't told us yet."

"But how did you get her out?" Jessica held her hand out to the baby, who grabbed her finger.

"She wasn't that deep inside the fog. The others are much deeper in." Joseph knelt on the ground, dug through the soil, and tugged at a buried plastic bag. "Mushrooms," he explained, handing out fistfuls. "They've been rotting in the ground for a week, so they'll be good. Take the wolves." He handed one pup to Mark, another to Jessica. Cricket squealed in protest, then darted into the gloom.

Mark, Elliot and Jessica awkwardly clutched their new cargo. The pup was downy-soft, and a surge of affection pulled Jessica from the buzz that pulsed under her skin. Tiny claws hinged from his little paws, and his nose glistened black. Mark petted the critter in his arms, dumbfounded. The baby lifted her head and stared at Elliot, eerily silent, then leaned against his shoulder and closed her eyes. Elliot patted her back, mouthing, "What the hell?" at Jessica.

"You're telling me we have to get these kids out of here with wolves and a baby?" Mark said, his glasses sliding down the bridge of his nose. "Can't we leave the wolves here?"

"No," Joseph snapped. "Everyone will freak out."

"Wait, where's Anthony?" Jessica turned full circle, searching.

"He went to bury the shitty diapers and find Big Moon," Joseph said. "He's supposed to be back by now."

"Who's Big Moon?" Elliot whispered.

"A wolf. A big one. He watches over us like the moon."

"We have to find him!" A streak of panic tightened Jessica's voice.

"Twigs, go get him!" Joseph yelled at the rake-thin boy, who ran out of the interior.

The flurry of activity calmed, and the kids formed a line behind Joseph. He pointed, gestured, communicating in silence again.

"I told them they need to wait in the writing cave while we wake up the others," Joseph explained.

"What's the writing cave?" Jessica adjusted the wolf in her arms. He was getting heavy.

"The cave with all the writing on the walls, of course. Where we wrote down all the messages from home. I saw you there."

"The cave with the candles?"

"Yes. Come on. Let's go."

After swallowing handfuls of mushrooms, they hiked the upward path in silence, feet scuffing stone. Joseph led the kids through the passageway. Elliot, Jessica and Mark followed, laden with backpacks, wolves and the baby, who remained quiet, even when she stirred, eyes shimmering over Elliot's shoulder. The passageway carried the earthy-sour smell of unwashed, soil-caked skin. Jessica was thankful for her brother's headlamp, as holding a flashlight with a wolf in her arms would have been impossible. Even so, she struggled to stay balanced and upright, clambering over rocks in her path.

Soon the heavy dose of mushrooms set Jessica's mind alight. The softness of the wolf's fur, his tiny heartbeat, the pitch and tone of shuffling feet, were consuming, intoxicating. It all hummed and strummed through her, permeating her, tangling in her nerves, bathing among her cells. Prisms of color flickered in the dark, and when she blinked, a screaming red sunset hovered at some invisible horizon beneath her eyelids.

By the time they reached the scrawl-covered cave, Jessica's arms and back ached, but she was strangely detached from the pain, only observing it. She set the wolf on the ground and unloaded her backpack. Joseph lit the candles with a lighter from his pocket. Bean and Cricket reclaimed their wolves and settled into a corner.

Slug and Sparrow sat against the cave wall, glowing in the flickering candlelight, quiet and orderly. Joseph took the baby from Elliot and lay her in Slug's arms. He rocked her, mumbling inaudibly.

Elliot and Jessica heaped the supplies into piles and stuffed their pockets with electrolytes.

"They know the plan," Joseph said, grabbing a gas mask. "If we stay calm, they stay calm."

Mark was lost in the dance of candle flames, the shadows streaking the tunnel walls, his mind just as afloat as Jessica's. Joseph snapped his fingers at him.

"How do we do this after eating so many damn mushrooms?" Elliot whispered to Jessica, and she swore she could feel the rhythm of his heartbeat, despite the inch between them.

"Just put one foot in front of another and don't overthink it," she replied, hoping she could follow her own advice. She swung between calm and fear, her mind in a hammock, swaying in sensation.

Jessica pulled her gas mask from her backpack, then followed Joseph down another narrow passageway. Elliot and Mark trailed close behind. They walked in silence, gas masks in their hands.

The drip and slap of water grew louder – they were approaching the tunnel where reptiles sliced through black water. Soon rivulets formed at Jessica's feet, and she skirted around puddles, steering left.

Chapter 56

"Stay close to the wall," Joseph whispered. "And stay quiet."

"Wait, why quiet? What do you mean?" Jessica whispered back.

"They can hear you." Joseph's eyes were sharp and crystalline.

"*Who*?" Mark whispered.

"The reptiles. They'll leave you alone if you stay quiet!"

"What the hell *are* those things?" Mark said in a raspy echo.

Jessica swung right into fear now. She remembered the whip-slick torso, the shiny scales, the red eyes, and it was all too clear, too visceral. Each moment was a tiny bomb of detail and dimension, sometimes mesmerizing and beautiful, sometimes horrifying. She was too open, too permeable – everything seeped inside her, swirling and colliding in the space between her ears.

Joseph sighed. "It's better if you don't know. They're mutants. If you fall in, just walk slowly, and don't say anything."

Elliot and Jessica exchanged flicker-quick glances. The acute, paralyzing fear slunk away, but now something more subtle crawled across her skin, like a chilly slither. Mark was stone-faced behind her, trying to hold himself together, as if he might crack and crumble from a sharp exhale.

They edged their way along the ridge, the water's onyx sheen rippling below, and reached where the ridge widened without slipping. Elliot squeezed Jessica's hand,

and they stole a three-second embrace, softening into a moment of relief, headlamps beaming over the granite at low angles.

They pulled the gas masks over their heads. Jessica stared at the black rubber on her brother's face, the bug-like lenses in the glow of her headlamp.

Joseph crept into the passage that led to the crypt. Jessica shuffled behind him, her breath loud and tinny as it filtered through her mask. Mark and Elliot followed.

The fog engulfed her when she cleared the passageway.

"I think I'm in hell," Mark yelled through his mask, climbing to his feet.

Joseph wove into the fog, navigating unseen obstacles. Jessica struggled to follow, her hands flying out to steady herself as she stepped over debris. Their headlamps cut into the fog like strobe lights, but they lit no more than a few feet ahead. Stones and bones crunched beneath Jessica's feet, and she edged around a fractured human skull, stifling her gag reflex.

Jessica remembered what Joseph had told her about the ground beneath her – the collapsed tunnel, and she told herself to forget it, to imagine she'd never heard it, but each step felt like a prayer for the granite to hold. *Two thousand years in, it can't decide to cave in now.*

Two minutes into the fog, Jessica felt a creeping impulse to run from the abyss surrounding her. It intensified with each step, as if some malevolence, some age-old presence, might emerge from the black and hold her there forever. But she stumbled on, rasping through the mask. Mark and Elliot were just feet away, faint and hazy, like misty specters with black rubber faces.

Joseph stopped and waved. As Jessica stepped closer, a heap of blond hair and a nightgown became visible through the fog.

"Annabelle!" Jessica yelled, muffled by the mask.

Elliot scooped up the girl. Her limbs flopped and swayed like a ragdoll. Joseph led them back to the passageway, and Mark and Jessica walked close behind.

Elliot pulled Annabelle through the passageway, moving backward with his hands clamped under her arms. Jessica followed, listening to him heave the girl over granite. Joseph and Mark trailed her.

Freed from the fog on the other side, Elliot lay Annabelle in Joseph's lap. They removed their masks, sucking in fresher air. Joseph placed his hand on Annabelle's forehead, and for two long minutes, Annabelle lay limp in his arms, eyes half-closed. But then Annabelle took a sharp inhale, opened her eyes and coughed, her small frame shaking as Joseph pulled her from oblivion.

Jessica sighed, expelling her tension. Joseph fished out electrolytes and mushrooms from his pockets. Annabelle drank, coughed, and drank again, rousing more with each sip, then climbed from Joseph's lap, dazed, chewing the squishy fungi.

"I tried to wake them up, but it got me," Annabelle mumbled.

Elliot showered her with questions, to which she mumbled even more and shrugged. But Jessica stayed silent, suddenly heavy with guilt. *She has a family at home, waiting for her.*

Annabelle blinked and rubbed her eyes, unsteady on her feet. Her hair was a bird's nest, and her skin was ivory-pale in the gold light from the headlamps.

Jessica kneeled and placed a hand on Annabelle's shoulder.

"I want to go home," Annabelle said, as if she'd already heard all the words Jessica was preparing to say.

"Home to your mom and dad?" Jessica said.

"No. I want to go to my real home," Annabelle squeaked.

Mark glanced at his watch. "It's already nine-thirty."

Jessica's pulse ticked faster. Everything felt too real – hyperreal. Too electric, too consequential.

"Someone needs to wait here with her," Jessica said.

"No, I can stay here by myself." Annabelle slouched to the floor.

"No—" Jessica began.

"We're running out of time," Mark interrupted. "We need everyone's help in there."

Elliot crouched to speak to Annabelle. "Promise you won't move?"

She nodded, swiping tousled hair from her cheek.

They put on their masks and returned to the passageway, glancing over their shoulders at Annabelle, who remained on the ground, arms hugging her knees.

Please stay put, Annabelle, Jessica thought, scraping her palms over gravel in the passageway. *Please don't go near the water.*

Joseph led them into the crypt again, this time toward a rock-thick oval on the ground – a cocoon-like pod, inscribed with strange symbols.

They crowded around the pod, and Joseph grabbed a slip of paper from his pocket and unfolded it. He lifted his mask and repeated a string of syllables, lit by a vapory halo from the headlights.

A long, lazy whine echoed through the crypt – an eternity released in one mechanical sigh. The hairs on the back of Jessica's neck stood on end. A thin crack appeared along the side of the pod, then slowly widened. Joseph muttered softly, then pushed back the lid of the pod until it opened like a casket.

A young boy, no more than six years old, slept in a bed of plush white fabric with a tangle of rubbery tentacles attached to his forehead. He was dressed in a white, buttonless shirt and tapered pants, his feet in thin slippers. The tentacles released their hold, dropping from his skin like dead suckers. Jessica grabbed Elliot's arm. Mark staggered back.

Elliot lifted the boy from his bed, and Joseph pointed to another pod two feet away. Jessica rushed to pull back the lid. With shaky hands, Mark lifted another child from a bed – a little girl as young as the boy, dressed in a long white robe.

"There's one more," Joseph yelled through his mask. Jessica followed him to a third pod, while Mark and Elliot vanished into the fog with the boy and girl, toward the passageway.

The boy in the last pod couldn't have been more than three years old, Jessica guessed, scooping him into her arms. A crown of white-blond hair framed his elfin face, and his fingers were long and delicate. He looked like a porcelain doll, draped in silky white fabric, but he was a deadweight in Jessica's arms.

"Let's go!" Joseph yelled.

Jessica followed him toward the passageway, clutching the boy, struggling over uneven ground.

The boy seemed heavier with each step, and Joseph moved so fast, he quickly merged with the black vapor. Jessica almost lost her balance, colliding with a rock at her feet, and her sense of direction evaporated. Panic paralyzed her, until a finger prodded her shoulder.

"This way!" Joseph cried, suddenly right in front of her.

Sweat beaded from Jessica's forehead, and her own heartbeat exhausted her, thumping into her throat. The boy's head bobbed against her shoulder.

They moved slowly through the passageway, gasping and grunting in their masks, pulling the boy through the tight crevice. On the other side, Joseph laid him in Annabelle's arms.

"That nearly killed me," Mark stammered, the girl still limp against his chest.

Jessica sat on the ground, dizzy from the exertion. Pain radiated from her back and shoulders. Elliot lowered the eldest boy to her lap, then peeled off his mask and leaned against the wall.

Annabelle held on to the boy in her lap, and Joseph placed his hand on his forehead. The boy stirred, silently, then climbed to his feet and coughed, frowning at the glare of the headlamps.

Joseph took a hold of his hand, talking to him without a sound. The boy blinked, confused. His lower lip trembled, and tears flooded his face. Jessica wanted to hug him tight, but there was no time for that – she couldn't let the moment swallow her. Joseph grabbed the bottle from his hoodie again, and the boy drank.

He moved to the girl, who let out a shallow cry in Mark's arms when she woke, muted and weary. The girl drank from Joseph's bottle, spluttering. She had a head of tight glossy curls and piercing amber eyes that reminded Jessica of Olivia. She stared at Jessica, squinting into the headlight.

After another round of coughing, the girl stumbled to her feet and held on to Jessica's free hand, watching the boy in Jessica's arms. Her small palm was cool and soft, and her trust, her innocence, filled Jessica with a sense of awe and dread. *We have to get them out of here. Anthony's right. They don't belong here. They'll be ruined, destroyed by all the spite and grit.*

More tears threatened to spill from Jessica's eyes, and she sniffed, suddenly buzzing again. *What time, what fleck in eternity did you come from?* she wondered, staring back at the glowing irises watching her. *A few more hours, and you'll be gone from this world forever.*

The thought unsettled her, like a shift in the earth beneath her feet. The stars shimmering at the edges of her vision wanted to multiply, become a whole galaxy, and blind her with a kaleidoscope of haloed colors. Her head felt like cotton balls, her bones like lead.

After Joseph had woken the youngest boy, stirring him so he clambered from Jessica's lap, Elliot handed out mushrooms. The kids chewed, pinching their faces.

"Do you remember them?" Elliot asked, watching Joseph swipe a tear from his face with his sleeve. "From before the crash, I mean?"

Joseph nodded, hiding his face in his sleeve. "They don't understand why I'm so much older. And last time they saw Annabelle, she was two years old. But I can't talk about it. We need to get them out of here." He set off toward the candlelit cave, the children walking in an orderly line behind him, all four in eerie synchronicity. Joseph pointed, silently guiding them to steer close to the tunnel wall. Mark, Elliot and Jessica followed close behind. Jessica ate another handful of mushrooms, fatigue washing over her.

They inched along the ridge, but the kids were much more sure-footed, moving swiftly and easily behind Joseph, until the smallest boy teetered. Jessica watched his legs dip and bend, his feet skid and slip, his mouth fall open. Mark lurched toward him, gas mask flying from his hand, caught the boy in a tight grip, then slid into the water below.

"Mark!" Jessica almost cried, but she stifled her yell, instead leaning into the tunnel wall, clutching her mask with one hand, throwing out her other to block the girl beside her from stumbling.

Elliot sailed in after Mark, and this time, a muted cry escaped Jessica's lungs. The kids on the ridge stayed quiet, staring at Jessica as if they expected her to do something, perform some miracle. She pressed her finger to her lips. *Shhhhhhh. Please stay quiet.* Joseph gripped Annabelle's hand.

Mark clutched the boy with his right arm, rigid with fear, thigh-deep in water. *He'll get it together, find his way out,* Jessica told herself, until his glasses slipped from his nose. A frantic desperation muddled his bearings. He sputtered and lurched, rippling the water as he searched. The boy clung to him, hands digging into Mark's shoulder, legs recoiling from the surface.

Elliot grabbed the boy, who grunted, as if he, too, could only just hold back the urge to scream. At last Mark found his glasses, but he struggled to fit them onto his face – his hands could only prod and swerve; he was all thumbs and hopelessness.

Their wade out was painfully slow. One step, another, a pause to glance over their shoulders. Each ripple and splash sent Jessica's heart leaping. The children on the ridge continued their shuffle, and Jessica moved slowly behind them, now stepping sideways with her back against the tunnel wall, scrutinizing the steps of the kids ahead of her.

They were just seconds from reaching the dip in the ridge when the scales appeared. Just a blink from safety when a slick, shiny torso crested. Mark let out a harrowing guttural cry, and the noise reverberated through the tunnel, into Jessica's marrow. For two full seconds, she forgot about the slinking reptile, whose head was now cresting, rising like a submarine from the water, and instead she worried that she'd broken her brother all over again – that he'd be even more wounded than he was before.

A hideous hiss froze everyone stiff. It sounded like hatred – a sour, venomous evil. Jessica didn't want to look at it, whatever it was that had risen from the surface. She wanted to do nothing but stare at Mark and Elliot, will them to get out. But a bright flicker snapped her head sideways, and she saw the hot-coal eyes, the thick snouted head. The snake, the dragon, whatever it was, reared its head two feet above the water, its thick neck and torso arched into an *S*. Screams whipped the quiet and bounced from the rock.

"Get out! Get out!" Jessica yelled, all self-control evaporating, until a piercing sound drowned her cries – high-pitched screeches and grinding howls, coming from the boy and the girl on the ridge. The noise seemed to warp and expand, as if their lungs were spreading and ballooning in their tiny chests. Jessica wasn't sure if they were humming or screaming or both – she only knew that it reverberated like a guitar, quavering in their throats, flying from their lips in a fierce, grating resonance. As their voices rose, building to a numbing crescendo, a strange pressure pinned Jessica, Joseph and Annabelle to the wall. A forcefield, which, Jessica realized, now glancing back into the water, had repelled the reptile, who slunk off into the inky water.

The girl and the boy stopped yelling, and as their voices faded into watery echoes, Jessica and Joseph exhaled, not moving from the tunnel wall. Annabelle whimpered. Mark was still locked in terror.

Elliot lifted the boy onto the ridge, heaved himself out, and Mark followed. They crouched on the ground, limp and jellied, water streaming from their clothes. Mark lost himself in tears and grunts, beating a weak fist against the granite. Elliot stared into nothing, his breathing labored. Jessica watched the rise of his chest, her own fingers shaking. The kids looked on.

"What the hell happened?" Mark stammered.

"It's a gift," Joseph said.

"A gift?" Mark coughed.

"An ability. A kind of self-defense."

"We need to keep moving," Jessica said.

They climbed to their feet, grabbed their gas masks, and shuffled to safety in silence. The children remained stoic and orderly, only the youngest boy whimpering.

"Thank God they're not like Earth kids," Mark murmured. His knees were weak, and he stopped now and then to lean against the tunnel wall. Elliot held it all inside somehow, until they reached the cave, where he slid to the ground and sat with his head in his hands.

The kids ran to the others, immediately taken into the fold. Small hands clasped around their shoulders, and they huddled together. Jessica looked away, before tears spilled down her cheeks again. Their relief, their happiness at being reunited, was so palpable, it felt like liquid swimming in Jessica's veins; a beat she felt in her chest, merging with her own heartbeat.

Jessica climbed to her feet. She handed out hoodies to the kids, while Joseph gave them granola bars and more electrolytes. Mark remained slumped on the floor until Cricket handed him a wolf cub. Jessica took the other one, allowing herself a few moments of comfort as she nuzzled against his soft fur. The tremor in her hands intensified at the thought of leaving the cave and entering the park. *Who's already out there, searching?*

"Tell them that they need to keep their hoods up and their heads down when we get outside," Elliot said to Joseph, scooping the baby out of Slug's lap, into his arms.

"It's 10:45," Mark said.

The children formed another orderly line, swamped in oversized sweatshirts, their glowing eyes peeking from under their hoods. Their fear and excitement created a new current, humming under Jessica's skin.

"They're ready," Joseph said.

But are we? Jessica thought, watching her brother clutch the wolf, haggard, as if the last few hours had stolen years from him.

"Let's go," Elliot said, the baby settling against him.

A sudden noise chilled Jessica – the sound of feet sloughing stone.

"Who's that?" Mark said, his voice cracking. "Don't tell me they've already found us!"

Twigs jogged out of the dark, but Jessica's relief didn't last long.

"Anthony says he's not coming until he finds Big Moon!" he wailed, panting.

"We don't have time! We'll get stuck here! I told him he had to be here!" Joseph snapped. Another surge fizzled under Jessica's skin.

"But— "

Joseph interrupted the boy. "We need to leave. Now! If we wait, we'll be here forever!"

The boy fell in line, sniffling.

They began the uphill trek toward the cave exit, the baby sleeping again on Elliot's shoulder. Jessica's heart still raced, but she slipped into auto-pilot, cold and numb, some other force guiding her forward, while her fears slept curled up inside. She watched Elliot's outline in front of her – the wet fabric of his shirt, the splay of light from his headlamp, the tiny fingers of the baby napping against him, her head bobbing to the rhythm of his stride. They stayed silent, because talking seemed too exhausting, too dangerous, somehow. It might have opened up the seam they'd sewn around themselves, allowing all the horror and overwhelm to seep right back inside them.

The children shuffled along in front, sleeves dangling at their sides, dirt-blackened soles and white slippers traipsing the granite. The kids from the crypt were already grubby, their silky clothes streaked with dirt.

The hike was tense but tedious, slowed by small stumbling feet. A toddler's whine, a cry here and there interrupted the long march out – the kids were growing tired, their self-control waning. Jessica's neck ached, and so did her feet, her clenched jaw, her burdened arms.

At last, the air cooled, and the moss creeping across the rock told Jessica they'd almost arrived at the exit. The children lingered by the piles of pebbles.

"They're saying goodbye," Joseph explained. "To the bones they buried."

"Someone needs to make sure no one's outside," Jessica whispered. The sound of rain slapping against stone filtered in from outside.

"Wait." Mark raked through his backpack, then pulled out a raincoat. "For the baby," he whispered, handing it to Elliot.

"No, your turn," Elliot said. "I can't keep carrying her."

"I—" Mark began, shaking his head. "Okay, fine," he mumbled, handing the wolf to Joseph, then taking the baby into his arms.

Elliot turned off his headlamp and disappeared through the gap in the rock, then returned. "Let's go. I didn't see anyone, but it's too dark to know for sure."

"How are we supposed to see without headlamps?" Mark pulled his lamp off his head.

"We'll just have to follow Joseph and the kids. They can see in the dark way better than we can. If anyone sees us, we're screwed." Jessica flipped off her light, too.

They threaded through the gap, passing the baby and wolves between them.

Outside, the forest was drowning. The rain came down in sheets, blurring the dark to a slick puddling haze.

The baby cried out in spurts in Mark's arms, splashed awake and threatening to wail. Jessica draped the raincoat around her brother and fastened it at the front, fingers fumbling in the dark, and formed a cape that shielded the baby. Joseph placed his hand on the infant's forehead, and her cries petered out, dissolving into the rain.

The wolves howled. Jessica tried to comfort the pup nestled in her arms, but he howled on, his tiny noise aimed at the sky. Joseph held onto the other, whispering in his ear like a mother to a child.

They scanned the forest, searching for Anthony, but the rain hid everything but swaying branches. The downpour had already soaked Jessica's clothes, seeping through her hoodie and jeans. But she was thankful for the gushing rain and rumbling skies, which drowned out the howling and whimpering.

They set off toward the clearing, Joseph in front, the children following him. Annabelle held on to the youngest boy's hand, guiding him forward. Mark, Elliot and Jessica walked close behind, on the lookout for flashlights. But the forest was a dark timbered abyss, its roots and bark as soaked as Jessica's bones.

Struggling to hike through the tall wet grass, Jessica grew more anxious about Anthony – time was running out. Elliot, who walked to her left, was a blur behind the blanket of rain-splattered darkness. So was Mark, who lumbered in front of her, just a large draped shadow, shoulders hunched around the baby hiding under the raincoat. The kids marched ahead, unmoved by the rain, fueled by excitement. Jessica's vision began to permeate the dark, and now she could see the sweeping limbs of trees and the tiny figures in front of her, scrabbling up the path behind Joseph.

What if we lose one of them? Jessica asked herself, devoid of most of her senses, which were drowned by the rain. Their absence made the thoughts in her head too loud, rattling her, just like the thunder claps. Lightning streaked the sky, illuminating their hoods and dangling sleeves in three rapid flashes. The baby shrieked and wailed, shrill tones ringing through thunder. Another voice carried over the storm – the youngest boy cried too now, and Jessica could just make him out in the dark, stumbling and struggling up the trail. Elliot jogged ahead and lifted him into his arms, then trekked on with the toddler clinging to him. The wolves howled again, and Jessica felt the rapid heartbeat of the one in her arms, beating against her arm.

Jessica's own heart beat faster. They were making too much noise, even in the rain. Had anyone heard them? Was someone already following them? And Anthony – they'd reached the incline in the trail that led to the clearing, and there was still no sign of him.

We're so close. We just have to keep it together. But what if we got it wrong? What if they're not coming?

The seam that Jessica had sewn around herself began to unravel, releasing waves of adrenaline that sizzled her nerves and tingled in her fingers. *We're trekking through mud with missing children, and I don't even know what we're marching to. What are we going to find at that clearing? A spacecraft, or a small army of police officers? Government agents? Andrew and Sheriff Clarke standing in the grass with handcuffs? Or a dozen men in hazmat suits?*

The trees and shrubs thinned – they were nearing the clearing. Jessica heard whimpering, this time from Cricket. It grew to a wail, see-sawing in pitch. Jessica ran to her, holding on tight to the pup in her arms.

"We can't leave without Anthony!" she sobbed, trudging through the grass. Now Bean joined her, cries building, floating over the beat of the rain. The baby cried in high-pitched bleats. Slug and Sparrow were quieter, their whimpers almost inaudible.

Oh Jesus, please stop. Jessica squeezed Cricket's shoulder, helpless. "We're not there yet, Cricket. He might be there already, waiting for us."

They walked on, the children stumbling up the trail, until the path flattened, leading to wind-swept wiregrass.

Nearing the clearing, Jessica froze. Lights danced in the corner of her eye. Flashlights panned the grass down below, near Evergreen Pass, sweeping, razoring the rain.

"Shit, no!" Mark yelled.

Lightning struck again, flashing white-hot, painting everyone as silhouettes in the grass.

Did they see us? Please tell me they didn't.

Cricket howled, sliding into the grass.

"Get up, Cricket!" Jessica yelled, watching the flashlights pan wider, edge a little closer.

"We can't leave him here! He'll be alone!" she cried.

"Three minutes! We have to keep moving!" Mark yelled.

The flashlights reached the incline, where the trail snaked up the hill toward the clearing.

In the blur of rain and tears, Jessica placed the pup in Sparrow's small arms. "Run!" she yelled, then grabbed a hold of Cricket, who was still wailing, slumped in the grass. "Cricket, get up, now!" She tugged at her, and Cricket writhed and screamed, lurching forward and collapsing on the ground.

"I can't leave him!"

"We're running out of time!"

Jessica knew panic. It had rippled and surged in her for the last four days. But now it gushed from her, dizzying and viscous, like blood from a wound. There was no ground beneath her, nothing but a whirl of darkness around her, and yet her feet seemed too heavy to move.

This is it. This is when it all falls apart.

The flashlights were now filtering through trees on the trail, headed straight for the clearing. Jessica felt like her insides were crumpling, collapsing like dough and matchsticks. Nothing worked – she was just knees and elbows and rubber in between. There were no right moves, no right ideas, just dread, crouched on her shoulder, as loud and unwieldy as a big ugly bird.

A few more minutes, and they'll hear us, even in the rain.

Feet and voices rushed by – Mark in the flappy long raincoat, clutching the baby, and a few hooded kids, small feet stocring through the wiregrass.

"Wait!" Jessica yelled, raspy, too faint to be heard. She gripped Cricket under the arms and pulled her to her feet.

Chapter 56

As Cricket found her footing, heaving through sobs, Jessica noticed the rain had stopped. She paused, blinking the puddles of water from her eyes. Yes, it had suddenly stopped, as abrupt as a faucet.

The leaves were shivering, and so was the earth beneath her. A low heavy whirr grew louder, louder still, until it tickled the soles of her feet, just as it had twenty years ago, when Jessica stood alone in the dark, watching Olivia run into the light.

She didn't dare look up, despite the flashlights, the boots trudging up that trail, now no more than minutes away.

Blades of grass emerged from the dark – dawn-gray to green. Soon Jessica was bathed in pale white light, casting her shadow across the grass.

Elliot's voice was almost lost to the noise. "Jessica! Jessica!" he yelled. But it was enough to snap her out of the whirr, which had locked her in its resonance, pulling her from everything else. She looked up, Cricket writhing in her grasp.

A discoidal ship hovered above, dark gray and monstrous, as wide as a storm cloud. A blinding beam fanned from the center, ethereal and terrifying. Small hooded shadows ran toward it, faded into it, along with their voices. *Hide in the dark, run to the light.*

Cricket climbed to her feet, now only whimpering. Jessica lost her grip on the girl's shoulder when she began to walk backward, then ran toward the beam.

"Jessica!"

A hand landed on her arm. She spun around.

"Jessica, we need to leave now!" Elliot took her hand and pointed at the trail, where the flashlights were nearing the wiregrass.

They ran toward the trees, searching for cover. Faint barking grew louder.

Shit, they brought dogs, Jessica thought, until a huge shaggy beast ran straight toward her, followed by a young boy. Anthony, charging toward the beam with Big Moon.

Run, Anthony, run. But where the hell is Mark?

Nearing the trees, a strange chill swept over the clearing, and the branches froze, abruptly ending their sway. There were no rustling leaves, no fluting wind, just a strange pale light. Only Elliot moved, still gripping Jessica's hand. The rest of the world was holding its breath.

Someone called Jessica's name again, but it wasn't her brother, or Joseph, or anyone else she recognized. She turned around.

A woman stood in front of her. In the pale light, her amber eyes shimmered, and so did the suit she was wearing – something metallic, clinging to her skin.

"Olivia," Jessica said, the name leaving her before she'd understood.

The woman nodded. "We're in a pocket of time. They only gave me a moment. When this is over, you need to run as fast as you can."

Jessica nodded.

"Thank you," Olivia said, hugging her, and tears tumbled from Jessica's eyes, streamed down her neck. The rulebook of everything – time, space and humdrum existence – had been tossed aside, and now its pages were fluttering free, for a few seconds, at least.

But the moment quickly ended, their bubble of time ripped open by helicopter blades and pummeling rain.

Jessica and Elliot ran deeper into the trees. Flashlights reached the clearing, panning the grass, filtering through branches. They crouched low, winding around the low arms of evergreens, steering clear of the flashlights, until they reached the trail they'd come from. The helicopter circled the clearing, its blades drowning the forest in a choppy purr.

Jessica and Elliot remained under the cover of branches, walking parallel to the trail, snaking around trees. Jessica's fear was waning, and now its pulse was weaker, like an animal dying inside her. A sense of triumph, and defiance, was washing her clean of the panic and hopelessness that had gripped her. But her impulses, her reflexes, were still whip-sharp, still shocked awake, and a dozen questions begged for answers. *Where's my brother? Did they all get away? Did they see us? Did we leave a trail they can trace?*

Movement ahead stopped them in their tracks, until Jessica recognized the hoodie, the backpack. They jogged faster, gaining on Mark, who'd ditched his raincoat.

"What the fuck happened?" Mark hissed when they approached.

"Did they all make it?" Jessica said, ignoring his question.

"Yes, but where the hell were you?"

"I saw Olivia," Jessica said.

"What?"

"Just for a second. Where the hell did *you* go?"

They paused, listening to the fading noise of the helicopter. The rain streamed from their hoods and shoulders, but they were too drenched to care.

"I asked them to take me with them," Mark said, now kicking the grass.

"What the hell, Mark?"

"I'm so sick of life here," he muttered. "But they said the food would make me sick, and that I wouldn't be able to breathe."

"Who's they?" Elliot said. "All I remember is handing that kid to Joseph and telling him to run."

"You didn't see them?" Mark said. "They were standing right under the ship, helping the kids. They were standing in that light."

"We didn't see anything. It was all a blur," Elliot replied.

"I felt so alive." Mark kicked the ground again. "That light..." He broke off, as if something had caught in his throat.

They trekked the remainder of the trail in silence, listening for the helicopter, for feet trampling grass. The night's electric buzz was still under their skin when they reached the edge of the park.

The rain eased. Jessica looked up, into the cracks between the clouds, where a few stars blinked through the haze.

They're already an eternity away. As if they were never here. But I'm still here, she thought, now looking at Elliot, who found her hand.

"Let's go home and sleep for a week," he said, and Jessica wondered what that really meant.

Chapter 57

Wednesday, April 19, 2022

Dawn washed the bedroom gray, its sullen light spearing the window between The Arbor's heavy drapes.

Elliot still slept, half-swaddled in the comforter, and Jessica listened to his steady breathing, trying to slow her own breath and match his pace. The night before haunted her. It would stay with her always, she guessed, like a ghost who'd crawled under her skin.

We got away. Everything's fine. No one's going to knock on the door. But then what? This morning next to him, these hours in the aftermath, nested in high-thread count bedsheets – are they just a glimpse of what could have been? A glimpse of what I could have had in another, better life? Will he kiss me goodbye and find his next muse?

Everything had happened in a whirl, a storm. A lightning-quick bond, fused by moments most people never shared. Jessica remembered Joseph sitting in the passenger seat, telling her what she wanted to hear about Elliot. But how much of it had been true? And now that the drama was over, would anything else hold them together? She knew so little of his real life. His friends, his family, his habits. Was there any room for her?

Pins and needles tingled her right arm. She turned to lie on her back and stare at the bed canopy.

Driftwood will seem so boring to you, when there's no cryptic mystery to solve. My life, my miserable job, my home, she thought, watching him sleep. *You'll wake up craving normality. Your normality. Your Manhattan apartment, your espresso machine. And I am a delicate teacup by the edge of a table, ready to crack and splinter with a swipe of your hand.*

Waiting for heartbreak seemed even worse than the panic and terror of the night before. She flung back the comforter.

When you wake up, you're going to tell me that there's too much waiting for you in New York. That this was fun, but could never last. And I'll retreat back inside myself, read some more books. I'll get over you, somehow. I don't need you. I don't need anyone.

She stared at him, refusing to let herself cry. *I can't fall in love. Not with the real you. Not with the version of you who lives and thinks and breathes. I can't be that teacup.*

Elliot stirred and reached for her. "Not yet," he whispered, pulling her back into bed.

She melted into him, letting go, giving in. He felt like heaven – every touch and flex and whisper against her skin. His lips on her neck, the slip and grip of his fingertips, coaxing her into putty.

Her tears still wanted to flow, and a fire built as she held them back, a pressure that craved release. *Who am I kidding? There's nothing I want more than you. I'll die wanting you.*

On the tail-end of a sigh, losing herself to the sensation of Elliot kissing his way down her spine, she heard her phone vibrate from the nightstand. She ignored it, but it buzzed and buzzed.

"I wish the world would leave us alone," Elliot whispered, rolling onto his back.

Us, she thought.

Tabitha's name lit up the phone screen.

"Tabitha?"

"Jessie! Are you okay? I was so desperate to tell you something, I dialed before I remembered you had surgery last night! Why are you even awake?" Tabitha's voice was husky through the phone.

Jessica paused to scrape lies together. "It went fine. Don't worry, Tabitha. I'm going to be okay."

"*Really*?"

"Yes, really. What did you want to tell me?" Jessica said, cringing. *I'm not fine. I'm not OK. I might explode at any moment, in fact.*

"Jessie, something weird is going on," Tabitha whispered.

"What?"

"They're setting up tents in the park."

"Tents?" Jessica sat up and put Tabitha on speakerphone.

"Yes. And no one knows why, but my cousin said she heard the sheriff say something about *quarantine*."

Elliot sat up, too.

"She says the parking lot's full of black SUVs," Tabitha gushed. "And there are all kinds of assholes in the building, drinking all the coffee and holding secret meetings. No one's telling her shit—"

"Tabitha, I have to go." Jessica hung up.

Elliot was already on his way to the shower. "We need to leave town."

The room blurred as Jessica's feet found the carpet. *We. Does he mean together, or separately?* She grabbed her purse from the floor, her clothes from the back of the chair, listening to the shower water hit the tile. Where the hell could she go? She had an alcoholic aunt in Virginia, and a few cousins she'd planned on never seeing again. She called her brother. He replied with a storm of obscenities, then hung up to pack his suitcase. *I assume you're going with Elliot?* he texted seconds later.

She hesitated on the carpet, suddenly feeling marooned and alone, lost between her hopes and fears, and the urgency unfolding. *You need to move. Shower.*

Elliot walked out of the bathroom in his jeans, his hair wet, a dark shadow lining his jaw. Jessica watched him pull on a shirt, then showered and dressed with hurried tugs and swipes.

She found Elliot in the living room with his packed suitcase. He looked up at her.

"Jessica..."

She swallowed. *This is it, I guess. Goodbye.* She took a final glance around the plush cabin. It was fun, for a while. Fun playing with what could have been.

"I guess you need to grab some stuff from your place before we hit the road?" Elliot snatched the car keys from the coffee table, and Jessica held herself together, staring at the shiny apples in the fruit bowl. Her sinuses hurt from holding back tears.

"What does this mean?" she said.

Elliot sighed. "I don't know. We'll just have to keep an eye on the Driftwood news and see what pans out. Stay in touch with Tabitha."

"I mean, what do I mean to you?"

Elliot dropped the keys on the loveseat. "I'm sorry, Jessica. I made a whole bunch of assumptions. I didn't even ask if you wanted to do this alone. Maybe you need some time to think, cool off from everything." He took a step closer.

"No, it's not that. I just need to know what this is. To you, I mean. Before we…" She kept staring at the apple glinting in the low light.

"Before we go on a road trip and possibly flee the authorities together?"

She smiled. "Yes."

He was suddenly next to her, reaching for her. "I almost left on Monday," he said, threading his fingers between hers. "I thought you had someone else. But I turned around anyway."

"Someone *else*?"

"You were always in such a hurry to leave in the morning."

"It was Andrew."

"*Harding*?" Elliot's hand slipped from hers.

"Not like that! He wanted to ask me some questions about Olivia. He drank too much and fell asleep in my brother's room. Twice. I was worried he'd snoop around my house," she blurted, her cheeks burning hot. "And he found me on the lakeshore, after I fell into the lake.

He carried me to a patrol car, and when I first woke up, I thought he was you. I wanted him to be you. All I do is think about *you*."

He kissed her, melting her again.

Minutes later, they were curving around the winding drive, heading for Pine Street.

Yes, Jessica replied to her brother's text.

I'm renting a cabin in the woods, he replied.

Nearing Pine Street, Jessica balked at the thought of Elliot seeing her dilapidated home. He knew nothing of her threadbare life, other than the slivers she'd shared. But she was more worried about what to pack. They hadn't even discussed where they were going, or for how long.

"This reminds me of the house I grew up in," Elliot said, standing in the hallway, slaying her anxiety with a few words. She focused on finding her mother's suitcase.

The blinds and curtains were still drawn, and the bookshelf stood at an angle against the living room wall, revealing the faded ink. The house felt static, abandoned. The empty orange juice carton sat on the kitchen counter. Elliot pushed the bookshelf back against the wall.

Jessica lugged the suitcase from her parents' closet. Inside, it smelled of her mother's perfume and laundry detergent. She packed the clothes that weren't pilled or shrunken.

"Do you have a passport?" Elliot asked. He leaned against the bedroom doorframe, the way she always imagined he would, if her daydreams could have escaped her mind and manifested. Right there, watching her throw socks and underwear into a suitcase.

"Passport?"

"Just in case."

She searched her desk drawer, grabbed the passport she'd last used for a trip to Cancun with her parents five years ago, and returned to the bedroom. She grabbed her journals, her folders, her laptop, and packed those, too.

"Meet me at the rental car office?" Elliot said, turning the car keys in his hand. She nodded and threw her luggage in the car.

Closing the garage door felt final – its clunk made her shiver. She'd ended a chapter, with no idea of what came next. The wind ushered leaves across the driveway.

She followed Elliot's car to the highway, past the city limits sign, where the rain began to patter and slap against the windshield – slow and sloppy, like a lazy encore. Her phone buzzed from the passenger seat – a string of messages from Jamie. Jessica ignored them. *Perhaps you belong in that last chapter of my life,* Jessica decided. *Maybe I don't have to tolerate you, right up to the end.*

She watched Elliot run into the rental car office, then reappear with his suitcase, which he tossed in the trunk of her car.

"Where to?" he said, fastening his seatbelt.

Jessica laughed. "I have no idea."

"Somewhere quiet, where we can disappear."

Jessica drove northwest, deeper into forested mountain slopes, tuning into the local news here and there. But whatever was going on in Driftwood had been kept under wraps.

Elliot napped, then offered to drive. The tight coil of anxiety unwound inside her, slackening, allowing her breath to fill her lungs, reach her belly. The whoosh of the wipers lulled her to sleep.

Hours later, as dusk spread its wings across the sky, Jessica and Elliot lay sprawled on a hotel bed, propped up by pillows, miles from anywhere, surrounded by Jessica's folders and journals. Jessica lay in the crook of Elliot's arm.

"I thought I was writing a novel," he murmured, engrossed in a journal.

"What do you mean?"

"I thought I was the author. I thought I was creating something new. Turns out, you already wrote it. This is your story, not mine. I'm just a character."

Jessica sat up. "What? When did you become a *character*?"

Elliot paused to think. "When I crashed my car at Evergreen Pass. When I flew right over that guardrail. That's when I lost control of the plot, and it took control of me."

"But these are just late-night scribbles and meltdowns." She studied Elliot in the lamplight. His rumpled hair, his fingers clutching her fifteen-year-old journal. When he blinked, she swore his irises glinted, brighter than usual.

It's just the light, she told herself.

"I always wondered what the characters of books do when the reader isn't around," he said. "What they get up to when no one's there to keep tabs on them. Turns out they do this. They lie around, debating the book like actors backstage." He sat up and studied her, too. "No, Jessica, this is your book. You need to help me write it. Co-author it."

"I spent all those years cataloging other people's books. I never thought about writing my own. But what if things get out of hand? What if we have to bug out? We can't reveal everything and just call it fiction."

"Then we'll publish it under a pseudonym."

He scrolled through his phone, then handed it to her. "It's the first chapter. But there's something missing. It's hiding somewhere inside your journals."

Jessica read the chapter, inhaling his words like nicotine. His fluid, polished prose. Then she began to write:

"It's all my fault. I promised we wouldn't go out.

Jessica ran along the back road, skinny shins slashing the dark. Her legs were numb. The rest of her was all nerves and swinging arms, bursts of ragged breath. She didn't dare look over her shoulder. What if the shadow tried to take her, too?"

FICTION

Put simply, we publish great stories. Whether it's literary or popular, a gentle tale or a pulsating thriller, the connecting theme in all Roundfire fiction titles is that once you pick them up you won't want to put them down. If you have enjoyed this book, why not tell other readers by posting a review on your preferred book site.

Recent bestsellers from Roundfire are:

The Bookseller's Sonnets

Andi Rosenthal

The Bookseller's Sonnets intertwines three love stories with a tale of religious identity and mystery spanning five hundred years and three countries.

Paperback: 978-1-84694-342-3 ebook: 978-184694-626-4

Birds of the Nile

An Egyptian Adventure

N.E. David

Ex-diplomat Michael Blake wanted a quiet birding trip up the Nile – he wasn't expecting a revolution.

Paperback: 978-1-78279-158-4 ebook: 978-1-78279-157-7

Blood Profit$

The Lithium Conspiracy

J. Victor Tomaszek, James N. Patrick, Sr.

The blood of the many for the profits of the few… *Blood Profit$* will take you into the cigar-smoke-filled room where American policy and laws are really made.

Paperback: 978-1-78279-483-7 ebook: 978-1-78279-277-2

The Burden

A Family Saga

N.E. David

Frank will do anything to keep his mother and father apart. But he's carrying baggage – and it might just weigh him down ...

Paperback: 978-1-78279-936-8 ebook: 978-1-78279-937-5

The Cause

Roderick Vincent

The second American Revolution will be a fire lit from an internal spark.

Paperback: 978-1-78279-763-0 ebook: 978-1-78279-762-3

Don't Drink and Fly

The Story of Bernice O'Hanlon: Part One

Cathie Devitt

Bernice is a witch living in Glasgow. She loses her way in her life and wanders off the beaten track looking for the garden of enlightenment.

Paperback: 978-1-78279-016-7 ebook: 978-1-78279-015-0

Gag

Melissa Unger

One rainy afternoon in a Brooklyn diner, Peter Howland punctures an egg with his fork. Repulsed, Peter pushes the plate away and never eats again.

Paperback: 978-1-78279-564-3 ebook: 978-1-78279-563-6

The Master Yeshua

The Undiscovered Gospel of Joseph

Joyce Luck

Jesus is not who you think he is. The year is 75 CE. Joseph ben Jude is frail and ailing, but he has a prophecy to fulfil …

Paperback: 978-1-78279-974-0 ebook: 978-1-78279-975-7